Praise for Tim Sandlin and *Sorrow Floats*

"Pound for pound, Tim Sandlin's stuff is as tight and funny as anyone doing this comedy novel thing."

—Christopher Moore

"A raucous, surprisingly original tale."

—*New York Times Book Review*

"A zany road trip across America starring an engaging heroine and two AA devotees occupies talented novelist Tim Sandlin in *Sorrow Floats*."

—*Cosmopolitan*

"Able storytelling and an engaging cast of dysfunctional modern American pilgrims animate this winning tale of the road... Sandlin fashions a convincing tale of redemption."

—*Publishers Weekly* (starred review)

"A rousing piece of Americana...rowdy, raunchy...A total delight."

—*Library Journal*

"Tim Sandlin's fiction packs a punch. The writer's fictional Wyoming town is a grungier version of Garrison Keillor's Lake Wobegon, a community where people ponder the difference between depression and despair."

—*Denver Post*

"Fans of Tim Sandlin's quirky, iconoclastic novels will remember Maurey from *Skipped Parts*...Maurey's adventures on the road... mix comedy and pathos effectively."

—*Booklist*

"Unforgettable...*Sorrow Floats* has a multitude of gifts to offer—laughs, real people, high drama, and a crazy cross-country journey that makes it hard to put aside for long, if at all."

—*West Coast Review of Books*

"Funny and poignant...Sandlin's sustaining insight and faith in humanity give the book compassion and hope."

—*Winston-Salem Journal*

"Although Maurey writes postcards to her dead father and drinks like a fish, she doesn't hit rock bottom until she forgets and leaves her baby son on the roof of her Bronco. In an effort to get her life back together, she leaves on a cross-country odyssey with two recovering alcoholics and an ambulance-load of illegal beer. Mr. Sandlin understands that black comedy is only a tiny slip away from despair, and he handles this walk without a misstep."

—*Dallas Morning News*

"Very, very funny...Sandlin has a deft touch with characterization and dialogue that keeps the reader right with him from the first page to the last. He's a pleasure to read."

—*Witchita Eagle*

"A little bit of Tom Robbins, part Jack Kerouac, and a whole lot of John Irving."

—*Missoulian*

"Hilarious...not since *Lonesome Dove* have I met such an enticing crew of booted misfits between the covers of a book."

—*Greensboro News & Record*

"Tim Sandlin just keeps getting better and better. *Sorrow Floats* is funny, raunchy, and heartbreaking."

—W. P. Kinsella, *author of Shoeless Joe*

"*Sorrow Floats* is about a trip you'll never want to end. It's blasphemous, cantankerous, full of insight and pratfalls and all the relevant human yearnings."

—John Nichols, *author of The Milagro Beanfield War*

"Sandlin can see that there is a kind of gruesome comedy in what happens to us, but the humor is never mean, and he loves his people too much not to understand that their grief and nostalgia and frustration is real."

—Nick Hornby

Sorrow FLOATS

TIM Sandlin

sourcebooks
landmark

Published by Sourcebooks Landmark, an imprint of Sourcebooks, Inc.
P.O. Box 4410, Naperville, Illinois 60567-4410
(630) 961-3900
Fax: (630) 961-2168
www.sourcebooks.com

Library of Congress Cataloging-in-Publication Data

Sandlin, Tim.
  Sorrow floats / Tim Sandlin.
      p. cm.
  1. Women travelers—Fiction. 2. Young women—Fiction. I. Title.
PS3569.A517S67 2010
813'.54—dc22
                          2010020943

Printed and bound in the United States of America.
       VP 10 9 8 7 6 5 4 3 2 1

For Flood and June,
Also Larry, my good example,
And Carol, who led me into the sunlight

Acknowledgments

I'D LIKE TO THANK MY HORSES, GUNS, AND TRUCKS EXPERTS—
Greg Harris, Brian Nystrom, and Chip Rawlins. Laurel
Denison helped me transform myself into a twenty-two-year-
old woman, and my research assistant, Teri Krumdick, now
knows more than anyone would ever want to know about the
spring of 1973. When the going got strange, Jedediah's Original
House of Sourdough fed me.

I also want to remember Perry Spray, who first brought
Moby Dick into the neighborhood.

Self-esteem, if it is to be enduring, can only grow out of steady faith. For writers, of course, self-esteem comes (or fails to come) from the books they are writing at the moment. At the moment I have just passed the mid-point of my fifth novel, and one little line from that novel has made me happy for weeks. The line is "Sorrow floats."

—John Irving

I told the analyst everything except my experience with Mr. Rinesfoos.

—James Thurber

My behavior slipped after Daddy died and went to San Francisco. I danced barefoot in bars, I flipped the bird at churches. Early one morning in April I drove Dothan's new pickup truck off the Snake River dike, and when the tow truck crew showed up they found me squatting on a snow patch in my nightgown crying over the body of a dead plover.

Not that I'd ever been the Betty Crocker showcase woman. All through my teens GroVont townfolk called me "that Maurey Pierce girl," then after I came home from the university it became "that Maurey Talbot woman." But by May I'd taken to midday drinking and the writing of a daily picture postcard to Dad. I mostly sent him photographs of the Tetons from various views at various times of year—sunset from the top of Signal Mountain in winter, Jenny Lake on a cobalt clear day. I searched the valley curio shops for pictures of fall because Dad always did enjoy golden aspens and red chokecherries.

What Dad didn't like was cute kids in station wagons feeding Yellowstone bears. He looked at Yellowstone as a big zoo of tame animals and lost tourists.

The pictures weren't all mountains and ain't-nature-wonderful shots. On Easter I mailed him the postcard of Clover the Killer with a rope around his neck sitting on a bow-back gelding surrounded by tourists in car coats and sneakers. Clover is wearing a red plaid shirt and he has only one eye; the other side of his face is an empty cavern that goes way in there to pink, wrinkled skin—no glass eyeball or black patch or anything, just a hole.

On the back I wrote: "As the one-eyed whore said to the traveling salesman after he nailed her in the socket, 'Hurry on back now, mister. I'll keep an eye out for you.'"

———

The tide of public opinion swung to my male slut husband, Dothan, after I cut my hair short and took to carrying Dad's gopher popper in my windbreaker pocket. Nine-tenths of the men in Teton County drive around armed to the armpits, but let a woman pack a little Dan Wesson model 12 .357 Magnum with a four-inch, satin blue barrel, and the feed store cronies commence rolling their eyes and gabbing on about the Pierce family tendency to fall off the deep end.

Everybody says you've got to have balls to get respect in this world, but I couldn't help noticing that with that satin blue barrel poking out, the service improved considerably at Kimball's Food Market. The guy at the Esso station moved right along when I said check the oil. Even Dothan cut down on criticizing my dusty kitchen surfaces.

Dad won Charley—that's what I call him—with two pair jacks high at a stock show in Billings. I didn't load Charley with bullets. What I did was pretend he's a penis without a man, which is the only kind I like. Probably some strange psychological word for carrying a disembodied prick in your pocket, but I don't care. Where other people knock on wood, I rub my rod.

———

Why did I fight the demon? Which leads to why did I drink? Why did the world in all its parts press down on me from every direction until I reached the point of personifying whiskey? "Whisky My Only Friend," "Let Me Go Home, Whisky," "Whisky River Take My Mind," "Tonight the Bottle Let Me Down," "Tiny Bubbles," "Wine Me Up," "Mean Old Whiskey," "One Hundred Bottles of Beer on the Wall, One Hundred Bottles of Beer."

On my fourteenth birthday, before my first ever period, I had a baby named Shannon. Shannon is now eight and a half and beautiful, living in North Carolina with her natural father because I couldn't take care of her. Let's stress that—because I couldn't take care of her.

My son, Auburn, the light of my dark, frigid nights, started existence by defying the poison of Delfen foam, came out breech, had jaundice at three days and an undeveloped esophagus that wouldn't close for nearly six months. Dothan blamed me, of course, and Auburn has howled at the colossal cheat that is life ever since.

Dad's dead; you know about him.

Mom is a story unto herself. Don't get me started on Mom. She cleans and perfects meat loaf recipes and hums show tunes. Every third year or so she takes her clothes off in public— usually rodeos—and goes to pharmaceutical heaven for a few days, where they give her sponge baths and take the laces out of her shoes. My little brother, Petey, takes care of Mom after these periods, and the very thought of him sponge-bathing her white, droopy body gives me the willies.

Dothan sells real estate. He has the dates and times of all the Kiwanis meetings penciled on his calendar, not because he's a Kiwanian, but because he knows those are safe days to visit the members' wives. That pretty much says it all about my marriage.

I'm making a point here. My downfall can't be blamed on histrionics. In May of 1973, the day it all got up and went, I had as much cause to drink lunch and write picture postcards to a dead father in San Francisco as anyone.

1

THE AIR MADE EVERYTHING FLAT. BUILDINGS, COTTONWOODS, and the mountains behind all had a two-dimensional glare, with shiny surfaces and a paint-by-number look to the colors. I sat in our window seat in my blue fuzzy bathrobe with my bare feet on a cushion, waiting for Paul Harvey News and watching the alcoholics wander in from different directions onto the lawn of the Mormon church across the street. Alcoholics Anonymous met at noon every day but Sunday, and whenever Auburn was at his grandma's I sat in the window studying the drunks and reformed drunks for signs of me.

The men carried a stretched look in their eyes, like old dogs—the look of punishment accepted. They wore caps instead of hats and mostly had long-sleeved shirts rolled up over their wrists. An Indian wore torn pants and moccasins, a long-hair had on a red-white-and-blue vest, one guy was in a wheelchair. A non-alcoholic pushing a manual lawn mower stopped to look as four AA members lifted the wheelchair like pallbearers on a coffin. The crippled guy perched above their heads, grinning and bobbing, playing a harmonica while they carried him down the steps into the basement, where they held the meetings.

Two women drove up in a blue-and-white Chevrolet that said BABE on the license plate. They sat for a moment, finishing their cigarettes. As they got out, neither woman checked herself in the rearview mirror, which I took as relevant. I still checked myself.

Paul Harvey's voice boomed: "Hello, America. Stand by for *news*."

Time. I poured myself a coffee cup full of Yukon Jack. Cradling the cup with both hands, I stared into the light molasses-colored liquid. Was there a connection between this and Dad? Closing my eyes, I brought the cup to my lips and smelled the fumes. The sweet fire swept around my tongue and under it onto the saliva glands, then to the back of my mouth, where, like advancing lava, it flowed into my body.

The shoulder muscles, the jaw tight from clenching in my sleep, the fist-size rock in my stomach—everything let go at once. It was better than a masturbated orgasm.

The empty cup dropped back to the windowsill as I opened my eyes on a softer reality. The church roof wasn't shiny anymore. The non-alcoholic had disappeared, leaving his lawn mower in the middle of a pass. One last AA member, an older man in a white ambulance, pulled up against the curb. I pretended I could see him but he couldn't see me, as if the window were a TV set. He had on overalls but no shirt, which is weird for ranch country, and sandals. I hadn't seen guys in sandals since the university.

While I poured another cup of Jack, I said a little prayer. I thanked God for Paul Harvey. As he plain-talked about the seal on Kerr canning jars, he was so sincere. Paul Harvey must be the sincerest man in the world. With all my heart I wanted to buy the jars. I could plant some lima beans and nurture them and watch them grow, and just at the perfect moment, I would pick my lima beans. I would boil them or whatever women do and can them in Kerr jars and stack them on shelves in the basement we didn't own yet, then my family and I would have security. Come avalanche or nuclear war, we would eat wholesome food.

Do beans grow above the ground like apples or below it like carrots? I knew horses, some about cows. I sure wasn't no damn farmer.

The old, skinny guy in the overalls had that farmer look. Before going down the steps he rubbed both hands on his legs, as if they were dirty. Farmers have dirt under their fingernails, ranchers have blood.

My cup was empty so I filled it.

The postcard was a photo of two girls in sunsuits on a chair-lift with Jackson way down behind them. The picture must have been old because they had ratted and sprayed hair and cat's-eye sunglasses with little oyster-shell fans at the corners. A California nightmare.

I didn't gulp the whole cup this time. Had to pick up Auburn at Grandma Talbot's later, wouldn't do to show up crawling.

Dear Dad,

Hank called yesterday to say Jenny Lind foaled a chestnut colt with a blaze. He opened the Miner Creek gate and flooded the south pasture, which I told him you didn't want flooded. Mrs. Hinchman hit a pole and wrecked her Rambler and broke her hip. Knocked the phones out up Buffalo Valley.

Come back.

Maurey

Hank Elkrunner was the only one at the ranch when Dad saddled Frostbite and went up Miner Ridge to find a cow and calf

9

they missed when they moved the cattle off the forest lease. He took an old dog named Arnold with him. Arnold was a mean little dingo mix anyone other than a sentimentalist would have shot.

Frostbite came home that afternoon dragging the saddle, so Hank walked up the ridge and found Dad. Near as Hank could tell after backtracking, Frostbite stepped in a badger hole and rolled over on Dad, who caught a rib through the lungs. Dad knew he was dead soon, so instead of trying to make the ranch, he coughed blood and crawled clear up to a spine with a view of the Tetons he'd always admired. Hank found him leaning on a rock with a bunch of blue penstemon clutched in his left hand and his black beard turned to the sunset.

Son of a bitch cowboy died like a fucking poet. I could have killed him.

Arnold did the loyal-cowdog-of-the-West thing and bit Hank when he first picked up Dad's body.

———

I named Frostbite. Dad said animals deserve the same respect as people, and he hated names like Spot and Fury. Our herd was big on thirties movie stars.

On my tenth birthday I sat on the top rail of the corral while Dad led this skewbald colt in from the barn and handed me the reins. The yearling stuck the left side of his face up against mine with his nostril flare right in my ear. He wasn't all that tall, but his back was broad and he had perfect hips for vaulting. I looked in his eyes and I knew. Sometimes you just know these things, like in college when I would meet a boy and know within five minutes I was going to nail him. That's how I knew about Frostbite. We would fall in love and have one of those Disney Old Yeller, Lassie-and-Timmy relationships.

We did, too. Frostbite and I trusted each other like no one trusts a lover. For three summers we spent almost every waking moment together, until the year I got pregnant. We were Intermountain Vaulting Champions for my age group in 1962. Champions. Me and Frostbite. He ran full blast across the arena at the Denver Coliseum and I did handstands, sidekicks, somi swings. We had a backflip dismount that knocked the collective socks off the crowd.

It's weird when your true love and loyalty horse rolls over on your father and kills him.

Paul Harvey was talking sincerely about Watergate. The Senate did this, Nixon did that, Sam somebody was outraged. I couldn't tell what side Paul Harvey was on, but whichever it was, he really meant it. I poured another cup of Claude. I named this bottle of Yukon Jack Claude after a boy at college who followed me around like a pet beagle my whole freshman year. He was sweet, with horn-rimmed glasses, two-tone sweaters, and a calculator case holster on his belt, and I could have brought him untold joy if I'd let him sleep with me. I should have. He deserved untold joy if only for his persistence, and I'd have hardly been compromised at all. Lord knows I got nailed by enough boys who didn't like me in college; it wouldn't have hurt to get nailed by one who did.

Paul Harvey had discovered a man in Missouri with a twenty-two-pound cantaloupe. If you only heard the sound of the words but not what they meant, you'd think cantaloupes and Watergate and Kerr canning jars were all equally fascinating.

As Paul Harvey came to the daily bumper snicker, my phone rang.

"You broke her heart again."

"Hi, Petey, how's Mom?"

"She's an obsessive compulsive with a thankless daughter."

Here is that day's bumper snicker: "Love your kids at home and belt them in the car."

Since I wasn't talking, Petey went on. "Yesterday was Mother's Day."

"I'm a mother."

"We spent all day in the parlor next to the phone. I'd planned to take her to luncheon at Signal Mountain Lodge, but she was afraid you'd call while we were out. We had her hair done nice, too."

"Petey, are you saying you wasted a whole Sunday sitting with Mom?"

"I knew you wouldn't call. Too busy mooning over Dad who's eight months dead to call your live mom on Mother's Day."

Got me with that one. "Nobody wished me a happy Mother's Day. You don't see me whining in the parlor." Which was sort of a lie. Shannon sent a Mother's Day card made out of construction paper with models cut from a catalog glued to represent a family—me, Sam Callahan, Lydia, and her. Lydia, Sam's mom, who more or less raised Shannon the first five years, held a cigarette, and I was in a bra and slip. Playtex Cross Your Heart. I bet anything Sam made her do it. Probably even picked out the models to cut, because the one was me had dark hair and big boobs. Last time Sam Callahan saw me was at Dad's funeral when I was nursing Auburn. He laughed at my breasts—not the comfort called for from a best friend.

"Nobody wished you happy Mother's Day because you're such a bad mother," Petey said. "You lost the first one and you'll lose this one too. Or he'll grow up like Dothan. I'd drown a baby before I risked that."

"Petey, do you like boys?"

He hung up.

Before Paul Harvey got through the list of those turning one hundred years young today, Petey called back. I poured more of Claude's soul and answered the fifth ring. He said, "Take that back."

"I didn't accuse you of anything, I just asked. Dot says she's never seen you with a girl, so I wondered if you like boys."

"No, I don't like boys."

"But you don't like girls either."

"Girls smell bad; they make me sick."

"That leaves Mom."

He hung up on me again, although I deserved it. No one likes being accused of having the hots for a parent. Especially my mom.

I went back to the window and looked at myself in it and tried to picture Petey and Mom kissing. It wouldn't come. I'm usually good at picturing really disgusting sex acts. I can just see Dothan with all those Kiwanis wives, especially Sugar Cannelioski. He'd be on top; Dothan can't deal with any other position. He'd stick his pointy Talbot chin in her right shoulder and grind. That's the only way he knows how to do it. I'm in the grocery store and I see a Kiwanis wife rubbing her right shoulder, I figure Dothan's been grinding again.

He has a little brother, Pud, that everyone says does it with animals. I like to picture that. Pud's kind of cute in a retarded sort of way. I picture him behind a calf with the back hooves tied to his boots and his arms around her belly. He has this look on his face like Tony Randall eating a bad lemon.

The calf looks as if she's had better.

Sometimes at sporting events I like to picture men in bed with each other. The one I have the hardest time picturing in bed lately is me. After a semi-loose three years of college, then a real short rabbit period when I first married Dothan, I lost enthusiasm for sex as a personal experience. Since Auburn was born I'd only woken up with pain in my right shoulder twice, and at least one of those I think Dothan sleep-fucked.

Yukon Jack was my kind of companion. Jack never lets you down, never comes and goes to sleep just as I'm getting started.

13

He's monogamous and predictable. A certain amount of Jack causes a certain amount of warmth. He's always there and he never calls me cunt.

The AA guys carried the harmonica player back up the steps. He grinned and nodded just like he didn't care he was a crippled old alcoholic who had to go to meetings in the Mormon church. The men stood around with their hands in their back pockets and talked, but the women adjusted foundation garments and drove away. AA over meant I'd lost some time and was late picking up Auburn.

Consistent as Tupperware, the phone went off again.

"I am gravely ill."

"I'm sorry I'm late, Mrs. Talbot. The Bronco wouldn't start, but I gave it a rest and it might now. How's Auburn?"

"Whenever I am late to the Great Books Club I get nervous, and when I get nervous I become ill. You know I become ill, Maurey. Why would you purposefully try to make me become ill?"

Always lie to in-laws. "The Bronco flooded, Mrs. Talbot. I'll be there in ten minutes."

"It's my day to deliver Lord Byron's eulogy, which I wrote myself."

"I'd love to read the eulogy if you have a copy."

"A rash is breaking out on my back."

"Spray some benzocaine. I'll be there."

I addressed the postcard to Buddy Pierce, General Delivery, San Francisco, and licked on a six-cent stamp.

In the bedroom, I shrugged out of the blue fuzzy bathrobe and into crack-climber cutoffs and a T-shirt. No bra, it was only Grandmother Talbot. No shoes for the same reason. I put on my King Ropes red windbreaker, checked myself in the mirror a second, then slipped Charley into my pocket and checked myself again. A before and after comparison.

Definitely better after. Charley's blue barrel complemented the red nylon of the windbreaker.

I counted from twenty to zero backward to prove I wasn't drunk—I never drive Auburn when I'm drunk—took one more hit of Jack-Claude, stuffed a Hershey bar in the other pocket, and I'm on the way to Grandmother's house.

2

DELILAH TALBOT'S FEET HUNG OVER BOTH SIDES OF HER
sandals like oozing Silly Putty. She stood next to the television
in her polyester slacks and matching jacket outfit, looking with
distaste at Auburn on the floor.

She said, "Greens."

Once you rose above the feet, the rest of Delilah wasn't fat
at all. In fact, from the knees up she looked kind of depleted.
"Green what?"

Auburn's face took me in, and he crawled under the kitchen
table where he turned around and stared through the legs of a
chair. My nose said he needed changing.

Delilah expanded her first statement. "In Alabama we had
green vegetables with every meal, but out west it's meat and
potatoes, meat and potatoes. Manners are a by-product of green
vegetables. That's why westerners don't have any."

She stood with one finger on her chin, watching me load
up his diaper bag, blanket, the stuffed Cowardly Lion, and a
sponge cake she'd baked for Dothan. She made no move to
help me chase down my child.

Instead, the woman gazed into the air near my ear and said,
"Manners." Often Mrs. Talbot stripped the front half and back
half out of sentences, leaving one word to fend for itself.

I shrugged the load onto my shoulders. "You mind handing me Auburn?"

"Are you feeding my son green vegetables? I don't mean iceberg lettuce. Iceberg lettuce is not a green vegetable."

I bent on one knee to look under the table, hit my forehead on the metal strip that held the linoleum in place, and dropped the diaper bag.

Mrs. Talbot didn't notice. "Dothan was rude when he dropped Aubie off this morning; I suspect you of not serving green vegetables."

Auburn smiled and put some floor gunk in his mouth. I reached a finger in and dug out a dried piece of elbow macaroni.

"I still don't understand why you cut your hair, Maurey. You were so pretty as a little girl."

One thing about Delilah, she didn't see anything she didn't want to see. I could show up at her house toilet-hugging smashed and she'd say, "What a nice shirt. Did someone give it to you?" Right now she had no idea I was getting the whirlies under her kitchen table.

She said, "Lord Byron."

I reached one hand around Auburn's waist, and he frowned. If I moved too fast there'd be a scream scene, which had to be avoided at all costs. Scream scenes drove me to drink.

I truly enjoy being a mother, only I'm not naturally suited to motherhood. I love Auburn and couldn't live without him; it's the motherhood itself—the smells, the lack of sleep, the humiliation. I'm not one of those women born to nurture.

Mrs. Talbot droned on about Byron—Byron's foot, Byron's legacy, Byron's death.

I said, "I heard Byron slept around."

"I can't gab all the livelong day. Toodles." The door slammed, and after a moment, I heard Mrs. Talbot's El Camino pulling out of the drive.

"Thank God," I said to Auburn.

He put three fingers in his mouth.

I lowered my cheek to the tile to look up at him through one eye. Auburn had Dad's forehead and my blue eyes and skinny fingers. I couldn't see any Dothan in my baby. I liked to pretend Dothan wasn't related to him. Maybe Auburn's father had been Frostbite's spirit or God or Yukon Jack. This beautiful person couldn't be connected to a man who sold real estate or a woman with fat feet who said "Toodles."

I lifted my head off the tile and crossed my eyes and cooed, "*Boo boo be doop*," in my Betty Boop voice.

Auburn laughed.

I did Olive Oyl. "Oh, Popeye, you're such a man."

And Wimpy. "I'll gladly pay you Tuesday for a hamburger today."

I would have tried any trick to make Auburn laugh because one smile from my baby was worth whatever other trouble my ridiculous life dished out. When he squeezed my nose I went into W. C. Fields. "Sure, I like children, I like them with whiskey for lunch. Speaking of whiskey…"

Leaving Auburn under the table, I back-crawled out, then front-crawled over to Garth Talbot's fake-maple liquor cabinet. I didn't drink his liquor—at least not much. I poured a single shot of ouzo but left it on the floor. What I did was I mixed. I mixed Scotch with Jack Daniel's and Jack Daniel's with Scotch, then gin with vodka and vodka with gin. Everything color-coded.

Auburn looked on solemnly.

"Garth will never notice," I said. Auburn took his fingers out of his mouth and crawled over to my lap. I held him with one hand and mixed with the other. One of my biggest fears, besides quitting Yukon Jack, was that Auburn would grow up to become a Talbot; that he'd obsess on TV football and

South-shall-rise-again. Worse yet, he might grow into the Talbot chin. The Talbot men have this sharp, jutty chin you could plow with. According to Sam Callahan, every night at sunset all Talbot chins point to Alabama.

Sam Callahan is Shannon's father and my best friend. My only friend. We were never lovers except in the loosest definition. At thirteen, Sam and I lost our virginities together. We would play Red Rover, Red Rover and Red Light, Green Light, then go inside and play sex—Sam gave me killer orgasms back then—then go back outside and play Kick the Can. It was like Paul Harvey on canning jars, cantaloupe, and Watergate—none of the games meant any more or less than the others. Our lost virginities had nothing to do with lost innocence, at least until I landed pregnant.

Sam had all the maternal instincts I lacked. After the birth, I went back to cheerleading practice, cutout magazine photos of Sal Mineo, and Coke dates, and Sam went on to changing diapers and two o'clock feedings. He always volunteered to baby-sit, then to keep Shannon for the weekend, then the week. Pretty soon she was with him and Lydia all the time, and I'd washed out as a mom. Hell, I still hadn't had a period yet, how was I supposed to have instincts?

Sam did. He was born to mother. Sometimes I wish I'd fallen for him on a nonbuddy level, but you can't fake that stuff. He was too considerate to get the hots for.

You know how whenever boys squirt, first thing afterward when you're feeling warmish and post-passion affectionate, they jump up and bolt to the bathroom? They go off and pee like horses and come back to bed with one urine drop hanging off the end. That's when the boy feels like cuddling, but he hops under the sheets and pulls you close and that wet piss-head pokes right in your thigh. Talk about killing romanticism. That's when I go home.

Well, at thirteen, Sam always toilet paper-blotted the end dry before he came back to bed so that wouldn't happen. Who taught him that kind of consideration? The kid was weird.

As I changed Auburn he gurgled and made little fists with his hands. I put my face in his and he pulled my ears. I blew on his belly and he laughed like an angel. He had the teeniest penis. I couldn't conceive of it growing up and getting hard and being used as a weapon against women. Or maybe I could since that's what I thought about.

"You better not act like a man," I said. Auburn burped.

Since Mrs. Talbot hadn't bothered to change him, I left the stinky diaper in the trash sack under her sink. The smell would remind her of what she didn't do.

Thinking of Sam brought back a certain warmness that I usually kept covered with Yukon Jack. Sam drinks ouzo. I chugged my glass and left it on the floor while I regathered the pile of stuff. I stood up too fast, and the room separated itself from me. Took a moment for the black spots to settle out. Auburn sat on one hip, balancing the pile of mother stuff on the other side. At the front door, I turned to look for lost squeeze toys and saw Dothan's cake on the table. To hell with it.

The deal is that Sam was, and is, just a pal, but those carefree young lays were technically the most dynamite sex I've ever had. Sam paid attention. And he was easy to boss around. I could say higher, lower, harder, no-you-can't-stop-now; give directions you can't give a lover. God, did that boy have a golden tongue. I bet he's popular down there in North Carolina.

I'd never gotten off, not once, with Dothan, and he never went down. Why did you marry the bum, you asked? I take a drink and change the subject.

The spring before I dropped out twelve credits short of graduation and came home to marry Dothan, my boyfriend was named Leon. Leon the Moron. I tried for weeks to get him down there, then when he finally went, he dropped way too low, all the way to the hole, and he like chewed as if I were gum or something. He lasted about ninety seconds before he whined, "Did you get off yet?" I said yes just to move him off my crotch. Leon couldn't find a clitoris with a map. Then, he jumped up like they all do and headed for the can. Only instead of peeing, Leon brushed his teeth. I caught him. Chewed me for a minute and a half, then practically ran for his toothbrush.

At the Bronco the diaper bag strap broke and stuff fell all over the curb. Clean diapers, dirty diapers, a plastic Indian, *The Little Prince* by Antoine de Saint-Exupery, Auburn's pacifier—a jar of Gerber strained fruit cocktail hit the concrete and broke. When I leaned over, Charley came out of my pocket and bounced under the car.

Auburn laughed. I put him and his blanket on the roof and dropped to my knees to reach under for Charley. I leaned my left hand on a can opener.

"Shit. Why me? Everything happens to me."

I found my Ortho-Novum pill wheel, which I'd lost during the green tablet section. Greens were blanks and peach pills stopped whatever had to be stopped so I wouldn't get pregnant again. The pill companies thought women were such idiots they had to take blanks because they couldn't be trusted to count to seven. I was three days late starting peach, not because I couldn't count, but because I'd lost the wheel and wasn't about to get nailed anytime soon anyhow.

I didn't care much for the Novum wheel—the wheel of misconception, Lydia called it. She liked Novums because they made her breasts bigger and she cared about stuff like that. My fantasy form of birth control would be to cut off all the peckers around the world. Stack them in a big pile next to Old Faithful in Yellowstone Park for men to sit around and mourn over. That'd teach the ingrates to use their tongues.

Diaper rash medicine and dental floss had landed on Auburn's spare pants, next to Cowardly Lion. When I picked them up, the stuffed lion clanked against the medicine. I unzipped his back and pulled out a half pint of tequila.

"Whoa, how'd you get here?"

The fact he was in Cowardly Lion wasn't so odd; sometimes I hid bottles and forgot them. The odd thing was that he was tequila. I was monogamous with Yukon Jack. I tested his weight in my hand, read his label, then squinted at the sun. Tequila and sun go together. Has something to do with Mexico.

I look for signs everywhere, and a bottle of tequila suddenly appearing under my car was a definite sign I should enjoy the sun. I'd had a hard day; no one was around to gossip.

———

The tequila didn't make me drunk at all. Driving the GroVont Highway, I noticed how sharp the houses looked, how alive the aspens. For the first time since Dad's funeral I felt alert, on top of the situation. The weather sparkled. I sparkled. There was the Killdeer Cafe, then a minute later the Tastee-Freez sailed by on the left, and the Forest Service headquarters on the right. Behind it floated the Sagebrush Lounge in the old Talbot Taxidermy building. I wasn't even driving, I was on a magic carpet rippling through my hometown.

I used to drink tequila in college, before I met Jack, but had quit for some reason I couldn't recall. The bottle in the stuffed lion was a message from the past. College days. Life had been so simple and easy then. We all loved each other. People didn't carry mean thoughts behind their eyes.

Today would be the day to drive up to the ranch. I owned it now, I guess. Or Mom did, but she didn't care. Jenny Lind had foaled, and I loved Jenny Lind. I loved all horses.

A man yelled at me: "Maurey, pull over."

I looked to the left through my open window at Mangum Potter in his white policeman's car. Someone had made Mangum a deputy sheriff a few years ago, and it went to his head.

"Leave me alone, Mangum."

"Pull over."

"Suck a bull."

"Please, pull over, Maurey. I won't arrest you."

A tourist car came in Mangum's lane and he had to drop back, but just as I thought he'd gone away, there he was again back in my window. "It's important, Maurey."

I stopped the car and looked at myself in the rearview mirror. I looked okay. Nobody could tell I'd been drinking. If I spoke clearly and didn't come off meek or anything, he couldn't bother me. The last thing I needed was a raft of crap from Mangum Potter.

"Mangum, you got a lot of nerve stopping me. Dothan can get your badge pulled if I tell him to."

His eyes wouldn't look at me. He said, "Don't be scared."

"I'm not scared of you."

Mangum's hands went to the top of the Bronco and came down with Auburn. Auburn looked in the window at me and started whimpering.

Mangum's eyes were not friendly. "You forgot something, Mrs. Talbot."

My stomach went knot and my face drained. It had to be a dream.

"We got calls on you through town. You frightened people."

My baby squirmed in Mangum's hands. The hands were dirty with burned-off wart scars on both thumbs. "Give him to me."

Mangum settled Auburn against his chest with its badge. "I can't do that, Mrs. Talbot."

"He's my child."

"You drove with your baby on the roof. You can't be responsible for him."

"Don't take my baby."

"If you were a tourist you'd be in jail, Mrs. Talbot."

"I'll go to jail, just give me my son."

Mangum stepped back from my door. "Don't do anything crazy now. I'll take him to Dothan at the office. You go home and get some sleep."

"Sleep?"

Mangum leaned over to peer down at me. "If you can't sleep, consider what kind of woman forgets where she put her baby."

I rolled up the window and started crying. "Mangum, you cruel asshole."

"Go on home, Mrs. Talbot."

3

BECAUSE OF THE JAUNDICE AFTER AUBURN WAS BORN, THE doctor put him next to my bed in a clear plastic box with bilirubin lights. A nurse taped a gauze strip over his eyes, and for some reason they wouldn't tell me, she stuck an IV needle into the top of his head.

Then they left Auburn, naked, alone, and blind, where no one could touch him.

Lydia had brought me a portable eight-track tape player, and I lay there on my side, looking at my baby and listening to the *Blue* album by Joni Mitchell. I started sobbing and couldn't stop. For six hours I cried and cried until the front of my hospital gown was soaked. How could that be possible? There aren't six hours' worth of tears in the human body. People say crying is good for you and after you let it out you'll feel better, but after six hours I was hopeless as ever.

That was the last time I cried until Mangum Potter drove away.

The afternoon Dad died Hank called Mom and Petey called me. I was giving Auburn a bath when the phone rang, and after I hung up I took Auburn out of the plastic basin to towel him dry. As I rubbed the towel up and down Auburn's precious body, I went kind of blank and forgot time. I just kept rubbing his legs, then his back and arms. I touched his belly and thought of Dad's skin. Dad's neck, his face above his beard, and the backs of his hands were dark as my corral boots, but the rest of his body was the color of banana pulp.

I talked to Auburn as if he were Dad. Said the stuff we all wish we'd said—I planned to plant a line of aspens at the ranch. The cigarettes he found in my saddlebags were mine. Was he disappointed in me? I asked if he thought we should get Auburn baptized even though we didn't belong to a church. Then I told Dad he was the only thing solid in my life, nothing would ever be real again. I said "I love you"—all this time rubbing Auburn up and down with the towel.

That was the numbest I ever felt, more numb than Yukon Jack ever made me, more numb than the last time I made love to Dothan.

But all while I dried Auburn I never cried. That night fetal-positioned in bed, and the next day, then the funeral and the days after that—nothing. At times I felt like a monster, but I was just too empty for tears.

———

Someone tapped on the glass. A man I'd never seen before mouthed some words and did a crank-your-window-down motion with his hands. At first I ignored him, but that didn't work so I cracked the window an inch.

He spoke distinctly, as if I might be foreign or deaf. "Are you okay?"

I nodded.

He pointed to a pickup on the shoulder across the road. A woman with her hair in foam curlers waved. The man said, "We were driving by and thought you might not be okay."

"I'm okay."

The man wasn't prepared to leave me alone. He looked at the highway behind the Bronco, then hunched over to squint at me through the crack. "You're in the middle of the lane."

I stared at him.

"A car coming along might rear-end you."

I was too tired to fight back. "Thanks for stopping. I'll move my car."

"You sure you're okay?"

"I'm unhappy."

His head moved back. "Then nothing's the matter."

"I'm fine."

Two pickups and an ambulance were parked outside the Sagebrush Lounge. Buck Fratelli keeps things way dark inside so a jealous cowboy coming through the door has to adjust long enough for snugglers to move apart or, in extreme cases, break for the back door. What it does is leave you standing up front until everyone present has copped their attitude.

Faith Fratelli sat on a stool behind the bar, studying *Password* on a color TV with a purple-soaked picture. The Sagebrush used to be Talbot Taxidermy, and Buck wouldn't buy the dump unless Dothan's dad threw in his mutant animal collection. Taxidermists have a unique sense of humor. Along a shelf on both sides of the TV stood an array of jackalopes, fur-bearing trout, unicorns, sage hens with huge breasts. Buck's prize piece was a Wyoming werewolf, which is a butt mount of a whitetail deer with glass eyes in the hips, the tail made into a nose, and a pair of razorback fangs set in the asshole. Vicious-looking creature when you first see it and disgusting after that.

A voice on the TV whispered, "The password is 'swordfish.'"

Faith blew cigarette smoke out her nostrils. "Why do

stupid people smile all the time? This guy looks like a Mormon missionary."

Other than the skinny tie and that shit-eater under his nose, the guy didn't look a bit like a missionary. His shirt was purple.

Three ancient timber wolves sat on stools nodding over Blue Ribbon beer. The oldest wolf of them all was Oly Pedersen, who'd made a profession of outliving sidekicks. He'd signed up with Grandpa Pierce back in World War I, and they did the blood brothers thing men get into living in trenches with other men, so Dad always went out of his way to take care of Oly—drove him to the doctor, had him over for dinner on Christmas, that sort of thing. When I was a kid Oly'd chain-sawed me a rocking horse that was really neat.

A kid too young to be in the Sagebrush slapped at a Home Run pinball game while a skinny guy in white overalls and a fat guy in a wheelchair shot pool. The wheelchair guy rammed the cue ball like he wanted to kill it and hollered "*Banzai, motherfucker*" on every shot.

I said, "Everclear."

Faith glanced at me for the first time. "Your makeup's a mess, Maurey."

"I'm not wearing makeup."

The wheelchair man spun around. "Hippy chicks don't wear makeup. Bras either. And they don't shave nothin'."

"Shut up, Shane," Faith said with no energy, as if she said it often and didn't expect to be heard. "You making purple passion, Maurey?"

"The password is none of your business."

Faith missed it—flew right over her head. "Kids buy Everclear cause it's 180 proof. They mix it with gallons and gallons of Hawaiian Punch, call it purple passion." Faith pronounced it the same as everyone else in town—High-wayan.

"I'm in kind of a hurry here."

"The boys use it to get the girls drunk." Faith had pitch-black hair pulled into a ponytail and two turquoise bracelets on her left wrist. She was pleasant and Buck was smart, and between them they made ends meet, which isn't easy in GroVont.

I waited while she rang up the fifth and slid it into a sack. The grinner on TV said, "Shark," and his female partner said, "Lawyer."

"What do you want with Everclear, Maurey?" Faith asked. "You're a Yukon woman."

"I'm gonna drink myself to death."

Faith laughed without taking her eyes off *Password*. "Don't you wish."

I dropped two dollar bills on the bar. "Get Oly a Blue Ribbon, Faith, tell him it's from Dad."

The pool players were conferring, and as I left, Shane, the fat one in the chair, wheeled into my path. His head twitched. "We have a wager."

"I'm sure you do."

"Lloyd claims that dime in your back pocket is heads facing out, and I maintain it is tails."

I stuck my fingers in the pocket in question. There was plenty of room, for fingers, anyway. "How much did you bet?"

"The next round."

"You both lose, it's a quarter."

"Heads or tails quarter?"

"Isn't there a rule against leaving an AA meeting and coming straight to a bar?"

Shane went into a laughter spaz where he bobbed up and down on his hands. "I told you she watches. Every day, sitting in that window, watching and watching."

Lloyd spoke for the first time. "It's Coca-Cola."

"Yeah, right. At least I put mine in a coffee cup."

The flab on Shane's face arranged itself into a pout. He held the glass toward me. "It is Coca-Cola. Want a taste?"

"I'd rather die."

"We don't drink alcoholic beverages, ma'am," Lloyd said.

"Then why hang out in a bar?"

The two glanced at each other, and Lloyd kind of shrugged. Shane looked back up at me. "Bars are all we know. We ceased alcohol consumption but can't decide what to do instead."

"When you find out, tell me."

Lloyd held his pool cue with one hand and rubbed his overalls with the other. "We'll do that, ma'am."

I stared down at the grinning Shane. "Now, wheel out of my way. I'm busy."

4

SAM CALLAHAN SAYS THE ONLY IMPORTANT DECISION IS whether to commit suicide and die now or not commit suicide and die later. He read that in a book. I decided to die now.

As I drove up the river road to our family place, deep blue plastered the sky all the way to Yellowstone in the north and the Winds in the east. Earlier I had been too drunk to notice the air or the silver-gray sagebrush. On the valley floor the cottonwoods had small, lime green leaves, then as I moved up the mountain the leaves curled in on themselves until, at the ranch itself, each naked twig was tipped by a furry bud.

I pulled off next to the Miner Creek culvert and dug under the seat for a Flintstones never-tip cup, then I walked over to our buck-and-rail fence. The TM ranch stretched up the rise to the frame ranch house Grandpa built to replace the one-room cabin where Dad and three brothers and a sister were raised. Hank had the mares and foals fenced in the east pasture and the geldings strung along the creek. Frostbite the Dad killer grazed in a bunch feeding on bromegrass near the far irrigation ditch. The pasture was a dull yellow veined by dark green along the ditches where Hank was already moving water.

I had almost killed my son. Next time he might not be lucky, therefore, I had to stop. Easy logic.

Only a heartbeat ago Dad made us bull boats by cutting the ends off watermelons and setting in chokecherry masts with bandanna sails. Petey and I squealed up and down the creek, crashing through willows, encasing ourselves in mud from the knees down. We turned pinecones into boat families of a Mom, Dad, two kids, and a horse. Petey's family usually sank, but mine bobbed clear to the river.

I lived for horses back then. My mare, Molly, followed me like a beagle, once right into the house and into my room. The night lightning struck her I cried till dawn. I thought I would never feel that bad again.

Here's what I couldn't grab: the string connecting that to this, how the girl who slept in cowgirl boots and played with pinecone dolls became the woman who dressed like a Salt Lake hooker and hid bourbon bottles in vacuum cleaner bags. I pried the lid off Auburn's cup and poured it to the rim with Everclear. Was the problem nothing but alcohol? I'd been drinking more or less regular since college, although I didn't drink a bit while I was pregnant with Auburn. I only began drinking on a daily basis after Frostbite killed Dad. Closing my eyes, I tried to call up what I felt like before booze. A few watery images floated past—watermelon boats, Shannon, myself in the mirror in my cheerleading outfit, riding—but I couldn't hold what I felt like, what I thought about in the gap between going to bed and going to sleep, how I met the morning.

The first Everclear went down like gasoline. Made me shudder, which alcohol hadn't done in some time. I'd only tasted Everclear once, and then it was mixed with a washtub of cherry Kool-Aid at a frat party in Laramie. That was my sophomore year after I got hurt by a boy named Park, short for Parker. One day when everything was going dandy he just dropped out of school and went home to Maine. I rebounded into a Phi Delt bed. Randy, the Phi Delt, taught me lost weekend drinking and sex without emotional attachment.

I tipped the cup and took in as much as possible in one long chug. The stomach burn was amazing. Park popping into my mind was a surprise, since he generally stayed on the fringe, where he belonged. Park had been sad and sensitive, probably my only true emotional attachment even vaguely connected to sex. With Park, I had the friendship of Sam and the teenage romance of Dothan. We talked about it for weeks before I took away Park's virginity, then when he discovered he wasn't my first, or second, or even third, something in Park closed.

Two Swainson's hawks flew down the river. As I watched, the darker, higher male dived into the female in a feather explosion. The hawks plummeted, fused together, wings beating each other instead of air, until, yards above the river, they broke into separate birds again. If people could mate like hawks—a midair crashing of bodies—I might give passion another try.

I poured and drank again. The bottle was over a quarter gone and all I felt was belly fire and a little wooziness in my forehead. When Marilyn Monroe committed suicide, Dad sat in his recliner and stared at the wall all morning. He liked movie stars, and I guess he really liked Marilyn. I'd never seen him sad before, never realized grown-ups got sad before that. I made him iced tea with lemon, but he said he wasn't thirsty. I don't think he noticed what I was offering.

Marilyn Monroe was into fucking. She was the symbol of fucking and she died naked; then John Kennedy died, the pill came along, Vietnam, silly drugs and hard alcohol, and suddenly I'm on a fence sending myself into a twenty-two-year-old's grave. Auburn wouldn't even know I died on purpose to save him. He'd grow up thinking his mom the lush drank herself to death.

Couldn't allow that. Suicide to save a child was brave, but drinking till you died was weak. All I had left that mattered was how Auburn thought of me later on, and I couldn't die and let him grow up blaming weakness.

A note. Had to tell Auburn it was for him. Without a note, Dothan could turn the boy against me. Life would have been wasted.

One more slug, straight from the bottle this time, and a fairly coherent walk back to the Bronco. Only ten, twelve steps, nothing to brag about. Trouble with the door, then big trouble with the glove box. Sunglasses, fuses, unknown key, corkscrew, burnt candle, DON'T VOTE button, four-inch bit from a busted bridle—no paper but the Bronco registration and a pink speeding ticket Dothan hadn't told me about. Eighty-five in a thirty-five zone, Pocatello, Idaho, March 2, 1973.

"March two," I said out loud, willing recall. The day was gone. Hell, March was gone, a shadow in the forest of my memory. Month not to eat oysters. In like a lion, out like a lamb; what the heck did that mean?

The heck.

I dug a red crayon from under the passenger seat, then barked my head on the rearview mirror. Sent the mirror askew. Askew. Crayon said SCARLET on the side, with evidence of slurpy sucking on the pointy end. God, I tried to keep foreign objects from Auburn's mouth.

I two-hand-rubbed the parking ticket across my leg to make it smooth.

Auburn my son

I did it to save you from me. Dad lies. I loved you.

I drew a scarlet line through *I loved you*, then wrote it again. *I love you.*

"Yeah, right," I said. Now—back to the bottle and down to business.

I nailed an entire cup of Everclear in one drooly gulp. Gagged. Choked back vomit. Ran my hand through my hair. We're talking tunnel focus here, an oil filter-loosening tool wrapped around my skull. The stuff was working.

I sat on the bottom rail and rested my cheek on the top. An infinitely small red speck came from a crack in the wood, then crawled out of vision. The wood texture was beautiful, real, and close. I put out my tongue to taste it. Without emotion, I wondered what death was like. Would it be a nothing, not even knowing I was nothing, or would I exist without need? It didn't matter. We're born from zip and go to zip. Born naked.

Marilyn Monroe died naked. That was the way to go—the way you came in. Marilyn Monroe was the symbol of fucking, and when she died naked, people she didn't know sat in chairs and felt sad. Even the people I knew wouldn't be sad at me. Sam Callahan, Shannon, Lydia, Hank, Mom—they'd all say "She lived a tragic, useless life. Too bad," then they'd eat supper and go to bed and get up the next day and nothing would be different. Dothan would have to find a sitter.

A truck rattled down the road behind me, going toward town. Scared me into pouring another cup of Everclear. What would I have done if the driver stopped? I hit the cup hard.

I wanted to be Marilyn Monroe and go the way I came. A person of substance would never die in a windbreaker and cutoffs. Had to move up the creek so no one could see me naked. Suicide was embarrassing enough without being laughed at. I held the bottle up to my eye, two-thirds empty. One-third full, said the optimist. Whatever. Could I make it up the creek to privacy? I could do anything requiring balance. I was Rocky Mountain vaulting champion of 1962—same summer Marilyn Monroe got naked and died. If she could do it, so could the vaulting champion.

Going across the fence, I caught my foot on the rail and flung over on my neck and back. The world spun and the sky was no longer blue, but a dun color with black-and-yellow shifting holes. My legs went bad, as in non-functioning numbness. I turned over but couldn't stand, which caused frustration. Dad crawled to die with a view; who was I to break tradition?

The bottle swung below my breasts, held by my teeth. As I crawled things stuck in my palms and I had to go over sagebrush because my head wouldn't lift to see the path. Must have looked like an anteater. The ground tilted, I went off a drop, and part of me was suddenly wet. Far enough. I crawled out of the creek and spit out the bottle. When I unzipped the windbreaker Charley fell out.

With the T-shirt pulled half over my head, a wave of nausea struck and I had to lie down. Inside the shirt was safe, all white, like being in a veil. To strip the cutoffs I had to lie on my back and shoulders with my hair in mud. Groveling to get naked. Groveling to die. Tawdry but with the idealism of the nude.

I rolled into the submissive end of doggie style and looked down at the body I was about to kill. Not that bad a body to spend a life in. It produced two children. It could feel sunshine and water and orgasms. My nails tended to split, and from where I knelt, the breasts sagged, but they had been a fairly good size when I was nursing. Which was another thing my body could do. Adios tits, farewell belly, later gater pubic hair. I'm outta here.

I raised my head and drank it all—sucked down the fifth. Then, naked, I lay on my side, looking across the surface of Miner Creek at some weeds and a tiny yellow flower on the other bank. First flower of spring. Life was a cheat and a bitch. The black holes grew bigger until they took the flower, then the creek. My fingers found Charley and pulled him to me. Like Mom's breast, I put his barrel between my lips. Affection.

5

WHEN I MET SAM CALLAHAN BACK WHEN WE WERE BOTH thirteen and starting seventh grade, he confessed this dream of someday being a deep and sensitive novelist who commanded women's love and men's respect. All through junior high and high school he scribbled in three-subject notebooks, filling them with scads of poems and short stories. Most of the stories mixed baseball and romance, with a few sliding over into science fiction.

Sam soon learned deep and sensitive is another way of saying lonesome, and the closest he'd come so far to commanding women's love and men's respect through writing was his job as sports and entertainment intern at the *Greensboro Record* in Greensboro, North Carolina.

My favorite story he wrote back in high school was the one in which Death turned into a cute little mouse named Bob. Bob wore green shorts and a red football jersey, and he skittered across people while they slept, which killed them so he could collect their souls. Sam said the human soul looks and tastes like Swiss cheese.

Dying from being touched by a mouse became known as getting Bobbed. People were so scared of getting Bobbed that they took to sleeping under loads of blankets with their head covered so no skin showed. Outside of bed they wore layers and layers of polyester mouse-proof clothing and hoods and masks and gloves up to here so no one ever saw anyone, which made them even more scared because they thought Bob might be among them in disguise. A carpenter invented a sealed wooden box that guaranteed nothing and no one could ever touch the person inside. So each and every person in the world crammed themselves into individual boxes and pulled the top shut so they could never be touched by Bob.

One hundred years later spacemen from the planet Asthmador landed on Earth. The aliens hopped on the radio and called their wisest elders back home to ask them this question: Since every single Earthling was dead in a coffin, who put them there?

The elders shrugged their mandibles and said, "Beats me."

After I read the story Sam said, "It's an allegory."

"How did the Earth people know being scampered over by Bob would kill them if everyone Bob scampered over was dead and couldn't talk?"

Sam went all sulky, said I didn't understand literature and he wasn't showing me any more stories. He was lying.

Mom is scared to death of death, but Dad took it with the attitude of a cowboy—if you can't understand something, turn it into a joke. Once at a Pierce family reunion up at Granite Hot Springs my born-again uncle from Dubois laid into Dad about his personal savior. My cousin Stella Jean and I were weaving lupines into a hula skirt when Dad's brother Scott stuck his face right up next to Dad and challenged him to accept Christ in his heart.

"Don't you believe in anything?" Scott asked.

"I believe I'll eat another hot dog."

Scott's face and neck filled up with blood. "Where do you think you'll go when you die, Buddy?"

Dad slid a willow stick lengthwise through a wienie. "San Francisco."

The Two Ocean Lake underwater record was four minutes, fourteen seconds, held by Kim Schmidt's cousin from Nebraska. I dived off the pier and kicked twice, found the bottom, then the root. Counting by Mississippis, I wrapped my right arm under the slick wood and held on with my left. Thirty-two Mississippi, thirty-three Mississippi, thirty-four Mississippi...At sixty Mississippi I started over. The water felt cold yet caressing, and in my mind I saw trout and weeds waving by, ignoring me. On the second sixty Mississippi my chest tightened to the point I had to release a few bubbles. The yellow came again. As a child running in circles till I fell, as a little girl bucked off her horse, now as a teenager breaking the Two Ocean Lake underwater record, yellow always preceded black. I exhaled more bubbles, but that didn't help the chest pain. I opened my eyes—no trout, no weeds, only water and the vague form of the downed aspen on the bottom. Lungs really hurt, I'd stopped counting but couldn't recall when. My fingers lost the root. I clawed the bottom, flailing arms and legs pushing me down as the water carried me up. Lungs screamed, panic choked my chest, I fought to stay underwater. My face broke through with a sob intake of air.

"Look who's alive."

"I wouldn't call that live yet."

No forgiving hangover blankness here, I knew the facts in a heartbeat—Everclear, the Flintstones cup, Marilyn Monroe. It took a second to come up with why, then I saw my baby on the roof.

Shit. I'd failed.

I even knew exactly where I was. Although I hadn't slept here in years, I knew Sam Callahan's bed without opening my eyes.

A male voice said, "I've got pipe to fix."

"You spend more time on her plumbing than mine." Her would be me.

"She pays and you don't."

I slit my eyes open a crack and saw Hank Elkrunner and Lydia Callahan kissing each other good-bye over by the door. Her hand crept up his back into his long Blackfoot hair. His hand slid to the base of her spine.

"Be home tonight," Lydia ordered.

Hank gave her a love spank. "Doubt it. Lauren Bacall is set to pop."

I closed my eyes. Watching other people's affection makes me sad. After he left, Lydia lit a cigarette, then came to the bed and touched my forehead. "Hank says you're alive," she said.

"He's too good for you."

Lydia's hand twitched, like it would when you think you're talking to a person in a coma and the person talks back. "Hank's the best."

"You don't deserve him."

"Yes, I do."

Lydia'd been a mess when she met Hank Elkrunner. Now she had that reformed-drunk-someone-good-loves-me smugness that turns me catty. Hell, I could stop drinking if someone good loved me.

Lydia sat in an easy chair next to the bed and opened a newspaper. Her drug of choice had gone from gin to current events. "How's your head?"

"There's a spike driven through my third eye."

"I shouldn't wonder. Did you kill the whole fifth?"

I didn't answer. My head hurt, my nose hurt, my crotch hurt, all the muscles in my back hurt—my advice is never botch a suicide.

The paper rustled as Lydia turned a page. "This guy John

Ehrlichman is frightening. He reminds me of your husband. The others are all lying snakes, but Ehrlichman's a lying barracuda."

I had no idea what she was talking about. "Where's Auburn?"

"He's home. Delilah Talbot moved in to take care of him."

That brought up a dozen questions, none of which I had the energy to ask. Lydia talked as she read the paper.

"Doc Petrov pumped your stomach, but he said it was too late to do much good. You went into respiratory arrest, then your kidneys kind of crumpled and they stuck in a catheter. You should have seen yourself, Maurey. So many tubes running in and out you looked like a chemistry experiment."

"How long?"

"Two days here and three in intensive care. When Hank brought you off the mountain you were choking on vomit and all that blood was gushing out your nose, I thought we'd lost you."

"Yeah, right."

Auburn and I are on top of Teton Pass in the early spring and I park the Bronco to watch a fantastically lit sunrise. Beams bend around Jackson Peak, snow on the Sleeping Indian glows with a fire of its own. I step out with my bottle to be closer to the beauty and breathe a prayer of thanks, but I forget to set the emergency brake and the Bronco, with Auburn in his car seat, rolls down the pass. I run—run harder and harder, reach for the back bumper, but the Bronco is inches beyond my fingertips. Auburn laughs, trusting me. I dive and catch the trailer hitch but still cannot stop the rolling as the car's momentum drags me down the highway. At the cliff the front wheels go over, wrenching the hitch from my hands, and I'm left flat with my head over the edge to watch the car flip front over back, over and over down the mountain. Auburn's cries fill the canyon until the final crash. Then, I'm swept by silence. Once again yellow globs rush me, turning black.

When I met Lydia she used to drink a pint of Gilbey's gin at ten-thirty every night. She and Sam would sit through the sports and weather—Lydia didn't give a hoot about news in those days—then Sam would fetch her bottle and a two-ounce shot glass with an etching of the Lincoln Memorial on the side. Lydia filled and threw down eight shots—bang, bang—one right after another before bed.

She never offered me any gin, so I can't claim she led me astray, although whenever us kids got way-rowdy or wound up she'd give us each a yellow Valium. I kind of liked those. They made everything fuzzy as the line between me and the rest of the world became less distinct.

When Shannon was teething Lydia showed us how to dip the pacifier in whiskey and honey. Shannon will probably grow up with the idea that pain is relieved by alcohol and sugar. It's not.

My own mom lives in a drugstore wonderland now, but as a kid the only thing I saw her drink was eggnog on Christmas Eve. The woman had a remarkably low tolerance—one cup and she's giggling like a ten-year-old and dancing the rumba to "Jingle Bell Rock."

Every year she and Petey would sing "We three kings of Orient are, smoking on a rubber cigar, we got loaded, it exploded—BOOM."

Dad drank beer at rodeos and football games. Since he died, I've been told in his younger days he could hook back the bourbon, but I never saw it.

The thing is, alcohol had become a factor in my behavior. It snuck up on me. I loved Yukon Jack in a way I wouldn't care to love a man, but I hadn't planned on needing him. I didn't ask for marriage.

———

The weekend passed in two slots—bad dreams and awake. Awake was a bad dream come true, so I preferred the other kind. Twice a day Lydia and Hank helped me into the bathroom, where I sat amid threats of another catheter if I didn't go.

"You've peed on your last sheet," Lydia said. "I'm tired of wiping up your social blunders."

Hank nodded in solemn agreement.

Social blunder is a term Lydia uses a lot. She'll be at someone's house and burn a hole in the rug with her cigarette or break an antique doodad, and she'll put one hand over her mouth and say, "Oh, my, I've committed a social blunder."

Hostesses doubt her sincerity, but I think she is sincere, she just can't deal with honest embarrassment. "Social blunder" is better than what she used to say, which was "Fuck me silly."

During one of the awake periods Lydia asked me if I'd meant to harm myself or if the rooftop episode had simply shoved me off the deep end, alcohol-wise.

"Didn't you read the note?"

"We thought of that and looked, but the only paper Hank found was a speeding ticket on the seat that Auburn'd colored on. Anything you wrote must have blown away."

———

I awoke soaked in sweat after a nasty dream, in which a bald eagle swooped down to pluck Auburn off a picnic blanket, and found Lydia smoking in her usual chair at the end of the bed, glaring at the TV. She must have sat there most of the week.

She said, "Dirty Dick Nixon is a boil on the butt of a sumo wrestler."

"Why watch if it upsets you?" I asked.

"Because if I relax for a moment, America will flush her freedom down the toilet. You've got mail."

Lydia flicked her cigarette at her jeans' leg and rubbed the ashes into the denim. She didn't believe in ashtrays. When she was done she'd balance the butt on its end so every table in the house was covered by little filter columns. Once a week or so Hank went around scooping the mess into a paper bag.

One letter was from Sam in North Carolina and one from Dothan across town. My name on Dothan's envelope was typed, evidently by his secretary Lurlene, since Dothan can't type, which I took as a bad sign.

Sam's letter was written in red ink.

Hey Maurey,

Alicia has a problem with foreplay. I met her covering an Up With People concert at Page High. This small woman with Judy Collins eyes and a tight sweater took my hand and led me to a crawl space under the stage. I could see the audience, from the knees down anyway, tapping their feet as seventy-five kids above us proclaimed their wholesomeness and Alicia tore off my pants.

Later at Sambo's she ate like it was Thanksgiving and told me she equates danger with sexual tension. Since then she's turned tigress on a ferris wheel, in a public toilet at a baseball game, in a booth at Dairy Queen, and on a coffin in an open grave at the cemetery. In bed, she's frigid.

Maurey, I don't know if I want a long-term relationship with this woman. She might be a poor role model for Shannon.

You should see our beautiful daughter grow. She gets prettier and more like you every day. Which scares the pants off me. *I caught a 14-year-old boy talking to her at the shopping center yesterday. I was her father when I was fourteen, I know what those little monsters think.*

Shannon gave a report on Wyoming the last day of school before vacation. Took my antelope heads into Mrs. Fenster's homeroom and told the class they were wild Yellowstone ibex. Even the teacher believed her. Where does she get this tendency to put people on? Surely not from my side of the family. We went to dinner at Tarheels and Shannon refused to eat off the kids' menu. She told Alicia and the waitress she was thirteen and I was lying about her age because I'm cheap. Alicia stuck her hand between my napkin and my lap and we had a fight later. I said perversion is big fun, only not with my daughter in sight, and Alicia called me a hypocrite. The woman who fucked under Up With People called me a hypocrite.

I'm ready to change girlfriends. Here's a repercussion of our actions I hadn't planned on, Maurey: Women go ape over single men with young daughters. Shannon's a better line than a big dog.

She put your picture in Grandma Callahan's silver locket and won't take it off even to sleep. I asked her what she wants to do for the summer and she said go to Wyoming. Fat chance with me on the stock car beat. We might slip out there for a week in August, but in the meantime I've signed her up for swimming lessons at the club and hired a black woman named Gus to stick around weekday afternoons and fix supper.

My expenses keeping this house almost exactly double what I make at the paper. Selling Grandpa's carbon paper plant and putting the money in golf carts was a smart move as the bottom is dropping out of carbon paper. I guess Caspar knew what he was up to when he left everything to me instead of Mom.

Say hey to her, kiss Auburn for me, and tell your husband to screw himself with a stick.

Your friend,
Sam

P.S. Here's my newest story. Don't tell me what you think.

The next page started with "Kiss Your Elbow Enterprises" by Sam Callahan.

I showed Lydia the letter. "I hate it when he calls me Mom," she said. "He only does that to piss me off."

"Shannon loves me. It's a good thing she can't see me," I said.

Lydia blew smoke at Henry Kissinger on the TV. "I spent most of my life jiving Dad to get money, and now I have to jive my son. There is no justice."

The letter from Dothan was a four-page official document deal with "Wyoming Family Violence Protection Act, Form No. 1" typed in the upper right corner.

I said, "Wyoming Family Violence Protection Act?" and looked over at Lydia. She was watching TV so intently I could tell she was really watching me.

The form had Dothan and Auburn listed as plaintiff and me as defendant. On page two Lurlene had typed the story about me getting drunk and driving down the highway with Auburn on top of the Bronco. Page three was an A through H list of possible things the plaintiffs could ask the court to do to the defendant. Dothan had X'ed A, B, C, D, F, and G.

Out of curiosity I read the ones I didn't have to do first—E) provide suitable alternative housing, and H) pay injunctive relief, which I took as child support.

Although it was all lawyer words, the things I had to do for the next ninety days boiled down to A) have no contact with Dothan or Auburn, B) give Dothan the house, C) get out of the house, D) stay out of the house, F) not kidnap my son, and G) not touch any joint checking or saving accounts.

The fourth page was all legal giz with words like *Es Parte Temporary Order of Protection* and more plaintiff-defendant stuff. A judge in Jackson signed and Lurlene notarized it herself. Under the notary stamp Dothan had written, "Send Lurlene your new address so we'll have a place to serve the divorce papers. If you try to see Auburn I'll have you in jail. There's no booze in jail." He didn't sign his name.

Lydia's eyes had a skittish look. "You knew about this," I said.

She breathed smoke out her nose to buy time. "I heard rumors."

"How'd you hear rumors? You haven't left the room since I woke up."

"Hank heard rumors." She lit a new cigarette off the old one, then set the butt on its end on the floor. "And the George brothers delivered your stuff last night."

My mouth didn't feel wet enough to talk. "Stuff?"

"Clothes, toilet articles, your books."

"How about my record albums?"

"I guess Dothan kept those."

I hadn't expected this, although I should have. I'd been awake two days and Dothan hadn't come around. Maybe I didn't expect it because I hadn't thought about it on purpose.

"Did he send over my black Tony Lamas?"

Lydia's head turned and she blew smoke at me. "You mean the boots with the pint of Yukon in the right toe?"

We looked at each other a moment. Lydia and I had never messed in each other's personal moralities before. When I thought I wanted an abortion way back when, she didn't lay out any version of right or wrong, just offered to pay for it and drive me to the clinic. I didn't say "Poor Hank" the time she had an affair, or "Give the old man a break" when her dad was laid up by a stroke and she went cold on all of us.

"Your kidneys will crumple again," she said.

I held the sheet hem with both hands. "The jerk is taking my baby from me. Isn't that reason enough to need a drink?"

"There will always be a reason."

"Just bring me my damn boots."

———

I didn't need a drink so much as I needed a drink close by. Jack smelled like a friend, and I took one sip to prove I could, then I screwed his top back on. Comfort isn't so much drinking whiskey as knowing where the next whiskey will come from.

———

I showered while Lydia fixed lunch. The water was so nice I sat in the tub and let it run over my head till the hot turned tepid. When Lydia brought the cold cheese sandwiches into the bedroom she found me dressed and ready, right down to my black Tony Lama boots.

She stood in the door with the tray in her hands. Lydia has these unbelievably long fingers. If she'd been born a man, she would have been a surgeon instead of a TV watcher.

"Going out?" she asked.

"Do you guys have a tent I could borrow? I need a tent." I had on jeans and a long-sleeved shirt that Sam had given me for one holiday or another.

"Petey called this morning. He said Annabel hasn't been told about your escapades—he called them escapades—but you're welcome to live at home awhile."

"That's nice of him."

"You'd have to pretend Dothan's at a religious retreat."

I wondered where I should pretend Auburn was, but it didn't matter enough to ask.

Lydia set the tray on the bed and took a bite of my sandwich. "Hank will need help at the ranch this summer. You could live there."

"About the tent."

"For that matter, you can stay here. Women Against the Bomb can always use another envelope licker." It'd been Mothers Against the Bomb until Lydia volunteered her way up to director. She changed the name so no one could accuse her of being a mother.

I talked as I loaded the bare necessities into Sam's old day pack. Tampons, toothbrush, flashlight, spare panties, pocketknife, notebook, pen, all the candy bars in Lydia's house, *Stuart Little* by E. B. White, and the Yukon. "I appreciate all you've done, Lydia. I really do, but I need to be near Auburn. He's my only connection. I'll be back every day to shower and change."

Lydia sat next to the tray and drank my milk. "Doc Petrov didn't want to release you to me, he wanted you in an institution."

"Mental or prison?"

"He didn't say. What I mean is, if you behave the least bit strangely out there, Dothan's going to nail your body to the wall. As it is, you have ninety days without a son. One colorful action and we're talking lifetime."

I thought about what she said, I really did. I just couldn't differentiate between ninety days and a lifetime.

"Look, Lydia, what I need most is a postcard. You got any postcards around the house?"

———

Dear Dad,

I'm sorry I haven't written in six days. The whole family
has been so busy I haven't had time to think. Auburn has an
earache and he's teething and Dothan picked this of all weeks
to go on a religious retreat. I even missed Paul Harvey.
    Be careful, Dad. San Francisco can be weird in the summer.
Don't buy chemicals from people you can't trust.

Love,
Maurey

6

THE TOWN TONE REARED ITS UGLY HEAD THE MOMENT I walked into Zion's Own Hardware. Men cut their eyes at me, women whispered. I felt surrounded by a four-foot buffer zone that no one dared enter. All I'd done was drink and mess up; I wondered how big a zone they'd give a person who did something truly awful—Charles Manson or Liz Taylor or somebody. The whole town, buildings and all, would shrink away.

I picked up three stakes, because Lydia'd said Sam's backpacking tent was short, some twine, and a canteen and went to the front of the store, where my buffer zone chased off the line at the cash register.

I placed my purchases on the counter, then slapped Charley down with his barrel pointed at Johnny Jenkins's belt line.

"Centerfire, 140 grain, silvertip if you got any, Johnny."

He put both hands on the counter. Whenever a salesperson decides they aren't going to sell you something, be it drugstore, liquor store, or dynamite outlet, they all hit the same pose—both hands flat on the counter, feet slightly spread and evenly balanced. It's a training thing.

"I can't do that, Mrs. Talbot," Johnny said.

I played dumb. "Oh, hell, I'll take hollow point, then."

"Dothan telephoned and said not to sell you any bullets or sharp objects."

"You always do what my husband says?"

Johnny kind of sighed. He's really not such a bad guy, for a Church of Christ deacon. He wasn't taking pleasure from my humiliation. Lots of people would have taken pleasure. "Mrs. Talbot, can you tell me anything other than tragedy that could come of selling you bullets?"

A crowd of locals stood outside my buffer zone, watching my life crash like this was an NBC movie of the week.

"A Hell's Angel motorcycle gang might rape me and I'd have no protection," I said.

Johnny raised up, then down on his toes. "Not likely, Mrs. Talbot."

———

Johnny Jenkins's wife, LaWanda, made a pass at me in 1967. She stopped me on the street and asked me to come in her double-wide mobile home for a piece of pineapple upside-down cake. In her kitchen LaWanda told me to read *The Feminine Mystique*. She took off her blouse and stood there on the linoleum in her green Dacron slacks and bra and asked if I thought she had nice breasts.

That Fourth of July she ran off with a barrel racer from Aberdeen, South Dakota, and stayed gone three months. Right after LaWanda came home she and Johnny were baptized Church of Christ.

———

I didn't realize what LaWanda Jenkins did was a pass until two years later at UW, where I met a lesbian-and-proud-of-it. Cynthia said the neat thing about being a gay freshman in the dorms was that she made all the eighteen-year-old Wyoming girls nervous so she didn't get stuck with a roommate. I liked Cynthia; she'd have been easier to live with than that dork Lucy Jane from Thermopolis.

I asked Cynthia a series of what must have been the most naive questions in gay history: How can you enjoy it if nothing goes in anything? Does one girl pretend to be the boy and one the girl, and if so, do you switch off roles or is the boy-girl always the boy? Do lesbians have a secret signal they flash so they can recognize each other?

Cynthia was from San Diego, where she said lesbians abound, so my curiosity must have seemed like Goober gone west. She said in the long run my life would be lots happier if I turned gay, and maybe it would have, but I wasn't born with the chemicals. I figure it's as hard to fake you are as it is to fake you aren't.

Even though Cynthia had only been nailed by one man—her grandfather—she knew that all men are shits. I had to get nailed by an even dozen to reach the same conclusion. Then I came home and married the biggest shit of the lot.

7

I SET SAM'S TENT UP NEXT TO MY RASPBERRY BUSHES IN THE corner of the yard, as far from the front door and walk as I could get and not be on the neighbor's land. The rain fly didn't perch right because I was three stakes short on account of Johnny Jenkins's strict definition of sharp object.

As I ditched the north end of the tent, Sugar Cannelioski came out the front door and stood on the porch with her hands on her hips. She shouted across the lawn. "What are you doing in my yard?"

"Your yard?" Sugar had fuzz on her upper lip and no breasts at all, but she compensated with this long blond hair she must have brushed six hundred strokes a day. She stood with her thumbs front and fingers back like city women do the hands-on-the-hips thing. Anyone who's used to wearing jeans does it the other way around.

"You heard me, get off my yard before I call Dothan. Scat."

I put my hands on my hips the way you're supposed to. "Come out and make me, you slimy bitch."

She didn't move. "I'm gonna call the police first, then Dothan."

I took one step forward and she took one step back. "Does your yard come with my husband and my child?"

Sugar's perky face went smug. Nobody liked her; she'd made a career of looking smug at women and stealing men. "Me and Dothan have a trial marriage, and yes, his child is part of it. You've messed that baby up but good, Maurey. It might take me weeks to straighten him out."

I pulled Charley from my windbreaker and pointed him at her tiny tits. "Bring me my son or I'll kill you."

Sugar laughed. "You got no bullets. Johnny wouldn't sell you bullets."

I pulled the trigger and made a harmless click. To myself I said, "God, I hate this town." To Sugar I said, "I don't need bullets to stuff this gun up your ass." I took three quick steps toward the porch and Sugar scooted back inside.

Dothan must have moved fast to bring in a replacement babysitter/whore in less than a week. Or maybe it'd been planned all along. I'd been fairly sure he was nailing Sugar Cannelioski—hell, everyone else who cheated on his wife did. Dothan didn't have the imagination to nail someone original.

Sugar had been the town tramp ever since she was sixteen and ran off to Idaho Falls to marry a marine. He got himself killed rolling a Jeep off Teton Pass. People said they were fighting over her morals and Sugar grabbed the wheel. Whatever happened, the boy was killed and Sugar came out with a VA survivors' pension.

A year later she seduced and married her sister's boyfriend. That marriage lasted a month, long enough for her sister to gain forty pounds and the former boyfriend, now husband, to lose his religion and thirty-five percent of all future earnings. Sugar was always bragging how she would never have to work again in her life, nothing to do but concentrate on her appearance. To me, outliving one husband and divorcing another before you're eighteen isn't grounds to brag.

I stretched out on the grass, soaking up sun and waiting for someone to come arrest me. I wondered where Auburn was—in the house or with Dothan or Dothan's mother or what. Would he be wearing his blue coveralls or the sailor thing or the Alabama Crimson Tide warm-ups? Did he miss me?

Sugar came back out and sat on the top step to do her nails. Now that the law was on the way, she decided to turn chatty.

"He's been waiting to ditch you for years," she said.

"We haven't been married two."

"He wanted me, only you're too worthless to pay alimony or child support. Those are Dothan's words, not mine, although I will always back up my man. You're too worthless, so he had to wait for you to provide an excuse so he could dump you without penalty."

It occurred to me that the whole time I'd been thinking Sugar was the town tramp, she'd been thinking the same of me.

Sugar held her left hand out to admire the nail job. "Boy, did you provide an excuse."

———

The neighbors' cowdog loped over to mark territory on the tent, and a couple of kindergartner types stood in the street sucking their thumbs and staring at me with blinkless eyes. The little one dragging the blanket shred reminded me of Shannon. I smiled at her and offered a bit of Mars bar, but the other child pulled her away. Curtains fluttered up and down the block, checking out the fallen woman, but no one ventured outside to give me grief. We were all waiting for authority figures.

Mangum Potter's sheriff's department Chevy came from the north just as Dothan's GMC half-ton appeared from the south. They parked nose to nose with Dothan on the wrong side of the street. As the doors slammed and the two men with power over me made their way across the lawn, I concentrated on the Teton Peaks above their heads. In spring the sky mostly rains or spits sleet and the land goes mud as the snow melts, but on clear days when the valley floor is green and the mountains are white, the whole scenery thing can be uplifting as hell, and I needed uplifting.

Dothan walked over with his arms folded. He had on a corpse-colored sweater I'd never seen before with the collar points of his shirt neatly placed on the outside like he'd just taken a shower after wholesome exercise. "Jesus," he said, "she can't even pitch a tent."

Mangum walked to the other side of the tent. "No privy, she must be squatting in the bushes."

"I always knew she would wind up crapping in public."

"Get away from my camp," I said. "I'm not breaking any laws."

It was like they couldn't see me, or they didn't realize I could see them. People talk that way around zoo animals and retarded children.

"Want me to arrest her?" Mangum asked.

"What law have I broken?"

Mangum took the macho thumbs-in-the-belt-loops stance. "We could run her in on public drunkenness."

"I'm not drunk."

Dothan stuck the toe of his boot under a stake and eased it from the ground. My rain fly went even droopier. "In jail where folks can't see what a wretch she is, they might feel sorry for her."

"Nobody feels sorry for her," Mangum said.

"I do," I said.

Dothan went on. "Let's keep her out front where she can dig her own grave."

Mangum nodded as he considered the wisdom of the plan. "Whatever you say, but I'd be more comfortable with her behind bars."

Dothan turned to look at the house. Sugar waved and smiled, and Dothan waved back. "If she approaches my son or my home, I want her nailed to the wall."

"Sounds reasonable," Mangum said.

Dothan always sounds reasonable when he's not. I started to stand up, but my knees got wobbly. "The part I don't understand," I said, "is why you want Auburn. You haven't spent ten minutes in a row with him since the day he was born."

Mangum and Dothan walked toward their vehicles. With his back to me, Mangum said, "What'd you ever see in that woman in the first place?"

Dothan opened his truck door and looked over at me. The expression on his face was like when you have to shoot a dog that's been chasing the neighbors' calves. He said, "I don't remember."

Dothan saw plenty in me back in high school. He acted half-crazy whenever I came around, although maybe he was at an age where he'd have acted half-crazy about anyone who let him nail her at will. The boy was insatiable—before school, during lunch, he came so quick back then we could hop in a mop closet after geometry, get him off, and not be late for social awareness.

He was two years older than me, so after he graduated they wouldn't let him hang around school anymore. He took a job at his dad's taxidermy. Dothan used to say he spent the days mounting elk and the nights mounting me. No matter how often he showered the alum brine smell clung to him like Saran Wrap. The stink nauseated me to the point where I refused to kiss him anymore, then he started splashing himself with Old Spice, which was like sucking Sterno.

My senior year I decided he was more trouble than fun, and I tried to break up. Dothan crumbled. First he said he'd kill me, and when that didn't draw the right response he said he'd kill himself. He said if I went out with another boy he'd join the army and get sent to Vietnam and die at the hands of gooks and it would be my fault. He also said no one would want me because I had the reputation of a slut. Which was crap; at seventeen every boy wants a slut.

I finally decided splitting up was just too hard and I'd deal with one more summer before escaping to college. It was a pretty lousy summer. I can't think of much worse than having sex in a car with someone you don't like.

Then, nightmare-come-true, he followed me to Laramie. I've never seen such a pain in the butt to get away from. I treated him mean so he would go away—didn't answer phone calls, stared through him in public, made fun of his pointy chin and old-man hairline.

To spite Dothan, I went out with an offensive lineman named Rocky Joe and slept with him. Isn't it amazing the number of motivations there are to fuck? Dothan and Rocky Joe got in a fight, and for the first time in his life, Dothan had his ass kicked. He limped back to GroVont and I never saw Rocky Joe off the football field again.

After that came the Park thing with all its deepness followed by two years of boys I needed but didn't much like who didn't much care for me either. College turned out such a bust that I figured Dothan was what I deserved. He'd gone from stuffing animals to selling real estate—not a step up, but at least he smelled better. So I dropped out, moved back home, got married, got pregnant, got drunk.

A kid from the *Jackson Hole News* dropped by to take my picture as a human-interest item. I crawled in the tent and refused to come out even though he whined that his editor would chew him out if he came back with nothing but a tent in a front yard. I didn't budge. Nobody says laughingstocks have to cooperate with the media.

On my stomach, I watched through the insect net as people walked up and down the street, pretending they had errands downtown. Or the dog suddenly needed relieving or something, any excuse to check out the Talbot spectacle. Cars drove by slow, as if my camp were a prizewinner in the Christmas outdoor display contest.

I ate two candy bars and drank half the pint of Yukon. Inside the tent was hot and airless, so I rolled Sam's sleeping bag into a pillow and took a nap until Dothan coming home for supper woke me up. When he slammed the truck door, I jumped like I'd been shock-therapied. Sleeping in the afternoon always makes me skittish.

The sunset was great. I may have been depraved, and I may have been a drunk, maybe I was even town tramp for a while, but I never lost my appreciation for the sun going down behind the Tetons. Even then, I had standards.

Besides, *town tramp* was a matter of perspective. We're talking a college coed between 1968 and 1971 here—the very height of the sexual revolution. I slid through that remarkably short gap between the pill and herpes when for the first, possibly the last, time in history the young reveled in sex without consequences. A dozen boys before age twenty-three was not that rare or squalid.

After dark I unscrewed the Yukon bottle, switched on the flashlight, and pulled the notebook from the pack. Between sips, I made a list—one dozen pricks I have known.

Sam
Dothan
Rocky Joe
Park
Randy
Lonnie
Chuck
Joe Bob
Joe Bob
Winston
Akeem
Leon

I went back and put a check next to the ones who sleeping with had made me feel better about myself instead of worse.

Sam ✓

Park ✓

Lonnie I'm not totally convinced happened because if we made it, he was a tequila screw that I blacked out. All I know is I woke up naked beside him in a Cowboy Joe homecoming float, and afterward he told anybody who would listen that we'd made it. Lonnie may have been lying through his teeth. He wouldn't be the first to say he did when he didn't or he didn't when he did.

One of the Joe Bobs was from Archer City, Texas, and the other from Great Falls, Montana, but I couldn't tell you which was which. The bigger one had a '58 Corvette tattooed on his chest. I remember that. I met him at a frat party, where he slammed a thirty-two-ounce Miller High Life and said "Lick my chrome, baby."

Winston was a married English professor specializing in Camus and Kafka. He's the one who denied me. Akeem was a black guy who collected white women. Honest to God, the headboard of his bed was covered with silver stick-on stars like you give little kids for doing their chores. I asked him what they were for, and he said it was to remind him of the night sky over Mecca. Then when we finished what wasn't near all it's built up to be, he jumped from the bed to add a star to the collection.

Even a tramp can be naive.

Sipping the Yukon so as to conserve warmth for the long night, I played with the flashlight beam on the roof of the tent and came to generalizations concerning the male gender. A few, a very few that I'd met, see women as individual people with both good and bad traits and unique fears and needs. The giant majority of boys said things to each other like "Gettin' any lately?" and "If she's ugly, put a flag over her head and fuck her for Old Glory."

Boys plied girls with whiskey in hopes of tricking them into doing stuff they didn't want to do. If a woman gave anything of herself willingly, boys interpreted it as proof of their manly superiority. The worst insult one boy could hurl at another was to call him female body parts—boob, pussy—or the action most wanted from a woman—cocksucker.

Was I the first female to figure this stuff out? Maybe Lydia knew and wouldn't tell me for fear of causing disillusionment. At nineteen I'd wanted someone to like me, so I came at this human connection thing open to sincerity, and now at twenty-two I was bitter, cynical, and smart. If I met any of them now, the good ones, the Parks and Sams, they would avoid me like walking gonorrhea. Five years out of high school and I'd lost hope. What a gyp.

———

I filled in the rest of the page with doodles, then I couldn't think what to do next, so I turned the page and did it again. My problem, besides retrieving my child, was that I could chug the Yukon and turn off my mind, knowing that running out meant we were in for a long night, or I could drink slowly, which meant sobering up between sips. The quandary was kill the bottle and be out of whiskey, or save it as security and never quite cop a proper buzz. I began to regret drinking in the afternoon as a nap inducement.

How I doodle is I draw pages of wavery lines with arrows on both ends. I'm very careful—no lines cross each other and every single arrow is a perfect wing-like V pointing the way to look next. I don't know why I doodle that way; I guess I never made the grade with faces.

Halfway through my third page of arrows, a sneeze exploded outside my tent. I would've liked to pee my pants.

"Who's there?" No sound came except the slight swish of someone trying to walk on grass without making noise. "I've got a gun."

"It's not loaded," a voice whispered.

Jesus, what good is a pistol if the whole county knows you don't have bullets? "Who's out there?"

"Pud." He waited a moment, then whispered again. "Pud Talbot."

Pud Talbot—all I needed was that retard sniffing around the tent. "Did Dothan send you out to bother me?"

"Dothan'll be real mad if he catches me here. Can I come in, Maurey?"

The whisper action seemed to indicate he was telling the truth, the visit was unauthorized, but I'd known the Talbot family too long to trust anything that seemed the truth. "What do you want, Pud?"

"I brought you food. Can I come in, Maurey? I don't want Dothan mad."

"Okay, but try anything weird and I'll break your nose with Charley."

Pud knew who Charley was. "I won't try anything weird." The zipper made its sound, then Pud pushed a greasy paper sack and a lit flashlight through the door. He crawled in head first. "I thought maybe you were hungry."

I hadn't considered it, but he was right. "What all did you bring?"

He shined the light on the bag. I picked it up and shined my own light inside—bologna and American cheese on white bread sandwich, a carton of chocolate milk, and a box of Milk Duds.

"Thank you, Pud." Maybe almost dying had made me susceptible to emotion, but I was kind of touched. Here was someone I hadn't known about who cared whether or not I ate.

"It's what I had for supper," he said.

"Didn't happen to bring anything to drink, did you?"

He raised up on his knees and flashed the light beam down the bag with mine. Our heads almost touched. "I put milk in," Pud said.

"I meant alcoholic to drink."

He lowered himself again. His voice sounded disappointed, as if he'd failed in his good deed. "I didn't think about alcohol."

"Wish I could say that. Thanks again, Pud. I do appreciate the food."

Pud sat quietly while I ate my sandwich. His flashlight beam explored the tent some, but he was careful not to illuminate me. He seemed to accept it when I shined my light on him. Pud was shorter than Dothan, with curly dark hair and eyes the same brown as the backs of his hands. I figured his age at eighteen or nineteen. I'd known him most of my life and married into his family, but I doubt Pud and I had ever had a real conversation. The guy in front of me was different somehow from the kid we'd mocked in junior high.

"Thank you," I said again. "This is what I needed."

He nodded twice. "I thought you might be upset and forget food. He took your baby."

What I saw when I looked at Pud that I'd never seen before was compassion. I never know what to do with compassion. Lydia had it, she'd give her right arm if you needed it, but she'd joke like it didn't matter and call you trouble as she saved you. Her compassion had to hold the illusion of hard ass or the whole Lydia image would collapse.

Pud's compassion was straight. Men too simple to hide themselves get to me. Right in the middle of chewing bologna I suddenly got the urge to crawl into Pud's arms and cry for six hours. I hadn't touched a human, when I was awake, anyway, in a week. Having a baby, you get used to skin-touching affection, even when you don't have a man.

But I was afraid if I touched him Pud would take it wrong— all other men would. He might think he could touch me back.

"Can I ask you something personal?" I asked.

His hands turned over, palms up, but he didn't say anything, so I went on. "For as long as I can remember people have said you're not smart, but I've seen you work on cars and stuff and you seem on the ball then. Why do people think you're not smart?"

He turned off his flashlight. "I can't read."

I turned off mine. It was kind of nice in the dark. The moon outside was bright enough that I could make out Pud's form, his arms and the outline of his head, but I couldn't see the expression on his face.

"Can't read at all?" I asked.

The head outline dropped and I could tell he was looking at the ground instead of me. "Not very good. I try, I used to try hard, but the letters don't stay still."

We were quiet a long time, aware of each other's presence. Reading books was important to me, maybe most important after Auburn, Yukon Jack, and horses. It was hard to conceive of not being able to read.

I was curious about something else, too. "There's this other thing people say you do, Pud, that I always wondered if it's true."

"Mess around with animals."

I was glad he said it. Even in my frank frame of mind I'd have had trouble saying "Hey, Pud, do you fuck sheep?"

Pud's flashlight came on and he shined it on me for the first time, although he kept the beam out of my eyes. "Do you believe it?" he asked.

"I don't know what to believe anymore."

"My brother tells everyone I mess with animals."

"I'll ignore what Dothan says about you if you ignore what he says about me."

Pud slid closer. I needed to hold his hand, nothing more, but I needed a hand.

He tapped a rhythm on the tent floor with his knuckles. "When I was a kid Dothan had a club, the Rough Riders, that he wouldn't let me in. He said I was too stupid."

I saw a glimpse of what being Dothan's younger brother must be like. I'd lived less than two years with him and already tried suicide.

Pud went on. "Dothan said I could be a special cadet of the Rough Riders if I'd give Stonewall a jack job."

"Wasn't Stonewall that God-ugly dog of yours?"

"He wasn't so ugly."

I didn't see any reason to fight over it, but Stonewall was ugly. "How do you jack off a dog?"

Pud held his hand in the light and made his thumb and first finger into an O. "I didn't like being left out, so I did what he said. The boys in the club laughed at me." His voice was sad. "Dothan said special cadet meant I had to jack off a different animal before every meeting. I wouldn't do it."

How could I tell him Dothan was the screwed-up one, not us? Everyone in town had it backward. "Jacking off an ugly dog isn't so bad, Pud. Hell, I've jacked off Dothan himself."

His head nodded. "He told everybody, too."

Pud's eyes came up and met mine. He moved his hand toward me, I closed my eyes and felt his fingers gently touch the side of my neck. I almost groaned.

Pud said, "You've got a tick."

"What?"

"Hold still, I don't want to leave the head inside."

I went rigid, afraid to even blink. Pud's fingertips on my neck turned slowly counterclockwise. He exhaled and drew his hand back to hold the tick under the flashlight beam.

"See," Pud said. "I got his head."

The tick kicked its tiny legs into Pud's palm, and its head rose and fell, like it was blind and wanted to re-enter my body. Pud pressed its middle with his thumb until the tick popped and blood splattered from the base of Pud's fingers to his wrist.

He wiped his hand off on his jeans leg and said, "You should check yourself. Stonewall used to get hordes of ticks this time of year."

8

TICKS AND DEAD BABIES ROAMED THE NIGHT. BLOATED, sucking ticks, crawling-out-my-ear ticks—my dreams reeked of the buggers. I found them in my pubic hair, hanging off my breasts, imbedded in my lower eyelid.

But the tick revulsion was diddly compared to opening my locker in GroVont Junior High to find Shannon smothered on my math book or lifting the toilet lid on Auburn with open eyes staring up from under the water.

Time after time I came awake choking, sweating like a stuck pig. Nightmares based on true fear must unleash a reaction in the sweat glands. Being in a coma was easy thrills compared to that night in my own yard.

The mid-morning sunlight caught me curled up against the far panel with the sleeping bag wrapped around my neck. My fist clutched the empty Milk Duds box.

When I crawled from the tent Mrs. Barnett was standing on the sidewalk holding a cut-glass bowl of candy. She wore a synthetic dress, and her tongue made those little click sounds you think of when you think disapproval from an old woman. She stepped past me and went up the sidewalk to where Sugar Cannelioski waited in her matching slacks and top outfit looking like the Barbie doll from hell.

"How thoughtful of you," Sugar said in this drippy southern accent she must have picked up overnight. "I just love pralines." Sugar held the door so Mrs. Barnett could totter inside, then she looked at me on my hands and knees in the corner of the yard.

"Don't even think about asking to use my bathroom," she called. I flipped her off, but she was already inside hostessing and missed it.

"My bathroom, you flat-chested slut," I said to the ground. Memories of that bathroom left a bad taste in my mouth, anyway. Every time Dothan went righteous the first place he looked for a bottle was the tank on the back of the can. What an insult. I may have been drunk, but I wasn't stupid.

I didn't even want Yukon Jack right then, which I took as a sign I wasn't an alcoholic but a regular person temporarily thrown off by her father's death. Or something. Something had thrown me off.

What I wanted was black coffee followed by a hot shower and more black coffee. What I had to do was get my butt upright and down the road.

Except for the Teton Mountains, the Killdeer Cafe had been about the only consistency in my young life. The dump had gone through maybe six name changes, but for me the cafe had always been Max in back slinging grease and Dot out front taking care of people who didn't eat at home. She'd quit for a couple years about the time Shannon was born, and I don't think I ever had my bearings the whole time she was gone.

Dot has all this curly black hair that goes with her rounded cheeks and chin. I wouldn't say she's fat, but fat is such a subjective deal. If I was shaped like Dot, I'd say I was fat. Half the single men in Teton County were in love with her. Single men will fall in love with any woman who brings them food.

When I came through the door she was sitting at the counter, eating a sweet roll and staring at a paperback book propped against a napkin dispenser. The first instant Dot saw me shock flashed in her eyes, but she hid it quickly. I appreciated the effort.

"Coffee, hon?" Without waiting for an answer she grabbed the pot and brought it to my normal booth by the window. Dot talked to fill in that uncomfortable space when you first see a friend who has screwed up.

"Have you read this *Teachings of Don Juan* book? Jacob picked it up somewhere and now he has his heart set on becoming a sorcerer. People turn into crows and fly over the ocean. They eat hummingbird hearts. I think it endorses drugs."

Booths, tables, and cracked-plastic-covered stools, the Farmer Brothers stainless-steel coffee urn, the pyramid made from single-serving cereal boxes, a calendar with the months framing a University of Wyoming football schedule—the name might change, but the restaurant had achieved a glacial kind of pace that gave me comfort. The newest decor addition was three years old. That came about when Max changed the name to the Louis L'Amour Room and the real Louis L'Amour threatened a lawsuit. Max framed the personally signed threat letter and hung it next to the Dutch Master box turned cash register.

The coffee cup kind of quivered in both my hands. "Taking drugs isn't healthy, Dot, no matter what that Mexican says. God wants us to drink whiskey."

Dot laughed like I was kidding. "What can I get you, Maurey? Max went to the dentist after the breakfast rush, so I'll fix it myself."

"Nothing but coffee, I only need coffee."

"Pooh on that, girl, you need nourishment. Why don't you freshen up in the ladies' room while I whip us up a snack."

Dot coming close enough to criticism to suggest I freshen up was the equivalent of Lydia telling me I looked like something the cat threw up.

"Yeah, maybe I will," I said, "but no food. I don't want your food." I took my coffee cup to the John. As I passed the counter I stopped to look at the Don Juan book. The cover showed a man and a cactus in burnt orange and burro brown. It was just the sort of drivel Park would have changed his life over. Myself, I distrusted all guru types. None of them wore jeans.

———

In the bathroom I stripped down for a tick check. From what I could see of myself it was easy to understand the shock flash I'd caused Dot. A week like the one I'd just gone through is tough on the old body. A coma, or wherever I spent Monday afternoon through Friday morning, is great if you're trying to lose weight but hell on the complexion. Only color on my entire body came from these bags under each eye. They were the same burro shade as the man's blanket on the Don Juan book cover.

I haven't been much for long gazes into mirrors since the self-inflicted haircut a couple months after Dad's thing. During the shower at Lydia's I'd kept my eyes on my feet, right where they belonged. In the Killdeer can I discovered brand-new, never-seen bones—mostly around the hips and sternum. My eyes looked like peach cross sections with the pits removed.

At fifteen I'd been regarded as the prettiest girl in the valley. Maiden aunts and horny politicians said so all the time. "Maurey, you're the prettiest girl in the valley." The only good to come of my downfall was to all those mothers who once said to their dogface daughters, "Just you wait. About the time you bloom she'll be mud on a boot." They must be dancing in the streets by now.

I came back to Dot sitting across the table from just what I didn't want—a rib-eye steak, mashed potatoes and gravy, and biscuits, and a quart glass of tomato juice.

"I said I didn't want food."

She doubled her chubby fists around the salt and pepper shakers. "You aren't leaving this room until that plate is clean."

The urge was to dump it all on the floor and say "The plate's clean," but Dot's round face was such a study, with her chin out and her eyes blinking. She reminded me of a mama sage hen that spread her wings and attacked my shins once on the trail to Taggart Lake. The hen hissed and spit while her babies peeped in tiny bird panic. One swing of my hiking boot and I'd have kicked that chicken to kingdom come, but bravery in the helpless always gets me, especially if the helpless is a mother. I went way back around the other side of the creek and scratched the hell out of my legs on wild rose bushes.

This time I sat down and cleaned my plate. It was really good. The steak was char rare running in blood, the mashed potatoes straight real stuff with lumps, no flakes added as a buffer. The biscuits were hot and homemade, and if they gave a Nobel Prize for gravy, which they should, Dot would have to learn Swedish.

It was the first time in ages I'd taken pleasure out of anything more wholesome than Yukon Jack and masturbation. Dot held on to those salt and pepper shakers the whole time I ate. I think she'd committed herself to violence if I didn't cooperate, and the relief from my not calling her bluff struck her silent.

I felt softer. "Dot, what do you think I should do?"

She watched me drain the tomato juice, then she got up and went after the coffeepot. I waited like a child while she poured the refill.

"Here's the truth, Maurey. You want the truth?"

People who ask that question generally go on to say something unpleasant. I blew coffee steam at her and nodded.

"If you stop drinking, you'll get your baby back, and if you don't, you won't."

I always knew Dot was stupid. "Look, Miss Holy Righteous Woman, I have problems. My husband is a sadistic prick, my mother's crazy, my brother must be a pervert although I can't figure what kind yet. Dad is dead. Drinking is a symptom of something terribly wrong. If you cure the disease, the symptoms take care of themselves."

She studied my face a long time. "Did I ever tell you how Jimmy's grandfather died?" Jimmy had been Dot's husband. He's kind of a local legend because he was the first boy from Wyoming killed in Vietnam.

"Is this going to be a pithy story illustrating a point?"

Dot went right ahead. "Jimmy's grandfather Homer had a mean Angus bull that could jump any fence and strut over any cattle guard. Homer and that bull hated each other like lifelong enemies. One day the bull got Homer against a loading chute and stomped him to bits. Broke both his legs, destroyed his kneecaps."

"Wasn't Jimmy raised by his grandmother down in Bondurant?"

"Homer was Christian Scientist and said the Lord would set his legs. The Lord didn't and they started to stink, so Jimmy's dad went against Homer's wishes and called Doc Heinlein. You remember Doc Heinlein, he delivered you and Petey. He was just a kid when this happened, straight out of Provo."

"How much are you charging for this steak?"

Dot looked at my plate. "You didn't order it, I can't charge for something you didn't order."

"If it's free, I'll sit through this story. Otherwise Paul Harvey starts soon and I don't want to miss the news."

Vexation skipped across Dot's face, but she plowed on

through her anecdote. "Doc Heinlein took one look at Homer's legs and said, 'Homer, you've got a problem. Those legs are gangrene and if I don't cut them both off, you're going to die.'

"Homer said, 'I've got a problem all right, but it ain't my legs, it's that blankety-blank bull.'"

I love it when Dot says "blankety-blank" instead of "mother-fucking" or whatever the people she's quoting really said.

"Jimmy's grandfather loaded his Winchester coyote rifle and drug himself by his arms—wouldn't let anybody help him—drug himself into the yard and across to the feed corral, where he gut-shot that mean Angus twice. Then he lay down next to it and watched for three hours while the bull died. Jimmy's dad and Doc Heinlein played dominoes on the porch."

"Dominoes? What is this, *Beverly Hillbillies?*"

"Finally the bull expired and Homer threw back his head and laughed. He looked over at Jimmy's dad and Doc Heinlein and he said, 'There, I solved my problem.'" Dot smiled at me, her face pink with conviction.

I bit. "So, what's the punch line?"

"Jimmy's grandfather died anyway."

"I don't get it."

9

I DECIDED TO BAG THE SHOWER UNTIL AFTER PAUL HARVEY. My only real challenge was to coerce Faith Fratelli into turning the TV off and the radio on, which would be a trick. Imagine the surprise when I walked into the Sagebrush to find her staring glumly at a blank screen.

"It's them stupid Watergate hearings," she said. "They're on every channel, all day. No game shows, no soaps. I feel like crying."

Nobody was in the lounge, unless you count Oly Pedersen. He did the wooden Indian number down the bar, the only sign of life the dull glow coming off his goiter. "Maybe the TV people think Nixon is more important than *Concentration*," I said.

Faith sent me a disgusted look. "If *All My Children* isn't back tomorrow, I'm zipping off a letter to the networks will make their hair curl. What are you steamed over this time?"

I hadn't realized I was visibly steamed. Must have been the sound of gritting teeth when I sat on the bar stool. "Dot Pollard pisses me off."

"The Dot Pollard I know? Works at the Killdeer? Wouldn't say a bad word about a mouse?"

"She thinks just because she feeds a person she can tell them how to run their life. I'll take a Yukon, up, and a Blue Ribbon for the old guy."

Faith rummaged in the well and pulled out a nearly empty Yukon Jack bottle. "I can't believe Dot gave advice without being asked to."

I reconstructed the scene in my mind. "I guess I did ask. But that doesn't matter, she's still a mean bitch."

Faith's lips moved as she counted out the shot. "One, two, three. You asked for advice and she said something you didn't want to hear?"

"She was mean about it."

Faith took Oly his beer. "No wonder Maurey's pissed, she asked for advice and got an answer."

I swear Oly smiled. You couldn't actually see where anything on his face moved, but there was a moment of cognizance at my expense.

What had my existence come to? I'm being ganged up on by an airhead whose quality of life is directly affected by *All My Children* and an upright catatonic. "Turn on the damn radio."

———

"Stand by for news."

I love Paul Harvey. Not for what he says. What he says is a bunch of founding-fathers, John-Birch-Society, welfare-mothers-enjoy-pregnancy, I-love-America-by-golly gush. It's his voice. God cussed out Moses in that voice. Dad used it to break horses. Even when Paul Harvey is wrong, I believe.

Just to prove I didn't really have to have the alcohol—I was only drinking because I wanted to, not because I needed it—I held off on Jack until "page two." That's the canning jar commercial. Page one is the real news, in this case more Watergate crud, page two the commercial, page three the outrageous thing the liberals did, page four another sincere commercial. Then comes the twenty-two-pound cantaloupes and lifesaving pussycats, then the daily bumper snicker and public commendations for survivors. Then another commercial followed by a punch-line story that farmers chuckle over and repeat endlessly at feed stores across America.

I was on my second shot and Paul was winding up for his big finish when the front door crashed open. A hand appeared low down on the door frame and a voice yelled, "*Banzai, motherfuckers.*"

Shane's radish face appeared as he struggled with his wheels. Behind him, Lloyd the farmer did whatever you do to push a fat man in a wheelchair through a tight door into a bar. While it was a grunt, the pair seemed experienced and sure of the outcome.

Shane's voice was a gush. "We visited your tent. It leans to port."

Lloyd gave a shove that popped the chair into the room and across toward the quarter-slot pool table. Behind me came the *pft* sound of Faith opening a soda pop bottle. Lloyd said, "Give Maurey a break. There weren't enough pegs. Can't set a tent proper without enough pegs."

"I wasn't criticizing Maurey, who's criticizing Maurey? Yo, Oly, you stud, got any yet this morning?" Shane did something with his right hand that spun the chair toward me. "Oly drives the high school chicks wild, we can't keep 'em off him."

I missed the end of Paul Harvey's story. He'd been booming about a weasely little termite exterminator in Nebraska with twelve wives and a fiancée. Somebody asked one of the wives—a fifteen-year-old named Trixie who worked in the laundry room at Holiday Inn—why all these women married the weasel and not a one wanted a divorce now they'd found out about each other. Even the fiancée still planned a white wedding.

And just as Paul Harvey came to her answer, Shane started in with the *Banzai* clamor. That's the kind of crap doesn't happen when you drink at home.

I decided to deal with it. "What are you doing nosing around my camp?"

Shane reached between his legs and pulled out a bottle of Coors. He held it high like a bowling trophy. "Feast your eyes on this, little lassie."

"Little lassie?"

"Coors beer, Rocky Mountain spring water at a dollar sixty cents a six-pack. What do you think of that?"

"Coors is cow piss in a can."

Shane belched this hoot that passed for laughter. "Of course, except in this case it's cow piss in a bottle. But, and this is a but to remember, I am also holding a lesson in life. Do you drink cow piss?"

Lloyd crossed between us to collect two glasses of Coca-Cola from Faith. Out of all the creeps to make fun of my tent, he'd been the one who saw why it collapsed. If only he wasn't wearing sandals.

Shane repeated himself, only louder. "Do you drink cow piss, Maurey Talbot?"

"I'd DT first."

The radish split into a grin. "As would any decent, God-fearing alcoholic. Thanks, buddy." He took the Coke from Lloyd. "But, I'm here with the truth, honey, easterners will pay five bucks for this bottle right here." He shook the Coors. "Five bucks for warm cow piss. And, little lassie, do you know why they'll commit this atrocity?"

"They're crazy." Wyomingites think anyone living in the eastern time zone is nuts.

Shane slammed the bottle on the pool table. "Because Coors is illegal in the East. Everyone wants what they can't have, even if it means drinking cow piss. They'd eat manure if the government told them not to."

Another trouble with drinking in bars is you run into the sort of people who hang out in bars. I gave a who-are-these-jerks eyebrow roll to Faith, but she'd gone back to staring at the blank TV screen. Evidently she'd heard the Coors spiel before.

"That's where you come in," Lloyd said. He had worn-brown eyes with wrinkles all over hell—one of those guys who hit the wall and reacted by staring at the sun.

I put both feet on the floor. "I don't come in. I'm sure you're both perfectly nice ex-drunks, except maybe him"—I motioned at Shane—"but I have no desire to continue this relationship."

Shane did the bob-up-and-down-on-his-hands deal. "Listen to the college girl firecracker. 'Continue this relationship.' I'll give you twenty dollars to see your tits, little missy."

"In your dreams, prick face."

Shane's face ducked low and went sly. "What if I said I was dying and I could go peacefully if only you'd give me twenty minutes of nice?"

"I'd say your death isn't worth twenty minutes of my time."

Lloyd stepped toward me. "Do you have a driver's license?"

"What are you guys, an act?"

He rubbed his right hand on his overalls leg. "We both lost ours to alcohol."

"I could get mine back if my legs worked," Shane said.

I said, "You shouldn't drink if you can't handle it."

The ripple passed through Oly again. Faith tittered. "Ain't it amazing, Lloyd's sober and can't drive because the law thinks he's drunk, and Maurey's a drunk but can drive because the law thinks she's sober."

"*Irony*," Shane shouted. "Get yourself planted in a wheel-chair and the world explodes with irony."

"What's a wheelchair got to do with it?" Faith asked.

This a-drunk taking for granted was wearing thin. Nobody said "Maurey's drunk"; they said "Maurey's a drunk." I hadn't admitted that yet, and everyone else's unquestioned conviction of the fact showed a lack of sensitivity.

I stood up from the bar stool. "None of this relates to me, I'm going home."

Shane hunkered down. For a man living on wheels, his head did an amazing amount of vertical action. "Where's that?"

"What?"

"That home you're going to? Is home the tent with the list?"

Lloyd took another step toward me. He's one of those guys who can make his eyes go totally unguarded. "If you have a driver's license, we can take you to North Carolina."

"I'm not going anywhere." I wondered if I slapped him would Lloyd blink. In the unnecessary-movement category, he was the exact opposite of Shane. "Why would I go to North Carolina?"

Shane hooted again. "Don't play stupid with us, lassie."

Lloyd said, "You have a daughter there you need to be with."

"How do you—"

"And the people in charge will never return your son if you don't get off the front lawn."

You know that tone you imagine Jesus talked in, that's Lloyd. I met a guy in college had deep-sizzled his brain on LSD who talked the same way. It's like the speaker is wearing a sweatshirt that says "I am gentle. Kick me, I won't mind."

"Why does the whole damn state know my business and feel the right to offer an opinion?"

Faith cackled. "You're the valley entertainment right now, Maurey. Unlucky for you it's off-season. Middle of July nobody would've cared that you've gone nuts in public."

"I'm not nuts."

Lloyd still hadn't blinked. "Nuts or drunk, you need to get out of sight and we need help hauling a load of Coors to North Carolina."

I looked over at the pinball machine and the jukebox. The jukebox had a picture of a ferris wheel on the back with a happy couple in the top chair. Next to them was a pay phone with hundreds of numbers written on the wall. "Why North Carolina?" I asked.

Shane wheeled toward me too. I was being surrounded. "Because the cur Ashley Montagu burned Granma's barn."

"I knew it would be something like that."

"And Lloyd's looking for his wife who ran off."

Faith spoke from the backside of the surrounding forces. "Watch out, he'll show you her picture any minute now."

Lloyd finally blinked with a moment of insecurity. I wondered what the picture of his wife looked like—a skinny-armed farm wife with a dust-colored face, or maybe a small-town beauty operator type. The kind who chewed gum and gabbed while they touched women on the head.

"You drive all the time," I said. "I've seen you show up late for AA."

I looked at the hair on Lloyd's arm while he talked. I've always been into hair on men's forearms. Lloyd's arm muscles were stringy yet tough. The hair lay dark and uphill instead of inside to outside like on most people. "I can drive fine, just not legal. Mangum knows I'm clean so he lets me loose on the north end of the county, but we can't take Moby Dick on the road without a licensed driver."

"And one hundred cases of Coors," Shane added.

All men want something from me, but usually it's out-front man-on-woman stuff. These guys had dreamed up some scam or another that involved more than sex or mothering. "I'm outta here."

"Maurey." Lloyd used his unguarded eyes as a weapon—like a sheep dog left outside at thirty below zero.

I neatly deflected his needs. "You'll have to save yourselves because you're not using me."

Pissed-off thunderheads piled up over Yellowstone, but the Tetons sparkled in the west, clear and real. I stood on the Sagebrush mud mat breathing fresh air and listening through the door for the word that always follows when a man wants something and a woman won't give it. "Holy Hannah, what a *cunt*." That was Shane. I couldn't hear Lloyd's answer. I remembered his eyes, though, and the hair on his forearms, and I pretended to myself he didn't say "Dumb bitch" or "Women." He probably did and I was just wishful thinking. Sometimes I'm not cynical enough.

The white ambulance out front was like an antique, the kind of bus you think about Hemingway nailing nurses in the back of while outside the Spanish civil war rages in the olive groves. Shaped like a loaf of Wonder bread, it had stretched windows along the sides, what appeared to be an extra layer of white sheet cake on top, and airplane running lights at the eight corners of the loaf. Over the two-pane windshield a sign read AMBULANCE backward, so when it came roaring up on a car the driver could look in his rearview mirror and see AMBULANCE written the right way. Below that was another hand-lettered sign—MOBY DICK.

That explained one of the out-of-the-blue references they'd tossed off inside. Lloyd had personified his vehicle. I did the same daily with bottles; that was natural. I guess he did it with cars. Lord knows the piece of junk looked like a white whale.

I cupped my hands around my eyes to peer in the back window. Engine parts and loose playing cards lay over ratty blankets and sleeping bags. They read a lot of magazines— *Playboy, Popular Mechanics, Reader's Digest,* and *Guideposts,* some others I couldn't see their covers. The prevailing motif was grease. Jesus himself couldn't have fit a hundred cases of anything in that back end.

The Dick did have a trailer hitch, which seemed odd for an ambulance. A trailer would solve the space problem, but I'd have to fumigate before stepping in the door. If only there was a way to tape Shane's mouth shut. Two thousand miles cooped up with that hoot of his and I'd commit murder.

"Whoa," I said out loud. "Don't even think it. Better to rot in jail."

The frustration came because the skinny farmer in sandals got to me with that daughter jab. He knew I needed Shannon. Was Lloyd intuitive or a lucky guesser or what? If he was so smart about human feelings, why had his wife run off? If somebody ran off from me, I sure wouldn't go chasing after them.

Here's the deal about love and children. A few people cared about me—Sam Callahan, Lydia, Mom in her limited way—but for them, caring was an in-spite-of situation. "Maurey is a mess, but we love her anyway." Mess might not be the exact word they used.

But Shannon and Auburn loved me without acknowledging flaws. Shannon thought I was okay. I could rest if I was around someone who thought I was okay.

It seemed the right idea to walk the block from the Sagebrush to Kimball's Food Market. Those two shots might be just enough excuse for Mangum Potter to crucify my ass. Besides, the day was pretty. Living in a land with seven months of winter, a person comes to appreciate spring. Alcohol use and a suicide attempt hadn't killed off all the fun of fresh air and nifty sunlight.

Mrs. Hinchman's wild rose bushes sported tiny pink blossoms. The day I lost Auburn the buds had been nothing but green swells. A red-tailed hawk wheeled over the grade school playground, searching for lunch in the jungle gym and teeter-totters. GroVont was a good place to raise kids, compared to

Idaho Falls or Utah, anyway. I'd been raised here and I wasn't evil or anything. Shannon was fine, although she'd left when she was four to go off to college with Sam.

Shannon was more than fine, she was beautiful. Inadvertently, I'd given birth to a bundle of curiosity and compassion. I don't remember having compassion at her age, at least not for anything other than a horse. If I lived in Greensboro, I could sit on the porch swing as she talked about dolls or cotillions or whatever girls talk about. In the evenings she would kiss my cheek and say "Good night, Mama." Nobody had ever done that.

It would be nice to hear Sam go on about God's relationship to baseball or writing stories or something equally as silly. Normally his girlfriends didn't like me any more than Dothan liked Sam. They couldn't catch on that we'd had a child together but we'd never dated or felt an iota of romance. This new girlfriend in the letter didn't sound any better than the last six, although I would bet the ranch she'd moved up the road by now anyway. Sam was too giving to hold a woman more than a month.

Outside Kimball's, Mary Ellen and Shawn McKenzie played on the painted mechanical horse. Mary Ellen had managed to balance her little brother on the horse's head while she sat on his stiff tail—born trick riders.

Shawn took his fist out of his mouth. "Nicgel."

Mary Ellen fleshed out the thought. "Can we have a nickel, Mrs. Talbot? We want a ride, but it takes a nickel."

"Let's see if I can find one." They waited patiently while I fished for change. Mary Ellen wore a pinafore that I know Mabel made from a pattern she cut down, because it had darts. I'd bought Shannon enough birthday presents to know dresses for seven-year-olds don't come with darts.

"Here you go, kids—two nickels for two rides."

Shawn held out his chubby hand, but Mary Ellen took the money. "Thank you, Mrs. Talbot."

Shawn said, "Tang you, Mrs. Talbud."

"You're welcome."

The deal is that Lydia is a personal appearance snob. She sends away to New York or someplace exotic for all her makeup and shampoo and conditioners. Her fingernail polish came from Paris and cost about two dollars a finger. Her shampoo was concocted from edible objects—eggs, aloe, and cucumbers—and made me smell like a salad. Time for some regular green Prell. I also picked up a comb, two Hershey bars, and a picture postcard of two girls in bikinis lying on lawn chairs set in a snowbank. Dad would get a kick out of that.

Reaction from the fellow shoppers was roughly the same as it had been at Zion's—titters, stares, or embarrassment, each in about equal doses. If you've ever been pregnant and thirteen in a small town, you know the vibes. I'd made myself fairly insult proof, but you never completely outgrow the leper thing.

Mr. Betts made a pass at me. On the canned goods aisle, he blocked my path with his shopping cart, held both my hands in his, and did a soul search of my eyes over frozen cranberries and his wife's Dexatrim.

"If you need anything at all, Maurey, don't hesitate to call me at the office."

"Sure, Don."

"I always told your father that if you ever came to a bad end, I'd be here to help. I think he took comfort in that."

"I'm certain he did."

Mr. Betts's hands gave a squeeze. "I'd do anything for Buddy's little girl."

At the checkout counter Lucinda Wright held up my comb for Mr. Kimball to inspect. "Is this a sharp object?"

Mr. Kimball peered down from the glassed-in box where he counts money and adds figures. "It's a comb, Lucinda."

"I thought it might be a sharp object."

"Look at her, she needs a comb."

Mary Ellen and Shawn still played on the horse that had run the course of its two rides. Mary Ellen had moved up on the horse's hips, only facing back the wrong way. Shawn smiled when he saw me and held out his hand.

"Sorry," I said. "Out of nickels."

Shawn kept smiling as if he'd expected as much.

"Say hello to your mother for me."

"She'll say hello back to you," Mary Ellen said.

I'd just reached the curb and was about to step into the street when Mary Ellen and Shawn broke into song.

> *How dry I am, hic,*
> *How dry I am, hic,*
> *How wet I'll be*
> *If I don't find, hic,*
> *The bathroom key.*

Shawn erupted into giggles while Mary Ellen stared at me with defiance, daring me to come back righteous. I looked from his five-year-old innocence to her seven-year-old experience, and I saw what had happened. The town had won.

10

"IF WE CAN'T LEAVE TOWN IN TWENTY MINUTES, I DON'T want to go."

Lloyd and Shane did a mutual freeze frame. Lloyd was bent along one of the Sagebrush's crooked cues, the tip of his tongue showing pink between his lips. Shane sat over past the phone with his finger in the pinball machine coin return and a bag of chocolate-chip cookies on his lap.

"It may take a bit more than twenty minutes to organize," Lloyd said.

Shane pulled a wheelchair 180. "No, it won't."

I stalked in, holding my shampoo-and-comb sack. "What's the scam on the beer?"

The scam was that Buck Fratelli would sell the boys one hundred cases of Coors for four dollars eighty-five cents a case, and a high school friend of Shane's in Gastonia, North Carolina, would buy it for ten a six-pack.

"Four thousand bucks for a four hundred-eighty-five-dollar investment," Shane bragged. "You can't beat that with a stick."

"You said they'd cough up five a bottle."

"That's what my friend retails it for out of his tavern. You can't expect me to move twenty-four hundred bottles one at a time."

"You'll need a trailer."

The Bobbsey Twins needed more than a trailer and a driver's license—they needed cash. Lloyd had the beer money, Shane had squat. I was expected to provide gasoline, food, and alcohol—soda pop for the men—for a two-thousand-mile run.

"What about motels?" I asked.

Lloyd looked slighted. "Moby Dick is self-contained, almost. We won't be stopping at motels."

"Self-contained means toilet, shower, and stove. Does Dick contain a toilet, shower, and stove?"

Shane hooted, which was the next subject I meant to discuss. Lloyd rubbed his leg. "We have sleeping bags. There's a separate bag for you."

"You bet there is."

Twenty minutes turned into seven hours, but, by God, we pulled it off. Who would have thought two dried-up ex-drunks and a housewife or whatever I was could get their acts together and bust out of a rut in seven hours?

First stop was the TM ranch for a double-wide horse trailer and cash on the barrel head.

I left the boys up by the house and walked across the west pasture to where Hank Elkrunner stood in a ditch, wearing jeans, leather gloves, and irrigation boots. He'd stripped off his shirt and had his hair down, so he came off all muscles and sweat and brown skin. I could see why Lydia went drippy on sight.

Hank looked up at the ambulance. "Somebody hurt?"

Shane sat shoveling cookies into his mouth while Lloyd lay on his back under the front end, checking something mechanical. "Those are my good examples. They used to be drunks."

"I figured the hospital expected you back so soon they decided to tag along on your adventures." The Indian thing about Hank is you never know when he's joking. Other than that inscrutability stance, he's fairly white—doesn't sleep with

89

bird parts next to the bed or drink bad wine or say "my people" like other Indians I'd met.

I said what I forgot to say Friday. "Thanks."

Hank bent at the knees and grabbed both sides of a head gate with his hands. His muscles bunched up as he lifted. "Arnold found you. I was trimming Charley Chaplain's nails when Arnold started howling. Thought he had flushed a porcupine."

With a grunt, the gate came up an inch and brown water swirled under the board, oozing into the sides of the ditch before it filled in around Hank's boots and started pushing dust downstream.

"Well, I appreciate you and Arnold saving my life."

"Couldn't leave a naked woman lying that close to the creek. Might spoil the water."

I'm way fond of Hank. He's worked for Dad since Shannon was born, and even though he's Lydia's boyfriend, which makes him a generation older than me, we've always been able to talk about life and boyfriends and horses and stuff.

Sometimes Hank was more of a dad than Dad. He taught me how to read scat and howl like a wolf and God is Nature/Nature is God. Dad drove me to Sunday school a lot, but he never taught me anything about God.

"Hank, I need to borrow a trailer and three hundred dollars."

His attention was on the mares next to the barn. "You will have to grant me an advance before I loan you three hundred dollars."

"Do we have three hundred dollars to advance you to loan me?"

He pulled off his irrigation gloves. "Barely."

Hank listened without expression while I outlined the Coors-to-Carolina gig. At pertinent points his eyes roamed up the rise to Shane, Lloyd, and Moby Dick.

"Why not call Sam and have him mail you the money to fly back east?"

"I don't want to owe Sam money."

Hank slapped the dust off his gloves on his left forearm. He looked over at the Tetons, which is what everybody in the valley does when they're thinking deep stuff. "Maurey, have you looked at the books since Buddy died? Sam financed the funeral and paid the inheritance taxes. He owns your mama's house."

"I don't get it."

"This ranch is supporting your mother, brother, me, and most of Lydia, and now it'll have to do for you. That many people can't live on horses."

"Why didn't anyone tell me?"

Hank looked right at my face, which, as I understand it, is a very un-Blackfoot thing to do. "You were preoccupied."

"Drunk."

He shrugged. "Sometimes you were just depressed."

You know, when your dad dies you can't simply stop functioning for six months. I mean, you can—I was the number one example—but you shouldn't. Somebody has to pay attention. At her sanest, Mom didn't know which end of a cow shits, and Petey was afraid of animals. That left me, and I'd flopped.

"I should surrender and give the ranch to Sam."

Hank crammed the gloves in his back pocket so only the tips of the fingers stuck out. "Don't do that, he might fire me and run the place himself."

The thought made even Hank smile. I'd seen Sam in a cowboy hat once. He looked like Woody Allen gone hombre. The only time he ever got it up to ride a horse, Mae West threw him into a barbwire fence.

"Still, I'd rather do this without Sam," I said. "He's been saving me for ten years. It's my turn."

As Hank and I walked through the shin-high grasses up to the house, I thought about why I didn't want Sam flying me down there. It was like, here in Jackson Hole people watched me.

And in Greensboro Sam's expectations would cause discomfort. If I got drunk, Sam wouldn't preach or anything, but he would think. Shannon had never seen the Mom-gone-bad either. I was worn out from disappointing people. I needed a gap, a rest between this and that where no one could pull me up, put me down, or tear off little pieces of my energy. Even though I'd just finished one, I needed a three-day nap, and being out of reach on the road with Laurel and Hardy might be the next best medicine.

———

Shane slid another cookie into his beak. "I don't see cows. You said there were cows and all I see are horses."

Hank nodded to the uphill side. "Cattle are on the Forest Service lease till October."

"I don't much care for horses. Never have since Katharine Hepburn insisted I copulate with her on one in 1942," Shane said.

I was dubious. "You nailed Katharine Hepburn?"

"On a stallion. Sweet girl, really, although she went to extremes for sensory experience." Shane lowered his voice. "She suffered from penis envy."

"We've got a filly named Katharine Hepburn." Hank waved his arm in the general direction of Frostbite and three or four quarter horse-Thoroughbred combinations.

Shane peered off toward the group. "Kate always was a bit horsey in the thighs."

I didn't for a second believe Shane had nailed Katharine Hepburn. Nobody—except possibly Spencer Tracy when she was underage—had ever nailed Katharine Hepburn. She wouldn't allow it.

Lloyd backed out from under Moby Dick. Some gravel was embedded in his bare shoulder next to the overalls. "Big hole in the exhaust," he said. "Thought I felt fumes inside."

Hank dropped to a haunch-squat to peer under Dick's guts. "Coke cans wrapped around the pipe will fix that. I've got some clamps in the barn."

"Much obliged," Lloyd said, and *Bingo*, they were male pals on the spot. Men can do that. "Carburetor's clogged," a man will say to a complete stranger, and instantly they're connected by a common language. I don't share a common language with women. Mildred Barber asked me what I thought of Final Net once and I had to say, "Huh?"

Lloyd and Hank wandered off for clamps and the trailer and left me with Mr. Delusions of Grandeur. Under the fat folds, his ratty eyes glittered. "This was right after *The Philadelphia Story*. She told me Cary Grant had vulture breath."

"So, if you got laid on one, why do you hate horses?"

He glanced at me. "Kate screamed, 'Give me more, big boy!' and the stallion panicked and reared. The end result was a life spent in this chair. It took all the Warner Brothers' resources to keep the story out of the tabloids. Can you see it?" He held his hand up to scan an imaginary headline. "Katharine Hepburn Cripples Stunt-man While Fucking on Pony."

"You were a stuntman?"

"Didn't you know?" He slid through another cookie.

The brown slime was getting deep, so I muttered something vague about checking a colt and walked over to the main corral. One of the mares had come up dry, and Hank had her and her foal penned so he could do the baby bottle deal. I did the baby bottle deal for Shannon, mostly, but Auburn was a breast baby. He'd left my tits tender—I could kind of excite myself by touching them. Sometimes I wonder if it's a sign of hopeless deprivation when nursing a baby gives you thoughts.

It felt weird to be at the TM getting ready to leave. What if I never made it back? All my innocence was wrapped up in this ranch, and innocence isn't something to leave on purpose.

Things happen outside Jackson Hole; you never know when you're going to get stuck somewhere and never again see the place that you'd always taken for granted would be the center of your days for life.

The corral poles were part of me, and the watering hole off the creek, and the boneyard where pieces of machinery older than Wyoming rusted into the sage. The ranch cycles were so soaked into my blood that on our land I always knew what time it was and which way was north. You feel those things when your identity becomes a location. The outside world made me nervous.

Back over at the house, Lloyd and Hank had pulled Dad's old rodeoing trailer over to Moby Dick and were in the process of winching it onto the hitch and hooking up brake and lights wiring. From the corral, I could see a big dent I put in the trailer by backing it into an A&W billboard. The billboard fell on an empty fireworks stand and knocked it flat. Dad laughed until tears dripped off his beard.

I didn't see any urgent need for Hank to loan us that particular trailer. Self-destructive tendencies can't possibly benefit from a father memory following your backside across America.

———

Shane had his back to the work, facing the horses and the sun. It was the time of year people liked to face the sun. He looked at me and popped a cookie. "Tonto says you used to ride horses."

"Used to?" I said.

"Tonto?" Hank said.

"You might think you're hot stuff, but even before you fell off the deep end you could never have matched Kate at horsemanship. There was a competent woman. You don't look so very competent."

I advanced on him. "Maybe it's time you and me duke it."

Shane was amused to no end. "I don't fight helpless women."

"I do fight fat cripples."

I could tell calling him a fat cripple earned me a little respect. Most people bend so far over backward not to say the wrong thing around the handicapped, to the point where the bending over becomes obvious and an insult. Shane was one of those cripples who wanted the same abuse given normal men.

He turned the chair so we weren't facing head on. "I did not mean to upset your feminine sensibilities. All I meant was Katharine Hepburn did things you couldn't do even before you became a drunk."

I looked over at Lloyd, who chose to stay noncommittal, then back at Shane, who seemed to be leading with his belly.

"Watch this, Humpty-Dumpty." Sticking two fingers in my mouth, I let out a whistle. Very little causes me pride, not since college, anyway, but my whistle does call 'em in for lunch. Not a boy in Teton County could out-blow me.

Frostbite's ears jumped alert and his head swiveled. As he came at a canter, you couldn't help but admire the skewbald Daddy-killer. The old guy was fourteen now, but he still lifted his feet like a colt, and his eyes still sparked with the glory of performance.

At a twenty-foot gap, I held my hand palm forward and Frostbite stopped on a nickel. A dime. World's greatest trick horse.

"Nobody's rode him since Buddy," Hank said.

Frostbite and I locked brown eyes on blue. Faith in each other leapt between us like lightning between a thunderhead and a mountain spire. Horse and woman became a unit.

Hank stepped next to me. "I advise against it."

Shane said, "If you break your neck, don't ask to use my chair."

I gave the hand signal for Frostbite to turn around. Exhaling calmly, I said, "No problem. We haven't lost a thing."

My rear mount was smooth as water over a rock. The instant my jeans touched his back, Frostbite became motion, I became Frostbite. We're talking exhilaration—the refinding of lost enthusiasm.

I grasped the mane with my left hand and did a right vault, then reversed it and bounced dirt on the other side. For the first time I wished I hadn't cut my hair. Long hair streaming in the wind is a trip when you go fast. You should see Hank do the arrow-beneath-the-belly Indian trick. On a full-blast horse death doesn't mean shit.

As he hurled toward the fence I gently tugged Frostbite's mane and touched him with my left leg. He did a flying leftward U-ey, and ZOOM, we're charging back toward Moby Dick. I placed both palms on his back between my thighs, straightened my legs, and lifted myself into a rear spin—same trick Mary Ellen McKenzie had been trying on the mechanical horse at Kimball's before she mocked me.

Forward again, I made a crowd appreciation check. Hank watched with both hands on his hips. Shane knocked his harmonica against his dead leg. He would say something tacky, but I would know I'd shut him down. The slug couldn't crap at me anymore.

I brought both feet under my body with my weight on my toes. Time for the free rump stand followed by the back flip dismount. This would knock their socks off—all except Lloyd, who wasn't wearing socks.

I came to on the ground in the shade of the ambulance. This time the progression went in reverse—black spots turning to yellow turning to three round faces staring down at me. Hank's was angry, Lloyd's concerned. Shane was so entertained he practically bubbled.

Hank said, "I won't bury another member of your family."

In times of embarrassment, always fall back on bravado. "Fucking horse broke stride."

Shane giggled. "That's what Katharine said." Hank knelt to manipulate my legs.

I must have landed on my shoulders because that's what hurt the most, other than my already battered ego. "Frostbite jumped a chiseler hole. He's lost his touch."

Lloyd didn't blink. "Would you have fallen if you hadn't had a drink?"

Shane gave his hideous hoot. All three chins contracted like a frog's neck when it croaks. "She'd have stayed up longer with more to drink, not less."

I closed my eyes. I'd crashed any number of times learning the tricks. This didn't mean a thing; I wasn't a washed-up, twenty-two-year-old has-been.

Hank touched my ankle. "Can you move your feet?"

"Of course I can move my feet. Let's get the hell out of Dodge, I'm tired of this godforsaken dump."

————

Dothan trained Mae West to buck whenever she heard "Chewy Chewy" by the Ohio Express. Dothan loved the Ohio Express, which tells you as much about his depth of character as the calendar with Kiwanis meetings marked by a star.

He used to bring his portable eight-track tape player to the ranch and sit on the corral fence listening to music while I exercised Frostbite and a couple others. Dothan was only there waiting for me to get done so he could take me up the hayloft and get straw in my pubes. Every now and then while I rode I'd catch him chunking a rock at Mae West's butt, always when the same song was playing. I didn't make the connection until after the incident.

I should have been suspicious when Dothan volunteered to wrangle the senior class trail ride. He told Sam Callahan that Mae West had once been ridden by Ernest Hemingway, so of course Sam had to have her. You should have seen Sam sit that horse—rigid as uncooked spaghetti. He posted constantly like we were in England. On turns he yanked the reins so hard she did a complete circle, then he overcorrected and circled her back the other way.

A mile up the Forest Service lease fence I was stalled behind Sam while he tried to stop Mae West from grazing. Her head would dip down to grass level and he'd jerk the reins, which she took as the signal to back up, so she would, and behind her, one at a time, the whole senior class of GroVont High would retreat down the mountain.

That's when Dothan popped "Chewy Chewy" into the eight-track.

Mae West's first kick grazed Frostbite's jaw and he spooked, so I missed a second or two of the action, but when I turned myself back around she was sunfishing and Sam was laid over on her side hanging on by the saddle horn. And screaming. You never heard such a noise.

He stayed with her quite a while, considering. I remember mixed in under Sam's screams and the horse's snorts, this whiny-ass voice going, "*Chewy, chewy, chewy, chewy.*"

Mae West charged the fence, dug in her heels, and Sam flew over her head and front-flipped into barbwire. All in all, I thought it was semifunny—one of Dothan's better sick jokes—but then I'd been thrown off my share of horses, and I knew the world doesn't end. You get back up and get back on.

Sam had no such perspective. He never figured how he'd been had, but in his heart Sam knew somebody other than Mae West caused him a backside full of holes. He wouldn't speak to anyone for days, not even me. Just sulked in his room and wrote stories about how all horses are minions of Satan and must be shunned or they will kill.

11

NEXT CAME A DRIVE ALL THE WAY INTO JACKSON TO CASH Hank's check, then back to GroVont for the beer. An argument broke out over who got to hold my money. My money. Imagine the gall. Shane said I'd spend it or misplace it or give it away to a worthy charity because that's what drunks do with their money.

"I've never misplaced money in my life."

"Just children."

Lloyd dropped the two of us off at Lydia's with the promise to come back in an hour with the load of beer and a pint of Yukon Jack.

"You won't on-purpose accidentally forget Jack?" I asked.

"Drinkers only quit when they want to; no one has stopped yet from being out of supplies at the moment."

"Well, I don't want to, so you don't forget."

On Lydia's two front steps, Shane taught me the tip-back, pull-up method of getting him into places.

"I go up stairs backwards and down stairs forwards," he said. "That way if I fall, I land on my face and don't get hurt."

"Is that supposed to be a joke?"

I set Shane up in Lydia's living room with a Dr Pepper and a *Progressive Peacemaker* magazine. He picked Sam's short story off the TV table and stared intently at the title—"Kiss Your Elbow Enterprises."

"My grandmother used to make my sister and me kiss our elbow every night before bed," he said.

"No one has ever kissed their own elbow. Unless their arm got ripped off."

From somewhere beneath him, Shane extracted a wicked little pocketknife. That chair was a general store on wheels. It was like in the cartoons when the coyote needs a weapon and he reaches out of the picture and comes back with an Acme anvil or six sticks of lit dynamite, only Shane did the trick between his legs.

"I used to kiss my elbow often," he said. "I was a special little lad."

Some crocks are better left alone. I went into Sam's room for shower paraphernalia, and when I came back out carrying my towel and Sam's old razor, Shane had pulled his right leg up so the ankle crossed his left knee and taken off his saddle oxford. He was intently reading Sam's story.

I stopped to check Shane out as a traveling companion. He wasn't grotesquely obese or anything, just your regular fat, but the slump posture in the chair and that dull ruby face made him appear grosser than he was. You know how a Scotch drinker's nose swells up red and laced with tiny exploded blood vessels? Shane's whole face was like that. And his head didn't sit on his neck steady; it sort of bounced or quivered or something.

His couldn't have been an easy life, what with ostracism for being hideous and all. Maybe the lies were compensation, maybe an insecure boy blustered from fear under all those flabs of suet.

Without looking up at me, Shane said, "I used to write novels. They were rather good, but the literary life is ghastly pretentious, so I quit. Pretension is the one flaw I simply cannot stomach."

Lydia came home while I was doing the legs and pits job in the shower. She walked right into the bathroom and sat on the toilet where I could see her through the semi-transparent shower curtain. She dropped her jeans over her ankles, but her black-with-red-lace-trim panties stayed up while she peed. Crotchless panties! On a weekday! The mind boggles at what perversions she and Hank must practice in private.

"Maurey," she said, "Aqualung is trimming his toenails in my living room."

"That's Shane. I think he's harmless."

"No guest who trims his toenails is harmless. Did he bring his own furniture?"

"He's in a wheelchair. Didn't you see the wheels?"

"I didn't look." She stood and pulled up the jeans that were two sizes too tight. "Didn't I tell you again and again Prell strips every drop of moisture from your head."

"Better than shampooing with vegetables."

She picked my Prell off the side of the tub and dropped it in the trash can. "Might as well shave your head again."

I managed to dry myself without looking in the mirror.

Cutting back through the living room, Shane sat waving Sam's story around, feeding Lydia this cock-and-bull about her son being a literary lion of the first degree. Unlike me, Lydia wallows in flattery. Tell her she has nice hands or is politically vibrant or was a good mother, and pretty soon she'll revert to southern belle and start batting her eyelashes and offering you canned cashews. Takes an insecure person to believe the compliments of strangers, I always say.

Packing consumed all of five minutes. I came through college when straining to look good was considered hypocritical. Powder and paint make 'em what they ain't. Paddin' and stuffin' don't add nothin': fallout from the Janis Joplin beauty school, I guess. I wasn't a hippy chick—no burned bras and body lice for me—but I was no sorority social climber, either. Two pairs of boots, corral and town; flip-flops for in the car; two pairs of Wrangler's; three shirts, two for regular everyday and a nice Neiman Marcus yoked deal with a fitted waist, mother-of-pearl snaps, and baby-doll puffed sleeves for rodeos and funerals; five pairs of cotton panties; a raft of socks that didn't match, but that didn't matter because they'd be under my boots; and two bras just in case we went somewhere I couldn't bounce.

After Dad died I fumigated his wicker trout creel to create a new style in purses. It was way cool with a deep place for my notebook, keys, pints, and whatnot and little places for Carmex and change. I slid Hank's three hundred dollars into the waterproof pocket up top where you're supposed to keep your fishing license and extra leaders.

I put in a pair of silver hoop earrings Shannon gave me for Christmas. The last time she came to Wyoming we bought a gallon of ice cream one night and pierced each other's ears. You should have seen it, the seven-year-old and the twenty-one-year-old, both terrified of running a knitting needle through our body, yet giggling like sisters. I don't know which scared me most, sticking Shannon or Shannon sticking me. We ended up with blood and ice cream all over both of us. Being a mom can be more fun than sex or alcohol put together.

———

I carried a suitcase, Sam's day pack, and the creel purse into the living room to find Shane with his claw dipped in a bag of Pepperidge Farm gourmet crackers and Lydia hovering, ready to serve his smallest whim.

She didn't seem surprised to see the suitcase. "Did you know Mr. Rinesfoos practically began the civil rights movement? That's how he lost the use of his faculties, in a Klan riot in Birmingham."

"Who's Mr. Rinesfoos?"

Shane popped a fistful of gourmet crackers through his lips. "Three sheeted racists held me while three more forced my Negro pal Isaiah to bite the curb. As they stomped the back of his curly head, I broke free and began pummeling the Grand Wizard, but their bedpost clubs crushed all the vertebrae in my spine."

Lydia bought the rap. "That is so admirable. I'd love to give my body for a cause."

Shane and I let that statement lie between us on the floor. I think it was such an obvious opening that he suspected a trap. Or maybe Lydia was too easy for an all-star lech to bother with. Instead I blindly jumped into the good-bye thing. I'm not big on good-bye things. Every vacation when the time comes for Sam and Shannon to head back south, I make an excuse and bag out a few minutes before they leave. I never even said good-bye to Dad, and he's dead.

Lydia hugged me and told me not to commit suicide or buy flowers from hippies on city street corners because the money went straight to the Moonies. I can tell I'm not latently gay or anything because I don't initiate hugs with women. Men either, come to think of it.

"You heading straight out from here?" she asked.

"After we pick up the tent and drop by the post office. Might as well take Sam his tent."

"You tell that overgrown horse's turd to send me money. It's a disgrace how he treats his mother."

"I thought the story was written by a youngster. Surely you are not old enough to have an adult child?" Shane asked.

Lydia's forehead wrinkled in spite of all that Swedish paste she glops on it. "Of course I don't have an adult child. Will you see Annabel before you leave the valley?"

I wanted a drink right now. "Doesn't seem to be much point."

"Maurey, there's not much point in anything you do."

———

Dear Dad,

*I told Hank to shoot Frostbite and sell his hooves to Purina.
We'll use the guts for bearbait and give the hide and meat to
the religious fanatics up in Buffalo Valley. I'm leaving on a
tour of southern cities tonight. You can reach me through Lydia
Callahan.*

Write, wire, or call,
Maurey

———

Loaded, oiled, and gassed, our trio in the belly of Moby
Dick headed across Togwotee Pass and into what people in
Jackson Hole call Out There. Shane babbled nonstop from his
perch in back, Lloyd held the steering wheel with both hands,
his head cocked, listening closely to M.D.'s engine as it strained
against the trailer and Coors. My Jack bottle that I'd named
Scout after Tonto's horse snuggled in his position between my
thighs on the passenger seat.

On the long curves, I looked back at a killer spring sunset
between the Grand and Mount Moran. The peaks were
majestic, the valley floor a warm, dark green. Auburn did not
know I was no longer a cry away. This was stupid. I almost
told Lloyd to pull it over and let me go. Only a true idiot
would walk away from paradise. Only a total idiot would
leave her child to smuggle bad beer and go into hiding from
somebody. Who was I hiding from? Dothan, my son, my
hometown, myself?

Shane rambled about a snuff queen in Denver he violated with a .44-40 caliber Colt Peacemaker. Her method of finding fulfillment was to have herself nailed by a loaded handgun. Those were Shane's words—"violate" and "fulfillment."

"She made me flip off the safety," he said. "Is it not peculiar the lengths some people will go to for sexual stimulation?"

I drew on Scout. "Did the Colt have a sight?"

Shane blew the first seven notes of "Tumbling Tumbleweeds" on his harmonica, then he stopped. "Of course the Colt had a sight. What woman would screw a pistol without a sight?"

What woman indeed? I fingered Charley's barrel in my wind-breaker pocket. No sight, but he didn't need one. I'm not that kind of girl.

Lloyd leaned toward the stick shift and said, "Spark plug wires are arcing. Hear that?" All I heard was the sun going down on my home.

12

LLOYD DROVE, I DRANK, SHANE TALKED. WHILE ALL THREE musketeers were practiced professionals at our chosen tasks, Shane was beyond practiced. Shane was a Renaissance talker. An eighth-degree black belt of the mouth.

In the Wind River Canyon he lectured on Manuel Lisa and early explorations of Yellowstone, including the Hayden Expedition of 1872, then he went on to reasons why the South could have won the Civil War and proper procedures for cooking a peacock—boil it forty minutes, then hang it by the neck outside for three days. Otherwise treat it like a turkey.

Between pronouncements he blew six or seven notes of "Tumbling Tumbleweeds" on the harmonica, sometimes eight notes. Lloyd's face never changed, and he never gave comment. I think he was listening to the engine, which he found more interesting.

Shane gave a blow-by-blow account of flax farming in Nicaragua—figures he was part farmer—and why women went nuts over Steve McQueen. He proved the first five lines of the Lord's Prayer is actually a limerick by reciting them in singsong:

Our Father who art in heaven
Hallowed be thy name

Thy kingdom come
Thy will be done
On Earth as it is in Heaven

"Second line doesn't rhyme right," I said.

"Does in Hebrew."

I turned to Lloyd. "Does he always talk this much?"

"Only when he likes someone."

"But I don't like him."

"Shane doesn't take that into account when he decides who to like."

Shane spoke in essay form as he compared the Grateful Dead, Allman Brothers, and Willie Nelson. "The most influential bands of the last five years, and each has two lead guitars, a keyboard player, and double drums. Can you name another band with that configuration?" He convinced me Lou Gehrig was better than Babe Ruth, male birds are more beautiful than female, and the space program failed to ignite the public's imagination because none of the astronauts was named Buck.

"Buzz wasn't close enough?" I asked.

"Do not insult my intelligence, lassie."

Shane said Ringo Starr was the greatest Beatle, then named the mothers of Adam, Hoss, and Little Joe on the *Bonanza* TV show—Elizabeth, Ingrid, and Maria—and the last picture show to play in *The Last Picture Show—The Kid from Texas*, starring Audie Murphy and Gale Storm.

"Have you ever noticed Australian women are made particularly ardent by anal entry?" Shane said. He blew the second phrase of "Tumbling Tumbleweeds." "The French have seven words for a man going down on a woman. We have *blow job* for a woman on a man or, God forbid, a man on a man, and *sixty-nine* for everybody on everybody, but the English language does not recognize the male giving pleasure to the female."

The radio was broken, of course. I should have known. I tried drinking faster, but Shane's voice was a fog cutter. Lloyd tuned him out to the point where he might as well have been driving alone. Lloyd had practice, I think. The familiarity level was hard to pin down. They might have formed the team two days before I met them, or twenty years.

If Shane ever came up for air, I meant to ask him why he thought Ringo Starr was the greatest Beatle. I thought so, too, and I'd never met anyone who agreed with me. The idea that Shane and I might have something in common was fairly disturbing. Sam Callahan said George Harrison was greatest for spiritual reasons, and Park wanted to be John Lennon because he aspired to darkness. Dothan hated them all.

The spring of our freshman year, John Lennon went on the radio in England and said the Beatles were more popular than Jesus. Sugar's sister, Charlotte, organized a record-burning party on the basketball court behind the Foursquare Gospel Church in Jackson. Dothan and I had our first major fight over the Beatles and religion. I owned all the Beatles albums and most of their forty-fives, and he didn't own any, and he wanted to burn mine.

"People will think we're Catholics if we don't," he said.

"I'm fifteen and have a daughter nearly two years old, what do I care what people think?"

Sam and I steamed the labels off my Beatle albums and glued them on Sonny and Cher albums, then we slipped Sonny and Cher into the Beatle covers. On the forty-fives we switched Beatles for Sopwith Camel, the Detergents, and Sam the Sham and the Pharaohs.

While I was at cheerleading practice my mother let Dothan steal everything I owned by the Beatles. That night Sam and I stood back from the glowing crowd and cheered as "I Got You, Babe" went up in smelly, melted plastic. I kept those

Beatle records right up to the day Dothan moved me and all my stuff he didn't covet out of the house.

"Have you seen her?" Without looking at me, Lloyd handed over a three-by-five color photo, the kind with the ragged border developers were into back in the sixties. "Sharon might be going by Carbonneau, or Gunderson. That's her maiden name. Gunderson."

A girl, maybe eighteen, stood next to a sign that read CASINO SALVAGE in front of a brightly lit stucco building. She had straight chestnut hair with these thick bangs that hid her eyebrows. Her face was happy as she vamped the camera by pulling her brown skirt up over one knee, revealing a bony leg and a tooled cowboy boot. She was thin, but not anorexic, only her shoulders slumped. Could have been somewhat pretty if she concentrated on posture.

"Is this your wife?"

He nodded. "Someone in Salt Lake saw a girl like her in a Teton campground last summer."

There were hundreds of girls like her in Teton campgrounds last summer—size sevens with brown hair aren't exactly unique—but I didn't want to tell Lloyd that. He obviously took the deal seriously. His eyes were probing the darkness beyond our headlights, but I could tell he was watching me.

Behind us, Shane finally broke through the second phrase of "Tumbling Tumbleweeds" and into the meat of the song. I had a terrible intuition he was one of those harmonica players who learns one song and goes no further.

I sipped Scout. "She's pretty."

Lloyd glanced at the picture, then back ahead. "She was FBLA Sweetheart in high school. That's Future Business Leaders of America. Sharon can type ninety-two words a minute with only two mistakes."

She had that secretarial look around the temples. "Was the picture taken a long time ago?"

"June 7, 1966—the day we opened our salvage yard. Las Vegas is paradise if your interests run to redemption of abandoned automobiles." Lloyd stepped on the floor dimmer switch as two semis came at us, then past. He glanced at their rear ends in the mirror and said, "Sharon sure was proud of our junkyard."

"Everybody's proud of something."

Behind us, Shane went quiet, for him, anyway. He muttered under his breath and made a thump sound as he slid to the floor. When I checked it out he was sitting on the pile of unrolled sleeping bags, digging furiously through a blue backpack. Probably searching for food.

"If Sharon was so proud and junk in Vegas is so lucrative, why did she leave?"

Lloyd turned and looked full at me. Without the Jesus eyes, he came off as any other farmer beaten to nonexistence by weather and banks. But the glowing eyes made him appear to know things the people he looked at didn't know. Imagine you go to tip the pizza delivery boy and you suddenly realize the kid is Nostradamus. That's the feeling Lloyd causes.

"You know darn well why she left me," he said. "I'm a drunk. Only a fool stands by a drunk." His eyes went back to the road. "Sharon took it a long time, longer than she should have."

Scout was committing foreplay with my frontal lobe. He caused the white stripes rushing into the headlights and under Lloyd's side of the ambulance to go hypnotic. I really liked that.

Nineteen sixty-six meant Lloyd and Sharon were your basic May-December romance. Or March-October. What would it be like to live surrounded by dead cars with a lover old as your own father? Lloyd had to be at least forty-five, probably hadn't had a hard-on he didn't wake up with in years. I read in *Cosmo* that girls with old lovers are actually trying to nail their dads.

Lloyd kept his voice noncommittal. "We met at a demolition derby in Prescott, Arizona. I'd been drinking beer all afternoon and got in a fight with a mechanic who said fuel injectors decrease acceleration. Sharon picked me off the arena dirt and three weeks later we were married."

Lloyd swerved to miss a mule deer and just about sideswiped two more. Ever since Dubois, we'd been passing antelope, but these were the first deer. One thing I don't understand about Wyoming is why, the minute the plains get dark, all the animals make straight for the nearest asphalt.

"Sharon and I had our junkyard and each other, and nothing else mattered until I betrayed her for the bottle. I blamed the pressure of running a business, or the Nevada heat, or my hangover—a scraped thumb gave me excuse to shoot the whole day. Whenever Sharon gave me her sad look I said 'Be glad you have a husband who doesn't gamble.'"

Lloyd's talk had the rhythm of a rehearsed speech. I'd bet my next drink this story usually started with "My name is Lloyd and I'm an alcoholic." You'd never catch me spilling my guts to a bunch of drunk losers turned coffee-swilling losers. "Here's how far down I went. Ain't I princely for not dying so I could sit through this meeting."

I'd rather be interesting and pathetic than boring and pathetic.

"She stuck by me for fourteen months. Then one Sunday while I was breaking an automatic transmission off a brand-new Lincoln wrecked by some high-roller, she packed her overnight bag and ran away. Didn't even leave a note."

"At least Sharon didn't steal your child and throw you into the street."

Lloyd didn't comment on my tragedy. AA people consider it bad form to one-up during the other guy's talk. "I don't remember hardly any of the next two years. I know I stole and ate dog food. I changed my oil without replacing the filter. Once I was hospitalized for drinking transmission fluid.

"One morning I found some whiskey in a couch at a Manpower temporary employment office in Memphis, the next thing I woke up in a hotel room in Mexico City with a broken leg. I'd lost two months."

It's really not so bad driving through Wyoming at night while a gentle man's voice drones from the seat next to you. The towns are mostly eighty, ninety miles apart, so there's no slowing down or speeding up. Cars and trucks came at us one at a time with plenty of gap between lights. Lloyd's voice was calm, like a bubbling stream, only his was a stream with words you could listen to. His pitiful story showed me the degradation of real alcoholism. It reassured me that I wasn't a real alcoholic.

I got intimate with Scout and waited for more been-there-and-back stuff, but none came for a mile because Lloyd seemed hypnotized himself. I guess he was dwelling on his days of glory.

"So," I prompted, "you woke up in a hotel with a broken leg."

His face snapped back from somewhere. "The management thought since I couldn't walk they'd send Shane to take care of me."

"Our Shane? He couldn't take care of anyone."

Lloyd gave me a some-people-are-naive shrug. "Shane stayed with me every moment for two weeks. He held me together through the shudders and stomach pain, the termite attacks, the suicide waves and night terrors. He convinced me I lost Sharon because I was a drunk and if I stopped being a drunk I could get her back. He's stuck with me through more than three years of searching for her."

"A regular Ralph Nader."

Lloyd took the picture from my hand and returned it to the breast pocket of his overalls. "I chose to live. I'd never have made that choice, or even known I had the choice, without Shane Rinesfoos."

The subject of this Drunks Aglow account had been unnaturally quiet during the testimonial. Could the same grotesque fatso who offered twenty bucks to see my tits lead a double life as a selfless savior? I turned to look back at the saint and screamed. Shane had his penis out. *Yuck.* He was bent over like a zoo monkey playing with its wienie, only Shane was rolling on a condom.

I screamed again. "Let me out. Pull over, goddammit, let me *go.*" I clawed the door handle. *"Fucking perverts."*

At my first scream, Lloyd swerved right, but he didn't slow Moby Dick. "What's the problem? Are you sick?"

The handle came up, the door popped open, and pavement raced under my eyes, but when the dramatic moment said *Bail out,* I went chicken. After all, we're talking overweight cripple here. Exposure would be in character, but rape? There was no sense in a road burn death over an exposed pecker. I refuse to be killed by a penis.

I swung my anger back on Lloyd. "You old men are sick with your games. You think because I drink and ride off in your mobile slut house that I'm like that. Well, I'm not, Bucko. Like that."

"You lost me," Lloyd said.

"Lloyd," Shane said.

Lloyd glanced at Shane on the floor, then at me. He reached toward my shoulder and I flinched—almost fell out the door.

Lloyd said, "He has to change his plumbing twice a day to stop infection. He's not a pervert."

"I am, too," Shane said, "only not this time."

Bent over, his belly had all these horizontal folds with his little penis sticking out of one like a zipper on a down-filled parka. How could he hang a rubber around that worm?

This was more insult than threat. "What kind of exhibitionist uses a condom?"

He leered up at me. "This would be easier with your help."

"Yeah, right."

"I could hold it while you tape the root."

"Have you ever priced nursing homes?"

Where most condoms have the ego-boosting large-tip reservoir, this one had a rubber straw. Maybe Shane was into being sucked off from three feet away.

His pink face broke sweat from the exertion. "If I were a pervert, I would certainly pick a girl younger than you."

A plastic bag was taped to the inside of his thigh. Another hose came off the bottom of the bag and ran to a twist clamp taped to his ankle.

"This is how you pee," I said.

"Urinate to you," Shane said, which made no sense when he said it, and still doesn't. His balls were hairless and the same color as his face.

"You may observe this process," Shane continued, "and say to yourself 'incontinence,' but you would be incorrect. I control when I go and when I don't go, more or less. The problem is simply the world and all its toilets are designed for the ambulatory. Imagine, if you can, finding an acceptable commode every half hour when you are twenty-eight inches wide and on wheels."

Longest speech I ever heard from a man with his pecker in his hand. "What's incontinence?"

Lloyd almost smiled. "He pisses on himself."

Shane yanked the rubber with both thumbs and index fingers, his butt bouncing off the floor with each tug. "I do not piss on myself. How dare Lloyd of all people accuse me of helplessness. This is merely a convenience."

As I watched him tape the rubber to the base of his worm that seemed intent on crawling back inside, I understood the lack of hair on the balls. "Doesn't look convenient to me."

13

When Lloyd stopped to gas up at a truck stop near Rawlins, I volunteered to drive and he hurt my feelings.

He said, "I've come too far to depend on a drunk driver."

"You brought me because I could drive."

"We brought you because you have a driver's license. You'll get a chance, but only in the mornings before your first drink. One sip of alcohol and you're in no more shape to sit behind the wheel than him."

Shane slept like the world's loudest snoring baby. We're talking cattle trucks on the overpass. At first, I thought he was shaking the ambulance, until I realized the wind outside whistled along about seventy miles an hour, which is average around Rawlins.

"I am not drunk," I said.

"Same thing I used to tell Sharon every night before I passed out."

"I'll damn well tell you when I am drunk."

"My words even as she undressed me because I couldn't undress myself."

When it came time to pay for the gas, I found out why they really brought me. "If I have to buy food, he's going on a diet."

Lloyd rubbed his leg and looked in the mirror at Shane the sleeping slug. "An alcohol addict with control over a food addict—should be interesting."

"Just tell him if he wants to eat, he better cover up while he pulls his plumbing."

As Lloyd double-clutched us onto the interstate and into the wind, I saw a grotesque vision of Shane's nail in the night sky, right up near the handle of the Little Dipper. Repulsive sights have a way of burning themselves into my brain.

"You think Shane gets hard-ons?" I asked.

"He talks about them often enough."

"But does he get them?"

Lloyd cracked his window. "Do witches fly and leprechauns pass out gold?" He seemed to think that answered my question.

———

I have an ambiguous relationship with the penis. Love/hate. Make that fascination/disgust. Fascination to touch, disgust to look at. Fascination at what they can do, disgust at what they do do. The dick is so comical, dangling in space like a lost thumb. And so vulnerable. It simultaneously begs to be cuddled and castrated.

Sam Callahan's wasn't the first penis I ever touched, although I told him it was. When I was seven, almost eight, we went to the county fair and a log peeler named Walt Walsowski started talking to me in the livestock barn, next to the goat pen. He said if I closed my eyes and held out my hands, he would give me some M&M's.

Until I peeked, I thought he'd handed me a trout.

In the car going home, I told Mom what Walt had done. "The second I touched his thing he peed gobbledigook all over my shirt."

She acted as if she didn't hear.

"What was that stuff, Mom? Walt laughed and said next time he would melt in my mouth, not in my hand."

She was furious—at me. "Maurey, you are disgusting and evil. Don't you ever talk like this again."

Can you believe it? The man blows his wad on a seven-year-old girl and the girl is the one made to feel dirty. No wonder I take my romantic episodes from bottles.

———

Scout and I consummated our love on the downhill side of Elk Mountain, west of Laramie. Weak knees, nauseated stomach, and uncontrollable eyelids—the signs of orgasm and drunkenness pretty much match. Only difference is you don't have to tell a pint how great he was.

We expressed our passion quietly, hiding our secret from Lloyd, who stared unblinking into the Wyoming night. By closing one eye, I could focus on his cheekbone and bare shoulder, at least for a moment, but Moby Dick had the spins. The red running lights fell through the roadway, and Interstate 80 heaved. I enjoy a good buzz, but Scout was making me sick. After great effort, I cranked the window down and got the vent open. Lloyd glanced over without a question.

Should I throw up? Pass out? I could always die again. I held Scout to my lips and inhaled from his mouth. Wetness ran off my chin onto my lap, and when I looked down Scout fell to the floor.

———

The first time I passed out from alcohol was Labor Day night before the start of my senior year at GroVont High. Kim Schmidt drove a Ford load of us to a sixteen-man rubber raft padlocked to a dock where Jackson Lake Lodge launches their Snake River float trips.

Dothan mixed this obscene southern half beer-half wine concoction he called a scrotie-oatey. Even more obscene, the beer and wine was Colt 45 and Ripple. Stuff stagnated in your mouth like swamp water.

We leaned on the inflated sides of the raft and laughed too loud while the moon came over Mt. Leidy and put shadows all up and down the river. The boys bragged about other times they'd gotten drunk and told Spanish fly stories. The only other girl there chain-smoked Larks and said her daddy would smash the first boy who tried to touch her. I watched the water until the illusion of our raft moving upstream made me queasy, then I watched clouds cross the moon, but that made me feel funny, too.

After three, maybe four scrotie-oateys Dothan said he'd throw me in the river if I didn't show the guys my breasts. I didn't care. I thought I had okay breasts because I'd had a baby. Most of the guys had never seen a tit—I made their summer. The girl called me revolting and said she was going to tell the pep club board, which she never did because three minutes later she was barfing her brains into the oar frame. My advice is never mix beer and wine in the same can.

Everyone but Dothan disappeared. He tried to nail me, but I stopped the son of a bitch—threw up right in his face. He called me a frigid slut, then I was all alone crying in a half inch of water on the bottom of the boat.

Next thing I remember is looking up to see two Jackson Lake Lodge boatmen and a family of tourists as they started loading for a breakfast float.

———

God, I had to pee. I ran from store to store in the shopping center, begging for a bathroom. My bladder felt knitting needle pain, my thighs quivered, but at each stop the hollow-faced cashiers shook their heads and said, "No restroom." Liars. Assholes. Somewhere, every store hid an employees-only closet with a commode, sink, pink powder soap in a dispenser, and a sign that said workers must wash their hands before returning to the job. I ran into the central plaza, searching for a place to go. People were all around. They flew kites; they threw Frisbees. They watched from the edges of their eyes. I stood in the courtyard and shook as ravens landed on the church roof in a mass of squawking black. Staring people circled me. They held their children back so I couldn't affect them. Shannon placed her hands over her mouth while next to her Pud Talbot pointed at my feet. The crowd broke into jeers and threw garbage at me—banana peels, used condoms, the centers of golf balls. From beneath my bridal gown, a pool of pale yellow liquid spread across the concrete floor into an ever-expanding half-moon. Dothan stepped from the crowd to wrap my face in Saran Wrap, over and over. Through the layers I saw Shannon and Auburn turn to leave, then my lungs burned and I woke up.

———

God, I had to pee. I came awake in morning light in an empty ambulance. When I raised myself to look at the day a metal pressure stuck me above the bladder. Somebody'd fastened a seat belt on me. I wasn't used to seat belts.

The ambulance was parked beside a brick building with a red roof. My guess was church. The building was set down in a wide prairie of low juniper and big, round boulders that seemed sprinkled from the sky. In college we used to cross the pass to Fort Collins, Colorado, for basketball games and parties at Colorado State, although more often they came to us since the drinking age was nineteen in Wyoming and twenty-one in Colorado.

Anyhow, bushy junipers meant Colorado to me. Church. Colorado. Not bad reasoning for someone about to pee their pants. The part I didn't know was the whereabouts of my crew.

The back end looked like a bomb had gone off, same as it did yesterday, but Shane's chair was missing. Lloyd should have left a note.

I took Scout with me, more for security and companionship than a drink. A lot more, actually, because he was empty and the ambulance floor smelled of Yukon Jack. I hate careless drinkers. The church door opened into a hallway with two doors on the right and one on the left. Left proved to be the side door to a sanctuary, the door for the priest or reverend or whatever. The casket-looking altar was covered with a green rug but the cross didn't have anybody dead on it, which ruled out Catholic. My guess was Episcopal or Presbyterian. The lectern came with an attached pencil-thin reading light, and Fundamentalists don't go in for reading lights. Gets in the way of Bible thumping.

I can't say I was still drunk, but early morning equilibrium was a problem. Back in the hall, I lurched left, grazed the wall, then got up momentum and more or less fell sideways through the second door and into an AA meeting.

Even though I'd never been to one, I knew right away what it was. Drunks in bars had told me how well lit the room would be and how everyone would be smoking cigarettes and drinking coffee from Styrofoam. Eight or nine people stopped whatever interesting thing they'd been doing to go into those blank-faced stares that strangers do when you show up somewhere unexpected. Lloyd sat on the left in his overalls with no shirt. Shane was at the head of the table in his chair. He was leaning toward a pregnant woman who looked about seventy years old. Maybe I'd get pregnant at seventy to balance off having been pregnant at thirteen.

"Toilet." My voice was a crack.

"Through there on the left," said a man in a Century 21 gold blazer.

I pointed at a door by the coffee urn and he nodded.

What a leak! Sometimes the pain is almost worth the release. About twenty seconds into the deal I realized how it must sound in the meeting room, so I leaned forward to turn the cold-water tap in the sink. No lie, I went two full minutes of continuous stream. That's one of the dangers of drinking to unconsciousness.

Afterward, when I leaned over to splash water in my face, I glanced up at the mirror and flinched. We're talking gruesome. I tucked in the left side of my shirt where it'd come out, but that didn't help much. I still projected degeneracy.

On my return to the little extended family of formerly lost souls, none of the faces had changed—same who-is-this-dead-beat-with-the-Yukon-bottle stares. They looked infringed upon.

"Thank you," I said.

"Would you care to join us?" the man in the gold blazer said. He seemed to be group leader. "Have some coffee."

"No, thank you. I can't drink out of Styrofoam."

"You're welcome here."

"I just had to use the restroom." I turned to Lloyd. "We'll be waiting in the truck." He blinked.

Outside the church, the day was pretty and fresh smelling, like real spring. Real spring doesn't come to Jackson Hole until June, and then it only lasts like two days. Our falls and winters are glorious, and summer is a short paradise, but spring is mostly mud.

I breathed deeply a couple of times, then dropped the dead Scout in a trash can, crawled into Moby Dick, and went back to sleep.

I dreamed I was an alligator.

Interstate Stuckey's. The more lanes on a road, the lower the standards in curbside cafes. Once through the Safe-Tee glass double doors you could turn left and throw money away on "The Traveler's Prayer" decoupage plaque, five-pound boxes of piñon nut brittle, bumper stickers to announce where you've been and how your profession does it, or coffee mugs for the WORLD'S GREATEST MOM. I didn't qualify.

Or you could turn right for food that would start a riot if they served it in prison. How do you make hash browns out of fiber-board, anyway?

The waitress with fire-colored hair and a name tag that read HOWDY on top of a peanut and DOROTHEA on the bottom said we were in Raton, New Mexico, gateway to Capulin Mountain National Monument. Right off she accused Shane of being a hypochondriac.

"I bet you can walk fine."

"Bless you, my good lady, I only wish it were so."

"Let me see the bottoms of your shoes."

Shane pulled an ankle up over one knee, and Dorothea examined his sole. She didn't comment on what she saw.

"My cousin Glenna is a hypochondriac in a wheelchair. When Mr. Delvins got killed by a Coke truck, the moment Glenna found out she collapsed on the floor and hasn't walked a step since."

"Maybe she has a psychosomatic disorder," Shane said.

"Not likely, Glenna's from Dallas. We took her to four kinds of specialists and Oral Roberts's 'Hour of Faith,' and nothing helps. Reverend Roberts got her to stand and fling away the chair, but then she fell on her face right on camera."

Dorothea sucked the tip of her pencil as she examined Shane for signs of health. "Glenna broke her nose on TV. Goes to show there's times you should let well enough alone."

Lloyd ordered coffee, I had a chocolate shake, and Shane

pigged on a cheeseburger and French fries so greasy they dripped. When he bit down on his burger the side facing me spit juice.

"Trouble with Wyoming," Shane said, "is no one there can cook meat properly. This excellent morsel reminds me of a cheeseburger I ate one August afternoon in San Bernardino, California. An Italian woman named Lucy cooked it on the sidewalk to show how hot the concrete was. She asked me to father her child, but I was in a religious order at the time that forbade impregnation. Needless to say, the pressure was too great and I eventually fell from grace."

Lloyd blew across the surface of his coffee. "We need a water pump. One we got won't last two more days."

The radio finished a Goodyear tractor tire commercial and went into the noon farm-to-market report—hogs down, sheep up. A woman from the next booth dragged a little boy towards the ladies' room while the kid yelled, "I'm a big boy, I don't have to go in yours." The father or whatever he was chewed three toothpicks and stared out the window at a Peterbilt with the engine running.

I signaled Dorothea over to our table. "Do any radio stations around here carry Paul Harvey News and Commentary?" I asked.

She chewed her lead a moment, then said, "My husband, Donnie, used to listen to him, but he can't find it anymore."

She'd have gotten away with that if not for a Spanish-looking busboy who was hovering nearby. He said, "KRMC."

"Pardon me?"

"KRMC has him just before 'Lobo Sports Shorts.'"

I turned back to Dorothea. Notice how polite I came on with the pardons and pleases. "Please, would you mind changing the station for a few minutes? I'd like to hear Paul Harvey."

"Yes, I mind."

"You're interested in alfalfa futures?"

"I'm not interested in changing the station."

From polite, I moved to understanding. "I notice you are varicosed. Being pleasant to customers might increase your tips and you could afford to have your legs stripped."

She pointed the wet pencil tip at my face. "Don't be getting snappy with me, little girl. You're from out of state."

Lloyd and Shane chose not to participate in the exchange. Intrusive son of a bitch that he was, even Shane knew not to step between two irritated cat women. But I was more than irritated, I was fed up. Last-straw city. People had been pushing me and stepping on me and tearing at me for weeks, and Stuckey's was the place to stop it.

I said, "I demand Paul Harvey."

"You can demand all day, honey, but you can't have him."

As Dorothea turned back to the kitchen, I screamed.

Remember Estelle Parsons in *Bonnie and Clyde*? She was subtlety personified compared to my howl. All activity on the dining side, the curio side, and, I'd bet, out in the parking lot came to a halt. Even the little boy in the ladies' room shut up.

I didn't stop with the scream, either, but kept up a series of bloodcurdlers. I learned my scream from Dothan's father, who used to call in coyotes by cutting toes off rabbits. Rabbits can really scream.

Dorothea dropped her pencil and covered both ears with her hands. She shouted, "What's wrong with her?"

Shane stopped gorging himself long enough to raise his voice. "Hysterical digitalis. Her mind must be fed Paul Harvey's voice once daily or she goes insane. If you have some liquid Demerol handy, we might be able to calm her down."

"We got no liquid whatever you said. Shut her up, she's scaring the customers." Which was true. All except the man with three toothpicks. He looked bored, a seen–it–all type with a reputation to uphold.

Shane wiped the grease off his mouth with a napkin. "The alternative would be to tune in Paul Harvey."

———

Paul wasn't worth much that day, anyway. All Watergate and a pithy story about his crusty neighbors in the Ozarks—one of those wisdom-of-simple-rural-folk deals. He didn't even give a daily bumper snicker.

14

Dear Dad,

*The Indians in the picture are Navajo or Zuni or something, one
of those tribes Hank calls Blanket Boys. He says anyone whose
ancestors didn't charge bareback across the plains killing buffalo
is a wimp. Whatever they are, the sight of turquoise gives 'em
a hard-on. They're like pickup truck-driving dope dealers, only
these guys deal blue rocks.*

It takes all kinds.

Maurey

———

"You want to try your hand at driving?" We stood—or
Lloyd and I stood while Shane sat—in the Stuckey's parking
lot, looking upwind at New Mexico. About all I could see
between us and the mountains was brush and highway and
used Pampers. Sparkles from broken beer bottles lined the
road, giving a bleak fairy-tale look to things.

"Sure, I want to drive. Listening to his blather could bore a
person back into a coma."

Shane smiled up at me. He was relieving his fluids bag on the rear tire of a white Thunderbird with California plates. I took it as a political statement. Shane was smug because he'd hustled me for a bag of Chips Ahoy cookies based on that hysterical digitalis rap. I'd have gotten Paul Harvey without his help.

"You ever drive a stick shift?" Lloyd asked. "Moby's steering is somewhat loose, takes muscle on the turns, especially to the right."

"I can turn Dick. You're worn out. Hop in back with the pervert and take a nap."

"Sharon used to love this ambulance. I can understand why she left me. I was a drunk like you are now, but I'm still surprised she left Moby Dick."

"Women don't marry cars," Shane said as he wheeled over to the side doors for load-up. "You think houses and drapes and dinette sets mean more to them than people, but get down to it, and men are the only gender can have meaningful relationships with objects."

"It has a manual choke," Lloyd said. "Are you familiar with the manual choke?"

Driving Moby Dick was a trip. Where the ignition should have been there was nothing but a blue wire, a red wire, and a switch. The stick shift was a four-foot rod with a hollowed-out nine ball stuck on top. Made changing gears into a sport. Reverse was where I expected first, which led to initial grinding that almost lost me the wheel. Lloyd would have taken it back, but he really was worn out from driving all night. The Jesus eyes were more puppy-after-electroshock. Or what I imagine puppy-after-electroshock would look like.

He didn't nap in back with Shane but took over the passenger seat to keep an eye on me. Maybe he thought I had a hidden bottle and would drink on the job. If so, Lloyd was wrong. After a bottle makes me good and sick, I swear off forever, which generally becomes ten or twelve awake hours.

Not long by AA One-Day-at-a-Time standards, but for most of those ten hours, sincerity is my middle name.

Every now and then after Dad died I took a shot at quitting completely. I didn't tell anyone because they'd give me guff and know if I failed. If you can't do something, it's best to pretend you don't want to. The extended sobriety spells were generally kicked off at the end of a several-day binge-out when I did something so disgusting, so bottom-of-the-slime-barrel, that I turned on myself.

The last time was in March when I was faking constipation so I could drink behind a locked door, and I dropped my Yukon on the bathroom floor and broke the bottle. Without even thinking, I grabbed an old hand towel, soaked up the liquid, and proceeded to suck that dirty rag dry. Cut the crap out of my tongue on broken glass.

After that I made a deal with God, but he let down his end of the gig, which was to give me strength, so I let down my end, which was don't drink.

"Where'd you learn to scream like that?" Lloyd asked.

I told him about Garth Talbot and the coyotes and rabbits. "He sold the coyote pelts for bounty and used the rabbits to make jackalopes. You may not have noticed, but every jack-alope in Teton County is missing two or three toes."

Shane was popping cookies like he was in a competition. "Are you aware that if you slice the big toe off a person you effectively cripple him just as completely as I was crippled when that semi-truck jackknifed on Monarch Pass?"

"What semitruck?" I asked, but it was too late. Shane was already off on the woman from Montana who'd lost a toe in a Sears Roebuck lawn mower. She liked doing it in apple trees or some-such nonsense. Taking my lesson from Lloyd, I was learning the tune-out technique. I didn't acknowledge the words but let Shane's sound float over me like a TV in the next room at a motel. Or say you live next to a motocross racetrack all your life, pretty soon you won't be able to hear it. Park said the sun makes a loud roar, but we've all heard it all our lives and no one has ever not heard it, so no one knows it's there. Except him.

When I met Park he was sitting under a tree in the snow, crying. His childhood dog had died back in Maine, and his mother used an ink stamp to record the dog's paw on the letter telling Park what had happened. So, I'm bopping along and there's this boy with curly blond hair and pretty fingers holding a letter. I sat down next to him but kept it cool by not saying anything.

He showed me the letter with his dead dog's footprint at the bottom. He said he hadn't cried in years and it felt kind of good to finally let go. Since then, I've discovered that's what they all say when you catch them crying. "I haven't been able to for years and it feels kind of good to finally let go."

Sam Callahan says the cowboy code allows for tears on two occasions: when your horse dies or when you hear "Faded Love" played on twin fiddles.

With Park I took it as vulnerability beneath the hard, society-imposed shell of manhood. I was nineteen.

Park and I talked for ten hours, first in the snow, then in the student union over countless cups of coffee, then on a lobby couch at my freshman dorm. After the Dothan-Rocky Joe fiasco I guess I was ripe for a sensitive man. He told me he'd read *Siddhartha* by Herman Hesse, he listened to jazz, and my hair was the color of dolphins dancing off the New England coast. He showed me a poem about God and death that he'd never shown anyone.

I told him about a man I saw die. I told him about Frostbite and my secret warm springs and that I had a five-year-old daughter named Shannon.

We met the next day for breakfast, then we both skipped

morning classes. I wanted to touch his hair and feel his lips, but after my recent history I thought it best to let Park make the first move. We must have been together two hundred hours before he held my hand. In the dark, watching *Butch Cassidy and the Sundance Kid*—he yawned and pretended to accidentally bump my fingers during the bicycle scene.

That same night he asked permission to kiss me, and I said okay.

Two weeks later he showed me a poem and asked permission for another kiss. Maurey is a nickname. My real name is Merle—after the actress Merle Oberon—and Park had rhymed Merle with pearl and girl about thirty times.

"This poem proves I love you," he said.

"I love you, too," I said, which was a first.

"Perhaps we should consider expressing our love in the physical sense," he said.

I almost said "Fuck my eyes out," but this was true love, right? The rules were different. This was what Sam Callahan and I had practiced for all those years ago, so that now I had found it, my innocence wouldn't botch the deal.

We did it Park's way. We discussed the implications, the level of commitment, the possibility of pregnancy and options thereafter, the details of us both living in dorms where intermingling was against the rules. I suspect he was stalling for time while he figured out how to lay his hands on a rubber. I had one in my purse, but I couldn't just whip it out. You don't do that to a boy who writes you a poem.

Finally, the selected evening arrived. His roommate was off at a debate tournament, and I could sneak up the stairs while the dorm counselor was watching *Hawaii Five-O*. Park had arranged like two dozen candles and lit so much incense the neighbors must have thought we were smoking pot. Freshman lore held that girls don't do it unless you get them drunk, so

Park paid someone to buy him a pint of peach brandy. I didn't want to drink, I wanted to get nailed for love.

He went into the bathroom for half an hour. I took off my clothes and hopped in the sack. He came out wearing a knee-length flannel robe with a rope belt and put *The Sea* by Rod. McKuen on his roommate's stereo. Park asked me for the third time if he was pressuring me into something I really didn't want to do.

"I couldn't live with myself if we did this and afterward I lost you," he said.

I reached out and grabbed his dick through the bathrobe.

Afterward, I felt great. I don't mean he was hot stuff or anything. He was nervous at first and couldn't get a stiffie, then I did some advanced manipulation. He came practically on contact, but that didn't matter. He was trainable. What mattered was how much better it had been with love involved. I got all emotional and tingly when he touched me, and just looking at the skin on his back excited me in a way Dothan couldn't have pulled off with an hour's worth of foreplay. Not that Dothan ever had time for foreplay.

But Park was skittish. Something hadn't lived up to his idealism.

He got out of bed, put on his robe and tied the rope, and stood with his back to me looking out the window. "That wasn't your first time," he said.

I should have smelled trouble. An alert woman would have caught the scary note in his voice, but I still felt way fine and close to him. "No, was it yours?"

His sounded ready to cry again. "Of course not. I screw every girl I pick up."

By now I knew there was a problem. "Park. Hon, you know I have a daughter. How do you think I got her?"

His shoulders slumped. "I knew you weren't a virgin,

but I didn't expect you to be experienced. You had her so young, I hoped you'd been abused or raped against your will or something."

"Park, it's okay. I didn't love him and I do love you." I patted the bed where we'd made love.

He came and sat down next to me but didn't touch my body. "Was I your second?"

"No."

"Third?"

"No."

He stood up and went into the bathroom. After a long while I got dressed, blew out the candles, and sneaked back down the stairs.

I only saw Park once more, in the cafeteria. He acted as if nothing had happened. We had one of those "Are you okay?" "Of course I'm okay," "You sure you're okay?" "Why wouldn't I be okay?" conversations.

Then he dropped out of school and went home to his mother in Maine. For several days, I wanted to die. I cried and ate, cried and ate, relived every moment we'd been together in my head, imagined his touch on my arm.

One morning as I went over that crucial night for the hundredth time, it hit me. Park had said, "I hoped you'd been abused or raped."

Fuck him. Fuck love.

I got out of bed, showered, stole some of my roommate's makeup, and went to a fraternity party where I got drunk out of my mind and sucked off a jerk named Randy.

The next day I made two rules: 1) Avoid poets and 2) Never fuck sober.

———

You look at Lloyd in his sandals and overalls with no shirt

and his brown shoe-polish-colored hair and you think he's not the intelligent sort. But get to know him and he's smart in the ways he needs to be smart. East of Clayton we came upon a cluster of gas stations at the Texas state line.

"Better fill up here," Lloyd said from the passenger seat.

"We can't be half-empty yet."

"See these three stations in New Mexico and none up ahead in Texas. That means state gas taxes are lower here, gasoline will cost a good deal more once we cross the line."

So I pulled over for gas and a Coke and some cashews. Shane finagled me for a pack of peanut butter-filled crackers. Lloyd looked under the hood.

"Give me the map," Shane said.

I'd already studied it and knew the way to I-40. "We're not lost."

"I enjoy knowing where I am at all times. It keeps me oriented."

I pretended to ignore him. I was approaching hour fifteen without alcohol—hour six of being awake—and the familiar knot was forming below my sternum. The skin on my forehead was tightening, and my breasts were nervous. I didn't need a drink yet, maybe, although I wouldn't have turned one down, I guess, but the uncomfortableness and unfairness made me cranky.

"Lassie, would you please pass along the map?"

"Are you faking Irish roots or calling me a TV dog?"

A *Popular Mechanics* sailed into the windshield. "Why must every exchange be such a struggle with you, woman? Simply hand over the damn map."

He was right. No use being a jerk about it. I held the map toward him but out of his reach. "The name is Maurey. It's not lassie, not honey, not little missy, and certainly not woman. See if you can say Maurey."

He glared at me. Lloyd opened the door and climbed in. "Bearing on the impeller shaft is about gone, I hope they have a water pump in Amarillo, " he said.

"Maurey, will you pretty-please mind passing the map back here?" Shane asked.

I gave it to him. "Isn't life more pleasant when you're polite?"

"Up your heinie with a stick."

One reason I was cranky was the heat. We'd moved in and out of spring in Colorado—I slept through it—and now we'd entered summer. Jackson Hole doesn't prepare a person to deal with heat. Sweat trickles into my eyes and down my ribs. I get paranoid that my crotch stinks.

"Keep an eye on the temperature gauge," Lloyd said. "We might have to stop and drive at night."

The thought of getting stuck in this oven-ugly barren country made me crave whiskey. "I'm not stopping for nobody."

Twenty miles or so from Dalhart we passed a billboard that said DOUBLE AUGHT RANCH with a sideways figure eight thing under the words. The next fence post had a dead rabbit hung on it, then the next a dead bird—crow, I think—then the next a dead armadillo. Every fence post on the right side of the road was decorated by something dead and decaying.

"This is gross," I said.

Lloyd blinked. "I've heard about this ranch. The owner has a fetish with predator control."

Less than a mile later the death-on-a-stick thing started up on the left side, too. Ranch kids see death often, so they don't have the romantic Bambi-Daffy Duck notions of city kids, and you don't marry into a family of taxidermists if you tend to be squeamish, but this was disgusting. Mile after mile of rotting corpses. Some posts had two animals of different species, some little more than a picked-over skeleton. At first it was only distasteful, but as the minutes passed and the dead flashed by faster than white lines on the highway, I swung from nauseous to scared.

A great iron arch with the Double Aught brand in the middle marked the main ranch entrance. On each side of the brand two coyotes hung by the neck from hangman's noose knots.

"I'm going to cut them down," I said.

"They'll just kill more to replace them," Lloyd said.

"The right thing to do would be to cut them down." I wanted to stop, I tried to stop, but we were already by. The coyotes retreated into the rearview mirror, farther and farther away. I wanted to swing around and go back. I meant to, but the upshot of the deal is I didn't.

"There are some sick people in the world," Lloyd said.

"Sick people in Texas. They'd never get away with this in Wyoming."

Lloyd looked at me with sad eyes. "They get away with it everywhere. Nothing changes except in degrees."

I didn't get it. Lloyd probably had in mind a deep symbolic lesson about the state of the world. If so, he was too profound for me. All I saw was two lines of slaughtered animals leading into the horizon. Far as I'm concerned, dead stuff is dead stuff. Doesn't symbolize squat.

I glanced back at Shane to see why he wasn't relating the scene to some perverse woman he knew in his youth, but he had the map spread on his lap and hadn't even looked up. Too busy figuring where he was going to see where he was.

Lloyd rubbed his hand on his overalls leg. The material on the right thigh was shiny and soft from all that rubbing. "My father was an alcoholic," he said, "and his father before him. It generally runs in families."

"None of the Pierce family has ever been alcoholics," I said. "Until you."

"I'm not an alcoholic." The north end of the Texas Panhandle must be the most bizarre country on Earth. All flat and scorched, makes you feel like a ladybug stuck on a dirty burger joint grill. A foreground full of rotting animals made the outlook disorienting. What was I doing outside Jackson Hole? Lloyd went on in an inflectionless voice. "Grandfather Abe volunteered for World War One. In New York City, the night before he was supposed to ship out, he got so drunk that he missed his boat. The army gave him two months in the stockade, but Germans torpedoed the troop ship he should have been on and twelve hundred soldiers died."

"There's one hangover he won't regret."

We reached another DOUBLE AUGHT billboard, and the parade of corpses finally came to an end, replaced by a view of cattle grazing around oil pumps and stock ponds.

Pissed me off. "How can my ranch compete with these peckerheads? They've got year-round grass and money pouring out of the ground."

Lloyd wasn't listening. "Old Abe stayed polluted most of the next forty-five years. In 1959 he drove his truck off an overpass in L.A., landed smack on a woman and two children in a station wagon."

"Dad bought Mom a station wagon in 1959—army green with wood trim. Petey and I pretended it was a fort."

"The mother lost her spleen, one lung, and her eyesight. Abe broke his arm. He still had a fifth between his legs when they cut him out of the wreck."

The Dalhart silos showed up on the horizon. Made the town appear as a thriving city off across a sea of winter wheat. I had to ask the question, even though I knew the answer and knew Lloyd was telling the story because he wanted to change me.

"What happened to the children?"

"Dead as those coyotes back there. They were so squished their daddy couldn't separate out the parts to bury them in two caskets." Lloyd rubbed some more. "Abe lost his driver's license." The deal was a gyp. People were all the time telling me grisly tales of alcoholics accidentally killing kids and swamping themselves with guilt. Why tell me? I wasn't an alcoholic, and I sure as hell didn't drive drunk.

"If Abe hadn't gotten soused in 1914, I wouldn't be alive today," Lloyd said, "but that family in L.A. would be."

"What you're saying is God moves in mysterious ways."

Lloyd's head snapped back and the cloudy look in his eyes went sharp. It was an amazing transition. "I'm saying God doesn't work at all. Everything that happens to you, me, Shane, my Sharon, everyone everywhere, is nothing more than luck. The universe is random."

What a thought. "How can you say that and not drink?"

He let his arm slide out the window into the wind. "AA every day."

15

As we passed a sign that said "I'm a Ding Dong Daddy from Dumas," Shane threw what Lydia calls a conniption.

"Turn right at the next highway."

"That's no highway, Shane, you could barely call it a road."

"I don't give a flyer what you call it, turn right."

I barreled on through, and that's when Shane started screeching. "Stop her, Lloyd. Turn around. Are you going to stop? *Stop this fucking car.*"

I stopped. It was either that or risk giving the guy a heart attack. I didn't like the slob, but I didn't want to kill him. My life had enough guilt.

"Turn off the ignition," Lloyd said. There wasn't an ignition, so I popped the clutch and we lurched and died. Lloyd turned around to face the back. "Now, what's the problem?"

Shane's face had gone from radish to beet. He looked like he might blow up. "The problem is I told her to turn and she didn't turn. I said all along we shouldn't bring a women's libber. I hate libbers, they never do what they're told."

"What makes you think I'm a women's libber?" I asked.

"You don't wear a bra. Probably burned it in a protest march."

"Hippy girls don't wear bras," Lloyd said. "Maybe she's a hippy girl."

"A hippy girl would have helped with my catheter. She's a libber with no respect for the crippled."

Lloyd looked at me. "Why don't you respect crippled people?"

"It's him I don't respect, he's a warthog."

We all stopped talking for a moment. Outside the ambulance, locusts or cicadas or something Texan made an insect buzz-saw noise. Inside, the only sound was a tiny, irritating whistle whenever Shane exhaled.

"Turn Moby Dick around and go back to that road," he said.

Lloyd was patient. "We'll be happy to if you give us a reason, Shane, but this is a long trip. We can't make detours based on whims."

They stared at each other. I said, "I'm not a hippy or a libber. I just don't like bras."

Shane's head bobbed and jerked. "I came on this drive for you two. You're searching for your precious wife, and she has to see the other baby she threw away. There's nothing in it for me; you should honor my sacrifice by turning right when I say turn right."

I pointed at Shane. "He has bigger breasts than mine, make him wear a bra."

Lloyd ignored me. He was always ignoring me. "What about rebuilding Granma's barn that was burned by the cur Ashley Montagu?"

"*Ah-ha.* That's what I mean. We can't save Granma unless you make her turn down that road."

"Who is Ashley Montagu?" I asked.

"The cur who stole his granma's photo albums and set fire to her barn," Lloyd said.

Shane had almost no control over his head. I didn't know if that was a neurological deal connected to his lack of legs or over-excitement. He spit when he talked. "I hate it when people jabber when they should be taking action. Do you have any notion the frustration a cripple suffers in a world of fools?"

He was trying to hack me off. "Who are you calling fools?"

"Do you know what time it is?"

Lloyd and I glanced at each other and did a mutual shrug. Time was meaningless in the belly of Moby Dick. May as well go down one road as another.

"Can you back a trailer?" Lloyd asked.

"Can I back a trailer? I've been backing this very trailer since I was twelve." Which was true, only I was a rotten backer at twelve and I hadn't improved with age. Hadn't even tried the maneuver since Dad died. I got her bent across the yellow line, and a semi just about splattered Coors and us all over U.S. 287. Finally, I pulled forward into Dumas, where I did a U-turn through the A&W and drove back to Shane's road.

"This better be good," I said.

"I hope it's not the hideout of Ashley Montagu," Lloyd said.

Shane pulled himself up high enough to peer across us and out the front window. He said, "My breasts are perfectly normal for a stout man."

———

Shane's road was made of black tar and had all these craters that back home we call frost heaves, though they must have been something else because I don't think Texas gets cold enough for frost heaves. It was one of those roads that ten years ago was in the country and ten years from now will be in town, but at the present nobody knows where it is.

We passed a muffler shop, an irrigation systems warehouse, a mini-garage rental building, and a salvage yard that seemed to deal exclusively in pickup trucks. I slowed down at the junkyard so Lloyd could do a head swivel. He grunted like an expert inspecting inferior goods, but he didn't say anything.

Shane had opened his chair facing forward and humped into it. Every street sign he would demand I slow down, but I wouldn't and he'd hit the back of my seat with his open hand. After a couple miles of this his arm shot into a point. "There, make a left there at those mailboxes."

I glanced at Lloyd, who nodded. The new road led into a semi-rural neighborhood of old houses in red brick and new houses in blond brick. Most of the new houses didn't even have yards, just dirt so black it looked fake.

"This is a suburb," I said. "We don't have any suburbs in Wyoming, except maybe over by Casper. The boom towns have trailer parks, but those people never plan on staying longer than it takes to buy an in-state hunting license."

"Must you chatter incessantly?" Shane said. "This entire journey you've done nothing but talk, talk, talk."

"That might be an exaggeration," Lloyd said.

Shane's arm came by my ear, on point again. *"Banzai, motherfucker!"*

Up ahead, a woman holding a baby sat on an upright suitcase. Next to her a redheaded kid in paisley shorts and a Baylor sweatshirt threw rocks at a German shepherd chained in the next yard. The kid held a leash that wound around another suitcase and a bowling bag and ended at what appeared to be a wet rat.

Shane's voice was a bark. "Pull over."

I rolled Moby Dick to a halt like this was a bus stop and they'd been expecting us. Which, evidently, they had been. When Shane popped open the side doors the woman started handing in suitcases.

She said, "You're late. He'll be home soon."

Shane blamed me. "It's that woman up there, she can't drive. Maurey, Lloyd, this is Marcella."

Marcella put out a weak smile. "And this here is Hugo Jr., that one over there is Andrew. We think Andrew has emotional obstacles to overcome. Hugo says it's because I ate tainted shellfish when I was pregnant, but I think it's caused by fumes from the refinery. A number of children in this area have emotional obstacles to overcome."

Andrew ran up and leaped into Moby Dick, dragging what turned out to be the ugliest cat in America. The kid shouted, "I'm hungry. You're so greedy you never let us eat. *Pee-U*, it stinks in here." He looked suspiciously at Shane. "Somebody cut cheese."

"I gave you tacos, but you were too good for them," Marcella said. She wore a Dacron print dress with white pumps, and the hair in her bun was the same color as the dirt in her yard.

"Tacos make me puke. People who eat tacos turn into Mex'cans."

"You said you didn't want a cucumber sandwich."

"Cucumber sandwiches are shit."

At the word *shit*, Shane faked like he might backhand Andrew upside the head. Shane didn't touch the kid, but Andrew collapsed on two spare tires and some loose crescent wrenches and proceeded to burst into tears. This scared the baby, who started howling on its own.

Marcella raised her voice over the chaos. "I'm not coming to North Carolina if you're going to abuse Andrew."

Shane looked down at the writhing boy. "The little lad used the B.M. word. I really will whomp him if he uses the B.M. word again."

Andrew screamed, "*Shit.*"

I looked over at Lloyd. "Coming to North Carolina?"

His eyes had gone glass. "Interesting experiences happen when you're on the road."

I really don't like loud noise or family violence. They make me nervous, and the general melee in the back end was making me way nervous. My first thoughts ran to the escape of Yukon Jack. I could handle colorful crud like this with a bit of whiskey.

Marcella piled the suitcases into a kind of chair and sat down. She dug into the bowling bag to pull out a baby bottle, which the baby rejected with authority. "Hugo will be along soon," Marcella said. "He might shoot us all."

Shane turned on me with some fierceness. *"Drive."*

———

Dumas to Amarillo was forty miles of flat during which the rock in my belly went from warm to hot and the nail in my lower spine dug in another inch. The process was awful—one minute I'm fairly fine, a little uncomfortable and nervous. I'm thinking, I don't need the stuff, who's boss here, anyway? Then the next instant God calls my bluff and nothing matters, not love, not my children, not my own health or death, nothing matters but drinking whiskey. Now. Lots of whiskey. Life is disappointing when your mind hates your body.

And added to a high-intensity case of Jack withdrawal, the moment I saw him I wanted to strangle that kid. He cried, he demanded, he browbeat his mother. He called everyone in the ambulance "stupid." We'd gone two blocks when Marcella yelled, *"Duck,"* and tackled Andrew. She stayed on the floor until an oncoming Oldsmobile passed and moved out of sight.

"You think he saw us?" Marcella asked.

Imagine Jesus stepping serenely through a race riot. That was Lloyd. "Who saw us?" he asked.

"Hugo. He'll get home and we'll be gone. As soon as he gets hungry he'll come after us. Hugo has a double standard."

Meanwhile, Andrew is howling from being knocked onto crescent wrenches for the second time in five minutes, the baby is howling, the cat is *mew*ing like it's lost its mother, and Shane decides the excitement is over, time for a tune on the harmonica. If I don't get whiskey in the next three minutes I'm going to yank Moby Dick across the center line and shut them all up by plowing head-on into a cattle truck.

Lloyd must have sensed a problem. "You want me to drive?"

"I can drive, goddammit. Just keep your mouth closed and leave me alone."

Longest damn forty miles of my life. A lot of information flew around the Dick in that forty miles, practically all of which I missed. What I did catch was Hugo Somebody took mug shots of grade school kids for a living and he'd nailed Annette Gilliam, who may or may not have traveled with him to all these Texas schools taking orders for two portrait, four large-, eight mid-,and sixteen billfold-size picture packets. I got the idea Marcella's main complaint wasn't so much that Hugo nailed another woman as he nailed a woman who wore cotton flowers in her hair.

Marcella's voice reeked of defeat. "She gets the flowers from her sister, who works in the Odessa Woolworth's."

"You don't have any alcohol, do you?" I asked her.

She stared like I was talking French and Shane said, "Drive," again. Lloyd asked me if I was okay.

"No, I'm not okay. Who are these people? Am I expected to feed the brat from hell back there? Why is that woman dressed like my grandmother? I suppose she's one of Shane's floozies he butt-fucks with a pistol while she knits baby booties and begs for more of the barrel."

"*Butt-fuck, butt-fuck,*" Andrew shouted. "*Floozie, woozie, Mama wants a butt-fuck.*" He ducked out of Shane's reach. The kid was a fast learner.

Shane sounded like he was gargling. "I'll thank you to watch your filthy mouth in front of my sister and her brood. Simply because you live in the gutter is no reason to oink like a pig."

"Sister?"

"You sure you're okay?" Lloyd asked.

"I have to potty," Andrew yelled.

An armadillo appeared on the road ahead. I slammed brakes and everybody and everything in the rear end slid forward until they piled into something. The trailer full of Coors kind of buckled into a jackknife, although it didn't roll. Thank God it didn't roll.

I killed that armadillo dead. My lower lip was bleeding on the steering wheel. Andrew and Hugo Jr. were howling yet a third time, and the whimper sound turned out to be coming from me.

I twisted in my seat to check the mess in the back. "Is the baby all right?"

Marcella was on the floor on her back, holding Hugo Jr. to her chest. "He's better off than me. What'd I do to make you stop so fast?"

"Where'd you get your license?" Andrew yelled. "From a Cracker Jacks box!"

Lloyd touched my arm and said, "I better drive from here."

16

I DON'T REMEMBER MY FIRST DRINK IN AMARILLO. IT WENT
down in a two-handed chug. The second Yukon Jack straight
up disappeared just as quickly, only by then I was partially
aware of the surroundings—bar, black floor, a row of stools,
scattering of tables, and a dance floor. Dust. I noticed the dust.

By the first sip of number three I knew I was in Pepi's
Lounge next to Pepi's Motor Court and the Golden Sandstorm
Cafe, which I later discovered was also owned by Pepi. Maybe
he got tired of naming buildings after himself.

After the initial sip, I set number three on the bar to think
about what had happened. I'd needed a lot of drinks since
Dad died, but they'd been based on nerves and knots, mental
stuff, nothing like the last few minutes after Lloyd took over
driving. Out-of-control panic. And pain. Lots of pain. I had a
problem here.

The drag part about admitting you are an alcoholic is that
once you say it out loud, each drink becomes a moral battle-
field. You find yourself glued to binge-or-starve consumption.

I knew a boy named Mike in college who rode motorcycles.
Mike admitted he was an alcoholic. He would fight it and fight
it and make himself a pissed-off mess, then he'd surrender and
drink that first drink, just to relieve the pain. But one drink

made him feel like such a failure that he'd say, "Hell, I've lost my self-respect, I might as well get drunk, comes out the same either way." So he'd get blasted and stay that way for days, afraid to sober up for fear he'd have to rejoin the battle and relive the pain.

I considered my philosophy of daily maintenance doses more practical. At least I finished the semester. Mike left for Denver, and I heard later he died from something—an accident, I think.

However, staring out the window at the motel where my ever-expanding crew was cleaning up after the long drive, the person in me who observes my screw-ups when I drink had to face the truth.

"Shit," I said.

"Huh?" asked the bartender.

"Never mind." Truth isn't all it's built up to be. If everyone who is certain they are honest with themselves suddenly became honest with themselves, the streets would flow with the blood of suicides. And I sure as hell wasn't going to commit suicide.

Pepi's Motor Court was made of fake adobe almost the same white as Moby Dick. Why would anyone create fake adobe? It's like a teenager going to Montgomery Ward and buying a fake pimple. What's the point?

Marcella came out of room five and walked toward the cafe. Andrew had one of Shane's harmonicas, which, thank the Lord, I couldn't hear from the bar. He appeared to have his little heart set on bursting the baby's eardrums while simultaneously riding on his mother's insteps. Now there was a woman with a self-image problem. Marcella was so used to shouldering guilt that she'd thought I stomped the brakes because of something she said. The perfect mom for a kid who blamed her for every discomfort. Sort of a mother-son S&M combo, only in most families the mother takes it on herself to make the children guilty instead of the other way around.

I still didn't believe she was Shane's sister. People born in hell don't have relatives.

Dad would have loved Pepi's Motor Court. When Petey and I were kids the family used to drive to horse shows and rodeos, or sometimes we'd vacation at Grand Canyon', and at night when it came time to stop Dad would circle whatever town we chose for like forty-five minutes, searching for a motel with the exact tacky shade of rosy-purply neon he preferred.

Mom would be tired from riding herd on two kids in a pickup truck all day, so she'd say, "Buddy, you just passed a perfectly good Holiday Inn." Back then Holiday Inns were twelve dollars for two grown-ups and kids stayed free. But Dad had an instinctive distaste for chains—motels, restaurants, even gas stations. Right from its start he didn't trust the franchise system.

Actually, Dad didn't trust a lot of things in motels. If the sign out front said CLEAN ROOMS, he reasoned anybody who had to tell you so was suspect. He avoided motels that accepted credit cards. Even though we didn't travel with a dog, we never pulled in if Dad spotted a NO PETS warning. He'd once been burned by a cafe with a "Recommended by Duncan Hines" notice out front, so he wouldn't stay anywhere that was recommended by anybody.

My favorite was a motel in the middle of the Arizona desert where the rooms were shaped like concrete tipis. Nothing grew within miles of the place. Petey and I would run round and round the tipi, whooping and shooting invisible arrows at the other guests. The heat in the tipis was always broken, which Dad liked, but one night the desert was cold as the dickens and all four of us had to sleep in the same bed. Mom let us eat marshmallows under the sheets. Mom could see humor in situations back then. In 1961 we moved off the ranch and into the house in town, and Mom lost her sense of irony. Nowdays, she might literally die if someone ate a marshmallow in her bed.

———

Shane wheeled through the room five door and sat in the parking lot staring off west at the sunset. His hair was slicked down à la TV evangelist, and he had on a clean shirt buttoned right up to the Adam's apple. His head bobbed and weaved, making him look mechanical—an extension of the chair instead of the chair being an extension of him.

Assuming he wasn't lying like a dog and Marcella really was his sister, I wondered if they'd ever whooped and shot invisible arrows. If a person is handicapped when you first meet them, it's hard to conceive of them the other way. At what age had Shane turned pompous? Ten? Six? You wouldn't think a six-year-old had the capacity for pompous, unless you'd met Andrew. Which led to another question: Wouldn't most people with the ego to name a boy Blah-blah Jr. use it for the first son?

"Shit," I said again.

"Huh?" asked the bartender.

"I'm avoiding my truth-facing session."

"You want another shot?"

"Of course."

———

The three-piece band played "Jambalaya," "Stand By Your Man," and "Big Balls in Cow Town." Some oil field rough-neck types shot pool while some cowboy types tromped a circle around the dance floor. The few girls present seemed to prefer cowboys to oil—who can blame them? The farmers nursed beer and looked sullen. Who can blame them, either?

I did my own drink nursing, determined not to waste myself before the appropriate time. Only amateurs throw up before last call. I wondered why they call making a drink last "nursing." I can see the baby-on-Mama's-tit analogy with alcohol, but in my experience babies are hungry. Auburn sucked it down fast as I put it out, as if I might be yanked away at any moment. What little I nursed Shannon she was slower, somewhat like a bar nurser. Sometimes she fell asleep at the wheel.

On "Across the Alley from the Alamo" the energy level of Pepi's picked up a couple of notches. It was a noise deal—the dancers shuffled louder, the pool player broke rack with more oomph. Took a moment to figure out what was waking people up, until I heard the harmonica riff twisting in and out of the guitar lead. Shane sat at the base of the band platform, puffing his rosy cheeks into a hand-held microphone. He had two harps cradled in his left hand, different keys, I guess, and a jailbait cowgirl on his lap. Shane, the jailbait, and all three band members seemed especially pleased with themselves.

The bartender paused in his lemon cutting. "The old guy can really blow," he said.

"That's one way to put it."

"I heard he lost his legs riding Tornado."

Anyone even vaguely connected to rodeo in the sixties knows who Tornado was—the Babe Ruth of Brahma bulls. The most famous cow athlete of all time. Cowboys still take their hats off at the mention of his name, which is a bigger deal than you think. Those old cowboys never take off their hats except for showers and sometimes sex. A hard-core code follower even tips his over his face to sleep.

To say Shane rode Tornado was akin to saying I danced the two-step with Hitler.

"You really believe that?" I asked the bartender.

"If Mr. Rinesfoos says he rode Tornado, you better know he rode Tornado."

"Mr. Rinesfoos?"

After his break, Shane spun circles on his left wheel while the cowgirl in his lap squealed and did nose-to-nose bumps. I'd wager tomorrow's bottle she'd never been on a horse. As he flashed in the circle, Shane pinched butts all around. The fluttery girls took this as an honor bestowed on them by the life of the party. The boyfriends grinned like a bunch of good sports. Crippled or not, if the pervert ever touched my ass, I'd wheel him through the jukebox.

It's weird when the whole world takes delight in some guy you think is a dirtbag. Everybody's-wrong-but-me doesn't wash when other people make the claim, but I'm different.

Shane played "Setting the Woods on Fire" with the band, then did a solo version of "I'm So Lonesome I Could Cry" that was pretty moving in spite of coming from a man with three chins. I was raised country but broke loose in college when I discovered Jimi Hendrix, Joni Mitchell, and the Mothers of Invention. Those frat boys I went out with were big on Bread. Psychedelic wonder rockette as I became, some elemental deal from my upbringing left me susceptible to Hank and Patsy. I tried to outgrow sentimentality and failed.

Just as Shane had me dewy-eyed, he spoiled the mood by leading the crowd into a round of "Cotton Eye Joe." That's the one where everybody drapes arms around each other's shoulders and hops up and down, and at the proper moment they all shout *Bullshit*. I hate "Cotton Eye Joe" above all things rural in America.

The jailbait in his lap raised both hands high when she shouted *Bullshit*, practically sticking her tits up Shane's nose. Some guy with sideburns down to his armpits grabbed my hand and tried to drag me onto the dance floor. He wouldn't take "No" for an answer, so I said, "No, cocksucker." He left me alone after that. Drugstore cowboys hate it when you call them cocksucker.

Through the noise and cigarette smoke, I saw Lloyd working his way down the bar, showing the picture to each hunched-over nurser. He had on a clean pair of overalls that looked exactly, down to the soft right thigh, like the pair he'd had on since we met. His hair was Vitalis slicked, with the part running straight as a knife edge. Gave him that untrustworthy look of a door-to-door Bible salesman.

When he came to me, I said, "I've been thinking this over seriously and I've decided that I'm not, technically speaking, an alcoholic."

He had the photograph in his left hand and a bottle of Coca-Cola in his right. "I'm happy to hear that," he said without a smile. "What made you decide?"

I set down my drink and held up three fingers. "First, it doesn't run in the family. Second, when I wake up with a hangover, I never crave a drink right off the bat. None of that hair-of-the-dog jive for me."

Lloyd looked me in the face. I'll never quite get past those eyes of his. "And third?"

"Third, I never black out. Real alcoholics black out entire days, and I remember every move until the moment I fall asleep." Third was partially a lie. Only partially since I never lost an entire day, but there were times I went from A to B with no idea what happened in between.

Sipping drinks, I'd come up with a fourth reason that I didn't tell Lloyd because it's an old bar joke: How do hospitals define alcoholic? Anyone with insurance. I didn't fit that description, either.

Lloyd kept staring at my face; made me nervous. "I'm glad you discovered you're not an alcoholic," he said.

"So am I."

"Answer me one question. This afternoon, if I'd told you I had hidden a bottle of whiskey somewhere in Moby Dick, what would you have done?"

"Did you really?"

"Reality is not the point, Maurey."

I stared at my drink in search of answers. I had none, then I had six, all of them lies, then I had none again.

Lloyd held his hand out toward the tattooed truck driver on my left. "Have you seen this woman? Her name is Sharon Carbonneau, but she may be calling herself Sharon Gunderson."

———

From there the evening took on a fuzz mode. Cowboys danced as roughnecks chain-smoked around the pool tables and farmers sulked. Shane sang a few songs in a voice like a cartoon frog. The women ate it up. Lloyd finished the hopeless quest number and sat alone at a table drinking Cokes. I had another Yukon Jack and ate a pickled egg.

I thought about something Sam Callahan said in one of his short stories: "You can't be paranoid unless you once trusted; you can't be cynical unless you once believed; you can't hate unless you once loved." I wasn't paranoid, cynical, or hateful, so I must not have ever done those other things, either. I missed out.

A narrow-hipped boy in a Rainbow Radiators windbreaker asked me to dance on "Walking After Midnight," and I did. The boy had lovely fingers and sweet breath. His eyes reminded me of Auburn. At the end of the song I allowed myself two seconds of resting my cheek on his shoulder, but when he asked for a second dance, I said, "No thanks. Two in a row is more of a commitment than I can handle." The boy looked at me funny, which was to be expected, and went away.

I felt flat. I didn't want to drink more, didn't want to stop drinking, wanted to find the motel room and take a shower, didn't want to leave the anonymity of the crowd. I wanted to think about the children I'd had and lost and the men I never had but lost anyway, only I was too tired to sink. Even depression takes energy.

What I really wanted was to be young again—before sex, before whiskey, before anyone I loved died.

"Where's Shane?" Lloyd asked.

With effort, I raised my eyes from staring at the dew ring my glass left on the bar. "Hustling jailbait on the dance floor."

"No, he's not."

I looked over toward the band. Three or four couples had their eyes clenched in ecstasy or desperation or something as they slow-dance-hugged across the floor, but none of them were sitting down. "People disappear from the bar, they're either outside drinking, outside doping, or gone somewhere to get laid."

"He's not drinking."

"Can you be sure?"

Lloyd rubbed his leg. "I'm sure."

"That leaves doping and nailing."

Lloyd's eyes went into their dubious wrinkle. "Shane doesn't take dope."

My head lurched an inch, then bounced back up, kind of aping Shane's twitch. "Can a man in a catheter nail?"

"Maurey, you're more obsessed with Shane's sex life than he is."

"What a disgusting thing to say."

After Lloyd left the fuzz turned dense fog and lights coming out of the darkness. Time and space imploded. So to speak. As it were. I asked the bartender for a dry napkin and a pencil. I drew a map of the Pepi's complex with an arrow going from the bar across the parking lot to Moby Dick, then I wrote, "Take my body to room five. I have friends there."

17

I BLINKED AWAKE TO ANDREW POINTING A TOY PISTOL AT MY face. "Bang, bang," he said. His other hand clutched a single-scoop ice cream—chocolate—on a sugar cone.

"Didn't anyone ever tell you not to point guns at grown-ups?"

"The people with the treasure map wanted to shoot you, only the lady wouldn't let them. But I did. I shot you good right between the eyes."

Shot me good. "Little punk, I'll show you what grown-ups shoot back with." I felt around and found my windbreaker next to me on the sheet, but no Charley hidden in the pocket. He wasn't on the narrow nightstand between the two beds, either. I hate it when I wake up without my gun.

Andrew crawled onto the bed and settled down next to my knees. "The man said you could be easy pickin's. He smelled like throw-up."

"Look, kid, I'm not responsible for your ice cream, you understand? You'll lose it any second now, so don't scream at me. It's not my fault." He nodded without looking at the cone. I went on. "Have you seen a .357 Magnum? The bore looks blue when you hold it in the light."

I scooted to the edge to look under the bed—no Charley, but enough dust bunnies to start a hutch. When I lifted my head the room filled with yellow-and-black balloon-like scum. I realized I was naked with a six-year-old mini-Shane staring at whatever slipped from under the sheet.

Chocolate drips came across Andrew's grubby little hand and soaked through the sheet over my thigh. "He told Mama you were ripe to bang-bang."

"I was ripe for a gang-bang, Andrew. Not bang-bang."

He shrugged, knowing the difference didn't matter. The cone leaned at a fifty-degree angle or so, and I really wanted to be out of bed when it dropped. But Marcella wasn't the type to ignore a floozie flashing her kid. I know those passive women. They turn tiger where their children are concerned. I could say "Close your eyes and I'll give you a surprise" like Walt Walsowski did when he handed me his trout-penis, but Andrew was way too interested in staring at my weak cleavage to fall for the deal.

"Where's your mother, Andrew?"

"She's outside fighting with Daddy."

"Your daddy?"

"Uncle Shane says my dad porks on the side. Do you know what pork means? It means he kisses girls with his mouth open. I saw him kiss Mrs. Gilliam like that. I was disgusted."

"Will you look over by my suitcase for my pistol? I can't get up without him."

"When you kiss with your mouth open it makes you married. After that the daddy has to pull a plow."

The chocolate fell off the cone onto my crotch area. I flipped the sheet—ice cream, windbreaker, and all—over Andrew's head, then made a dash for the John. His howl barely started when I slammed the door.

———

Desperate people often mark time in days and nights. "If I can make it through one more day/night, I'll be okay." Which is a lie, of course. Desperate people are never okay. In the last few days I'd developed a similar system of marking time using showers. "I'll be fine if I can just get a shower." Or, "I remember talking to Pud. It was between the first shower at Lydia's and the second." Time had transcended the sun.

The shower in Amarillo was pretty good, as far as showers go. I ran out of hot water with a head full of soap, and Pepi should call the Culligan man for a softener, but on the whole I was satisfied.

Sam Callahan says women mark time by meals, but he's usually wrong. He wrote a short story where all the women in the world were divided between those who stopped eating under stress and those who ate like pigs under stress. The men built a tall wall between the two groups with guard towers every hundred yards with machine-gun nests. Only the women who stopped eating under stress were allowed to have babies, so within three generations obesity was bred out of the human species. The only problem was the men had to keep the women under stress at all times. Sam said his story was set in the past.

After my shower I dressed in clean stuff, searched the room high and low, and went out into the absorbent Texas sunlight to watch Marcella and Hugo Sr. fight.

They'd reached that point where you've run through all the loud accusations and rebuttals at least twice and you've fallen into tense silences. Time out for rearmament. Marcella and Hugo Sr. both held ends of the bowling bag strap, as if they'd given up on a tug-of-war. Marcella stared at the white gravel next to the horse trailer while Hugo Sr. blinked at her through rectangular eyeglasses. He was rectangular in many ways— bread box-shaped head, squared-off shoulders, square-cut boots with loop buckles like the dope dealers wore back in college. Only Hugo sure didn't look like a dope dealer, he looked like a rectangular man who took mug shots of grade school children.

Marcella held Hugo Jr. on the arm that didn't hold the bowling bag. Andrew knelt by an eighteen-wheel Otasco semitruck, letting air out of a tire with a wooden matchstick. His parents were too busy being tense to notice.

"The driver's liable to yank off your arm and beat you with the stub," I said to Andrew. That was Dad's favorite threat. I was eight years old before I realized he couldn't actually do it.

Andrew looked up at me. "I saw you naked."

"Call the police."

"You have freckles on your butt."

Which was a lie if I ever heard one. Lloyd's sandals stuck out of Moby Dick's hood as if the ambulance had eaten him alive and was just sucking up the last morsel. With the hood up, M.D. looked more like a pelican than a whale. When you're comparing things to animals I guess size is irrelevant.

His head popped out and looked down at me. "The map to your room trick was a good idea. When I passed out in bars they used to roll me out by the trash."

"I've used it before."

"One of the waitresses spotted it or you'd've been rough-neck mincemeat. Those oil field guys don't care if their dates are awake."

I looked into the engine. Lloyd was tightening something to something. I'm not real mechanical for a ranch girl. "Where'd you and Shane sleep?"

Lloyd stuck a socket wrench on a knobby thing. "I spread my bag in Moby Dick, same as I always do. Figured since you paid for the room you ought to have a bed. Marcella and the kids took the other one."

When had I paid for the room? Behind me, Marcella said, "What's Annette Gilliam got I don't?"

Hugo Sr. said, "She thinks I'm interesting."

"The tulip behind her ear is cotton, Hugo. Didn't you realize that?" When I turned to look they'd switched with his head down and her staring at him. The motel was on the edge of Amarillo—I wasn't about to pass a bar yesterday—so across the road the fields stretched out flat and black. The sky wasn't even the same color as home; it was a bleached-out blue like the eyes of a malamute.

"Why would people live in this godforsaken land?" I asked.

Hugo Sr. glared at me like I was being snippy. "I live here," he said. Marcella dropped her end of the bag and turned around to cry. I could see she was crying; Hugo Sr. couldn't. For all he knew she was admiring the view.

"Water pump was forty-five dollars," Lloyd said. "Receipt's in your basket. Shane didn't make it in."

"I hope he didn't spend the night outside," Marcella said. "He knows in his condition he's prone to pneumonia and death."

Every conversation I had with Lloyd seemed like two unconnected conversations spliced together. "What were you doing in Dad's creel?"

He looked up from his hands. "You threw it at me, remember? You said take what money I needed and you sprinted off to the lounge."

"I don't think I sprinted."

Marcella turned to me with tears tracking down her cheeks. "You sprinted. We all agreed that was the word."

Hugo Sr. let the bag drop. He said, "If you leave, I will follow to the end of the Earth. My baby shall never cry without his father hearing and coming to his aid."

Andrew crawled under the truck with another matchstick. His voice came from behind the inside dual. "I saw you pork Mrs. Gilliam."

My body speaks its needs in one-word sentences. "Shower," it says. "Whiskey." "Sleep." Right then it said "Coffee." Whenever I need something I need it right now and I need it real bad.

I sat in the Golden Sandstorm Cafe in a window booth, listening to "Tie a Yellow Ribbon Round the Old Oak Tree" on the dishroom radio. Some joker leaves prison and the whole darn bus cheers when his girlfriend takes him back. Had to rank with "Cotton Eye Joe" as the worst songs in world history. I'm not a snob or anything, but bad taste offends me.

Here's what I thought about over coffee as I looked out the window at trucks kicking up dust on U.S. 287: I thought about the ever-closing gap between the time I first feel the urge for something and the absolute last moment I can go without it without screaming. My body needs were becoming Nazis of immediate gratification.

Except in the one area where gratification used to count most. It'd been many months, maybe even years, since my body said "Sex." Had I lost the need, let it slip into wistful-stuff-from-my-youth, or had it merely gone into hibernation, someday to awaken with a hungry roar to devour whatever object with a penis happened to be standing nearby?

Sometimes I hoped it was lost forever, other times I hoped to roar again. More starve-or-binge mentality. For someone who didn't want sex I sure thought about it a lot.

———

"Stand by for news!"

All right. I hadn't known what time it was or what station carried Paul's show or anything, and here he was. My lucky day. Of course, Amarillo might be the one town with Paul on every station, but you take your omens of an upswing wherever you find them.

Paul's voice, or God's, or Dad's, depending on your suspension of disbelief, came echoing across America's heartland with the Truth. All the Truth, nothing but the Truth, so help us God.

I wasn't sure, didn't even care, about Truth's content—Paul was against hijacking, obscenity in schools in Illinois, and the nation of Argentina, for the workingman and Kerr canning jars, and split on Watergate. I think he took the everybody-does-it-so-get-off-Nixon's-back stance. Or maybe he condemned the stance, the dish machine made it hard to follow. Paul had a funny line about Chuck Colson's grandmother.

Content didn't matter. What mattered was one person in the whole universe who was sure of something. Paul Harvey gave my life consistency. Like showers and Yukon Jack, he was there when all else broke up and floated away. When Paul read the daily bumper snicker—"Have Grandchild, Will Baby-sit"—I almost wanted to cry. Cliff and Marjene Henderson were celebrating seventy-five years of wedded bliss. Take that, Dothan Talbot. A street woman in Little Rock had searched thirty years for the son she gave up as a baby, then was arrested for vagrancy and when she went up before the judge, glory be, there he was. The woman is now living comfortably in the judge's guest room, cared for by her doting baby boy.

Only in America. How many mothers gave up their sons before one of them made it as a story on Paul Harvey News?

Marcella did her timid entry thing with Hugo Jr. through the screen door. After Paul, and the reunited family story, I actually didn't mind her joining me. When Marcella ordered breakfast, I said, "I'll take whatever she's having."

———

What she was having was skimmed milk, Texas toast, and hash browns. Texas toast is when you take a loaf of white bread and drop it in the French fryer.

"Shane tells me your marriage failed also," Marcella said. Her bun leaked strands of black hair across her high cheekbones, and she hadn't fixed her face after the tear session. Hugo Jr. drooled on her shoulder on this smock thing that covered her chain-store blouse. Gave her a *Grapes of Wrath* look.

"Yes, my marriage failed also."

"Did your husband commit adultery?"

"Dothan nailed anything that didn't fight back."

Her hands reminded me of a lawn full of grasshoppers in late summer. On first glance you think *Peaceful lawn*, but give it a second look and you realize peaceful is actually chaos.

Marcella's face was void of a sense of humor. "Hugo Sr. is adulterous."

"Throw his ass into the street."

We both paused over our fried bread to picture Marcella throwing anybody's ass anywhere. She adjusted the collar of her smock. "Is that how you treated your husband when he was"—pause—"with another?"

I thought about Dothan and Sugar and whose ass wound up in the street. "That's what I would do, not what I did. What I did was drink whiskey until I didn't care anymore."

She stared into her milk the way I did coffee or alcohol. I don't see how you can fathom deep stuff in milk because the surface doesn't let in light.

"I'm tempted to drink whiskey, I really am." Her eyes lifted to mine. "Only I don't think I could ever drink enough not to care that Hugo was intimate with Annette Gilliam. I'll never be able to look at him again without seeing her kissing his lips. They even did it in the Oldsmobile once. Can you imagine doing it in a car—like an animal."

The tendency was to belittle—"What animal does it in a car, Marcella?"—but I squashed that tendency. The woman left her husband because he nailed on the side. Timid flower or not, she had more courage than I did.

"I can't sleep," she said. "Whenever I close my eyes I see them in the public schools taking memory photos of the little children, then they go out in the parking lot and she touches him in the Oldsmobile, and he says, 'I love you, Annette Gilliam.' How could he do that, then come home and kiss our babies and touch me with the same hands that touched her?"

I gave my explanation. "Men are scum."

Marcella's eyes were all need. "My life is a nightmare."

I'm no good at eye contact with women. I always think they can see what I'm hiding. I don't know what I'm hiding, I never looked at it myself, but it's dirty and weak and I can hide it from men but not from women.

I pulled away from her eyes to look out the window at Andrew, who seemed to be peeing into a Cadillac's gas tank. "When I came back to GroVont from college, I decided I'd been hurt as much as I could stand. I married Dothan because I thought nothing he did would ever hurt me."

"If he can't hurt you, you don't love him."

"That's the point, Marcella."

She stared at me. I know her background. She was raised to believe marriage for any reason other than love, even if the reason is to avoid pain, is the worst sin a woman can commit.

"Was it true?" she asked. "Has he ever hurt you?"

Andrew finished peeing and began stuffing gravel into the gas tank. I could see Hugo Sr. sitting in his Oldsmobile in front of the Zippy Mart next door. He was drinking something from a thermos. I thought about Dothan and the Wyoming Family Violence Protection Act that took my baby and gave it to him.

"No," I said. "He hasn't found a way to hurt me."

"There's Shane," I said. The wheelchair came around the west corner of the fake adobe motel. Far as I could tell, nothing existed beyond that corner but black dirt. Marcella slid from the booth and stood up with Hugo Jr. on her hip. "I hope he didn't spend the night outdoors. My brother is prone to pneumonia and death." Shane didn't look prone to death. He was playing his harmonica and bobbing his head as a little girl in a costume pushed the chair.

"The doctors told him to get rest and never catch a cold."

"Why should Shane be more prone to pneumonia than you or me?" I asked.

"It's his disease." Marcella fished in her vinyl purse and came out with a couple of crumpled dollar bills. At least someone else had money on this trip. "He has baseball disease. He'll die of it for sure someday, but most people with baseball disease catch pneumonia and die before the other stuff gets them."

I did some extensive two-plus-two work. "You mean Lou Gehrig's disease?"

"One of those players. I always forget which one." She leaned forward and squinched her eyes up to peer out the window. "Who's that with him?"

18

THE LITTLE GIRL IN COSTUME WASN'T A LITTLE GIRL AT ALL, at least not in the sense most people give *little girl*, which is *young girl*.

"You think it's a blond Indian?" Marcella asked as we crossed the gravel lot between the cafe and motel.

"More like a surfer chick," I said, having never seen a surfer chick except on TV. The girl was blond, but not wheat blond, more legal-pad yellow, and she had a tan the color of granola. Her bangs were long and thick as the hair on the back of her head—the bowl look. She wore wire-rim glasses, a red rag bikini top, and an ankle-length skirt made from a tapestry. With every step she bounced on her toes, as if she had more energy than her body could handle. Between her head-bobs and Shane's they looked like a pair of toys you'd set in the back window of your car.

When Marcella and I came within earshot, Lloyd was rubbing his leg like crazy. His voice carried a pitch high. "Does she have drugs on her? We can't transport no drugs."

Shane took the girl's hand off his shoulder and kissed her knuckles. I don't know if he'd scored or what, but he sure wanted us to think so. His flabby face was all atwitch with winks, grins, and eyebrow arches. "Certainly she has no drugs.

Critter is into pure nature highs. You aren't transporting any illegal drugs are you, Critter?"

"Heck no, I promise." The girl with the god-awful name did a cross-my-heart-hope-to-die thing with her right hand. "I did them all up in Tucumcari. We fixed psychedelic mushroom spaghetti with ground hash meatballs. Was a bit chewy, but boy, did it fuck your head. I was in Tucumcari for a Captain Beefheart concert." She leaned her face toward Marcella. "Are you into Captain Beefheart and His Magic Band?"

Marcella didn't nod yes or shake no or anything, just looked at Critter like you look at a snake in a zoo. Even Andrew came over to give her his openmouthed attention.

"Captain Beefheart is my role model," Critter said. "Everything he does is meaningful on the third level. Have you ever listened really close to 'Frying Pan'?"

She put her palms atop Shane's head and lifted her eyes to the Texas sky. *"Go downtown, you walk around, a man comes up, says he's gonna put you down. You try to succeed to fulfill your need, then a car hits you and people watch you bleed."* She bent to kiss Shane's forehead. "Think about it," she said.

Shane pumped up proud enough to have an aneurysm. Both his shoes were untied, and his shirt was buttoned wrong. I didn't put much stock in that. Shane's the kind of guy would button his shirt wrong on purpose to call attention to the fact he'd recently been disrobed.

He bent his head straight back and looked up at her chin and said, "I understand."

Critter raised on her toes and swiveled to me. "You're the alcoholic, aren't you? It's not your fault, at least not the fault of the you you are now. Addiction is the spirit's way of working out karma from another life."

I blinked twice and decided she wasn't real. "We about ready to pull out?" I asked Lloyd.

He aimed his Jesus eyes at the gravel, which gave me a funny feeling. Bad news was on the way. Lloyd said, "Shane offered Critter a ride to Oklahoma. We're going that way."

Her voice was an Okie accent mixed with fried brains, if that's not a redundancy. "I really appreciate it, man. The chick Glenda I hitched out with split with one of Beefheart's roadies to homestead in Canada. Land is free there. The guy knows a place that sells Jeeps packed in grease all the way from World War Two for fifty-five dollars. Wrap your mind around that. Homesteading in Canada would be such a trip. The guy has wolves in his yard and everything."

I broke in. "Wrap your mind around fat chance. Lloyd, what's she, sixteen, seventeen tops?"

"Eighteen," Shane said.

"That's runaway, not to mention statutory if Bozo here got his dipstick wet."

Shane winked. "I'll never tell." Critter kissed his greasy head again.

I plowed on. "We've got a hundred cases of illegal Coors in the trailer. We can't turn Moby Dick into a teenie-bopper bus line."

Critter touched me. I couldn't believe the nerve. She reached across Shane and touched my arm. "You're carrying some incredibly heavy medicine on your second level. I have a massage technique that may ease your pain."

I said, "Jesus Christ."

Shane leaned back so his ear brushed her red bikini top. "The beer isn't illegal until we cross the Arkansas line. Besides, little missy, it's not your say, you are simply along for the ride. Moby Dick belongs to my good friend Lloyd."

"I'm buying the gas, I say she stays."

Shane took a stand. "If Critter stays, I stay."

We—me, Marcella, Shane, Critter, even little Andrew—looked to Lloyd. He made an unlikely leader, with his Adam's apple and stringy arms, but we made an unlikely gang of followers. He gazed off across the Panhandle awhile, then nodded once and looked back at me. I knew I'd lost the power play. People forced to choose always first look at the person they're about to disappoint.

He said, "Shane's stuck with me for three years. He stood by me through detox. I can't leave him behind."

Shane's whole face went gloat.

Critter said, "Far out, man, I'm into loyalty."

———

Dear Dad,

This picture is either a cowboy riding a very large rabbit or a rabbit under a very small cowboy. Proportion in Texas is shot to hell. The state is like Wyoming, only flat and the sky and earth are the wrong color. Makes for disorientation.

I am living in an ugly cartoon.

Wish you weren't dead,
Maurey

———

Critter scampered back into the fields to fetch her duffel bag, and I walked over to Zippy Mart to drop my postcard in a mailbox. On the way back Hugo rolled down his window and motioned me over.

"Where are you taking her?" he asked.

I lied. "Mexico. We're going to Mexico first, then maybe Costa Rica."

He said, "I'll never stop following her."

I leaned one hand on the door handle. "If you want her so much and can't live without her, why nail Annette Gilliam?"

He rolled the window shut.

Back at the motel Shane was circling the rig, organizing the transfer of Marcella's suitcase, several spare tires, Sam Callahan's tent, and a couple of engine parts I couldn't identify from M.D. to the horse trailer. Whenever I tried to talk to him he pretended something urgent had come up and he took off, arms pumping.

I discovered a really neat way to get the attention of a man in a wheelchair. You take a tire tool and stick it between his spokes.

"What?" Shane demanded.

"Where's Charley?"

"I loathe a woman who talks in riddles."

"My Dan Wesson model 12 .357 Magnum with a four-inch barrel, which is longer than yours, by the way. I want him back."

Shane sputtered and twitched. I never met a man yet couldn't be put at a disadvantage by making sport of his dick size.

"I don't have your precious pistol," Shane said. "You probably got drunk and lost it."

"That's impossible. I would never lose Charley."

"You got drunk and lost your baby, why couldn't you get drunk and lose your gun?"

———

Andrew had to use the bathroom twice between the time we loaded him into Moby Dick and we left the motel. Right then I could foretell the next 1,500 miles. For some reason, Marcella handed Hugo Jr. to Shane. Hugo Jr. reacted by going into high wail. The kid wouldn't shut up, not even when Shane gave him back. First thing Critter did in Moby Dick was light incense—smelled like Dothan's hands during his taxidermy period. The kitten peed on a sleeping bag.

Lloyd asked me to drive the first shift. "I have something for you," he said. He leaned in the passenger door and opened the glove compartment to show me a half-pint of Yukon Jack. "When you need it, tell me and I'll take over the driving."

"Isn't there a rule against you AA guys buying booze for other people?"

"No." He pulled himself up into the seat. "You will stop drinking when you decide to stop. I see no reason for us to repeat yesterday afternoon."

"Good point."

He turned his eyes on me and it was like being under a full moon. "When you are ready to stop killing yourself I will be there to help."

"I'll keep that in mind."

———

The trip boiled down to a leapfrog from bathroom to bathroom. We didn't even make the Amarillo city limits before Andrew started hopping on one foot and whining.

"Why not hook him up with one of Shane's catheters," I suggested.

Marcella said, "Maurey," and Lloyd cut his eyes at me like I'd made a social blunder.

Critter pretzeled her legs and made her thumbs and index fingers into little O's and hummed into the smoke. Shane explained the sex life of armadillos.

"The egg is fertilized months before the female attaches it to the uterus wall and begins gestation. She always has quadruplets, and they are always all four the same sex. I once saw two armadillos having oral sex, but I don't know if they were the same sex or not. The woman whose car I was riding in refused to stop after we ran over them. I've always regretted not returning to inspect the bodies. Homosexuality is fairly rare in animals."

"I knew a dog that would hump anything or anyone," I said.

"That's what you said about your husband," Marcella said.

Shane didn't like being interrupted. "We're not discussing dry-humping dogs. We're discussing oral sex in the animal kingdom."

"What's dry humping?" Andrew yelled. He was coloring Moby Dick's interior walls. Gave the ambulance the feel of a hippy bus, but Lloyd didn't seem to mind. He was staring at Sharon's picture, searching for a clue, I guess.

"Why chase after a wife who's hiding from you?" I asked.

Lloyd didn't answer—just looked at the picture, then out the window, then down at the picture again.

Critter's home was in Comanche, Oklahoma, which she showed me on the map as a dot down south near the Red River. Way the heck out of our way, but I didn't say anything. I didn't really care where we went so long as we didn't get there. Getting somewhere would mean I had to start feeling again and figuring a way to wrest Auburn from his evil prick of a father.

"Is Hugo still following?" Marcella asked.

I could see the big Oldsmobile in the side mirror. He'd dropped back behind two pickups and a black limousine, tailing us like a detective in the *Mike Shane Mystery* magazine. "Yeah, he's back there."

"He's just being stubborn. He's afraid losing his family will make him look bad at the Presbyterian church."

"Hugo's a religious adulterer?"

"He joined the church to play softball. The Northside Presbyterians have the best team in the Panhandle."

Critter said, "God is in us all."

———

The road was weird. It was a four-lane divided highway but with curbs like a town street instead of shoulders like a normal highway. I kept being afraid the right trailer tire would drift over and scrape, so I tended to keep it close to the middle, which pissed off the Texans who wanted to pass. One man shook his fist at me. After years of watching people flip each other off, his expression of anger seemed almost wholesome.

In Memphis, Texas, we turned east on this state highway about the width of a Ping-Pong table. Every time a semi-truck came at us we about crashed mirrors. Made me tense.

A billboard for MILDRED'S MANURE read "We're Number 1 with Number 2." Four white crosses next to the road marked the spot where four people had died in traffic accidents. In Hollis, Oklahoma, a sign outside a church read "The road to God is always under construction."

"I know a man in Hollis can cover his entire nose with his lower lip," Shane said. "Maybe we should stop and see him."

I felt fingers on my neck and almost jumped through the windshield.

Critter said, "Relax, think about a cool place where the grass is green and the water pure and cold."

Home. "What the hell are you doing? Did I say you could touch me?"

"These muscles are tight as guitar strings. I've never met anyone so Saturn-squared. Even Freedom isn't this tight after an all-night run to Dallas."

My automatic impulse was to reject kindness from an airhead—it seemed the strong thing to do—but her fingers felt nice. All the way through the muscles and blood to the bones, everything gave an inch. "What's Freedom?"

She kneaded the base of my neck. "He's my man. Freedom is kind and gentle. He travels freely on the sixth level. Wrap your mind around that. I've never even seen past the fog of level five. Sometimes I have corporeal thoughts, jealousy, hunger, yangy stuff like that."

"Nothing wrong with jealousy and hunger if that's how you feel."

"Freedom is immune to pain. He has surrounded himself with an invisible hedge of protection."

Her fingers were firm and strong. Her words were the droolings of a droid whose brains had been scooped at birth, but I ignored the words and heard the voice. Her voice was a ballad sung to a baby by a mother who didn't take her clothes off at rodeos. It was like being in the mountains alone. I must have been starved for human touch because I didn't care that Critter was a girl or, even worse, a girl who said "karma" and "yangy" and had a man named Freedom. You know, sometimes it's good for people to touch each other without sexual undertones. Some of my best friends are people I haven't fucked.

Critter's voice drifted into a soft rhythm punctuated by the bass of Shane's lecture on trucks or truck drivers or whatever. Driving the divide in the geometric design of road, telephone poles, fences, fields, I floated back to Lloyd's offer to be there when I decided to stop. I'd taken the offer as a nose-in-my-business, but he meant well. Lloyd was wise to the point of being guruish when it came to things other than his wife.

Fact: Someday, in the distant future, I would have to face reality and stop drinking alcohol. It would be a pain in the ass but I could stop. I could. Lloyd had stopped. Shane had stopped. Surely if old winos could pull themselves together enough to get off the juice, so could I. But it was such a cheat to be forced to stop. Other people drink whiskey all the time and no one says they are killing themselves.

I would stop as soon as I hit that bottom they all talked about. What could be more bottom than driving with your baby on the roof?

It's just that I couldn't conceive of living every day from now on until I died without a single drink. What would I do with my time? Watch TV? Bowl? I was too young to stop taking risks.

Dothan, the jerk, was divorcing me, and soon I would find myself pushing thirty and single. Alone. Someday I might want male company again. How do non-drinking women find dates? Join a church? Come on, I wasn't the type. What did non-drinking couples do on dates? I didn't like men who didn't drink. They were boring, insecure, uptight, and often weird; and you know what single men think of non-drinking women—frigid fish.

Lloyd didn't have to tell me I must stop drinking someday; I knew that damn well, only today wasn't the day. I had to find a friend first. I'd never find one afterward.

Critter dug into my shoulders with her thumbs. "Freedom could give you a prescription to relax your vibrancy points. He's very good at mixing pharmaceuticals."

"I really would be in trouble if I started dabbling in pills."

"You really are in trouble now."

Shane couldn't handle not being the one being rubbed and consoled. I heard him do the flop-on-the-floor thing, then he said, "My first level needs its plumbing changed. Critter, would you be the angel of mercy and assist with my catheter?"

"You betcha." Her hands moved off my shoulders, and I almost groaned. My touch neediness is so intense and the pay-out so sparse, maybe that's one reason I substituted Yukon Jack for affection.

"He doesn't need help with his plumbing," I said. "He's using you to get his crank felt."

"What a sordid accusation," Shane said.

"He can fix it by himself."

Critter had already turned away from me. She said, "I know, but it doesn't harm me and it makes Shaney happy."

"Shaney won't appreciate you. He'll think he took advantage of you and treat you like a fool."

"No, I shan't," Shane said. "I'll think nothing of the kind."

"There's no shame in giving a man what he wants," Critter said.

"Jesus, are you naive."

Andrew shouted, "She's touching Uncle Shane's wienie!"

"Uncle Shane has a disease," Marcella said, "and Critter is a nurse. Nurses are allowed to touch wienies."

"She's no nurse—nurses wear shoes. Someone call the police and throw her in jail for touching Uncle Shane's wienie."

"The penis is a beautiful and sacred object and should be held in glorification," Critter said.

I repeated, "Jesus, are you naive."

Shane and Marcella hit it in unison. "Don't say 'penis' in front of Andrew." That's when I decided they really were brother and sister.

Critter's attitude of penis glorification may be warped, but no more than Shane and Marcella thinking it's okay to whip it out for medical purposes but not okay to call it by its name. I never have figured the shades of decency that say it's kosher to call an object one word but not another that means the same thing. Why is *wienie* harmless but *penis* filth? The thing is still a dick. Or take *make love* and *fuck*. What, one's holy and beautiful and the other scummy dirt? They feel the same to me. How about *passed over to San Francisco* as opposed to *dead*? They both mean somebody I need disappeared.

Something brushed my leg and I jumped like I'd been hot-shotted—second time in ten minutes.

Lloyd said, "Only a cat."

I'd forgotten about the no-name kitten. He, or she, I think it was a he, crawled into my lap and broke into heartfelt purrs. Soon as my stomach settled, I scratched the little sucker behind the ears. He was a gray, short-hair, bony thing with normal whiskers on the right side of his nose and minuscule whiskers on his left, the result of Andrew and a pair of nail clippers. I don't know if the whisker amputation caused it, but the cat couldn't walk right. He had a way of lurching and catching himself, not unlike the way Shane described people walking with their big toe cut off.

When the kitten tucked his chin to his chest to receive my scratches, he reminded me of Sam Callahan's old cat. Sam's cat was cool, but she couldn't, or wouldn't, differentiate between a litter box and an open suitcase, which caused no end of unpleasant scenes with guests over the years.

Shane launched into this story about a job he once had driving a school bus in Santa Teresa, California. I missed the front part and came in on the weird section.

"I was driving the football team home from a victory over Palo Alto High. The September evening was incredibly hot, or the tragedy would have been averted."

"What tragedy was that?" Critter asked. "Lift up so I can clean under here. I've never seen one that wasn't circumcised before."

"I came over a hill directly onto two Best Buy milk trucks parked on opposite shoulders. The Highway Patrol measured later, and they figured the drivers left the bus less than one inch of clearance. The press called it a miracle of driving skill that I slipped the school bus between them going fifty miles an hour without any of the three vehicles suffering so much as a scratch."

"My hero," Critter said. I didn't hear a drop of sarcasm in her voice.

Shane went on. "Unfortunately, all the windows were open. As I flew through the gap, I heard this whap, whap whap sound. Sixteen boys on each side of the bus lost their arms."

Lloyd and I exchanged one of those looks that bind people later on.

Critter said, "Yuck, why are you telling me this?"

Shane seemed oblivious of the fact several people were about to get sick. "The screams didn't start for three or four seconds. I don't think even the boys who'd lost their arms knew what had happened. Then the situation reduced to chaos. If you pinch it some, the rubber slides on easier."

Critter said, "Like this?"

"I thought perhaps some of the arms could be sewn back on, so I jumped from the bus and ran to the milk trucks. I'll never forget the sight if I live to a hundred. Thirty-two arms lying on the highway. They didn't look real, more like broken mannequin parts. Except for the blood and exposed muscles."

"I've heard this story before," Marcella said.

"I haven't," Lloyd said.

Andrew was still fascinated by the wienie. "They'll put you in jail."

"I told the milk truck drivers to throw the arms in their rigs and follow me to the hospital." Shane lowered his booming voice. "Here's the miracle: not one of those poor boys died. We saved every last soul. Of course it took the doctors too long to sort out which arm went with which boy, so they weren't in time to sew any of them back together.

"At graduation that spring the school gave me a special award in appreciation of my quick action. Whenever a boy came onstage for his diploma you could tell which side of the bus he'd sat on by which arm he had left."

Thirty-two arms on the roadway made an interesting image. Even Critter was grossed into a moment of silence. I asked Lloyd, "Why does he tell these lies?"

Lloyd's eyes were closer to Jesus than ever. "What makes you think they're lies?"

"The next spring the California Legislature passed a law against school bus windows that open from the bottom. It's been almost twenty years, but the one-armed members of that football team still come together every September on the day they beat Palo Alto. They send me an invitation, but I don't go. It doesn't seem proper since I'm whole and all."

19

"YOU MIGHT OUGHT TO PULL OVER," LLOYD SAID.

"Why?"

A red light flashed in the mirror, then I heard the siren. My impulse went to flight. "Let's make a run for it. I'll stop and wait for him to get out and walk up, then I'll peel out."

"Peel out?" Lloyd rubbed his leg and blinked, as if I might really go Bonnie and Clyde on him. "We aren't breaking any laws."

"Oh, yeah, I forgot." As I opened Moby Dick's door I glanced at the mess in the back end. It was hard to believe in that pile of trash and humans on the run we weren't breaking a law. "Pull your pants up."

"This is a legitimate procedure. I shall not be rushed."

Lloyd spoke up. "I've kicked around a lot of years, Shane, and I've found no matter how legitimate the procedure, it's always a mistake to show your dick to a cop."

Conjecture leapt to mind as to how Lloyd came by this experience. Too much conjecture. Handling the Highway Patrol would be less complex. Police figures are easy to deal with—don't make eye contact, act dingy, dumb, and flirty, and tell them what they want to hear. In other words, fulfill their definition of feminine.

The patrolman—thirty, sunglasses, nice ass—stood off to the road side of his car, writing on a clipboard balanced against his belt buckle. Mick Jagger lips—I swear they were plump and red as whole pimientos glued to his teeth.

"You look like somebody," I said.

He opened his mouth and the sound came out Okie instead of English rock star. "You know that gentleman?" he asked.

Hugo Sr. sat in his Oldsmobile fifty yards up the road, staring off at the lime green wheat.

"I met him this morning. His estranged wife and children are in the ambulance." I couldn't come up with more explanation. I mean, I could have come up with more, but it was complicated and involved personal lives.

The patrolman didn't ask for explanation. "May I see your license, ma'am."

"Only if you call me Maurey. I'm not used to being called ma'am. Makes me nervous. What's your name?"

He didn't answer my question, but I spotted a silver name tag on his pocket flap that said BEN LAWSON, OHP. Good western sheriff-type name, nothing English or prissy like Mick. He held out his hand. "License."

I dug in my back pocket. "The picture's not very good. My eyes came out red and the camera made me look ten pounds heavier than I was. I've heard they always do that."

The lips flexed. "Your license plate on the trailer is expired, ma'am."

Sure enough—1972. "It's my father's trailer. He got killed last fall. It was awful and I guess we haven't taken the trailer on the road since then. I'm truly sorry." I hate talking to sunglasses. You can't tell if you're getting goodwill or contempt or what. All you can see is two versions of yourself playing the fool.

Ben Lawson compared the picture on the license to me. "Merle Pierce?"

"Maurey Talbot. Maurey's a nickname and I forgot to change the license after I got married. It didn't seem to matter, or maybe I knew the marriage wouldn't last. Little signs like that make you realize the deal was doomed from the start. Don't you think so?"

Ben Lawson stood close with his thumbs deep behind his belt buckle. "Get one thing straight, Mrs. Talbot. I'm not related to the faggot."

"You sure look like him."

"You are in no position to tell me I look like a faggot."

"I didn't say you look like a faggot. He nails more chicks than any two men in Oklahoma."

"You're in no position to make fun of Oklahoma, either." Ben Lawson walked along the trailer, inspecting scratches and rust spots. At the wheel well he stopped and took off his sunglasses to stare at Moby Dick. Andrew waved from the rear window, but Ben Lawson didn't wave back.

He nodded at the trailer. "Hauling horses?"

Lloyd's door opened and Lloyd came hopping over the hitch, bony hand extended. "Hi, I'm Lloyd Carbonneau and I'm a recovering alcoholic. I own a salvage yard in Las Vegas, Nevada. The vehicle belongs to me, but I don't drive it." The hand not shaking with Ben Lawson offered Moby Dick's registration.

Ben Lawson sized up Lloyd from his sandals to the no shirt under the overalls, then he turned back to me. "What's in the trailer, ma'am?"

A horse lie would have led to proof of inoculation and interstate livestock permits. "Household goods. My friends are moving to North Carolina and I offered to drive them."

He put his sunglasses back on his face, where they definitely doubled as a psychological prop. "Let's see."

"What?"

"Open the door, ma'am. I'd like to see the household goods."

"Wouldn't you rather look at my registration?" Lloyd said.

Thirty seconds of hemming and hawing later, Ben Lawson looked in at two battered suitcases, a tent, three bald tires and one rim, a dead battery, and one hundred cases of Coors. I hadn't actually seen our contraband yet. It was in boxed cases with the Coors logo, which I think was ripped off from the Coca-Cola logo, above the script thing about pure Rocky Mountain spring water. The cases were stacked four wide and five high. Quick math put them at five cases deep back in the double-wide horse trailer. Plenty of room for more. I wondered why we didn't buy more.

Ben Lawson said, "Some household, ma'am."

"That's not beer in the beer boxes. They packed those with books and dishes and stuff. Beer boxes stack nice," I said.

He stepped into the trailer to gently shake the top box of a stack. Glass clinked.

"Sounds like we broke Marcella's china," I said to Lloyd, who did nothing to back me up.

Sunglasses and lips hovered over me from about eight feet in the air. "Let's go look in the vehicle."

As I followed him to the ambulance I once again reminded myself that a cute butt does not a nice guy make. You always hope beautiful people will behave themselves accordingly, when, in fact, it may be the opposite. I haven't known enough nice guys to work out a pattern.

I said a little prayer to God to please make Shane hide his private parts. My prayer was answered and wasted at the same time. Sam Callahan says be careful what you pray for because God has a preset quota of granted wishes for each person and they shouldn't be wasted. It's like when you enter a contest you don't really care to win; you lower your odds in the contests that matter.

The very instant Ben Lawson pulled open Moby Dick's side door, a butter-knife-slicing-cardboard voice shrieked, "Arrest her quick. Use your gun and arrest her."

"Who, son?"

"That lady touched Uncle Shane's wienie."

Critter beamed like a sunflower. "Far out, it's Jumpin' Jack Flash. You're the spit-image of Mick Jagger. I mean, you two are twins."

Andrew yelled, "Shoot her with your gun!"

I viewed Critter through Ben Lawson's eyes—dirty bare feet, tapestry skirt, rag bikini over the pertest little breasts you ever saw. And that haircut. She cried out to be shot or fucked, it would be a tough choice.

The babble continued: "I can tell you're death karma on women. My girlfriend Longina would suck you off on sight, man. One line from 'Satisfaction' and she'd drop to her knees and stick out her tongue."

I broke in before she got us all shot or fucked. "Critter, he's kind of sensitive on that subject."

"Longina goes to Velma-Alma High. She's seen the Stones four times. Wrap your mind around that. She'd die to meet Mick, and stud, you're as close as anyone in Velma-Alma will ever come."

His hand went to the sunglasses, but he changed his mind and left them on. "How old are you?"

"Seventeen."

Andrew stamped his foot. I couldn't believe it. Nobody outside women in Russian novels and trained horses stamps their feet. "Arrest her and throw her in jail to rot, and arrest Uncle Shane, too. He beats me."

Shane's head bumped up and down as he did the good-natured laugh deal. He was sitting on Critter's duffel bag, the perfect picture of a pervert. I'd have thrown the whole bunch of us in jail. Everyone had faces of atrocity, even Marcella and the baby.

"We're hoping Andrew grows up to write TV shows." Shane laughed. "Such an imagination." He held out his hands, which he'd twisted into gnarled, useless claws. "As you can see, I'm afflicted. My niece was helping me change my catheter, and little Andrew misinterpreted. Do you have any notion what it's like to wear a catheter?"

At *niece*, Andrew started to brat out, but Shane gave him a shut-up-or-die look and Andrew shut up.

My feeling is Ben didn't buy the gnarled hands or catheter rap, either one. He asked, "Are you sick?"

When Shane shifted off the duffel bag, part of the folded-up wheelchair came into view in the junk behind him. Ben said, "I didn't realize."

Shane stared glumly at the floor. "I lost my capacities fighting a forest fire in Montana. A deer had panicked and run into the fire and become trapped. I had to go in after it, otherwise I couldn't have lived with myself." He lifted his eyes to his twin reflection in Ben Lawson's face. "I saved the deer, but a falling tree severed my spinal column."

Marcella said, "I am a Christian, Officer."

This time when Ben Lawson took his sunglasses off he folded them and slid them into his shirt pocket, right below the name tag. You could read his thoughts in his lips. Sympathy, cynicism, duty, resolution. He turned back to look at Lloyd standing next to me. "Are any felonies being committed here?"

"We're just simple travelers."

"You carrying any dope?"

"Would someone driving this getup and hauling all that beer risk carrying dope?"

Ben Lawson locked into Lloyd's eyes. His lips kind of quivered at the experience. I knew what he felt, I'd locked into

Lloyd's eyes myself. That much sincerity makes a person weak in the stomach.

Finally the lips formed speech. "I've got real criminals to chase. A bunch of clowns smuggling Coors must be harmless enough."

"That's us," I said. "Harmless clowns."

He backed away from Moby Dick, feeling his pocket. "One thing. Disguise the damn beer. You don't have a chance in hell of making the East Coast without someone pulling you over. No use in being too stupid."

"We try not to be too stupid," Lloyd said.

Ben Lawson turned away and walked toward his patrol car. "Have a nice day, folks."

As I pulled Moby Dick onto the two lanes of asphalt, Shane went gleeful. "*Banzai, motherfucker*, we showed him. It's all in the timing. I unveiled the chair at the perfect moment to maximize guilt."

"What's a motherfucker?" Andrew demanded.

"You told me you lost your legs in a motorcycle wreck," Critter said.

"I rode my motorcycle into the fire to save the deer. Let me explain the details."

Hugo Jr. started crying, the de-whiskered kitten sneaked back onto my lap to nurse on my shirt buttons. I drummed a finger rhythm on the steering wheel, considering what to name the precious half pint in the glove compartment.

Lloyd leaned back and smiled for the first time since I joined forces with the AA duo. "Oklahoma's pretty," he said. "I could get used to this."

20

COMANCHES ARE ONE OF THE TRIBES HANK ELKRUNNER approves of. He has strict standards when it comes to authentic Native Americans. The best are the mountain tribes with four-pole foundation tipis—Blackfoot, Flathead, Nez Percé— although he looks at Crow as a short step from Communists. He says the Plains tribes—Sioux and Cheyenne—are overrated because of the Custer thing, and Apaches are the only south-west Indians worth dealing with.

"I dated a Hopi once," he said. "All she talked about was TV. She watched *Truth or Consequences* while I humped her."

Bottom of Hank's list of real Indians are the Civilized Tribes of Oklahoma, especially the Cherokee. "No better than white farmers," he said, which meant no better than anyone.

Comanche, Oklahoma, was a three-gas-station town with a Korean War air force fighter plane mounted on concrete in the city park. Critter had me turn right at this Humble station with old-fashioned pumps where you actually see the gasoline in a glass bubble on top. It was neat. Lloyd wanted me to stop so he could make the owner an offer.

A mile or so west of town we came to a peeling white-frame farmhouse with a full-length porch, two huge pecan trees in the yard, and a half dozen Volkswagen buses and bugs parked at random, like they'd been tossed by a tornado. Every one of the Volks was painted with garish designs and hippy code words—LSD, PEACE, SPEED KILLS, WOW, LOVE, 13, GATORADE.

I'd seen hippy houses before. In Laramie we called them train stations—one bunch of people constantly coming and going, another bunch sitting there with nothing to do, and nobody cleans the bathroom.

It was late afternoon and hotter than a popcorn popper when Critter's arm came by my ear and she yelled, "There's Freedom."

I spotted right off which one of the seven or eight vagrant types was Freedom. He stood dead center on the porch, hands on his hips and what you would have to call a sneer on his face. "Why isn't Freedom's hair long like the others?" I asked.

"He hasn't been out of jail long enough to grow it out." Critter stuck her face out my window—which put her mouth at ear level—and shouted, "Freedom!"

A couple of longhairs stood up to watch me park next to one of the pecan trees. A tanned woman with no shirt on came out the door and sat on the steps, nursing a baby. A dog rolled onto his back with all four legs sticking straight up.

I said, "It's Tobacco Road."

"No, that's Zig Zag. He wants his belly rubbed, but don't touch him unless you don't mind fleas."

The dog looked the least flea-ridden of anyone in the yard. I'm not normally prejudiced against the counterculture, but there's freaks who have long hair and get high but otherwise think roughly along the same lines as the rest of us, then there's the other kind. These freaks were the other kind.

Before Moby Dick came to a complete stop the side door popped open, and with a squeal, Critter streaked across the dirt yard and up the steps where she latched on. Freedom draped his right arm over her shoulders. He didn't seem as happy to see

Critter as she was to see him, because the expression on his face stayed the same. He didn't even look down at her, just stared over her shoulder in our direction.

"Maybe Sharon came through here," Lloyd said.

"Let's go see what a guy who travels freely on the sixth level is like," I said.

Shane was strangely quiet. When I looked in back he was shoving his chair through the door with a bad-taste pucker on his mouth. Marcella was bent over, changing the baby's diaper. She'd tightened her bun, as if we were making a social call. Andrew, amazingly enough, was asleep.

All the way from Anadarko through Fort Sill, forty miles, he beat two rocks on an upturned plastic bucket and sang, "*Here comes the bride, big, fat, and wide. Where is the groom, he's in the dressing room. Why is he there, he forgot his underwear,*" over and over and over until I was about ready to stop Moby Dick and strangle the kid dead in front of his mother.

On the thirtieth *big, fat, and wide* I heard a clump. By the time I looked back he was asleep on a ratty army blanket, using the bowling bag as a pillow. I'd have given all the money I would ever own to be able to fall asleep like that.

I climbed out my side and walked around to join Lloyd where he stood rubbing his leg and inspecting a charred Volkswagen bug.

He touched the door handle and peered in the broken window. "It was the battery under the backseat. Sparked into the stuffing. I've seen a dozen burned like this."

Critter was on a rave. "Beefheart was totally cool, you wouldn't believe the energy. I mean, when he sang 'Dachau Blues' waves of love washed from the crowd onto the stage. He picked up on it, too, I could tell by his aura lines."

Freedom kept his eyes on Shane's wheelchair. "Where's the stuff?"

"Glenda split for Canada and I got a ride to Amarillo, where these straight people picked me up. I told them they could crash here tonight. Meet the straight people, Freedom. That's Lloyd and Maurey. She's an alcoholic, Shane's the dude getting in the chair. There's a whole family inside, but I forget their names."

Something about the way Critter said *straight people* made me think she was making a point in code. Freedom didn't care. He said, "Where's the goddamn stuff?"

"Can't we talk about that later?"

"We'll talk about it now." He came down the steps and moved toward Moby Dick in these long strides—real purposeful, manly.

Critter followed, childlike. "I got your stuff, Freedom. It's okay. Now's just not the time."

Shane threw his hands up in self-defense, but Freedom marched past the chair, reached into Moby Dick, and pulled out Critter's duffel bag. She didn't say anything, just stood there looking underage.

Freedom had on a sleeveless undershirt, the kind Grandpa Pierce used to wear. He wore sandals, which matched him up with Lloyd. When Freedom's hands yanked things out of Critter's bag, you could see the brown stains on his fingertips. The knuckles of his left hand had LOVE tattooed in blue ink, one letter to a finger, and the knuckles on his right hand had HATE.

Another tapestry skirt came out, and a pair of thongs. He pulled out a glass bulb thing with rubber tubes off the sides, which I took as a high-tech water pipe. Then Freedom started pulling out brown paper packages, each one shaped like a brick.

I was pissed. Critter stared at the ground, where she could avoid eye contact. Lloyd's eyes were on the wrapped bricks, and so were Marcella's from the door of the ambulance. Shane looked at the ground, too, about the same spot as Critter.

"You knew she had dope," I said to Shane.

Marcella squawked, *"Dope."* She turned quickly and held her hand over Andrew's eyes. He was asleep, but she wasn't taking any chances.

"Is that true?" Lloyd asked Shane.

Shane looked at Lloyd—he still couldn't face me. "We couldn't leave her there. You would have left her if I told you." I was way pissed. "We could have gone to jail, you fat jackass. Even your own sister. You risked all your friends just to impress a hippy dopehead you wanted to nail."

Freedom's voice was harsh. "There's only eight here, where's the other four?"

I knew right then he was a jerk because Critter was more afraid of him than she was of me, and I was ready to kill her. "I told you, Glenda split for Canada. She went for the free land."

"The cunt."

"It was her money, Freedom."

Can you believe a guy with the name Freedom using the cunt word? Here's a truth: There's not a man alive, no matter how liberated or advanced, who, when the conditions are right, won't call a woman a cunt.

——

"Owsley, go get me my pipe," Freedom ordered.

A boy I hadn't noticed before said, "Get it yourself, I'm doing something." The boy sat against a pecan tree trunk with a drawing notebook in his lap. Thirteen, maybe fourteen, he was the Hollywood version of an angel. Pure skin, soft cheekbones, eyes a light blue sliding into silver—but the beautiful element that jumped out and touched your heart was his hair. His hair was sunshine blond and thick and fell like a Yosemite waterfall over his shoulders to his waist. How this angel ended up in a yard full of scuzballs was the great mystery of Oklahoma.

Freedom's fingers tore into one of the packages. He didn't raise his voice, but I got the idea he didn't have to. A truly chilling threat works better as a whisper than a scream. "Owsley, bring me my pipe. Now."

"Why can't somebody else fetch your stuff? I'm the only one out here doing anything."

"Owsley."

The boy pouted, but he moved. When he stood, he had the body of a football halfback. Good shoulders, no hips, just a trace of ass. He was about the same age as Sam Callahan when he and I de-virginated each other, but they were as different, visually, as a Kentucky Thoroughbred from a llama. Emotionally, they both tended to sulkiness.

After Owsley went in the house, I drifted over to check out the drawing pad. It was a charcoal picture of a hawk with its wings spread and a snake in its claws. Came from one of those DON'T TREAD ON ME flags, I think. The drawing was really good for a kid. Really good for anyone. He knew how to fine shade with charcoal, which is something I never pulled off back at GroVont High art class.

"Is that a narc?" Freedom pointed down the road at Hugo Sr. sitting in his Oldsmobile.

I was flipping through Owsley's art pad and took a moment to frame an answer that wouldn't get Hugo Sr. shot at, but before I came up with anything Shane jumped in. He'd been quiet too long—extended contriteness was not his deal. "That's my sister's husband. She left him in Amarillo and he's been following ever since. He's harmless, unless you are married to him."

Freedom's eyes went squinty. "Looks like a narc to me."

Marcella's head came out of Moby Dick. "Hugo Sr. is a children's portraitist, a very good one. Whatever a narc is, he isn't that."

"He makes me nervous out there. DeGarmo, take care of it."

One of the anonymous scuz-types went into a whine. "You'll smoke while I'm gone."

Freedom's eyes snapped at the chosen scuz. "Jesus Christ, what is with you people today?"

DeGarmo trotted off down the road toward Hugo Sr. His jeans had leather patches all over the butt, and some were peeling away so you could see the top half of his crack.

"What's he gonna do to Hugo?" Marcella asked.

Freedom wasn't even watching to see what DeGarmo did to Hugo. He was more interested in the pot sifting between his fingers. He said, "I better not have to send someone after Owsley."

The scuz lieutenant was still fifty feet away when Hugo Sr. started the Oldsmobile, did a three-step U-turn, and drove off toward Comanche. Guess he wasn't as stupid as I'd assumed. Hardly anyone ever is.

Cocktail hour. The day was one to be proud of, so far; I'd driven all the way from Amarillo, Texas, with scarcely a tremor. My neck muscles hurt, and I had that fluttery stomach only alcohol can un-flutter, but I'd said, "No whiskey till Comanche," and here I was. An alcoholic could never have shown my level of self-control.

You want to talk addicts, you should have seen that pack of lost dogs that circled Freedom as he finger-sifted marijuana. Not a functioning frontal lobe in the bunch. I'd have been shocked to hear a two-clause sentence escape from any of those chapped lips. Their eye pupils were huge black holes—as compared to Freedom's pupils, which were pinpricks. Most of their mouths weren't quite closed. The *Duh* look.

Winston, the married English professor, had pinprick pupils like Freedom's. I think he was self-medicating or something because he couldn't get a stiffie unless the girl was on top and he took frigging forever in coming. Or maybe that was an age thing. Winston would lie there, his arms thrown over his head, and babble something from Camus like "Mother died today. Or, maybe yesterday; I can't be sure. The telegram from the home says: 'Your mother passed away. Funeral tomorrow. Deep sympathy.'"

I'd look down at his curly armpits and think, What've I got to do to make the intellectual dildo come? Christ, no grade is worth this.

When Winston gave me a C, I put a full rubber in his car ashtray where I knew his wife would find it. Us self-proclaimed victim types can be nasty.

21

YEARS AGO THERE WAS A FRIED-FOOD DRIVE-IN IN JACKSON named the Purple Cow. The carhops wore uniforms like Swiss milkmaids yodeling over burgers named after strains of cattle— Angus, Holstein. The Charolais Burger came with bacon and Velveeta cheese. Whenever our family drove by the Purple Cow on our way to church or someplace, Dad would recite: "'To each his own,' said the old lady as she kissed the purple cow."

At the time I thought the saying was meaningless silliness meant to amuse us kids, like Mom's "Mares eat oats and does eat oats and little lambs eat ivy," but now I see the old lady in a deeper vein. Dad was never meaningless like Mom. I think what he meant was weird people are okay. Just because your brother is gay, or worse, or the only nice boy you've run into in months has a reputation for jack-jobbing animals, that's no reason to condemn them. Some people live in Wyoming, some in New York City. Some people eat TV dinners off aluminum foil trays, and some people kiss cows. There is no better or worse, only to each his own.

I considered the different-strokes-for-different-folks stance as I put Dustin in my mouth and Freedom put his pipe in his. Dustin was the name I'd chosen for Lloyd's half-pint because Dustin Hoffman played a half-pint in *Midnight Cowboy*.

Freedom's pipe was a real pipe, the U-joint kind plumbers find things in under the sink. It was two feet long with the hole out on the end covered by a scooped piece of screen from a screen door. It held a fistful of pot at once, and when Freedom exhaled his nostrils blew like Frostbite on a twenty-below day.

Dustin was ice cream, fresh air, pretty dresses on little girls, and riding Frostbite over a fence, all rolled into one fine swallow. I took delight in whiskey.

When Shannon was eight months old she would shake her head side to side and laugh the cutest laugh you could imagine. Sam Callahan said she was making herself dizzy on purpose for fun, which proved the need to get high was innate in the human species, as inbred as the sucking reflex and crying when you stub your toe.

Lydia said Sam's nature-wants-us-stoned theory was nothing but an excuse for stealing her Valiums.

Park told me anthropologists have studied hundreds of cultures around the globe and there are only two universal characteristics: every culture has a way to get fucked up, and they all have a rule against nailing your mother.

So—I wasn't to blame. Freedom's method was illegal, mine was addictive, Indians used peyote, and scaredy cats used Jesus. It all came down to reality avoidance.

"Really prime stuff, huh?" Critter said to Freedom, who didn't appear ready to share with the milling pack. "I handled it just the way you said, tested from two kilos, weighed them all, pretended it was commercial crap, which was pretty hard, believe you me. That stuff had me seeing tracers."

Freedom hit deep twice more. "Clean up the kitchen. Dog Whiffer made chili and left a mess."

"Did I do good, Freedom?"

He squinted his eyes at her through the blue smoke. "You're four pounds short."

"I need to pee." I said. "You got a bathroom in the house?" Critter's eyes weren't the same flashy, pert sparkles they'd been in Amarillo. It's like we'd entered a zone of stagnation. "Sure," she said. "All houses have bathrooms."

"Toilet's plugged," Owsley said from under the tree.

"I just fixed the toilet last week," Critter said.

Owsley didn't look up from his drawing pad. The angel face showed remarkable concentration. "Dolf got paranoid and flushed the plants."

Freedom said, "Dumb shit."

Lloyd already had Moby Dick's hood up, and Shane was zeroing his chair in on the topless nurser. Looked as if they planned to stay awhile. As I walked toward the house with Critter, she touched my arm. Touching seemed to be something she was used to and I wasn't.

With her other hand she tugged the red bikini top up on her mound breasts. "I feel real yangy about lying about the pot. The karma adjustment will have me lotused all afternoon tomorrow."

"I'm not mad at you, you needed a ride and did what had to be done to get it. Shane's the one I'm pissed at. We've entered this business partnership and he can't be trusted. The jerk."

"You should be kinder to Shane. He says you are racked with guilt because he quit drinking and you can't even though you are young and healthy."

Shane was leaning forward in his chair, pretending to admire the baby while he poked his nose into tanned cleavage. His body kind of spazzed and he went into a coughing fit that left drool off his chin.

I said, "There's enough guilt in my life. Shane isn't on the list."

———

Inside, the house was typical of what I'd seen of train stations—four thousand dollars sunk into the stereo system and maybe fifty cents on the rest of the furnishings. Everything was close to the floor. The two couches and a chair seemed to have their legs cut off. Some corn-on-the-cob crates were covered with pop cans and paper plates on which ashes and dried chili made a holocaust-colored mess. The rug had multiple burn holes, especially in front of the couches and stereo, and the only decoration higher than my waist was a hand-painted sign over the kitchen door: *Getting a job means admitting that you can't take care of yourself.*

Five or six versions of the people outside sprawled around the room in big-pupiled stupor. One guy was frozen in an uncomfortable kneeling position in front of the record stack. He'd gone catatonic with two fingers stuck in a Doobie Brothers album cover. Another guy lying on his back on the floor suddenly hurled his hand at the ceiling, then drew it slowly back in until it touched the tip of his nose, then hurled it up again. A girl with EAT ME written in red fingernail polish on her forehead danced to no music in the corner.

One December back in Laramie, Joe Bob's fraternity elected him Finals Week Procurement Officer. That meant Joe Bob had to find and buy diet pills so the frat boys could wire themselves into all-night study sessions where they talked nonstop, chewed gum like cows, and sweat the stinkingest sweat that ever came off a man.

Joe Bob took me to a train station out by the Medicine Bow Mountains where some needle people had a speed factory set up in what used to be a tack room. The needle people had a black Lab with about thirteen two-month-old puppies that wandered the house eating anything that hit the floor and crapping.

That much shit was way beyond hippy handling capacities, so they'd bought a hundred-pound drum of lime, and whenever someone vaguely coherent spotted puppy poop they'd dump a McDonald's medium soft drink cup of lime on the pile and forget about it. The system worked pretty well so long as you looked where you stepped, but personally I was disgusted. Hundreds of white, dusty piles gave the house a surrealistic, moonscape appearance.

Disgusting as the needles-and-dogshit people were, this bunch in Oklahoma had them beat.

"Don't sit on that couch," Critter said, indicating a Forest Service-green divan being slept on by a person of unknown sexual persuasion. "That's Arlo's couch, and anyone else who uses it is in big trouble."

"Is Arlo dangerous?"

"This science professor at OU is studying body lice, and on Wednesday afternoons he pays a dollar apiece for every live one Arlo brings in."

"The couch is a crab farm?"

"Arlo is a crab farm. He made seventy-five bucks off his pubes last week but spent it all on drugs to numb the itch. I wish Freedom would make him split. I hate little spiders. I better not find any on me."

"Fuck you, Critter," Arlo said. He wasn't asleep after all. "Give me any more grief and I'll sit on your pillow."

———

Let's skip a detailed description of the bathroom. Some things are better left unexamined.

———

Back in the kitchen, the EAT ME girl danced and ate ice cream out of the carton with a fork. You can always tell a train station where the people are into narcotics by the shortage of spoons. Her dance was a kind of Tibetan hula thing with lots of flow and no rhythm.

Critter stood in front of the electric stove holding a steel wool pad that looked remarkably like my mother's hairdo.

"Maurey, this is Dog Whiffer."

The notorious Dog Whiffer who made chili and didn't clean up after herself. "Freedom's in the crappiest mood. He got ripped off or something in Dallas. Went down for five thousand Seconals and came back with twenty-five hits of mescaline."

Critter stared at the brown crust on the burners, apparently stymied by where-to-begin. She asked, "Save any for me?"

"Freedom said not to. He says you get funny on mescaline."

"I like that."

"Last time you went deep on us."

Critter gave up on the steel pad and dipped herself a bowl of chili. "Want some? It's not vegetarian or anything. We transcended the petty divisiveness of moral judgments based on food."

I went into what-the-hell, you-only-live-once, and accepted a wooden bowl and a fork. To be safe, I sloshed in some Dustin before I ate.

Dog Whiffer did a counterclockwise twirl on her toes. "Freedom was ungodly till he copped some Dilaudid. You should have heard the fight with Owsley. The kid hasn't been going to school and a truant officer showed up at the door."

"Kids today don't know how easy they got it," Critter said, as if her generation walked barefoot through the snow to a one-room schoolhouse.

"What's the age difference between you and Owsley?" I asked.

"Three years. But they're vital years."

The chili was tasty stuff. Dog Whiffer had put in more beans than most cooks in Wyoming. Wyomingites eat lots of cow, especially the men. Usually men consider other men who cook as effeminate, only the stigma doesn't count with straight cow things—chili, rare steaks barbecued outside, whole calves reamed lengthwise and turned slowly over hot coals.

Shane's voice boomed from the living room. "South America, the southern tip of Paraguay, I contracted terminal malaria. A native shaman mixed up a cocktail our Negro guide said was used to kill zombies. With some uncertainty, I quaffed the brew. In less than an hour, I was free of malaria, but I've had no feeling in my legs ever since. I'll give you twenty dollars if you let me tweak those exquisite breasts."

Critter's fork stopped in midair as we listened for an outcome. A moment later, Shane went into W. C. Fields. "I'm a little short today, but I will gladly pay you next Tuesday." He got a laugh instead of a slap. Rankled me no end.

"You think the others might do food?" Critter asked.

"I'll take a couple bowls to Marcella and Lloyd. You can ask Shane yourself."

Critter dipped a tin cup into the pot. "You better work out this envy thing with Shane. If he dies before you've reconciled the friction, the burden may slop as far as your next three lifetimes."

"That blob's not going to die."

Shane's stupid, lying story must have unstuck the catatonic because the walls suddenly vibrated with Doobie Brothers. I slid Dustin into my back pocket and took the two bowls from Critter. That's the up side of half-pints—they fit in the back pocket of a pair of Wrangler's.

As I left the kitchen, Dog Whiffer shouted over the music, "I hope you don't mind, but I balled Freedom while you were gone. He said it was okay."

22

MARCELLA WOULDN'T TOUCH THE CHILI. SHE SHIED BACK TO the far side of Moby Dick as if I'd offered her a bowl of smallpox. "Don't you go giving Andrew any of that stuff, neither. He's too young to be addicted."

Take it from me, you're never too young to be addicted.

"Where is the sprout, anyway?" I asked.

She pointed across the yard. "He refuses to come inside. They won't give him dope, will they? I'll be real angry if they give him dope."

Andrew was playing over by some of the more energetic hippies who were taking turns flinging painted horseshoes at each other. Seemed to be at each other because no one hit within five feet of the ringer poles. They held bottled beer—thankfully not Coors—in their left hand, threw with their right hand, and alternated between saying *Wow* and *Shit*. Freedom sat on a folding chair, smoking cigarettes and scowling at the ineptitude of his troops. A man wearing nothing but Jockey undershorts *ohmed* dangerously close to the flight path. He had erect posture, his feet pretzeled over his knees, his fingers poised in prayerful O's, and his eyes closed in on his soul. So to speak. As it were.

Andrew studied the meditator closely, then stepped up, drew back his child-size cowboy boot, and kicked him in the sternum.

One eye opened briefly, then closed again. *Ohm, ohm, hairy krispy, hairy krispy.*

Andrew yelled, "Eee-yah!" and karate-chopped the guy in his Adam's apple. No reaction. We're talking Don Quixote's attack on the windmill.

I took Marcella's bowl over to Owsley, which was more or less what I'd planned all along. He sat under the pecan tree in the dying Oklahoma light, concentrating on his eagle and snake.

When I handed Owsley the bowl he said, "You're the alcoholic, aren't you?"

"No."

"Tell the scared lady there's an all-night truck cafe out on Highway 81. That's where I eat when everything at this house is poisoned."

"Does that happen often?"

He shrugged and went to work on the chili. I stood next to him, looking down at his unbelievably beautiful hair. I wanted to touch it the way you want to touch a pulsating coal in a dying campfire. "Is that a golden eagle or an immature bald?"

Owsley glanced at the picture, then up at me. "What's it to you?"

"The golden has feathers all the way to the toes, you've drawn the legs bare."

"Well, I guess it's an immature bald eagle, then."

I tried to take my eyes off his hair and look at the drawing, but it took effort and I wasn't in the mood for effort. "But you didn't know you'd drawn an immature bald until I told you. That's sloppy art. I looked through your work while you were inside and you're good, way too good to put a golden body on bald legs."

The angel eyes snapped in such a way that I knew for certain Freedom was his father. "You touched my stuff while I wasn't here?"

"Are you listening? A person with your talent has a responsibility to draw nature the way it is and not cross animals or put things where they don't belong. You can be Picasso and screw it up, but only if you know the right way first."

He threw the bowl and what was left of the chili toward the mailbox post. "People in this dump touch anything they please. It makes me sick. If only straight pigs have privacy, I'd rather be a straight pig."

Evidently, I'd rubbed a sore spot. "Owsley, I'm sorry I touched your personal pictures. I was just looking at them. You have a great talent."

"Don't let it happen again." With that he picked up his charcoal and went back to studying the picture. I'd been dismissed.

Can't leave without one last shot: "You want to grow up to be a straight pig you better stay in school. Fool."

———

Andrew had found a tree limb and was beating the religious zealot across the head and shoulders. Several of the horseshoe throwers stood in a rough semicircle, watching without judgment. Beating had no effect, so Andrew jabbed the ragged limb butt in the guy's chest and twisted. The guy showed amazing self-discipline, not something I would have expected to run into in a train station.

Lloyd leaned his back against Moby Dick and watched Andrew's antics while he ate. His fingers were black grease to the knuckles. "Sharon hasn't been here," he said.

"You're lucky on that one."

His head went down and up in what passed for a nod. "I suppose. Only, I wish I'd find one person who'd seen her, even a year or two ago would be enough. How could a girl that beautiful disappear without anyone remembering her?"

I'd seen the photo, and Sharon was nice, but not beautiful,

which just goes to show you the old eyes-of-the-beholder thing is true. And Lloyd had the eyes. His eyes under Owsley's hair on Steve McQueen's body would be God his own self.

"It's a big country, Lloyd, assuming she stayed in the country."

"I'll find her in Florida. I know."

Andrew picked up a horseshoe and started for his target, but one of the hippies intervened—first sign of involvement from anyone on the place.

The chili bowl was empty. "Spark plug wires are arcing," Lloyd said. "We ought to replace them."

"Will they hold to Carolina?" Lloyd didn't answer, which I read as yes. "I've spent my quota on car parts. It's gasoline and maybe oil from here on."

He handed me the bowl, careful that our fingers didn't touch. "How about hay?"

Andrew was trying to light a match and failing. "Cars don't run on hay, Lloyd. Even I'm not that dense."

"The patrolman was right, we have to disguise the beer."

"We could draw a funny nose on each bottle."

Lloyd didn't smile. "I figure twelve bales of hay will seal the Coors from view. Freedom says a place down the road will sell it to me. He buys manure there for his marijuana plants." Lloyd knew the power of his eyes. You could tell because he held them back until he wanted something.

He used them now. "I'll be needing some money."

Freedom must have heard his name. I smelled him behind me before he spoke. Smelled like burned rubber.

"Hey, man, I can use that stuff."

I jerked away from his voice. Anyone else would have sensed my repulsion and gone away. "Just what I've been looking for," he said.

"What's just what you've been looking for?"

He leaned under Moby Dick's hood, over the battery. "This'll teach those bastards."

Freedom produced a pocketknife and a clear, plastic globe, the kind toys come in for a quarter at the grocery store. Shannon used to see a toy halfway up the dispenser machine and beg for quarters, hoping that particular toy would drop out the slot. Once, it even did. Sam Callahan took this as a sign that Shannon was born to win. He ignored the five hundred times the machine spit out the wrong toy.

Freedom carefully scraped the white corrosion off the battery poles, positive first, then negative. Dad told me if I touched that stuff it would eat off my fingers, then I would go blind. I don't know if Dad exaggerated, but I noticed Freedom avoided direct contact with the moldy powder.

Lloyd realized the deal. "You're going to sell that to someone as drugs."

Freedom tapped the globe with his finger. "Fuck, no, I'm not selling this to no one. Honest men need not fear my medicine."

"You'll carry it on you and let them steal it," I said.

Freedom grinned, exposing gaps between his teeth. "You're pretty smart for a wino."

Lloyd's voice was soft and sad. "When they shoot it up they'll die."

"Ain't that a shame," Freedom said.

I'm hard to shock by weirdness, but, Jeeze Louise, there has to be limits. "Stealing isn't worth killing anyone over," I said.

"Is when they steal from me."

"No, it's not."

Freedom turned on me, crouched like a rabid dog—or how I imagined a rabid dog would crouch. "Nobody rips off Freedom. Got that? Nobody. Any asshole fucks with me dies and damn well deserves to."

"You just went off the disgusting scale."

"Oh, yeah? Which one of us is the alcoholic?"

——

Freedom had never-ending depths in which to sink. I was beginning to think this sixth-level jive meant sectors of hell. After I got Lloyd's money from the creel under the front seat, he asked me which one of them I was boffing.

"Boffing?"

"I bet on the cripple. You're the kind of butch bitch who wants control. I bet you sit on his face, give him a smell, then run around the room making him crawl for it."

"I'm not sick enough to imagine the shit you take for granted."

"Or you're doing it for both of them—fuck the skinny one and make the fat one watch."

"You're right, Freedom. I fuck the skinny one and make the fat one watch."

23

I TOLD LLOYD TO BUY THE CHEAPEST STRAW THEY HAD. "Don't get hay," I said. "This is for hiding, not feeding." "What's the difference?" he asked.

What's the difference? A guy moves his hands with deliberation and shines Jesus eyes on people and keeps his mouth shut while others talk nonsense, and pretty soon you attribute wisdom to him. Lloyd had lost true love, he'd survived a multi-year drunk; people who hit the bottom and make it out alive are supposed to come back with insights. Deep knowledge.

Here's this skinny old man sets himself up as a junkyard guru, and he expects me to emulate his grand sobriety, expects me to trot right along following his vision of the pure life. I'd been thinking about stopping drinking because Mr. Gentle here said I should. Why, I wouldn't follow George Washington himself if he didn't know the difference between straw and hay.

"Pick up another half-pint," I said. "I'm out."

———

I couldn't go back in the house. I'm used to being the one dirty thing in an otherwise wholesome environment—not counting Dothan—but in that house the environment itself was putrid. Crabs in the couch. Drugs in the toilet. Women who regarded sex with less romanticism than even I did. Heck, I'd never been in a scene where I was the health nut.

Depressing thought. So, I stayed outdoors, where, except for an occasional tinge of marijuana, the air gave the illusion of cleanliness. I sat on the front porch, draining Dustin and watching Marcella urge her son to come in the ambulance before they turned him into a junkie. She was so distraught, strands of hair popped from her bun. Marcella was the sort of woman who used a cookbook featuring quick meals you can make with canned mushroom soup.

When Lloyd started Moby Dick, Andrew ambled on over, ignoring his mother, making sure the hippies knew that leaving them was his idea, not connected to that hysterical woman with the crow voice who wouldn't take a step outside. The instant he came within reach Marcella grabbed him, and as she jerked him through the open side door, the *Ohm Ohm* man came to life.

He shouted in the voice of prepuberty, "Tell the boy that I who am one love him, I have always loved the boy and shall always love him across the passages of dimension and space."

Marcella's face looked as if she'd received a death threat.

Lloyd had to back up twice to get turned around and gone without running over Owsley—not a simple deal considering the Dick's gearbox. Owsley was just the kind of kid who wouldn't move, and Lloyd was just the kind of guy who wouldn't ask him to. It felt kind of weird watching Lloyd drive away, leaving me alone in the sloth zone. Another abandonment. My days had been a series of abandonments: Sam Callahan, Shannon, Auburn. Dad.

A half block away Lloyd turned on Moby Dick's lights. One of the rear lights on the trailer was way dimmer than the other one. Not dead yet, but dying.

Dad had majored in art in college, after World War II and before I was born. He never let me see his work, so I have no idea if he was any good, but he had definite opinions of good art and trash. He thought Andy Warhol soup can art was trash. Impressionism was guys painting with their glasses off. He would have liked Owsley's stuff because he liked animals with lots of details. Details were big with Dad.

While the eagle legs would have pissed Dad off to no end, maybe it wasn't all Owsley's fault, maybe Oklahoma didn't even have eagles. Owsley had probably never seen one— golden or bald. He was drawing a picture of a picture he'd seen somewhere, a dollar bill, maybe. The dollar-bill eagle has toes the size of its head and legs spread like a woman screaming "Nail me, baby! I want a big hot one!"

Dad said you couldn't draw nature secondhand, you had to look at it and concentrate on seeing what you're looking at. When I was a little girl and sober I used to study nature so closely. I spent hours lying on my belly next to Miner Creek—almost the exact spot and position of my botched suicide—inspecting each hair on the leg of a spider or each vein in the face of a leaf. One summer I added seventeen sparrows and juncos to my life list. How many alcoholics can tell the difference between a rufous-crowned and a tree sparrow? Answer me that. Somewhere along the way I'd lost my life list, probably left it in a box over at Mom's.

The screen door slammed and Critter settled in next to me on the porch steps. She held a mug in each hand. "You want coffee? I made a pot and figured you might be in the mood after driving all that ways."

"I thought hippies only drink chamomile or jasmine or some other good-karma Kool-Aid."

"Heck, this is Oklahoma, can't get away from coffee in Oklahoma. Coffee and football."

I looked at the barefoot, directionless children on the lawn. "This bunch follows football?"

Critter laughed that unguarded giggle of hers that turned

guarded around Freedom. "You should see them in the fall. When OU makes a touchdown half jump up and cheer and the other half who were nodding out say 'What happened? Did we score? Who's got the ball?'"

The coffee was hot and pure, just the ticket after sucking Dustin dry. "Critter, I hate to tell you, but this is not a healthy place to live."

She made a sigh noise, as if one of those lower levels agreed. "It's my home," she said.

"For one thing, that boyfriend of yours is an A number one jerk. There's no excuse for nailing the Dog Sniffer bimbo."

"Whiffer."

"Whatever."

As the lawn darkened, the horseshoe game seemed to move farther away. A couple of fireflies expressed sexual desire by lighting their asses over by Owsley. Fireflies are rare in GroVont; we have them, but for the most part they stay unlit.

"I didn't think you were the type to make value judgments," Critter said.

"This is a special case. Freedom is a villain, and I'm the expert when it comes to sleeping with villains."

"He's my man."

"There is nothing you can do to make it come out right."

She blew across her coffee but didn't drink. "Freedom's under a lot of pressure, these people depend on him."

"When a man says he's 'under a lot of pressure' it means he's given himself license to nail anyone he damn well pleases. I was under pressure, you didn't see me fucking the neighborhood."

"Freedom says jealousy is middle-class Puritanism repressing the full joy of life."

Men must learn these lines from a secret book. How else could they all come up with the same garbage? "Critter, listen to me. I'm twenty-two and more experienced."

I swear to God she said, "Yes, ma'am."

"Finding the full joy of life by rampant and random coupling is for males only. They demand their women find full joy through exclusive service to one cock." Jesus, I was starting to sound like one of Shane's bra burners.

Critter's voice caught an edge. "Freedom doesn't care who I sleep with."

"That's even worse."

———

The first time I knew for certain Dothan was playing both sides of the fence I was eight months pregnant with Auburn. Eight and three-quarter months. I'd suspected before when he came home from the real estate office with a sunburned butt, but he said I was being a silly, neurotic woman.

"I wouldn't lie to you," Dothan said.

He lied to his boss, his clients, his parents, and his friends—I thought I was different. I gained thirty pounds that last couple of months and sex wasn't fun, it hurt, but old Dothan had his needs. They all have their needs. He said my being pregnant put him under pressure—hell, I was the one couldn't sit, stand, or lie down, what's he talking pressure for—and if I couldn't fuck, it was my wifely duty to suck him off.

So the beached walrus dropped to her knees. Three days before Auburn was born I'm down there uncomfortable and bored, and I open my eyes on this blond hair, about a foot long, weaving its way in and around the curly Alabama pubes. Maybe it was Sugar Cannelioski's hair, I don't know. One end was black, which meant the color came from a bottle.

I stared at the blond hair and thought, Jesus, what do I do now, then Dothan grabbed both my ears, wrenched them, and squirted pus down my throat. Tasted like dirty dishwater.

He said, "Thanks, babe," and walked into the kitchen for a beer. Didn't even help me stand up.

"How can he keep drawing in the dark?" Critter said, nodding at Owsley's shadowy form.

Another shadowy form detached itself from the horseshoe game and came over to the porch. It was a guy maybe a year or so older than most of the others, with imperfect skin and pitch-black hair pulled back in a long braid. Probably a percentage Indian, or possibly Italian; some percentage of him was swarthy, anyway.

"Hey, Roy," Critter said.

"Hi, Critter."

"Roy, meet Maurey, she's an alcoholic."

Roy didn't look at me. He didn't look at Critter, either, but not looking at her was on purpose, whereas he didn't look at me because I didn't count.

"Freedom came back from Dallas with bad vibes," Roy said.

"You can say that again."

"He really needed an opiate to mellow out, and I had some Dilaudid, so we made a trade."

Critter didn't say anything. A half-moon came up almost straight east, or what I thought was straight east, and a night bird sang from one of the pecan trees. You could tell Roy was embarrassed yet determined to plow ahead.

"Freedom traded a blow job for the Dilaudid."

"A blow job?" Critter said.

"From you. He said you wouldn't mind."

She stood up too quick and spilled coffee on the step. "He traded me for drugs?"

"Freedom do that often?" I asked.

"He's never...I don't understand. He doesn't own my blow jobs, how can he give them away?"

Roy looked at the porch steps and shrugged.

Critter's voice jumped a note. "We'll see about this crap. That asshole traded me for drugs. Roy, the Red River'll freeze before I ever touch your balls." She took off across the yard. "Freedom!"

Roy stood right where she left him, staring at the porch with his hands in his pockets.

I said, "Don't you feel like the scum of the earth?"

He did the shrug thing again. "I paid twenty dollars for the Dilaudid."

An argument broke out across the yard. I couldn't hear the exact words, but you know how arguments are, exact words don't mean much. It's tone that counts. From the sound, Freedom was walking away from her and she was trying to force him to listen.

The question I've never given myself an honest answer to is this: Why didn't I cut off Dothan's dick and stuff it up his ass? Or to be somewhat less dramatic: Why didn't I leave the bastard?

The easy answers are lies. I was eight months pregnant, and all my energy was going into my body with none left over for a crisis. I had no money or job skills. I hadn't let him nail me in a month, and a man left without sex for a month has a right to get it where he can—that would be the one he told himself. I'd known he was low class when I married him, so I was getting what I deserved.

Why is it when women get cheated on, or left behind, or raped, or even cancer, a tiny voice somewhere beneath the intellectual, together woman whispers, *You deserved it, sweetie?*

Lying fucking voice.

"I'm so bad I deserve bad stuff." Nobody deserves bad stuff—not drunks, not sluts, not women who marry for something other than love.

Or maybe it's not women, maybe it's only me; I'm the only

one in the world who thinks, My husband cheats and it's my fault because I'm pregnant and ugly.

Who the hell got me pregnant and ugly?

Critter rematerialized from the dusk. She had bad posture and was crying, one cheek was shiny pink from where he'd hit her. We were three people who would have died rather than make eye contact.

"Come on," she said to Roy.

"Should we get high first?"

"Let's get it over with."

He gave the shrug again. If Roy ever came close to normalcy, got married, got a job, that shrug would irritate his wife to an early divorce. It was a false pretense at innocence—"My asshole behavior is out of my control. Don't blame me."

I said, "Critter, this is crazy. Nobody can turn another person's sexual performance into a credit card."

"Freedom can," Roy said.

"He's a pimp forcing you to whore for him. Do you really want to be a whore?"

She touched her sore cheek. "I don't have choices."

"Everybody has choices. Come away with us in the ambulance, there's always room for one more. I don't care if he is your *man* or how much you love him, if he gets away with this, he'll never love you."

A tear ran down the bridge of her nose and hung off the tip. She was lost and seventeen, only a few years older than my daughter. "You didn't want me. You said I was a statutory teenybopper and shouldn't be allowed to come along."

"Heck, Critter, I was just hung over and mad at Shane. All of us in Moby Dick are in trouble, and when people in trouble travel together they have to take care of each other."

"Where would I go?"

"A person whose house is on fire doesn't sit in the flames

whining 'Where do I go? Where do I go?' She gets the fuck out. And honey, your house is on fire."

She bit her lower lip and looked from me to Roy, who was no help, then back to me. "I'm stuck," she said. "I can't run away from Freedom."

"Sure you can. Everyone in trouble thinks they're stuck, but no one really is, no one out of jail, anyway."

"This is jail."

"No, it's not, Critter. It's a bunch of sad people wasting their time."

Roy said, "You're taking all the fun out of this. It's only a blow job."

Critter reached over and touched my arm, first time I've ever felt natural touching another woman. She said, "I can't leave Freedom."

"Why not?"

"He needs me."

She led Roy into the house.

24

THE DAY JOHN KENNEDY GOT KILLED, DOTHAN TALBOT BEAT me up. Technically, I threw the first punch, but I maintain to this moment that Dothan had it coming. After we heard the news, Dothan and that idiot sister of his raced around the playground taunting the way kids will who have been raised by redneck ignoramuses from Alabama.

I wasn't in the mood. So I decked him.

American folklore considers it quaint when a thirteen-year-old girl hits a boy, he hits back, then they go steady. By Critter's age, at seventeen, the same scenario is sick. Boys who hit their girlfriends are abusive apes, and girls who stay with boyfriends who hit are spineless chickens.

Dothan never hit me again. After I got old enough to realize the humiliation of violence I always swore that if he ever laid a hand on me I'd be out the door, but that's one of those blank declarations almost every woman makes while the situation rests in theory. I'm done with blank declarations. Like the death of a father, or alcohol addiction, no one knows for certain how they'll behave when reality rears up and blows theory to the wind.

Critter, obviously, had given herself an excuse to stay. I'd created an excuse for Dothan to make the decision for us.

We, Critter and I, were supposed to be the vanguard of the first generation of smart women. I was the Be-Here-Now chick of the sixties, she the free-soaring spirit of the seventies, yet neither of us did squat about our cheating, controlling men. It took Marcella, the Betty Crocker of the fifties, to stand erect and shout, "Fuck you, jerk, I'm outta here."

Or whatever was the cookies-and-milk equivalent of "Fuck you, jerk" in Amarillo, Texas. Maybe she called him a lout.

Whatever she called him, it worked when our way didn't. Hugo was following like a puppy who'd been slapped in the nose with a newspaper. Where was Hugo now? Had he given up and returned to Amarillo and the cotton flowers of Annette Gilliam, or, like the Shadow, had he simply faded into the night?

I kind of hoped he was lurking in the darkness; I don't know why. All cheating men should be castrated—the cynic could make an argument that all men should be castrated—but the thought of Hugo Sr. hovering somewhere out of sight, never with us yet always nearby, struck me as kind of sweet.

———

The music changed from Doobie Brothers to Deep Purple— "Hey, Joe," a song about a man with a gun in his hand. One unassailable truth, Freedom held Critter, not me. Time to get the hell out of Dodge. More coffee—coffee would knock me off my natural state of high center and give me the impetus to get Lloyd and Shane on the road. I needed a liquid impetus.

Inside, Shane was bent over his harmonica, blowing blues notes that didn't match with Deep Purple. The tanned girl, who'd put on a tank top, sat at his feet next to a very intense-looking young man who held the baby. The others still sprawled in various postures of decadence, but you could tell from their body language that Shane was center of the deal.

Midway through a riff, Shane broke off and said to the intense young man, "Don't throw your blame for the uptight bearings of Christianity on Jesus. Jesus was cool, he taught love your enemies, love your neighbors, love yourself. He never said a word against mixed swimming. Or getting high."

The young man clenched his eyes. "But the Buddhist theory of nurturing negates my Nazarene upbringing. I'm left with emptiness."

Shane raised himself on his hands. "Christianity was noble for one hundred years, until that anal repressive St. Paul started writing letters. He's the one took sex off the cross."

The tanned girl raised a fist. "Right on."

Dog Whiffer twirled in her corner. "Tell it like it is."

I had a doll once that talked with more creativity when you pulled a string out her back.

"Andrew and Thomas were gay," Shane said. "Jesus didn't care."

"Who were Andrew and Thomas?" Dog Whiffer asked.

In the kitchen a kid with a totally bald head and hoop earrings sat staring at the closed refrigerator door. As I poured coffee, he exhaled. "Heavy, man."

"What?"

"Listen to the rhythm. It's like Africa. I'm really into black people."

I listened. "The refrigerator motor?"

"Very heavy."

"No, it's not."

He looked at me. "It's not heavy?"

"It's a refrigerator motor." I narrowed the space between our faces to four inches. His pupils were huge, unfocused pits. "Listen, my son. I am a messenger sent from God."

He nodded. Hell, he was on mescaline. People on mescaline are like old Blackfeet, they expect messages from God.

I pronounced distinctly. "God said to tell you: Grow up."

The boy repeated. "Grow up."

"Stop taking drugs. Get a job with the post office. Plant trees. Buy a lawn mower."

"I don't know if I can remember all this."

"Say it aloud so you don't forget."

He licked his dry lower lip. "Who did you say you are?"

"I am the Virgin Mary."

"A real virgin?"

"You better believe it. Say the words."

He licked his lips again and chanted in a near whisper. *"Stop taking drugs. Get a job with the post office. Plant trees. Buy a lawn mower."*

"Very good. Now, do it." For the first time since Dad died, I felt proud of myself.

———

Back in the living room Shane was doing his Socrates-to-the-students thing, sort of what I did in the kitchen, only I did it from good motives to help the poor kid while Shane did it because he got off on adoration.

"'Love your neighbor as yourself' means it is proper to love yourself," he lectured. "Jesus often practiced masturbation. It was a regular ritual of early Christian ceremonies until the fourth century, when Pope Pius the Second dried his stem and proclaimed self-love a sin."

The intense young man gazed at Shane. "You know so much information."

"Hey," I called over the loadies, "when Lloyd comes back, we're leaving."

His chins formed a frown. "I like it here."

"You would."

The tan girl leaned back on her hands to look straight up at me. I could have poured coffee down her cleavage. "Father

Rinesfoos is explaining the smooth-side-up, rough-side-down balance of astral perspective. It's totally amazing."

Captain Beefheart must not be as deep as Hank Williams. "Father Rinesfoos?" I said.

Shane said, "I am a priest of the One Day at a Time Chapel. Where's Lloyd?"

At that point confusion broke out on the porch. What sounded like lawn furniture hit the side of the house, Freedom's voice rose, then Owsley's above it, then Freedom's, then the door opened and Lloyd popped through.

"I'd like to go now," I said.

Lloyd's eyes took in the room. "Marcella wouldn't come back. She and the kids are waiting at the cafe."

"I like it here," Shane repeated. "These people recognize my worth."

The door burst open and Owsley did a headlong into the room, followed by Freedom holding the boy's art pad.

"You're going to school!" Freedom shouted.

Owsley crouched on the floor, eyes jumping like a beautiful coyote. "School sucks. The kids make fun of my hair."

Freedom tried to rip the pad asunder, but it was too thick so he went to tearing out a page at a time. When the destruction wasn't fast enough he threw what was left out the door. His voice was Moses, pissed off. "I won't have you bringing heat on this house. One more truant officer shows up here…"

He left the threat unfinished, but from what I'd seen punishment would not be "You're grounded."

Owsley was brave though. He barked, "Ha! There's more cops in those woods than squirrels. I couldn't possibly bring more heat than you do."

"I won't go back to prison because of you."

"I won't go back to school."

Freedom doubled his fists and advanced on Owsley. Shane cut his chair between the two. "Let us meditate on peace," Shane said.

"Get your ass out of my way."

"Fat chance." Shane set his hand brake.

Freedom hesitated, then came around my side of the chair. Owsley darted low around the other side and took off out the door. Freedom made a two-step run after him, then gave up. He turned on Shane.

"Don't meddle in my affairs, cripple."

"I can take you, shit-for-brains."

Something in Shane's demeanor gave Freedom a flash of insecurity. His slit eyes did a room scan, searching for support among the followers, but they returned only blank stares, although whether they sided with Shane or were too stoned to process the action is a toss-up.

Freedom came back to Shane, whose face gave an involuntary tic. As they sank into the macho male stare-down thing, I looked around for a weapon. A coffee cup isn't worth much when you're used to a bottle.

The upright man blinked first. "Jesus," he said.

Shane answered, "Yes."

Freedom stomped off down the back hall, making as much racket as you can in wimpy sandals. I heard him fling open a door, and his voice: "How long does it take to suck off an asshole?" The door slammed, more stomping, then the back door of the house crashed open and shut.

———

Shane reached down to cut off the stereo. You never realize how quiet a room full of people can be until you contrast it suddenly with a room full of noise. He pivoted his chair to face the tanned mother.

"That man has more problems than any of you. Don't follow him," Shane said.

"But Freedom takes care of us," the woman said.

"You may now take care of yourselves. Arise, gather your child, and leave this house tonight." Shane swiveled slowly, making eye contact with each member of the group. "Getting high is okay, making love is okay, but that man's hatred will destroy everything near him."

He didn't know the half of it; he hadn't seen the battery-acid-powder and blow-jobs-for-drugs tricks.

Shane's voice thundered. *"Arise and flee!"*

They didn't flee, but they dispersed. I'd been so proud of the one kid I saved in the kitchen, but Shane was set on converting the lot. The grandstander.

"You want some coffee?" I asked Lloyd.

"Yeah, that would be nice. I got the straw bales. You can't see Coors from anywhere."

Some gathered clothes from what I'd earlier thought were trash heaps. Others wandered away, shoeless, shirtless, clueless. From outside came the knock of a Volkswagen engine kicking in, then another.

"What's going on?" Critter stood in the doorway. The tapestry skirt had been replaced by a pair of cutoffs.

"The cripple told them to leave," Arlo said. "They were all on mescaline, so they did."

Arlo was like the old Indians Hank Elkrunner told me about who could shut down their auras or charisma or something so as to make themselves functionally invisible. The guy was missing a self.

"They'll be back tomorrow," he said. "How did the slurp job compare to others you've given? I'll front you three Quaaludes to do me."

Critter didn't even look at him. "Get lost, Arlo."

"If you don't take them, Freedom will."

I crossed the room to stand in front of her. "When will you escape?" I asked.

"When it's time."

"Don't wait too long, you'll lose your innocence and end up like me."

Her glazey eyes came to rest on my face. "You're not so bad, Maurey, you just think you are."

I hugged her. Never, in my whole life, have I initiated a hug with a woman.

She spoke over my shoulder. "I'll be okay."

"Leave the bastard," I said.

"Someday, not today."

Behind me, Shane celebrated the mass exodus. *"Banzai, motherfucker."*

25

I SAT IN BACK AND NURSED JESUS. HAS A NICE RING, DOESN'T it? I sat in back and nursed Jesus. I'd never thought about naming a bottle Jesus until I told the skin-headed tripper I was the Virgin Mary. Spanish people name each other Jesus all the time, although they pronounce it "Hey-soos," but for some reason you never hear of English speakers named Jesus. Maybe he's off limits to white guys.

Whatever, Jesus and I were in back with Marcella and the kids because I was drinking and would soon sleep, and Shane was in front because he had a cough. He pretended he didn't, of course—"Must be an allergy. I have an allergy to cumin that manifests in the lungs, and, no doubt, the chili was spiced with cumin"—but the truth was old Shane looked a bit peaked. The head twitches had taken on a rhythmic pattern. I'd have been concerned if he hadn't called me *little missy* when I helped him in the passenger's door.

"I need no assistance, little missy," he said, then he pulled a harmonica from somewhere and went into "Hey, Joe."

"Don't sit on my Etch-A-Sketch, little missy," Andrew snapped, and I almost nailed him with Jesus.

I hadn't seen his Etch-A-Sketch. A person could have hidden a small pony in the back of Moby Dick and I wouldn't have seen it. Up to the Comanche exit scene, I'd managed to avoid any close looks at the Dick's cargo section, but now I had to notice a few things just to find a stretching-out spot.

Shane's chair was folded against the back of the driver's seat next to his built-in perch. Marcella had created a kind of family nest from blankets, clothes, sleeping bags, cookie packages, and magazines with their covers torn off. She'd even rigged an orange-crate crib lined in socks and Jockey shorts for Hugo Jr., who lay on his back staring up at a Snap-On socket wrench calendar featuring a breasts-and-ass floozie in a cleavage-stretcher top, shrink-wrapped hot pants, and painted fingernails caressing a socket wrench the way I used to caress Charley.

"What'd you do with my pistol?" I called up front.

"I've never seen your pistol in my life," Shane called back.

"If I find him in your stuff, I'll shoot you."

"Little lady, if that dratted cannon is in my possession, you have my permission to gun me down."

"Thief."

"Harlot."

I propped myself next to the side doors against a hundred-pound bag of bad potatoes. They had erupted eyes and these white tentacle things that would cause me trouble if I ever DT'ed. From the spud sack to the back window was like an avalanche had swept through Lloyd's Salvage City. Fan belts, hub caps, clamps, more blankets, more slick-to-bald tires, piles of *National Geographies*, *Guideposts*, Max Brand and Ian Fleming novels, an empty gerbil cage, loads of clothes—why would two men who appeared to wear the same outfits every day need a thrift store wardrobe? From deep in the pile came the petite *mew* of the unnamed kitty.

Andrew screeched, "Don't look!"

Of course, I looked. Marcella was pulling a jammie top down over his upstretched arms and head, while his bottom half was little boy naked. White fanny, remarkably skinny legs, dirty feet—I felt a pang for my Auburn. Who pulled on his Hopalong Cassidy jammies now and tucked him in and said Lay-me-down-to-sleep for him until he was old enough to say it himself? Dothan sure as heck wouldn't stoop to mother work, and I couldn't stand the feeling of Sugar Cannelioski touching my son.

The best of all bad possibilities would be Dothan's mother. At least she'd give him a bath. They'd all three be telling Auburn what a sick, scum-sucking Yankee his mother was. If I never saw my baby again, the Talbot family would probably invent a story where I died. Probably in a car wreck. Car wreck is the story most people make up when they create a death myth.

"Read to me," Andrew demanded.

"Mrs. Talbot is cultured. She doesn't have time to read," Marcella said. "I'll read your bedtime story."

"No. I want Maurey."

He stood in his red cotton pajamas with black oil derricks pointing every which way, clutching a Golden Book. I'd been raised on Golden Books. Sam Callahan and Shannon had both been raised on Golden Books. If I didn't pull my act together and get back there to save him, Auburn would probably never know the smell when you first crack open a brand-new Golden Book. Dothan would raise him to converse fluently on cubic inches of truck engines and the Boone and Crockett point system for rating trophy heads.

I said, "I'll read him the story. I used to read stories to my children."

Andrew's face puckered in disbelief. "You have children?"

"A girl and a boy."

"Are they dead?"

I held the book in my left hand and Jesus in my right with Andrew snuggled on my lap in between. He smelled clean, like children do even when they're dirty.

Snow White and the Seven Dwarfs—not my favorite selection. It encourages passivity until a man comes along to save you, and I think Dopey is a caricature of a kid with Down's syndrome. I wouldn't let Shannon read it back when I had some control.

The cover showed a flat-faced girl surrounded by seven midgets holding hands in a circle. They all had bulb noses like Shane and plucked eyebrows.

"'Once upon a time, in a faraway land, a lovely Queen sat by her window sewing,'" I read.

Andrew shifted against my left breast and popped his thumb in his mouth. Page one was about a woman dying in childbirth. On page two the King gets lonely and marries the biggest bitch in literary history. Why was he lonely? He had Snow White. Men always want more than loving daughters, they want bitch women to nail.

And where was dear old Dad later when the Queen shipped Snow White off to scrub floors in the basement?

Mirror, mirror on the wall
Who is fairest of us all?

"'If the mirror replied that she was fairest, all was well. But if another lady was named, the Queen flew into a furious rage and had her killed.'"

Andrew's thumb came out of his mouth. "How did the Queen kill the other lady?"

"Crucifixion."

"Like baby Jesus?"

"She made them go swimming during their periods and they died of shame."

Marcella gave me a look, but Andrew seemed satisfied. He either knew the implications of swimming during your period in the olden days, or he didn't care.

I read, "As the Queen was a dog, soon the kingdom had a shortage of women."

"That's not the right way it goes."

"This is the way I'm reading it."

He slapped the book, right on the Queen's mirror. "Do it right. The story goes one way."

Marcella looked over from her baby maintenance. "Andrew has all the books memorized, you can't change a word."

"Then why read to him?"

She looked at me funny. "I thought you had children."

Put me in my place. I took a sip of Jesus and read the right way. "'As the years passed, Snow White grew more and more beautiful, and her sweet nature made everyone love her—everyone but the Queen.'"

I didn't really need Jesus. I mean, I needed Jesus the half-pint, what I didn't need was to get drunk. Three of my favorite things—a book, a child, and a bottle—were all within reach, and I was content to wet my mouth with him every few minutes to stabilize the buzz.

Shane had told the hippies that Jesus masturbated, but Mom took me to Sunday school every week for years, and *The Upper Room* daily meditation guide never mentioned self-love in the physical sense. When I was Andrew's age and going through a precocious stage, I asked the teacher if Jesus was a virgin because Mary was and it followed that a virgin mother would have a virgin son. I had the deal mixed up with Virgo. The teacher made me pray for God's forgiveness.

A lesbian from San Diego I knew in college told me Jesus was homosexual, like her. "Look at his gang—twelve guys, two whores, and a mother who claimed she'd never done it."

"Is that a normal configuration to turn out gay guys?"

"Put it this way, would a person with an extended family like that one be into man-on-top, get-it-over-with-quick?"

I told Sam Callahan about my lesbian friend's theory, and he wrote a short story in which two anthropologists found some scrolls that proved absolutely, beyond any doubt, that Jesus was homosexual.

"My story explains how this discovery would affect Fundamentalist Christian faiths," he told me.

"They would crucify the anthropologists and ignore the truth," I said.

"The ending is too obvious?"

———

The concept that God might involve himself in retaliation for bad acts came to me the summer after I graduated from high school, one stormy day on the Forest Service lease when Dad, Hank Elkrunner, and I were fixing fence.

It was between showers, and Dad was using the wire stretcher, his muscles all bunched up and sweaty, and I had a semi-incestuous thought. Nothing disgustingly incestuous like me-and-him—don't you just hate a dream where you're romantically entangled with a member of your immediate family? God, that makes me feel icky. This was a daydream where I wondered what Dad was like with a woman. Was he any good? Did he grunt? Did he dig his chin into her right shoulder?

In my wildest imagination I couldn't picture him with Mom, so I ran through all the possible women in the valley and ended up with Lydia Callahan. She was with Hank, but he wouldn't mind. It was only a daydream.

Hank was working the crimpers and I was leaning on the post hole digger with one hand on the barbwire fence; I'd just come to the part where Dad uses his tongue on Lydia, and I couldn't decide if his beard tickled, when lightning hit the fence about two miles up the mountain.

Here is a verifiable scientific fact: Electricity travels through barbwire faster than thunder through air. The jolt paralyzed my arm for like a half second, then blasted me ten feet into the sagebrush.

I was on my back, doing yellow-and-black spots, when the thunder passed over. Two of the spots gelled into Dad's and Hank's faces. They were both grinning, which was the only way I knew I wasn't dead.

Dad's beard split. "God give you a wake-up call?"

Hank touched my ozone-smelling hair. "Maurey, what did you do to anger the thunderbirds?"

I closed my eyes and swore to Father, Son, and Holy Ghost all three that I would never fantasize my Dad naked again.

26

I SWALLOWED A COKE BOTTLE TOP. SHANE PULLED OUT HIS *little knife and said, "You need a tracheotomy." Then I lay on the floor while he cut my throat.*

———

I slept on my back using an old army blanket as a pad and Jesus as my pillow. Around dawn I blinked awake and looked at the fuzzy light on Moby Dick's ceiling. Oklahoma, I thought. Andrew slept with his head on my left shoulder and Owsley slept with his head on my right. I thought, Gee, Owsley has gorgeous hair. Look at how the highlights shine when he breathes.

Then it hit.

"Owsley!" I sat up fast and *clonked* both boys' heads on the blanket.

"You aren't here," I said.

He came to his knees sleepily and wet his lips with his tongue. His eyes were the silver-gray color of aspen ashes. "I'm here."

"You aren't supposed to be here. How did you get here?"

"He slid out from under the junk pile after you passed out," Marcella said.

"Went to sleep."

She sat with her back against the far wall, nursing Hugo Jr. "He said you said he could come."

"I said no such thing."

Shane pulled himself around the passenger seat to face back. "Tsk, tsk, another alcohol blackout."

That's another problem with drinking. People can claim you forgot something you didn't forget and you're supposed to trust their memory over your own.

"I didn't black out anything, I never said a word to him about coming with us."

Owsley kept his eyes down. "You said there's always room for one more in the ambulance. When people in trouble travel together they have to take care of each other."

"I said that to Critter."

"I'm in more trouble than she is." His lower lip kind of quivered, and his hair hung in that limp dejection thing that women use to look forlorn. Men shouldn't be allowed to express themselves with their hair.

I was confused, but then I'm always confused before I've brushed my teeth. "We can't take on a runaway boy, Freedom will call the Highway Patrol."

"Not a likely supposition," Shane said.

Owsley brushed hair behind his ears. "Freedom don't care about me. He had Mary Beth claim me for Aid to Dependent Children, but the social worker found out she was only three years older than me and cut us off. Now, Freedom don't care what I do."

"Mary Beth is…"

"Critter. He was mad on account of he got ripped off in Dallas and the truant lady come out to the house. Last thing he'd do is call the law to fetch me back."

I looked from Marcella to Shane. The brother-sister duo

seemed to take for granted we'd added a passenger. Where was Lloyd, anyway, and why were we stopped in the country? Outside was hardwoods and bird sounds and the distant chug of a pump. One disorienting day sliding into another.

"We have to take him back," I said.

Owsley raised his eyes. "I ain't going back to Freedom."

"Yes, you are."

Shane pulled himself farther around. Owsley and I were directly behind his seat, so he had to twist his chins to peer at us. "Maurey, stop your yammering and think about it."

The back side of my brain knew Owsley was here for the duration, but the front side rebelled. I wasn't that much against having him, I just wanted some illusion of control over these changes. When things come at you like rockets the tendency is to cower down and refuse to be moved—but Shane was right. Freedom was an evil son of a bitch, and anyone we could save from his clutches had to be saved. He'd already traded his girlfriend's sex for drugs; how long till he traded his son's?

I hated it when Shane was right.

Owsley broke the quiet. "I'll get out and walk from here, just don't send me back to Dad."

"That's all right," I said. "One more mouth to feed won't make much difference."

Shane did a throat-clearing guttural sound. "There's another reason Freedom won't be anxious to drag our band back to Comanche."

I could see a red-brick farmhouse off through the trees. "Where is Lloyd, anyway? Does he know we picked up an extra lost soul?"

Any silence in Moby Dick was eerie, but this silence out-eeried the norm. Andrew slept, Hugo Jr. nursed, everyone else feigned distraction.

Shane broke first. He never could deal with silence. "You are to blame, Maurey. Normally, I'm not the type to say 'I told you so,' but in this case I will make an exception."

"Where's Lloyd? Is he okay?"

Marcella switched tits. "Lloyd took some beer off to trade for gasoline and food. I hope he comes back soon, before someone sees us and calls the police."

I felt nauseous, like the post-nausea nausea you feel at the first inkling of pregnancy.

"Pass my creel back here," I said.

"Freedom took your money," Owsley said.

"Just hand me the damn creel."

"I was hiding in back and heard him. I couldn't have stopped him; if I'd tried, he would have the money and me."

I stared into Dad's creel. Not only was the cash gone, but the jerk took my Ortho-Novum wheel. I spoke rashly. "I'm stuck in godforsaken hell with six people I don't like and a hundred cases of cow piss."

Hurt leapt into Marcella's eyes. Shane snapped, "You like Lloyd, and it's only ninety-eight cases now."

Screaming would not have accomplished anything. Instead, I descended into a great calm, the calm that comes between knowing something bad happened and believing it. Everything that could go wrong had, which meant I was in safe harbor. To analyze the deal to death, I was almost relieved. Freedom had given me an excuse to drink.

———

I popped open the side cargo doors. "Time for me to take a walk."

Shane lectured. "Did I say you would lose the money? Did I say you are much too incompetent to be trusted?"

"Fuck off, Shane," I said quietly.

"Why is it whenever a woman makes a dreadful error her first reaction is to tell a man to fuck off?"

Outside Moby Dick, I turned right, instinctively heading for Wyoming. But Hugo Sr. lurked in that direction, watching over us like an Oldsmobile-shaped vulture. The man was getting on my nerves. Left led nowhere, which seemed appropriate at the time. I picked up a fairly big stick because Jackson Hole doesn't have rattlesnakes and I have an irrational fear of the buggers. People who live in a town without grizzly bears develop an irrational fear of grizzly bears. It's part of Sam Callahan's displaced-persons theory.

When Sam and Lydia moved out from North Carolina they had no background for treeless vistas or seven months of snow or even horses. As a result, Sam used to make a major deal out of alienation. He wrote a story about a boy named Tippy who flew to the Land of Oz, and when the Munchkins asked what he wanted to eat, he said, "Grits and eggs." They brought him kitten heads on rice.

If you asked me, Sam leaned too heavily on Stranger-in-a-Strange-Land—used it as an excuse for weird behavior around women.

The one thing stranger than waking up in a strange land is waking up in a strange land without any money. Made me feel vulnerable. The stick didn't feel like any stick I'd ever felt, the pavement was made of shiny stuff I'd never seen in pavement, the humidity was suffocating. Back home we keep our air and water separate.

The question that reared above all others: Would this have happened if Frostbite hadn't killed Dad? Would I have taken to naming bottles or driven with my baby on the roof? Or say I had done that stuff, and Dothan had banished me from child and home, would I have gone to Dad for help? Would he have helped? He got really mad for a while when I was thirteen and pregnant, called me a whore, which is understandable considering the situation, but then he walked away from me until the day Shannon was born. Wouldn't the high-quality father have said "You're a whore, Maurey, but I love you anyway. Come home and I'll take care of you"?

I'm not comfortable questioning Dad's perfection. In fact, deep questions in general make me nervous. My former true love, Park, used to go on long walks where he contemplated the universe and took stock in himself.

"The unexamined life is not worth living," he said. Sam Callahan agreed, although he claimed Park stole the line. Personally, I think the line's a crock. People who spend all their time wondering how they're doing are like these tourist photographers who exert so much effort taking pictures they can't see what they're looking at.

———

Lloyd walked toward me carrying a red five-gallon can and a brown paper bag. The weight of the can had him leaned over to one side. His hair was mussed up, making him look for all the world like a scarecrow with an Adam's apple.

"Won't make Carolina on five gallons for two cases," I said.

"This should carry us into Arkansas. Coors is worth more there."

"It's also illegal. I don't do well in jails."

"There's worse places." Lloyd didn't elaborate, so I used my fertile imagination. The only place I could think of worse than jail would be jail in Arkansas. Or the drunk tank, which is a subspecies of jail. I've heard some grisly stories about life in the drunk tank.

Lloyd said, "Farmer was milking or I'd never've got the gasoline. He said his wife would make him sleep in the barn if she caught him trading necessaries for beer. She wears a white feather on her Sunday dress to signify that alcohol has never crossed her lips."

"Sounds like an unpleasant woman."

As we walked back to Moby Dick he gave me the bag and shifted the gas can to his free hand. "I wouldn't have lost Sharon if I wore the white feather."

"You'd never have met her if you hadn't been drunk," I pointed out.

Lloyd didn't disagree. He hardly ever disagreed with much of anything. He was like the Tar Baby in the Uncle Remus stories who sat there taking each punch until his attacker was absorbed and beaten.

"Lloyd, have you ever been without money before?"

He nodded. "A few times. It's no big thing."

"Dothan worries about money constantly, and Lord knows ranchers live one step ahead of or behind the bank, but that's for mortgages and truck payments and stuff. I've never been in a place where I had no money at all."

"We're not going to starve."

I stayed alert for rattlesnakes. "How do you know?"

Lloyd rubbed his leg as he walked. "Only free people in the country are the filthy rich and the filthy poor. Everyone else is in debt."

"I'd rather be filthy rich."

"Surviving without money will give you confidence, make you feel self-sufficient. You could use some confidence."

"I could call my friend Sam Callahan collect, have him wire out some money."

Lloyd's eyes squinted as if he were looking beyond what I could see. "It's not healthy to get rescued every time you make a mistake. You tend to forget actions have consequences."

"Is that from one of your AA books?"

Moby Dick came in sight. "Just because it's in a book doesn't mean it's wrong."

Taking advice from a book makes me feel run of the mill,

like my problems are so common they can be tossed aside by words from a bumper sticker. Same thing happens when I go to the doctor and he says what I have is going around.

Lloyd nodded up the road at Hugo Sr.'s Oldsmobile. "Besides, can't hurt to have the cavalry a hundred yards off the rear."

———

When we got back to the ambulance, Andrew and Marcella were outside having a fight. He said she'd put his shoes on the wrong feet, and she said she hadn't. Marcella patiently explained big toes in, little toes out, but Andrew wasn't interested.

"When I walk they're crooked. If you make me walk with backwards shoes all day I'm gonna ride with Daddy."

Sounded good to me. "The shoes are okay, but your T-shirt is inside out and backwards," I said. "See the tag?"

I touched the tag on his throat, and when he looked down to see if it was true I *plonked* his nose with my finger—one of Dad's favorite tricks. Andrew got upset and called me *stupid*.

"Are you carrying drugs?" Marcella said to Owsley. "We had a girl said she wasn't, but she was."

"I hate drugs. Only scums use drugs."

"You might have pounds of heroin on your person."

"Lady, where would I hide pounds of heroin?" Owsley made sense on that one. He'd escaped Freedom with a dirty pair of corduroys, his art pad, and a chunk of charcoal. If we stopped at a No Shoes, No Shirt—No Service joint, we'd have to root through the clothes pile before we took him indoors.

"You better not contaminate my babies," Marcella said. "They aren't sophisticated like you, this family was raised on fried okra and Jesus."

Andrew yelped. "I hate okra."

No one was happy with the contents of Lloyd's breakfast bag—three catfish and two dozen fried cornmeal globs he called hush puppies, the theory being if you threw one at a barking dog, it would shut up.

I was justifiably cranky. "I can't function without coffee. Don't expect me to drive."

Shane ate six or seven of the yellow globs, whining through every bite. "You promised you'd find Oreos. I'm a sick man, I deserve to eat what I want. Cold catfish is beneath my dignity."

I said, "Everything is beneath your dignity."

Andrew took one bite of hush puppy, screamed, "Onions!" and commenced to dry heave. Marcella cupped her hand under his mouth while she patted him between the shoulder blades and chirped, "Spit it up, honey. Spit it up."

When I said no one was happy I forgot Owsley and the cat. Those two went to town on the catfish.

I noticed Lloyd didn't eat anything. I think his feelings were hurt by the abuse we heaped on breakfast. It's probably not easy to approach a farmhouse at dawn with two cases of beer. As he poured gasoline into Moby Dick's tank, I asked, "How's it look?"

He saved enough to prime the carburetor. "I need a meeting."

"I'd rather have coffee."

Shane broke into a song called "Me and Bobby McGee," the line that goes, "Freedom's just another word for nothing left to lose." Nobody laughed.

27

GROUP MORALE ROSE CONSIDERABLY IN DE QUEEN, Arkansas, where each of us in the ambulance fulfilled short-term needs. Lloyd circled town streets named after Indian tribes until he found an American Legion hut with a nine a.m. AA meeting. I have no idea how he found meetings in unfamiliar towns; he must have a nose for alcoholics the way I have a nose for alcohol.

Lloyd and Shane did the chair-up-steps deal and disappeared for a few minutes, then Lloyd came back out with two Styrofoam cups of coffee for me and a box of store-bought doughnuts for the boys. Owsley drank some of my coffee, and I ate one of his doughnuts. Andrew tried climbing the sandstone rock wall of the hut, reached an exposure of a foot and a half, and took a leader fall. Marcella shoved Hugo Jr. into my arms and ran over to do the comfort routine. I guess her short-term needs were fulfilled too, because, far as I could tell, all she needed was to mother.

She didn't need coffee or sugar or whiskey or Hugo Sr. It's somewhat spooky meeting a woman who isn't addicted to substances. Me, I'm addicted to everything, except cigarettes. Lydia Callahan set such a good bad example that I managed to avoid that habit. And tranquilizers—Mom turned me against pills that transform the brain into a potted plant. And cocaine, and marijuana. Maybe I wasn't as addicted as I thought.

If God had descended to GroVont and said "Maurey Talbot, thou art strung out on alcohol, coffee, and men. Thou must this moment choose one and stop two," I'd have stopped alcohol and men in a heartbeat.

"Who told you bald eagles have bald legs?" Owsley asked.

"My dad. I must have been nine years old, we took a pack trip up Crazy Woman Creek and came on a bald eagle feeding on a baby elk carcass. Dad had me list every field mark different from a golden."

"When I was nine my dad taught me how to mix a gram of pure LSD with a gram of PCP to make six thousand hits of mescaline."

Up to that point I'd avoided any personal attachment with Hugo Jr. When you've recently been stripped of a one-year-old, the last thing you want is a one-month-old calling in the memories. But H.J. was a lovable little bug. No hair to speak of, wide blue eyes, a nose so tiny you could have hidden it beneath a pop bottle cap—some people say kids all look alike till their third month, but I protest that broad statement. I get off on tykes so young they can't hold their head up.

Here's the difference between having a baby in 1964 and having a baby in 1972: Pampers. When she was four months I accidentally stuck a safety pin in Shannon's thigh. Scream, I thought the girl would never stop screaming. Sam Callahan forbade me from ever changing her again. I felt so awful I couldn't face cheerleading practice. I suppose an alert psychiatrist would have tabbed me as a future child abuser right then.

Marcella appeared in my reverie. "I'm gonna take Andrew inside, find a bathroom to clean him up. You okay with Hugo Jr.?"

"We're buds."

"If he gets fussy, pacify him with a tit."

"But I've been dry for over a month."

She wrinkled her nose. "By the time he figures that out, I'll be back with the real thing."

You don't need women's intuition to figure what happened next. The moment Marcella dragged Andrew, kicking and screaming, through the door, Hugo Jr.'s macaroni noodle fingers formed fists, his face turned Shane's-nose red, and he went into high wail.

"She said to put him on a tit," Owsley said.

"You just want to see my boob. I know how boys your age are."

Owsley spit on the ground in disgust. "I saw tits every day at the house in Comanche. Yours won't be a thrill."

I always thought nursing somebody else's baby would be like chewing somebody else's gum, but it wasn't gross like that at all. Whatever instincts a woman has come out in nursing, I suppose, although I've known women who hate it. Lydia Callahan says nursing is nature's way of making you droop.

When I offered Hugo Jr. the right side he latched on natural as a foal on a mare. The effect was truly bewildering, on one hand breathtaking, like being part of something primeval, while on the other hand the ache below my breast for my own baby was almost more than I could stand. That ache separated into an ache for Dad, then an ache for what I'd missed with Mom, then an ache that kind of billowed out to include everything wonderful and impossible about life.

I looked down at Hugo Jr.'s closed eyelids and his upper lip on my breast. The areola was almost back to normal, pre-baby size, but at his touch my nipple hardened, as if the last year hadn't happened. His eyebrows were delicate as a spider web, and the hollow atop his head looked so vulnerable. They put an IV in Auburn's head the day he was born—I cried for six hours.

Hugo Jr. brushed my skin with his hands, and the aches formed into one bubble that rose to my throat and burst. I touched his tiny nose and connected.

Damn, I thought to myself, the first step back. I'd hoped to avoid this at least until fall.

When Marcella returned with the newly scrubbed Andrew to feed Hugo Jr. honest mother's milk, I walked the hundred yards west to where Hugo Sr. sat in his car eating a Stewart sandwich. I couldn't get over what a block-shaped person he was, like a 1950s sci-fi robot. Square chest, block chin, nose like a quarter-stick of butter imbedded in his face—I hadn't seen any of that in Hugo Jr.

"Loan me twenty dollars," I said.

He chewed with his mouth slightly open, staring up the road at the American Legion hut. "Was Andrew hurt bad? I'd never have let him climb that building if I was there."

"You are here, Hugo. Loan me twenty dollars so I can buy your kid milk."

"She'll never manage without me."

"She's done fine so far."

He glanced at me in his window. "Make her come back to Dumas and I'll give you the twenty dollars."

"You think I'd sell out my friends for twenty bucks?"

"Okay, thirty."

Yellowstone has millions of trees, and they're so thick in the Bitterroot you can't ride a horse off trail, but the mountains around Jackson Hole and GroVont are way-high deserts with loads of open space between stands. I need open space. Denseness gives me claustrophobia.

Arkansas was the densest land I'd ever seen. The trees and shrubs, flat shimmering with fertility, were pressed from all sides by intense humidity and these low, off-gray clouds. Driving Moby Dick up, down, and around the hills was like swimming through a lake of sperm.

We passed an unpainted house with a full-width screened porch and three little black kids playing next to a garden. The two girls had yellow ribbons in their hair, and the boy was riding a stick horse with a stuffed-sock head. I knew a few jocks at Laramie who were black—even got nailed by Kareem, who kept score—but I'd never hung out around black children. They seemed exotic and sleek, like palomino horses. I wondered if they felt the heat and humidity the same as I did. Would that shiny skin attract or repel mosquitoes, and did black boys get stiffies younger than white boys?

All through high school this rumor floated around that Sam Callahan's father was black. The rumor was based mostly on misconceptions that develop in places where blacks are rare to nonexistent. Sam ate southern foods, natural enough since he was from the South, but people didn't see it that way. They said, "Cornbread! Why, he must be part nigger."

He liked Sam Cooke music, and later Jimi Hendrix. He liked basketball better than football. He said "y'all" when he meant "you guys." Pretty flimsy fodder to brand the boy, but in a town small as GroVont flimsy fodder is enough. Knocking me up at thirteen didn't help.

To tell the truth, Sam more or less encouraged the black daddy theory, especially when he got older and started dating.

"I want the girls swept away by the soul man stereotype," he said to me.

"You want them swept away by the big dick stereotype."

Actually, Sam's dick isn't that bad for a little guy.

One time Lydia fed us this long gang-bang story involving five football players—four whiteys and a black halfback—who got her drunk and raped her and peed on her face on Christmas Eve. She used the story as an example of all-men-are-pigs and said any of the five could be Sam's father. Sam used the story as an excuse to alienate himself from the entire male sex.

"What'd you and Hugo Sr. find to talk about?" Marcella asked.

"He offered thirty bucks for you."

"You think I should go back to him for the sake of the boys?"

"Staying with a bad man for the sake of children is the single stupidest move any woman ever made."

"You're always so certain, Maurey. I wish I was more like you. I'm never certain about anything."

Shane was busy on the maps again. "We shall cross the river at Memphis," he said. "I have a cohort from the music industry in Memphis. Elvis stayed with the stage when I quit to pursue my studies in medical school."

"That's Elvis Presley, no doubt," I said.

"You've heard of him? He was a struggling artist until I taught him to swivel his pelvis with the downbeat."

"Yeah, right. Was Elvis there when you nailed Katharine Hepburn on a horse?"

"No, but I did introduce him to his wife. Sweet girl, I dated her first, you know."

"I read that somewhere."

"Your sarcasm is quite gauche, little lady. No wonder you can't hold a man."

Between hills we passed a bunch of swampy-looking rivers. Stagnant brown water makes for bad fly-fishing. "Lloyd," I say, "I understand about needing whiskey or food or oil, or even love. Heck, Dothan needs help with his income tax form. What I don't understand is needing a meeting. What happens to fill a need at these meetings?"

The lines around his eyes looked like a topo map. "We talk."

"No good ever came from talking."

The eyes shifted focus to me. "Why not come to a meeting and see?"

I didn't say anything for two bridges. "No, thanks, I could never deal with truth while drinking coffee from Styrofoam cups."

He shrugged and faced forward. "Be on the lookout for someplace I might be able to trade for gasoline. We'll be low soon."

"Gauge says we're full."

"That gauge always says we're full."

Funny I hadn't noticed that before.

28

MASTURBATION IS MORE A SYMPTOM OF DEPRESSION THAN A function of horniness. I'd suspected this through the drab years of college and confirmed it three weeks after Dad's funeral when I found myself masturbating constantly without even the semblance of a fantasy.

Paul Harvey—Yukon Jack—masturbation—sleep. Take care of Auburn through the evening, then network sitcom—Yukon Jack—masturbation—sleep. After many years of reading several hours a day, the habit came to a halt. I told myself it was because reading took hands I needed for clitoral manipulation, but I think now it was because reading took effort.

Little on Earth is as depressing as the mechanical orgasm. God knows I tried developing fantasies. I pretended Steve McQueen and Clint Eastwood had tongues of fire, but the emotional energy needed to respond even to an imaginary man was more than I could handle. Sam Callahan was like kissing my brother, Park made me too sad on top of the depression, and Paul Harvey gave me the willies, like sitting on the dick of a dead man. I settled for an actor whose name I didn't know who played Meathead on *All in the Family*.

After a couple weeks of Meathead I gave up and went back

to nothing, to fingers without feelings going round and round until release and relief. Alcohol plus masturbation plus too much sleep equals depression. Einstein said that.

What brings the subject up is Malvern, Arkansas. Let's all recall that I was accustomed to daily, at the least, self-service and had been dry for two weeks come Sunday. Mother's Day, when I should have been discussing the moistness of pound cake in Mom's parlor, I climbed into the bathtub for one of those rushing water jobs that make you feel half acrobat, half drowned.

———

The sign read MALVERN, ARKANSAS—BRICK CAPITAL OF THE WORLD. I eased past the Oachita Oil Company gas station, right out of *Bonnie and Clyde*, and into a shady city park. You got your weedy creek, swing set with attached slide, permanently embedded croquet court, statue of a Confederate soldier waving a sword atop a horse with a massive barrel and no sexual identity, and a tire swing hanging from what Shane said was a sycamore.

Lloyd unloaded three cases of Coors and brought them to the picnic table, where all the gang but Shane had gathered. Shane stayed in Moby Dick on plumbing patrol. Since we'd lost Critter he'd gone back to changing himself solo. The thing bothering me was the upshot of having less than two dollars in my pocket and nothing in my creel.

"You plan on making me jump through ugly hoops every time I want a bottle?" I asked.

Lloyd looked at me for a moment. Our conversations were being reduced to questions followed by silence as the responder worked out what was really said.

"No."

"Thanks."

Shane's head bobbed out of Moby Dick's side door. "If she gets whiskey, I get Chips Ahoy!"

The three cases fit perfectly between Lloyd's outstretched hands and his chin. When he moved his head, the Coors moved with him. "Anybody else want anything?"

"I either need a Laundromat or disposables," Marcella said.

Owsley looked up from his pad. "I'd like a Coca-Cola if it's okay."

Andrew hung upside down in the tire swing with his head firmly in the dirt. "If the girl gets a Coke, I want one."

"I'm no girl."

"Of course you're a girl."

"Owsley's a boy just like you," Marcella said.

Andrew fell out of the swing, picked himself up, and came over to inspect Owsley. "Girls have hair, that's why they're girls."

Owsley said, "You must have been raised in a barn."

"Don't make fun of my children. In Dumas boys have short hair, how's he to know different?"

"Well, explain to him about the penis. It's the wienie makes the boy, Andy, not the hair."

"Don't call me Andy, Owsley."

"Don't call me Owsley."

The discussion scattered into several people speaking simultaneously about what to call them and what not to call the penis. Lloyd took his load to the gas station to play *Let's Make a Deal*. It was one of those stations you can look at and know right off they have pink Peanut Platters and soda pops you've never heard of sunk in a metal box full of water. He would be trading with cousins named Gomer and Goober.

I could hear Shane singing "Secret Agent Man" to himself as he cleaned up his thing.

"Don't touch my hair," Owsley shouted at Andrew, who

started crying, which made Hugo Jr. cry, which got Marcella all fussy.

I sat on the picnic bench next to Owsley. "You have beautiful hair. I'd give anything for hair like yours."

"You can have it."

He was drawing a large frog sitting in a wheelchair. The resemblance was amazing. I'd never much gone for boys with long hair, except Indians, but Owsley's was special—texture of a Blackfoot and blond as a Swedish fashion model.

"I used to have long, beautiful hair like yours, only mine was brown. After Dad died I went crazy and cut it off. Now everyone treats me different."

Owsley didn't look up. "Kids at school spit in my hair and rub mud on it. Girls touch it."

"Hell, if it's such a pain in the ass, get rid of it."

I don't think the concept had ever occurred to him. He concentrated on shading the frog's belly, but you could see his young brain trying out the idea. Marcella took her whimpering brood to the creek, where Andrew immediately fell in.

"Freedom won't let me cut it. When he was in prison he told my foster parents he would kill them if they touched my head." His eyes did the unfocused review-of-life-in-a-foster-home. I'd seen the look before. Owsley's voice was kicked-puppy. "They didn't care. They just took me in for the state allowance."

I reached toward his head. "May I touch it?"

He looked at me. "Do you have to, Mrs. Talbot?"

"I'd like to." I slipped my hand behind his ear and ran my fingers all the way to where the last couple of inches rested on the picnic bench. It was like bathing in a waterfall.

I said, "Freedom's gone now, I say if something makes you miserable, ditch it, no matter how beautiful it may be."

Andrew threw a rock that almost hit Hugo Jr. Marcella and

both kids went into high frenzy. Shane muttered to himself, "Take that, dirty Dick. Now I've got you." A backhoe lumbered by on the highway.

Owsley said, "Cut it."

———

First challenge was to talk Shane out of the scissors. "I'll coif the lad's hair. I'm a licensed barber in the state of New Jersey, you know."

"You're too short, Shane. The hair cutter has to stand higher than the head."

"I hate to break the news, little lady, but your tits are too small."

Then came the "Sit up straight, I can't do this if you're slouched over a drawing pad."

"Have you ever cut hair before?" Owsley asked.

"Can't be that hard, hairdressers aren't famous for brains."

Shane wheeled over to kibitz, and Marcella brought Hugo Jr. up from the creek. "Hey, Andrew," she called. "Want to watch Maurey turn the hippy boy normal?"

"I'd rather barf up."

I really got into the combing part. My fingers had never experienced anything so soft and smooth. It was like making snow angels naked, like riding Frostbite slow motion, like Sam Callahan licking between my legs.

Marcella let Hugo Jr. crawl across the picnic table. "Lonicera Mangleson had hair that long, and when she cut it a wig maker in Amarillo paid forty dollars for the leftovers."

"You going to comb all day?" Shane asked.

The longer I combed, the more Owsley tensed up. "I've never had a haircut, not since the day I was born. It won't hurt, will it?"

"I won't hurt you."

"I wish they weren't looking at me."

As I finished the comb-out, Lloyd came back for Moby Dick. "I got a tank of gas and some groceries, but I'll need another six-pack. We're out of Yukon Jack territory, Maurey. Southern Comfort's almost the same stuff."

"What time is it?" I asked.

"One, maybe one-thirty."

"I missed Paul Harvey. My life is in shambles. I missed Paul Harvey and we're trapped in a hell-hole where they don't sell Yukon Jack."

"I told you she'd fall apart in the South," Shane said.

"Janis Joplin drank Southern Comfort. She was hard core and she died. Make mine tequila."

Shane made a drooling snort sound. "If you drink tequila, you'll be hard core and die, too."

Lloyd hoisted himself into the driver's seat. "What're you doing to the boy?"

"Maurey's playing Samson and Delilah," Shane said.

Lloyd watched a few moments. "Don't cut his ears off. He'll bleed in the ambulance."

Sam Callahan says the two times men invariably make cornball comments is when they're watching someone get a haircut or watching someone change a tire. You ask me, there's more than two cases.

I started by forming a ponytail with my left fist and cutting straight across. Was the first ponytail I ever saw long as a pony's tail. Shane's scissors were little dudes he used to cut tape for his urine system, so mine wasn't an efficient beauty shop operation. My snips had the subtlety of a machete hack across Guatemala. But a weird thing happened as the scissors clipped their way through the ponytail. The world surrounding

Owsley and me shut down, went blurry. Everything focused into one cone of light where my hands intersected his hair.

There's a trance state that two beings can reach where the silly banter of nearby yahoos no longer exists. Time no longer exists. Nothing before, after, or around the immediate unity of the two matters. It's neat.

Frostbite and I achieved the trance in an arena filled with several thousand people dressed in western wear. I pulled it off while nursing both my babies, and once an old sheepherder and I found it dancing "The Tennessee Waltz" at a Fourth of July street party in Tensleep.

The moment you're supposed to transcend the reality of time and space is sex, but that's one area where I've never come close. Sex is complex—Will my birth control kick in? Why won't he slow down? Will he treat me like dogshit in the morning? The relationship works with horse and rider, mother and child, or two dancers who become one with the music and thus with each other. First time you start wondering who'll finish on top, the deal is blown.

"Why didn't you want Andrew to call you Owsley?"

"Freedom gave everyone stupid names, said a new identity would force a break from our hung-up pasts. He's the one with the hung-up past."

The hair between my fingers was clean mountain water; sunlight on the Tetons in winter; awakening at dawn and lying in bed listening to the birds.

"So where'd he come up with Owsley?"

"Owsley's the guy in California who makes LSD. Freedom wanted me to become a chemist. He said nobody gets high on art."

The scissors were a silver canoe gliding through a golden lake. All these metaphors made my clitoris throb.

"Do you have a real name?"

"You'll laugh."

"Why would I laugh?"

"Brad."

"Brad?"

"I knew you would laugh."

"I'm not laughing. Do you hear laughing?" What he heard was me gasping for air. "Okay. Owsley is dead. Out of the fallen hair will arise Brad. The normal boy."

"Will cutting my hair and saying I'm normal make me normal, Mrs. Talbot?"

"Sure. While we're taking new identities, call me Miss Pierce from now on. I'm done with Talbot."

"We'll be Brad and Miss Pierce."

By God if I didn't have an orgasm. Not your everyday gee-that's-nice orgasm, either. There's "I got off, dear. You can stop now," and then there's orGASm. OrGASm is when your eyes and ears ring. OrGASm is when you can still feel it hours later in the back of your knees.

"Are you done, Miss Pierce?"

"Yeah, let's find a mirror."

29

Marcella changed Hugo Jr. down by the creek where she could watch Andrew wade up and down promoting leaf races in the slow current. Owsley, now Brad, found a Safeway sack in the trash can for his shorn hair. I asked him what he planned to do with it.

"I might stuff it in a box and mail it to Freedom."

"You think he would understand the symbolism?"

Shane peeled off a toenail, put it in his mouth, then spit it on the ground. "In 1964, my hair was long as Brad's, before you chopped it off. That's when I was on the bus with Ken Kesey."

I went off to the park ladies' room to pee and wipe my upper leg—not all that stuff you feel afterward is boy goo. I didn't think Shane had noticed my Big O during the haircut. He wasn't the type to witness an orgasm and not comment on it.

The women's outhouse shared a wall with the men's outhouse, and some nitwit had drilled quarter-size peepholes the women stuffed with wads of toilet paper. I imagined an ongoing battle of unplugging and plugging. This game must be an Arkansas thing; Wyoming men have the class and style of a McDonald's burger, but at least they don't cop their thrills watching women piss.

The graffiti read MARILYN MONROE HAD A MASTECTOMY. You tell me what that's supposed to mean.

When I returned, Shane was waving his wicked little toenail knife like a conductor on a baton. "Due to an outbreak of lice in the trenches, burr haircuts were ordered for all soldiers in World War One. One French division mutinied and marched en masse to the bordellos of Marseilles."

Brad interrupted the lecture. "Is your name really Shane?"

"Of course my name is Shane. Shane is an ancient, venerated praenomen of my forebears, on the matrilineal side. There were Shanes among the earliest Rinesfoos in thirteenth-century Belgium."

I thought about pointing out his matrilineal side would hardly have been named Rinesfoos but skipped it. He'd have claimed twenty-six generations of virgin birth. "Five or six Shanes live around Jackson Hole, but none of them are older than the movie. I think you stole the name from Alan Ladd."

"As a matter of fact, princess, the man who wrote *Shane* took the name from me. We had adjoining lockers on the UCLA football team."

"Let's ask Marcella. I'll bet cash your name is Percival or Mordecai, something wimpy and embarrassing."

Shane's head bobbed up and down, with his chins floating slightly after the action. He raised up on his hands and took on the radish tinge.

"Go ahead," he said. "Ask her."

That's when Andrew screamed, which was nothing new, only his scream was followed by one from Marcella. *"Snake!"*

Lord knows what I thought I was doing, but I grabbed the scissors and ran down to the creek. Marcella, with Hugo Jr. clutched to her chest, pointed at the snake between us and Andrew. Long sucker with black bands and yellow spots. Slit tongue zipping in and out. Slithery movements. Andrew stood in shin-deep water, pooping his pants.

With a yell, I jumped on the snake and got his neck in a death grip, just like the guy on *Mutual of Omaha's Wild Kingdom*. The snake twisted and jerked, fighting to sink his fangs in my skin. Screaming the Blackfoot war cry, I straddled him and held his head at crotch level while his body writhed between my legs. Then I squeezed him with my left hand, plunged the scissors into his neck, and started cutting.

Yellow gunk flowed, then muscles popped out the slit— actually went faster than Brad's hair. After I cut through the spine I tore his head off and with one last shriek threw it as far as I could.

The only sound was Andrew whimpering in front of me. I turned back to find Marcella, Brad, and Shane staring like I was the mad serial killer of Tasmania.

"It was just a harmless king snake," Shane said.

Marcella ran over and pulled Andrew from the creek. She swatted him once on the rear, then hugged him until he recovered enough to burst into violent tears.

Brad was in awe. "You ripped his head right off."

I stared down at the snake's body, still writhing on the ground beneath my feet. Then I looked up and made eye contact with Shane. I said, "He looked like a big dick. I always wanted to tear the head off a big dick."

30

"I DESERVE THIS DRINK."

Lloyd wrestled the shifter rod into second and pulled out on U.S. 270. "You've said that same thing each day since we met."

"I've deserved a drink each day since we met."

"What happens on days you don't deserve a drink?"

On the edge of town we passed a stockyard jammed to the gills with pigs—Band-Aid-colored snouts and screwy tails as far as the eye could see.

"We raised a hog once," I said. "Dad named her Dolores Del Rio and she was gross, ate her own shit along with six puppies, a bag of charcoal briquettes, and my school copy of D. H. Lawrence's *Sons and Lovers*. I was never so happy to slaughter anything in my life."

Lloyd went into third and repeated himself. "What happens on days you don't deserve a drink?"

"Look. I just killed a snake and lost all my money. My hands are still shaking. If I ever deserved a drink in my life, I deserve this one."

"I'm not disagreeing. I only wondered what happens on days you don't deserve to drink."

"I don't drink." I said that before I thought whether it was true or not, but after a few moments' consideration I decided to believe myself. The last two weeks had been daily trauma—surely I earned my escapism after losing a child and blowing a suicide—and before that life had been so boring and tedious, alcohol made the unbearable barely bearable. Since Dad died the only days I didn't deserve a drink were the five spent in a coma.

"Deserving drinks is an interesting notion," Lloyd said.

"If you're going to lecture, I'll climb in back where I'm appreciated."

My tough-broad reputation had risen considerably in the back two-thirds of the ambulance. In an instant, Andrew changed from irritating brat to irritating hero worshiper—following me around the park like a lost lamb, crawling into my lap every time I sat down. He was only partially disenchanted when I refused to wear the dead snake around my neck.

Brad was too cool to actively fawn or anything, but when I twisted around in the passenger's seat to argue with Shane on the Eve-snake relationship in the Garden of Eden, Brad was bent over his art pad sketching my face.

As usual, Shane pontificated. "Woman has for all time been terrified of the serpent because of the distinct possibility that one could ooze into her womb and nest. It's an ovarian reaction."

I said, "Bull. Women are no more afraid of snakes than men. I didn't see you wheeling down there to save the kid."

"I knew the snake to be harmless."

"Maurey didn't know that," Marcella said. "What she did was just as heroic as if it was an adder."

"Oh, my God, an adder," Shane said with sarcasm. He tried to denigrate my snake battle, but even Shane looked at me a tad differently. He hadn't called me *little missy* in over an hour.

When Andrew dropped his Coke it blew foam on Brad's art work and Marcella's rayon dress, which caused a scramble. Andrew whined for another Coke while Brad dramatically ripped the soiled page from his pad and Shane explained how the FBI made Coca-Cola take the cocaine out of its secret formula but each year the company whips up a batch of original recipe for its upper-echelon officers and select members of the executive branch of government.

I turned to Lloyd. "Does it feel to you that we're establishing a pattern here on the road?"

He squinted into the side mirror. "I think we got us a family unit."

———

Dear Dad,

Here's what I think. I might pick a date, like three months from today, and that'll be the day to stop drinking and turn serious. Meantime I can get it out of my system. How does that idea strike you?

I need you now,
Merle Jean Pierce

P.S. I killed a snake.

———

I named the tequila bottle Elvis because Shane had been yammering about him off and on all day, telling bizarre stories in which he saved Elvis's life or career. Shane claimed to be the entire background chorus on "Blue Christmas." "I did four tracks of *Blue-blue-blues* in harmony with myself," he said. "Elvis said colored girls couldn't have done better."

I also named the tequila Elvis because he was the king and I'd killed a king snake, which metaphorically made me the Elvis killer. Personally, I'd never been hot for his music—too much hips for country, too much Brylcreem for rock 'n' roll—but it was an okay name for tequila. "Gimme an Elvis, straight up." "I shoot Elvis with lemon and salt."

The worst social blunder I ever made in my life—before the Auburn-on-the-roof deal—was made on tequila. You ever do something so embarrassing you relive it over and over when you go to the bathroom in the middle of the night? Something so rotten it affects your self-image from that day on?

Sophomore year at Laramie, I wasn't ready for a test in Psych 101, so I spent a snowy afternoon sitting in my dorm room staring out the window and doing shots of Cuervo Silver. My roommate, Betsy, was concerned about my welfare, and she convinced me to go downstairs to the cafeteria for supper.

Big mistake. Someone was ribbing Lucy Jane Andrews from Thermopolis about biting a boy's tongue when he French-kissed her on the first date, and she said, "At least I didn't get pregnant before puberty."

The other three girls at the table sniggered and slid their eyes at me. I'd been hearing that crap for six years and learned to roll with it as the price you pay for being different, but this time I cracked. I could blame Cuervo or cafeteria food, but the truth is no one is responsible for this gig but me.

"Lucy Jane," I said too loudly, "had an accident in her white linen skirt a few years back and now she wears tampons every single day and every single night of the month. She hasn't been out of the bathroom without a plug in since she left high school."

Polly St. Michel tittered. I turned on her. "What are you laughing at? Your stepbrother raped you when you were twelve and now you can't ever have a baby." I turned on everybody at once. "You cat women are always gossiping about my daughter. Well, at least I'm honest, I don't hide ugly little secrets."

Betsy defended herself. "We don't all hide ugly secrets."

"Who'll go upstairs in fifteen minutes and make herself vomit like she does after every meal?" The cafeteria got real quiet as I fired my final shot at Dory Crandall. The poor girl had never been anything but kind to me. One midnight she told me her secret because the guilt was driving her to meekness. "And who slept with her best friend's boyfriend the day before they got married? I'll bet the happy bride would love to know that one."

Only when I paused for breath and looked in their faces did I realize I'd gone too far. All my female friendships were dead meat. Even others who weren't at the table would never trust me now, for good reason. In cowboy terms, I'd shot myself in the foot. In the head.

"Tell me about your dad," Lloyd said.

"What?"

"You write him postcards every day, but he's dead."

"Who told you my father is dead?"

"You did, yesterday when the highway patrolman stopped us. Don't you remember?" *Don't you remember?* Always digging at me; sometimes I wished Lloyd were more like Shane. Shane didn't care whether I drank myself to death or not.

A picture of Buddy formed in my mind—six four, black bush of a beard, voice that reverberated with authority. "Dad was like what you think of as God."

Lloyd kept his Jesus eyes on the road. "What's that mean?"

I thought in terms of honesty. What are God's characteristics? "Remote. Perfect, yet remote. God knows everything you do, but nothing you do affects him one way or the other."

"Your God must not be Southern Baptist."

"The county only decided to plow the ranch road a couple years ago, so back when I started school Mom and Petey and I lived in town all winter while Dad stayed on the mountain. I didn't see him on a day-to-day basis."

"It's tricky loving someone you don't see. They tend to get built into dream people." I guess Lloyd was relating my deal to his wife, Sharon.

I two-handed a slug of Elvis. "Mom was petty. She couldn't stand a cat hair on her curtains, or she'd go berserk if a bee got loose in the car. She spent hours worrying about the characters on a soap opera."

"All moms are like that," Lloyd said.

"But Dad treated her like a fairy princess, even after she started flipping out. He took everything she said seriously."

"So, do you hate him or her for that?"

"Nothing I did affected him. When the baby was born, he still wouldn't come out of the mountains. Shannon and I lived at Sam and Lydia's while Dad took care of the horses."

I sucked in one hell of a good pull on Elvis. "Dad's not dead. He's gone to San Francisco on business."

Brad was listening in back. He spoke up in the voice of a fourteen-year-old. "My dad used to wake me up at night and make me hide in the bathroom while Mom turned a trick in my bed."

I said, "Oh."

31

I TRIED TO GET SAM CALLAHAN TO WRITE A STORY ABOUT DRY mouth once. He could have a character whose mission in life was to develop a drug that didn't cause next-day ashtray lips.

"It'd be a quest story," I said.

"I only deal in universal concepts."

"What concept is more universal than waking up with a dry mouth?"

Of course he didn't write my story; he'd rather write about Jesus playing baseball.

Lloyd shook me awake to darkness and a mythic dry mouth. He said, "We need gas."

My lips made a frog-stuck-in-mud sound. Lloyd handed me a canteen he usually saved for the radiator and repeated himself. "We need gas. You have anything to trade for gas?"

I didn't even swallow the water, just let it soak into my tongue like rain on dust. "How long have I been asleep?"

"Since you finished your bottle. We tried to wake you for supper."

Moby Dick sat in a parking lot on the edge of a dark town. A hundred yards or so away lights shone through the windows of an Alka-Seltzer-shaped building. "I'm disoriented here, Lloyd. You got a fix on time or place? Why is everything shiny?"

He bent to squint through the windshield up at the sky. "Been raining. Two-thirty, maybe three. Some town in Arkansas. That building says 'Trojans' on the front."

"Looks like a high school."

"There's a couple buses down there where we can borrow gas, only we need payment."

I unbuckled my seat belt, opened Moby Dick's door, and breathed in the wet night air. To tell the truth, I felt like honest death. A tequila hangover is more elemental than Yukon Jack's. Imagine six hundred paper cuts on your brain.

"What's wrong with Coors?" Behind me Andrew giggled in his sleep and Shane snored like a rhino.

"Nothing's open," Lloyd said. "We have to steal the gasoline, and it doesn't feel right leaving beer. What if the people we steal it from are AA?"

I tipped my head and drank nearly a quart of water. Lloyd stayed patient. If I had to sum up Lloyd Carbonneau in one word, that's the one I would say—patient.

"We're talking a narrow line of ethics here, Lloyd. It's okay to trade illegal beer for gasoline but not okay to steal it unless we leave something of value and not right if the thing we leave is beer?"

He thought awhile, then said, "Yes."

"Just wanted to clarify my thoughts."

"I have a battery charger we could trade, but we might need it later. Aren't you carrying anything worth a few gallons?"

Dad's creel was on the floor. In the hidden pocket I found the keys to the Bronco and what was now Dothan's house and the silver hoop earrings Shannon gave me for Christmas. I held the earrings in the palm of my hand. "There's these, but they mean something to me. I'd just as soon leave Coors and not worry about right and wrong."

"How about that box?"

"The creel?" I ran my fingertips along the wicker and saw Dad standing in the Firehole River in his hip boots holding a cutthroat by the gills for Mom to *ooh* over.

Lloyd said, "Bus drivers can use a fishing box; unless they're married earrings won't do them much good."

What would Dad want me to do? Hell with that, what would I want me to do? I started transferring Carmex and junk from the creel to Sam Callahan's day pack. "Another piece of Dad bites the dust."

"It's good for you to let him go."

"I won't let him go for less than twenty gallons."

———

Which was bravado. We only had a five-gallon reserve tank and two one-gallon Coleman fuel cans. "Let's make two trips," I said.

"Seven gallons will get us into Memphis, where we can trade for more. I used to know people in Memphis."

We stood outside watching the rain drip on puddles and shapes pass back and forth behind the windows of what I took as a gymnasium. Beyond it the school lurked the way schools lurk at night. Closer to us, three school buses lined up under a security light facing the highway.

"I'm new at this, Lloyd. How do we steal gas from a school bus?"

Lloyd reached in under the driver's seat to pull out a hose—four feet or so of that semi-clear stuff you string between beakers in high school chemistry. "We charge it on the Idaho credit card."

"You always carry a siphon hose?" I asked.

He reached back in for a flashlight, which he handed to me. "First time we ran out of gas in Mexico I had to use Shane's catheter."

"Ouch."

"This hose is the one auto accessory Shane paid for himself."

———

Lloyd squatted in the gravel and sucked hose. After a few seconds his head jerked and he spit gasoline.

"Good thing schools always fill buses at the end of the day instead of mornings," he said. "The hose wouldn't reach anything less than a full tank."

"Where did you learn schools gas up in the afternoon?"

Lloyd shrugged his bare shoulders. "You pick things up."

The flow of gas into the tank made a tinkle sound, like Andrew peeing in a puddle. This didn't shape up as a quick operation. I checked out the lights in the gymnasium—lit rooms on dark nights bring out the voyeur in me.

"Keep an eye posted for the police," Lloyd said. "If they come, we flatten and roll under the bus."

"They'll see our cans."

"Probably."

Streetlights from the town glowed against the low clouds off to the east. West, it was Moby Dick, Hugo Sr., then blackness.

I nodded at the idling Oldsmobile. "That guy's starting to give me the willies."

Lloyd glanced back at Hugo. "He's only staying close to his family."

"Can't he take a hint? Marcella doesn't want him close to his family."

"Maybe he doesn't know what else to do."

"Let's paint a sign on the back of the ambulance that says 'Too late, dickhead.'"

Lloyd bent to check the flow. "Forgiveness isn't one of your strong points."

"Forgiveness is for the pope. If a man nails around on his

wife, he deserves to pay. Else every man would be nailing every woman. Fear is all that keeps pistols in the holster."

"How about loyalty?"

"Sam Callahan wrote that a stiff dick hath no conscience."

Lloyd spit again and I handed him the water I'd been hauling around ever since I woke up. He swished his mouth, gargled a moment, and spit.

"We all made mistakes, Maurey. You more than anyone should understand forgiveness. You'll never get your baby back without it."

I couldn't settle on a rational comeback. After tequila, though, rational isn't necessary for speech. "My mistakes have excuses. Hugo's don't."

"How do you know his story?"

"There can be no excuse for adultery by males."

"As opposed to females?"

"I can think of several reasons a woman might have to commit adultery."

Lloyd smiled, pretending I was kidding. Maybe I was, maybe not, I don't know. In certain situations women do deserve more slack than men. That's because men made the rules. They're the house and women are the gamblers, and everyone knows the only way a gambler can beat the house is to cheat.

"If Hugo lasts another day or two, I'll vote that she takes him back," Lloyd said.

"That's because you want Sharon to take you back and you know she probably won't."

His head came up. "Why not?"

Words came in a rush. "Sharon was a little girl when she married you, Lloyd. She's grown up by now. You can't expect to find the same girl who loved you years ago."

"Yes, I can," he said.

"This search is stupid."

The web of lines around his eyes went hurt child. I swear, I should be quarantined from sensitive men. The government could create a pain zone one hundred yards away from me in all directions. Put up KEEP OUT signs like they do on the trails when a grizzly gets mean.

"I'm sorry," I said. "If anyone deserves forgiveness, you do." Lloyd reached out to make a minuscule hose adjustment. "We had a nice sunset this afternoon. Too bad you were asleep and missed it."

"I had that coming." He didn't disagree, so I said, "I'm going for a walk while this deal fills up. No use both of us loitering at the scene of the crime."

———

Lloyd had simplified life to Ivanhoesque terms: one single obstacle stands between me and happiness, and if I can overcome that obstacle, all problems will cease to exist. Lloyd's peace of mind through the hard times was based on the lie that if he found his precious Sharon, they would automatically come together in rapture and love and all would be right with the world. So to speak. As it were.

My ethical question, wandering aimlessly through the damp parking lot, was, did I do the right thing? Is peace of mind based on a he better than no peace of mind at all?

I'd known other people who blamed all misfortune on one fixable fact. Fat people, for instance. There's no one more depressed than a fat person who loses one hundred pounds and discovers the thin can be lonely, too. Or those southern women who are trained that by being pretty, sweet, and available, a man will swoop down and make everything nice. Ivanhoe swoops down and nothing changes except the women stop being pretty, sweet, and available.

I suspected sobriety of the same trick. Every chatterbox in

America took for granted that if I quit drinking I'd win my baby Auburn back. If I quit drinking I would fall in love with a prince rather than a shithead. And the prince would fall in love with me. They said if I quit drinking my life would find direction and everything in the vicinity of it would no longer be ugly, turgid, and meaningless.

How the hell did they know? Sober women marry creeps. Sober women lose children. What if the deal was a colossal hoax, I abandoned the only dependable lover I've ever had—Yukon Jack—and afterward woke up to zippo? Emptiness? I could get screwed here.

I did the moth thing and drew toward the light. Five or six cars of the decade-old variety were parked close to a double-loading door, which I avoided. My tack was to stay on the dark edge of the parking area, then drift around the side of the Alka-Seltzer away from the highway. I found some glass doors, but they only looked in on a lobby-like room with two trophy cases flanking a large mosaic of a Trojan soldier's helmet.

The trophy cases were lit by those tube lights they mount above paintings in art museums. The trophies were mainly for football with a smattering of fake-gold statuettes wearing shorts to indicate basketball and track. Not a skiing or rodeo trophy in the bunch.

Off left of the doors I discovered a ledge forty feet or so up that circled the building and passed in front of a bank of way-high windows. The fire escape was a piece of cake. I could have climbed it smashed.

The ledge itself was somewhat narrow for my tastes—I'm no mountain goat—and it was wet and sloped like five degrees the wrong way, but the windows were framed in concrete that made an okay handhold. Once past the side of the frame, I planted my elbows on the lower lip and cupped my hands around my eyes to peer in at the Land of Oz.

It was neat. Ten feet high, the Scarecrow, Tin Man, and Cowardly Lion stood on one side of an immense throne, facing Toto and Judy Garland. Toto had a Pomeranian look about the nose and ears. Judy Garland's hair was in pigtails.

Just guessing, I'd say tomorrow was prom night and the junior class or whoever does these things in Arkansas was transforming the gym into a theme park. Mainly the transformation required a heck of a lot of emerald green crepe paper.

A dozen teenagers moved around the room, drinking Cokes and laughing and putting on finishing touches. They must have had a glitter fight earlier because the kids sparkled, especially their hair. The girls wore shorts, the boys jeans; everyone was barefoot.

A boy who looked so much like Park my breath caught was painting a yellow brick road on an entire wall of butcher paper. The road receded up the wall through a forest filled with Munchkins and flying monkeys. At the bottom edge where the road came off the paper it met a yellow carpet strip that ran across the floor to the throne.

A girl straddling the top of a ladder called something to the Park-boy. He set down his brush and walked over to the ladder, where he picked a crown off the floor and, taking two steps up the ladder, lifted it to the girl. She had blond, bouncy hair and was wearing white shorts and an off-white pullover jersey. As she reached down to take the crown their fingers touched and they smiled in each other's eyes. *Bing.* I wanted to cry.

"You finished?" Lloyd's quiet voice came from below.

I looked down. "Are you?"

"Gas is in. All we need now is to prime the carburetor and hit the road."

I looked back in to where the girl was balancing the crown at an angle on the Scarecrow's two-dimensional head. Park was frozen, gazing up at her like a dancer in a musical who's been told not to move a muscle till the starlet finishes her solo.

"I'll be right down."

Back on ground level, Lloyd asked, "See anything interesting?"

"The Land of Oz."

"Was it nice?"

"At my prom we did Camelot better."

32

AT DAWN I DROVE MOBY DICK ACROSS THE MISSISSIPPI River into Memphis. That's one big river, especially for a woman raised on water you can throw a rock across. A couple of tugboats were passing under the bridge, pushing what looked like floating city blocks. The air was thick as Cool Whip.

"My dad had two rules when it came to choosing a place to live," I said.

"Listen to those plug wires arc," Lloyd said.

I didn't hear anything. "First, he had to have a house where he could piss off the front porch without affronting the neighbors."

"I burned a truck up on this bridge once. Fifty-four Dodge flathead-six vapor locked on me, then she blew. They had to close the bridge for three hours."

"And second, he couldn't stand anyone living upstream. Said he felt surrounded if people got to the water before he did."

Lloyd rolled down the window. "Your dad wouldn't like Memphis. Practically the whole country lives upstream."

"Dad also didn't trust anyone from east of the Mississippi— said if their kinfolk had an adventuresome spirit, they'd have gone someplace fresh."

"Your dad might get a kick out of the part of town where we're headed," Lloyd said. "Men piss off porches on Cleveland Street."

"Nobody sees?"

"Nobody cares."

———

Cleveland Street was the epitome of what us hinterland types think of when someone says *inner city stagnation*. From the river, the tree progression went roughly magnolia, oak, cottonwood, nothing, with nothing being the plants in sight of the Calhoun Arms Hotel, which is where Lloyd directed me.

And as the trees moved from genteel to dead, the buildings followed the pattern. Right on the river is the largest Holiday Inn in humanity—glass and chrome twenty stories high. Cracked cinder block would describe the style on Cleveland Street. You know you're in trouble when you look at a porch and think stoop.

Women dressed like Sugar Cannelioski leaned against parking meters and sat on the stoops.

"Are these hookers?" I asked.

"Not all of them," Lloyd said. "Maybe."

"Who needs a hooker at six-thirty in the morning?"

"International Harvester graveyard shifts. The men get off work and can't sleep."

"In Wyoming when we can't sleep we watch television."

Finding a place to stop wasn't the nightmare I'd envisioned, thanks to parallel parking and lots of open slots that time of day. As Lloyd fed pennies to the ambulance meter and I fed them to the trailer meter, a black woman in crack-climbers and a leather vest came over to complain.

"You're blocking the view."

I looked between the trailer and M.D. at an adult toy store

across the street—Sodom and Gomorrah's Sexual Paraphernalia Shoppe. The window was covered by brown paper.

"Not much of a view."

"No, sister, the customer's view of me."

"Move down a few feet."

"That's someone else's turf. Look, white lady, I got a baby and a junkie to feed, and I lose the territory at noon."

In the movies big-city whores are tough and ruthless, they'll knife a man in a flash and not let it bum out their evening. But this woman wasn't any more brash than Marcella. She reminded me of a carhop.

"Didn't mean to hurt your business," I said.

"I know that, you got a couple dollars I can have?"

Lloyd knew of a public parking lot two blocks away where a friend of his used to work, but when we got there the man at the gate had never heard of Lloyd's friend. Hell, it'd been three years since Lloyd drank in this neighborhood, ghetto parking attendant can't be a lifelong career. A case of Coors lighter, we found a place along a graffiti-filled wall. The messages read NIGGER, EAT ME, JESUS SAVES, and GO OLD MISS.

"Why must we stop at a hotel?" Shane complained. "Granma is only five hundred miles away. We can rest then."

Lloyd slammed the hood and came to the passenger window. "We need to rake up some money. There's times you can't trade beer."

Seven in the morning and sweat was already trickling down my rib cage. I'd never sweat, outside sex, anyway, at that time of day in my life. "How're we going to rake up money?" I asked.

"You and I are going to sell something."

"Not my silver hoop earrings."

Shane struggled to pull down his pants. By now I was so used to seeing his act, I didn't think twice. He said, "Perhaps I could secure a loan from Elvis, if you good folks swore to the Almighty you'd repay his kindness."

Brad said, "I can make some money." The kid was already bent over his drawing pad, working on the wings of a bird.

"Someday, somebody's liable to call your bluff on Elvis," I said.

Shane shot back, "No doubt the ladies of ill repute would present you with a parking meter for the afternoon. Professional courtesy."

———

Lloyd disappeared for twenty minutes, then came back to announce we'd spent two more cases on two single beds with bath.

"We have to be out by five," he said.

"In the afternoon?"

He shrugged and rubbed his leg. "They rent on an hourly scale. We'll be done by then, and it's safer to travel at night anyway."

"Done with what?" I asked.

Our gang made an interesting little parade moving down the sidewalks of Cleveland Street. Lloyd carried the Coors under a blanket, Marcella carried the sleeping Andrew, I carried Hugo Jr., Brad carried the bowling bag full of diapers, backup formula, rash powder, squeeze toys, washcloths, and the kitten, and Shane talked.

"Syphilitics have a distinctive odor," he said as he rolled. "That gentleman on the corner was one. If each of these lovely ladies invited me to sniff their wombs, I could give an instant diagnosis. Save the county a fortune in testing."

"How about gonorrhea?" I asked.

"Any fool can smell gonorrhea. Imagine a yeast infection with a touch of melted chocolate. I can also sniff pregnancy. In my younger days I differentiated the male fetus from the female, but I lost the touch when alcohol corrupted certain blood vessels in my nasal passage."

We—all except Shane—stepped over a woman passed out on the sidewalk. Shane had to wheel around.

"What do you smell from her?" I asked.

"A noble life flushed down the toilet of society. Do not condemn this poor soul. Pity her. Empathize with her. She was once an innocent child who wore pretty dresses and loved ice cream. That empty husk was once you. And someday you might be her."

He glanced over, expecting me to swallow the bait, but I stayed cool. It's like we were growing comfortable with each other's depravity—made both of us harder to outrage.

The procession paused while Shane backed off a curb, without asking for help. On the other side of the street, Lloyd set down the beer and gave him a boost. Shane kept talking.

"I too have lain unconscious in public places. To look at me now you may never believe I was once held up as a bad example."

I said, "You're still my bad example."

With a screech, Andrew went from sound sleep to ultra-awake. "Let me down. I'm thirsty. Why doesn't that man have arms? This place is the pits."

When Marcella set him down, he ran in the street. She yanked him onto the sidewalk and swatted his butt once. He burst into tears and accused her of being mean and not caring about him. "I'm gonna live with Daddy. He gives me presents." For a change, Daddy was nowhere in sight.

"You're not going to live with Daddy."

"I love him and I hate you."

Kids have an instinct when it comes to hurting parents. I know I did. Andrew pulled loose, ran over to a bum passed out in a doorway, and stole his bottle. I handed Marcella Hugo Jr. and went after him.

"Give me the man's bottle."

"I'm thirsty."

"You can't drink that, it has wino cooties."

Andrew looked suspiciously at the bottle—DeKuyper peach brandy—then back at the inert pile of clothes in the doorway. "I'll wipe the cooties off on my shirt."

I advanced. "It's the man's bottle. When the man wakes up he'll need his bottle."

Andrew skipped out of my range. "He won't wake up, he's dead."

"He's not dead, now give me the bottle before I yank off your arm and beat you with the stub."

Andrew whined. "I'm thirsty."

"We'll get you a drink of water."

Meanwhile, Shane had wheeled over and was inspecting the public pass-out. "Andrew is correct. The gentleman is dead."

Andrew went white and dropped the bottle. It shattered. Lloyd bent over the man and touched his neck. "You people take the beer on to the hotel. I'll find a policeman."

We gathered in a bunch around the doorway. Andrew clutched Marcella's leg. I stood between Shane and Brad with one hand on the back of Shane's chair. Lloyd turned and left.

The dead man was wearing a denim shirt, slacks held up by a cord belt, and black loafers with no socks. His brown hair was slicked down and neatly parted. His fiftyish face had no flesh under the skin, as if he'd started going skeleton even before he died. A trace of drool leaked from the corner of his mouth and his eyes were cloudy, the same color as the Mississippi River when we crossed.

"There, but for the grace of God, go I," Shane said.

I said, "Bull."

He wheeled back a foot. "You know nothing, little girl."

I couldn't very well challenge him on that one.

"I'm sorry I stole your bottle," Andrew said to the dead man.

I thought about Auburn.

33

TA-DA. I'D SURVIVED TO THE NEXT SHOWER. SMALL triumphs—like making it through an entire day without dying—are sometimes more commendable than the big ones. Showers had come to represent goals. Safe zones. Sam Callahan and the kids in the neighborhood played tag games where certain trees were Base, and It couldn't get you when you were touching Base. I'd always looked at Jackson Hole as my personal Base, but recently safety from It had shrunk to the shower stall.

Quality-wise, the Calhoun Arms shower was about what you'd expect. Tepid water, used soap, dribbly pressure, furry stuff on the wall—but I wasn't in a position for pickiness. I'd just seen a dead man; I needed to be washed.

I saw a dead man once before. Lydia Callahan and I were in the Killdeer Cafe, or whatever it was called back then, when an old logger named Bill fell across the jukebox and died. I don't remember where Sam was. I do remember everyone sitting in their booths looking vaguely put upon.

For a very short while after I saw Bill crumpled up dead on the floor, sensate-type things were ultraintense—chocolate malts tasted luscious, the snow outside was colder and whiter, radio music had a new crispness. Sam Callahan and I had the most dynamite sex we ever had, which makes it the most dynamite sex I've had so far because no one's wiped me out since.

Sad when your sex life peaks at thirteen.

———

Clean underwear, I had. I'd never sunk so low as to put dirty underwear back on after a shower. Clean clothes, I didn't have. The last jeans and the Neiman Marcus rodeos-and-funerals shirt went on in De Queen, Arkansas, so as of Memphis I have sunk so low as to wear dirty clothes after a shower. Could be better, could be worse.

Marcella and Andrew sat on one bed playing Old Maid. Whenever she won a hand he threw all the cards against the wall, so Marcella stopped winning hands. Hugo Jr. lay on his back on the other bed, gurgling and kicking his feet in the air. Being cute. The kitten with half whiskers was drinking baby formula from a paper Coke cup on the floor. She couldn't reach the milk with her tongue, but she'd learned the soak-a-paw, lick-a-paw trick.

I sat next to Hugo Jr. to comb my wet hair. It had finally grown out enough to cover my ears and look somewhat intentional, like a woman with a short hairdo rather than a grief-wallowing neurotic who'd tried to chop herself ugly.

When a man gives himself a burr haircut society doesn't rear up and scream *rampant instability*.

"Where's Brad?" I asked.

Andrew pulled a card from Marcella's hand and threw down a pair of Gus Gulps. He shouted, "Fooled you, meathead."

"He took off," Marcella said.

"Took off?"

"As soon as you turned on the shower he ran out."

"He say where he was going?"

She looked at her cards and said, "Oh, dear, the Old Maid."
Andrew cackled.

I asked again, "Did Brad say where he was going?"

"I don't think so."

"When he'll be back?"

"He didn't say a word."

"He take his art pad?"

"I suppose so. He had something under his arm."

I didn't see his art pad anywhere in the bare room. "I
wonder if we've been ditched."

Marcella shrugged. Andrew turned on me with fierceness.
"Would you shut up. I'm concentrating."

"Yeah, right."

———

The Jesus eyes came in a circle and hit me full in the face.
"We'll sell blood."

"Whose blood?"

To his overalls and sandals getup, Lloyd had added a ball cap
that said CAT. I didn't remember him wearing it when we left
Moby Dick. "Yours and mine," he said. "Who else's blood we
got to sell?"

"I'm not selling blood."

"It's easy, Maurey. Last time I sold it was fourteen dollars a
pint. Twenty-eight dollars and a few cases of Coors will get us
across Tennessee."

"Just trade more Coors."

"We're not getting what we paid for it. Imagine how embarrassed you'd feel to pull into Granma's farm with an empty trailer."

"Lloyd, I was a high school cheerleader. I don't sell blood.
During the Red Cross drive I might graciously donate, but
girls from Wyoming are not desperate enough to trade blood
for money."

Lloyd's face had a tireder than usual look, and he usually looked tired. He took off the cap, wiped dew from his forehead, then put the cap back on. I wondered if he stole the cap from the dead guy. What an awful thought.

"At least walk down to the bank with me," Lloyd said.

"Why?"

"What else have you got to do?"

———

Shane was outside hitting on the black hooker in the leather vest whose two parking meters we almost blocked.

"Meet Miss Ivory Tupelo," he said. "Miss Tupelo is a recent graduate of Duke University."

"Pleased, I'm sure," said the hooker.

"You better get in out of the heat," I said. "You want some help with the steps?"

Shane was sweating like a jitterbugger. "I have no intention of entering that establishment. It's disreputable."

"You staying out here to be reputable with the coed?"

"He'd have more fun with me than he does with you," the hooker said.

"God, I hope so."

Shane jerked his shaky thumb at a pay phone next to a shredded phone book. "I called Priscilla and she insists on sending a car. You needn't concern yourselves about my welfare, I informed her I must return prior to five o'clock."

I should have known better than to ask. "That's Priscilla Presley?"

"How many Priscillas do I know in Memphis?"

I think the dead man had triggered a fed-up-with-bullshit gland in Lloyd, because for the first time since I met them, he didn't humor Shane's rich fantasy life.

He said, "Shane, you don't know Elvis Presley."

Shane did the hurt slump. "Have you come to doubt me, too?"

"Get in out of the heat, I have enough problems without nursing you." Strong words for Lloyd. It occurred to me I should set him up with Dot Pollard at the Killdeer. They could be the couple who never offended anybody.

"*Credo quia absurdum est,*" Shane said.

The hooker said, "You tell 'em, baby."

He repeated. "*Credo quia absurdum est,* Father Tertullian said those words in the third century as proof that the Christian God exists. They mean 'This is too absurd to be made up, therefore it must be true.'"

"If shit's weird enough, it's real," I paraphrased.

"Correct. Elvis and I are buddies. I saved his life and his career, not to mention I introduced him to his wife. This all must be true simply because you cannot believe it."

Lloyd said, "He's got a point."

———

Lloyd gave me a bum's tour of downtown Memphis. "The gray building is where you apply for food commodities. They won't okay the application unless you can prove you're living indoors. Over there's a Catholic church where you can sleep on the floor if you don't look drunk, only they kick you out at six-thirty a.m. This block is thick with winos by the seven o'clock rush hour. Across the street there is the Manpower temporary labor office. Good place to hide on cold days."

"That's where you found the bottle that started your last bender," I said.

He looked at me. "You remembered."

"You blacked out two months before you woke up in Mexico City with a broken leg. My memory's not totally shot."

We stopped at a light and were quickly surrounded by urban types, lots of them black people. "Your midterm memory works," Lloyd said. "How's the short? Where did you brush your teeth yesterday?"

I ran my tongue over my teeth. I'd brushed them after my shower today, but yesterday was off the list. "Where'd you get that cap?" I asked.

Lloyd seemed surprised by the question. He took the cap off and studied CAT, as if noticing it for the first time. "Policeman gave it to me. He said a crystal freak left it in his car during a bust last night. I don't know what crystal is."

"Speed. Amphetamines you shoot up."

Lloyd shook his head. "Stay off the streets a couple years and they invent whole new ways to be self-destructive."

"It's more a college thing, I think."

The light changed and the urban herd moved. In the middle of the street we met another herd coming toward us, and even though no one actually looked at anyone else, the two herds sifted through each other without a single body bump. I was impressed.

"The dead boy was only twenty-eight," Lloyd said, which surprised me. He'd looked fifty. "Claude Kepler from Opelika, Alabama. He had a hundred and fifty dollars in his pocket next to a Western Union receipt for two hundred somebody wired him yesterday."

"Sounds like he had a friend somewhere," I said.

"Never give a destitute alcoholic enough money to drink himself to death, because he will."

"Kindness kills thing, huh?" I said.

"Kindness should come in one-bottle amounts."

———

A blood bank in Memphis is about as far as you can come from a horse ranch in Wyoming. Just goes to show how my life had gone to pot in two weeks. I was raised in a beautiful environment, and I still wound up attempting suicide; I don't see how people from ugly places do it.

The blood bank wasn't nonhygienic, I guess. It just felt filthy. The room had the ambiance of a janitor's mop closet— five cots, some folding chairs, a radio tuned to dentist music, a refrigerator, a cash register. The center of the room was taken up by this whirlyjigger machine with an ominous look—part carnival, part *Buck Rogers in the 25th Century.*

Two of the nurses were exhausted matrons, and the third was a teenager with braces on her teeth who testified for Jesus as she slid the pipe in your vein. Damn thing was thick as Shane's tube. Evil-looking sucker.

"What's that deal?" I pointed to the whirlyjigger machine.

"Centrifuge plasma separator," Lloyd said. "They give nine dollars for plasma and you can come back in three days, or fourteen dollars for blood, only you can't sell but once a week. Winos who think of their future sell plasma."

"But drunks who live for today sell blood."

"We'll do blood because we're not planning on being around in three days."

"We hell."

"Plus, you'll be amazed how wasted you get tonight drinking with one less pint of blood in your body."

"Who said I'm drinking today?"

A steady stream of alcoholics, drug addicts, and an occasional college student trickled in, waited their turns, and went out with an extra-large Band-Aid taped sideways in the crook of their arms. No complimentary orange juice while you rest afterward like the Red Cross does it—this place was more of a backward gas station than a clinic. You pull up, plug in the hose, fill the tank, get your Band-Aid and cash, and you're on the road again.

While I waited my turn an old codger the nurses called Carl

stumbled through the door and fell over a chair. The harshest of the matrons moved to throw him out.

"Come back when you're sober, Carl," she said. "Any poor patient gets your blood would die of alcohol poisoning."

"Fuck you," said Carl.

I don't know how these places judge too-drunk-to-give because Carl wandered back twenty minutes later and they took him. Maybe the difference was the second time he didn't knock over any chairs.

You notice I said "waited my turn" there? I don't know how Lloyd got me, but he got me. One minute I'm watching Nurse Harsh tie a rubber hose around his stringy upper arm and he says, "We'll need more money, Maurey. Sign up," and the next minute I'm filling out a form saying I've never had hepatitis and I'm not currently on medication—they take your word for that stuff—then ten more minutes and I'm dripping into a bag. Looked like the same brand of bag Shane peed in.

"Any chance of listening to Paul Harvey on the radio?" I asked the Jesus nurse.

"Sure. Don't you think Paul Harvey has depth in his voice? I'll bet he has the easiest veins to hit. I'd love to clamp him off and watch his antecubital vein swell." Different women rate men different ways. I suppose ease of hitting their veins is as good a method as any.

The winos and nurses got in a big argument as to what station was best for Paul Harvey, but finally the matter was settled and someone turned the dial. We'd missed Page One, which was okay by me, I didn't go for the real news anyway. Lydia Callahan was the news junkie; I preferred the twenty-two-pound cantaloupes on Page Two.

Paul congratulated a couple for staying happily married for eighty-five years. He insinuated they still had good sex, or maybe I just took it that way. Then he told an interesting story about his neighbor in the Missouri Ozarks who'd taught his pig to imitate Fidel Castro. Basically, the neighbor tied a fake beard and funny cap on the pig's head, then let it smoke a cigar. That hog of Dad's would have eaten the cigar, beard, and cap, then tried to bite the neighbor.

The story came out pretty funny, but you almost had to be there. With Paul Harvey, delivery is more important than content.

Here's the day's bumper snicker: "Never take a snake by its tail or a woman by her word." Sexist pig.

There's no better time in the world for evaluating where your life's been and how close the reality matches the dreams than the twenty minutes or so it takes to sell a pint of blood. You lie there on the cot, watching your bodily fluids drip away and you think, So this is what I've come to. My body has eight pints of blood and I'm selling one for fourteen dollars. Is that what I'm worth?

Then you think how fast you'll probably convert that pint of blood into a pint of whiskey, and the tendency is toward depression.

Two weeks ago I lived in a nice home and took care of a beautiful baby. I was surrounded by the wonderful mystery of the mountains. I showered in clean water and breathed faultless air. I had what half the women in America want, and I botched the gig. One lousy bottle of tequila shows up in a lion's stuffings and zip—no home, no beautiful child, no paradise. Now I'm surrounded by addicted men who don't bathe. I'm forced to walk on concrete, I have a needle sticking in my arm.

The contrast with Paul Harvey was too much.

"We didn't need money this bad," I said to Lloyd. "You brought me here to make a point about alcoholism."

He looked at me and said, "Alcoholism has no point." Pithy son of a bitch.

Carl raised up and started dry heaving and fell out of his cot, pulling the needle out of his arm and his own bag of blood down on his head.

34

Dead Dad,

This is the Mississippi River, butt crack of the entire nation. I
saw a dead boy. I sold my blood and met a woman who sold
her flesh. Which of us would a cowboy call sleazy?
My adventuresome spirit is flagging. Could use your help.

Maurey

———

I paddled my canoe through the glass-still waters of Jenny Lake.
At the far end of the boat a whore named Lily sunbathed on her back
wearing a black bikini bottom and no top. She was very tanned, but
I could see purple bruises on the insides of her arms. Lily stretched her
arms over her head and leaned forward to lick between my legs. "You're
a woman," I said. "Close your eyes and I'm anyone," she said. I
closed my eyes and we drifted across the lake with her licking below
and above my clitoris and me floating with the gentleness of the water.
I almost came, I wanted to come, but I couldn't quite get over the edge.
When I opened my eyes Lily had changed. She had a black, full beard
and hair on her arms and chest. I said, "You died," and Lily said in a
man's voice, "That was a mistake." Then I was in the lake, drowning.

I kicked, I fought, I screamed. Lily pulled my feet down where I no longer wanted to go. I was smothered again.

———

Neither Shane nor Brad were back by five. Lloyd woke me from a two-hour nap and some strange dreams, and got me out of the room by checkout. I stumbled down to the street to meet Marcella and the kids. The bottom half of Andrew's face was purple. They'd gone to a Zippy Mart for yet more Pampers and snacks, and Andrew went wild in the Kool-Aid.

"I got in trouble," he said, proudly showing off his purple hands.

"I turned my back for ten seconds," Marcella said, "to read the ingredients in Dolly Madison cakes, and he tore open all the packs of grape and half the cherry."

"They taste the same," Andrew said.

"Cost me every cent to get him out of the store. Now I still don't have Pampers."

I gave her five dollars of blood money and said I'd watch Andrew and Hugo Jr. while she made another run. Lloyd said something about electric taping the spark plug wires so they wouldn't arc, and walked on down to Moby Dick. That left me sitting on the stoop with Hugo Jr. on my right arm, Andrew on my left leg, and the *mew*ing bowling ball bag between my feet.

"Do you have a husband?" Andrew asked.

"Not anymore."

"Do you want one? My daddy knows lots of boys who want wives."

"None for me, thanks, I'm done with husbands. Would you take your hands off my shirt? You're making me purple."

"You're already purple." He touched a big sucker of a bruise on my arm. While the nurse had been telling me which day she opened her life to Jesus Christ, she slid the pipe through my vein and poked out the other side.

"Women are hard to hit," she said. "We don't get many women in here."

As Andrew came off on my clothes, a couple of hookers drifted over to admire Hugo Jr. By the time we got done with "Is he yours?" "No, mine's cuter," three more hookers joined the huddle.

"I had a baby when I was twelve," said a pretty Spanish girl who looked fifteen. "Social Services took her. I don't even know where she lives now."

The oldest one in the crowd, who might have been my age, said, "My parents took mine. I went out to score one morning and when I came back they'd kidnapped her."

"You shouldn't have left a four-month-old alone," the Spanish girl said.

"Better alone than take her to Lactose Larry's. He abuses children. I wouldn't go there myself, but..." She kind of tapered off.

After that each hooker had to tell her story of lost children. Every single woman, without exception, had gotten pregnant in her way-early teens and lost the child, just like me. Since then they'd had countless babies, miscarriages, and abortions, not to mention boyfriends who hit, husbands who stole, and cops, customers, and pimps who committed every disgusting act in creation, but I got the idea that the first lost baby was the one they mourned over. After that they'd given up on expectations.

"Felicia would be six now," the pretty Spanish woman said. "Bobby would be twelve."

Soon the whores were sniffling like a bunch of little girls. It was weird. Andrew didn't know what to make of being surrounded by a gang of weeping women. Neither did I. They weren't anything like movie whores, which is the only kind I'd had contact with. We don't have blatant, high-profile prostitution in GroVont. I suppose if I'd been raised in a city, I might have turned into one myself. Losing a child by fifteen seemed to be the only qualification.

About the time everyone but me was good and puddle-eyed, a battleship of a white limousine rolled up to the curb. The size of my garage, it had six smoked windows down the side and four radio antennas on the corners. The driver's door opened and a coal black giant in a snappy uniform with loops on the shoulders stepped with amazing decorum to the trunk.

"Shane pulled it off," I said.

Andrew jumped from my lap. "Uncle Shane is in there?"

"This is a scam. I don't know how he arranged it, but this is a scam."

The coal black lifted Shane's wheelchair from the trunk like it was balsa. He carried it to the sidewalk, opened it, and I swear to God he pulled a white hankie from his back pocket and gave the seat a whisk.

I said, "It's a scam."

Ivory came out first. The chauffeur/professional wrestler offered her his arm and escorted her to the parking meter. She ignored the gaggle of jaw-dropping hookers.

"Thank you, Milo," she said.

"Pleased to be of service, Miss Tupelo."

Marcella walked up with her purchases as Shane's hands appeared on the door frame. As effortlessly as I lifted the baby into Marcella's arms—and in the same cradling position—the black giant lifted Shane and carried him to the waiting chair.

"Will there be anything else, sir?" the giant asked.

Shane sent me a cutesy smile, then turned back. "Tell your mother to wash her hands in mustard with a little lemon, Milo. The smell will come right out."

"She'll be happy to hear that, Mr. Rinesfoos."

Shane rolled over to the parking meter. "Remember what I

said about vocational-technical school, Ivory. You're too much a lady for this business."

Ivory Tupelo couldn't resist a glance at the assembled hookers. You could tell her life was made. Whatever had happened would be worked into every conversation from tomorrow till the day she died of old age in a rest home. But right now Ivory had one more moment to play it aloof. "Thank you, Mr. Rinesfoos. I'm sure that because of you I shall stop being a morning whore and make something useful out of my life."

Shane reached for her hand and brought it to his lips. After applying a light kiss, he said, "Miss Tupelo, it has been a lovely day."

Frankly, I could have shit.

35

MARCELLA, ANDREW, AND I WALKED AND SHANE ROLLED A
block in silence before I couldn't stand it anymore. I whined,
"Because of you I will stop being a morning whore and make
something useful of my life."

"Ivory is actually a very talented young lady," Shane said,
although he didn't explain what that meant.

"Milo's mother cooks at an Italian restaurant on Beale
Street. She likes the work, only the odor of garlic adheres to
her fingers. Of course, I solved the problem."

Marcella asked the question I would have died before asking.
"Did you really see Elvis Presley?"

"We played miniature golf," Shane said. "He has an
eighteen-hole course embedded in the living room carpet."

Andrew caromed down the sidewalk, bouncing from parking
meters to building walls and back. He shouted, "I know Elvis
Presley. He goes to my school. His mother bought him a ten-
speed, but my mother's mean and won't buy me one."

Marcella picked her way through a pile of urban squalor
garbage spilling from a knocked-over trash can. "Was his
wife nice?"

"Priscilla is genteel as a southern breeze, refined as Hawaiian
sugar. She's even more gracious than when I dated her."

Which reminded me of a hole in Shane's story. "I read where she was fourteen when she married Elvis. How old was Priscilla when you two dated?"

Shane ignored me. I knew he would. "Lunch was black caviar on toast, with peaches and cream," he said. "The lawns are divine."

I crossed over another passed-out wino, careful not to step in at least two visible body excretions. Like me, he had a Band-Aid sideways on his arm. "Hey, divine, did your good buddy Elvis loan us any money?"

Shane stopped the chair and swung it to face me. His head kind of twitched constantly now instead of the bob motion of a few days ago. "Of course not. He tried to press a thousand dollars on me, but I refused. Using Elvis for monetary gain would taint the purity of our memories."

I held out my bruised arm. "I tainted myself for fourteen bucks, it wouldn't have hurt you to drop your pride a notch. Not that I believe for an instant you actually luncheoned with the Presleys."

His whole body twitched, except the legs. "Shane Rinesfoos never drops his pride."

Andrew marched over to the unconscious wino and stomped on his hand. The wino screamed, rolled over, and resumed sleeping on his back. Andrew looked at me, his face a sunbeam. "This one's not dead yet."

———

When we got back to Moby Dick, Lloyd was talking with the parking lot attendant, not the one we'd beer-bribed that morning. This attendant wanted his own bribe. He said our time was up and we were hogging two spaces and the owner of the lot might show up any minute, which would get him in trouble because we didn't have a ticket or a pass or something.

I searched the back end and found Brad's art pad on the pile of coverless magazines. "Brad wouldn't leave his pictures behind if he planned to ditch us," I said.

Lloyd rubbed his forehead with the bill of his cat hat. "If we wait for him, it'll cost us more than we made by stopping."

For a change, I wasn't in favor of dumping people. "We can't drive off and leave him. Brad looks at us as family."

"He only joined up yesterday," Shane said.

"Some people latch on fast."

Andrew shouted, "If we run away from Owsley, I'll break windows."

"Brad," Marcella corrected him.

"Who's Brad?"

So Lloyd rummaged through the horse trailer and came out with two more cases. The lug of an attendant hefted them up on one shoulder, but he didn't seem in any hurry to go away—just stood there looking at Moby Dick. Finally he said, "Even with these you've got to split by midnight. That's when the owner drops by to check on the lot."

Split. The clown said *split.* "You told us he might show up any minute," I said.

"He might, but it's more likely at midnight."

Lloyd turned to me. You could tell he was sad about the deal. "We can't wait longer than that anyway, Maurey."

"Brad's not used to cities. What if he gets mugged or arrested or picked up by perverts?"

Shane did the *huh* sound. "Brad's a lad who can take care of himself in a tight spot. Reminds me somewhat of myself when I was young."

"You were never young," I said.

Marcella took me literally. "Yes, he was. We were both young once." That may be Marcella's tragic flaw: she has no understanding of sarcasm.

———

While we waited she decided to mend all the clothes in the junk pile. There must have been a hundred shirts, slacks, coats, every stitch of it worn out and unwearable. Most of the rags didn't even fit anyone in the troupe, although she did dig out a cotton pullover shirt with three-quarter sleeves that covered my bruise.

"You think I should style my hair?" she asked. "Annette Gilliam's cousin is a beautician. Maybe if my hairdo had been modern as Annette Gilliam's, Hugo wouldn't have strayed."

"The last time I changed hairdos, I gave myself a crew cut."

Marcella tucked a loose strand back into her bun. "You always look like a model in *Redbook*, Maurey. Next to you, I feel frumpy."

Andrew played a pretend baseball game by throwing a tennis ball against the cinder-block wall. He kept a running commentary going under his breath, every now and then shouting *"Home run!"* or *"Slide, you jerk"* or *"In your face, ump."*

Shane pulled out his harmonica to play "Love Me Tender" seven hundred times. Felt like seven hundred, anyway. Between riffs he fabricated bizarre details to go with his Elvis story. "He has a servant whose only job is to dust his shoulders for dandruff...Priscilla bathes in warm champagne...I shouldn't tell you this, but the sideburns are tiny toupees."

Lloyd had spent almost all his blood money on STP Oil Treatment and various other cleaners, fluids, and lubricants. Every few minutes he had me turn the key or rev the accelerator, push in the clutch, pull out the choke. The engine always sounded the same to me.

Personally, I was antsy—nervous stomach. Felt the way you do when the signs are all there that your period is about to happen, but it's a week late and you've fooled around without protection. I sat on the side loading door ledge and studied Brad's art pad. The only new picture was me, and I'd just as soon he'd stuck with bald-legged eagles. I suppose the drawing looked vaguely like me—Marcella said it was a spit image—but if so, I'd lost cheekbones and gained pouches. The woman in the picture looked forty. I don't look forty. I'm twenty-two. Twenty-two is when a woman should be at her peak. The woman in the picture was way past her peak.

"When you were an alcoholic, what's the worst thing you ever did to get a bottle?" I asked Shane.

He knocked spit from the harmonica onto the ground. "Why do you ask?"

"I need perspective here."

"You need validation that you aren't a real alcoholic because you've never done anything as disgusting as I have."

"Something like that."

Lloyd's voice came from under the hood. "I pawned Sharon's hope chest. Her grandfather built it himself for a tenth birthday present, and one Sunday while she was in church I threw a brick through a window and took the chest down to the Strip and hocked it. Bought me a fifth of gin."

"Why'd you break the window?"

"I told Sharon the chest was stolen by migrants." His head came out of the hood. "She knew better."

Shane played a few bars of "Love Me Tender." He stared at the setting sun off toward the Mississippi River, then he cleared his throat with a bullfrog pop. "Juarez, Mexico. Cinco de Mayo, 1968. I was broke and ill, going through the DTs. You've never gone through DTs, Maurey"—he called me Maurey—"they're worse than whatever your imagination has constructed them to be. I traded my wheelchair for a bottle of mescal."

"Jesus."

"The day was hot as my hell and the old man I traded with left me lying in the dirt street. I pulled myself under a taxi and drank the whole bottle."

"What happened?"

He shrugged. "Man who owned the taxi was AA. He showed me the choice between dying and living. You may not believe it now, but considering the alternative, living can be a lot of fun."

———

After dark Shane wheeled off to find a pay phone and order a pizza. Didn't bother to ask anyone what kind they wanted, just rolled himself away into the dark. I was reading Andrew cartoons from a *New Yorker* magazine while Marcella fussed with Hugo Jr. and Lloyd sat in the driver's seat, staring at a photograph of Sharon.

Six-year-olds from Dumas have trouble relating to *New Yorker* humor. "You ever consider letting her go and getting on with your life?" I asked Lloyd.

"No."

A three-quarter waxing moon came up through the buildings. By moonlight Moby Dick took on a fuzzy glow, as if the white paint had been mixed with Woolite. The ambulance looked more like a loaf-shaped space module than either a whale or an ambulance. I'd about decided to hell with subtle ethical shades, money is money and whiskey is whiskey, and I needed whiskey more than I needed money. My guts felt like I was ovulating a baseball.

I deserved a drink for letting that sadistic Jesus freak stab me. I deserved a drink because I hadn't had one yet.

Shane appeared out of the dark, whistling "Heartbreak Hotel." He seemed in a good mood. I don't know why, none of the rest of us were. "Sausage and pineapple, it will be magnificent. They wouldn't deliver to a parking lot until I personally guaranteed a five-dollar tip."

Lloyd's sad eyes pulled away from Sharon. "How you planning to pay for this sausage-and-pineapple pizza?"

Maybe black caviar on toast for lunch makes a person happy. Shane's voice carried a lilt that had been missing since Amarillo.

"We'll offer the delivery boy a six-pack. East Coast children go rabid at the sight of Coors."

"Did you see Hugo Sr. while you were out there?" Marcella asked. "I'm worried about him."

"That husband of yours is the Phantom. You never see the Phantom until he's least expected, yet he knows your every move," Shane said.

"Like Jesus," Andrew crowed.

Marcella corrected. "Daddy is not Jesus."

Lloyd put Sharon back in his overall's breast pocket. "I wish you wouldn't buy things until we're sure they take beer."

"They'll take beer all right. Trust me."

If I'd had a brain, that very moment I would have leapt from Moby Dick and run like the wind for the nearest liquor store. No one you can trust says "Trust me."

———

The kid who delivered the pizza drove up in a Mazda mini-truck with no doors and a red rag stuffed in the gas tank hole. He looked Brad's age, wore thick horn-rims, both suspenders, and a belt, and he wouldn't have touched a bottle of Coors for love or money.

"No beer. That's nine dollars twenty cents cash, plus the five-dollar tip you promised."

Shane held a bottle with one hand on the bottom and the other in back like on "Truth or Consequences" when the girl wanted to showcase a prize. He'd started the bidding with a six-pack and was already up to three cases. "You can market three cases for a hundred and twenty big ones. This is Coors, Rocky Mountain spring water, so rare you can't buy it in Tennessee for any price."

"My boss wants money, not beer. Now cough up fourteen dollars twenty cents or—"

"Or what, punk?" Shane growled.

Lloyd came over and lifted the pizza from Shane's lap. Shane groaned as Lloyd turned and held the box out to the boy. "You'll have to take it back. Here's three dollars for your trouble. That's all I've got."

The kid didn't touch either pizza or money. "Listen, mister, no returns. I have to pay for every pizza I take out."

I was high-strung enough without this crap. "We don't have money, peterhead. It's Coors or take it back. Those are the choices."

He blinked really fast. I've never seen such a quick blinker in my life. The glasses magnified the blinks so they looked like wings on a hummingbird. "I have one other choice. See that police car down there?"

We all turned in the direction of the Calhoun Arms, where a white City of Memphis Chevy idled against the curb with a hooker leaning in the window.

"Officer Hazen is a steady customer of mine. If I tell him a pack of hicks with a trailer full of illegal alcohol stiffed me for a pizza, he's going to be real angry."

"Hicks." Shane covered his heart with his hand. "The extortionist called us hicks."

Lloyd rubbed his forehead and leg at the same time. Looked like Pinocchio in overalls. "Kid, we don't have money."

Blink-blink. "Fourteen twenty or jail."

The screw in my lower back drilled through another half

inch of spine. I said, "Shit. I knew this would happen. You owe me one, fatso. You owe me about a dozen."

Shane wasn't contrite at all—just grinned and yanked the pizza box out of Lloyd's hands. He said, "You'll thank me someday."

"Over your dead body."

I counted out the nine dollars. "There's twenty cents here somewhere, let me look in the glove compartment."

"And my five-dollar tip."

What I wouldn't give for Charley and one bullet. "You threaten us with jail and now you expect a tip?"

"The man who called promised a five-dollar tip."

"If I had five dollars, I'd stick it up your ass."

I needed a drink. The kid was about to cry. All he could get out was a choked "Officer Hazen."

Lloyd stepped between us. Lloyd was always stepping between pissed-off people—a regular human buffer zone. "Take this three dollars as a tip. That leaves us without a dime. You should be satisfied with breaking us."

Blink-blink. "I was promised five."

"You can settle for twelve and leave or cause our arrest and end up with nothing."

Shane opened the box. "Balderdash, they left off the pineapple."

———

Lloyd decided we better hit the road. "That kid'll get three blocks and come back looking for his cop friend," he said.

Marcella gave Andrew a piece, but he wanted a bigger one. "Why would he do such a thing?" she asked. "He already has the money."

"Because he's that kind of person. In his mind we cheated him."

Andrew decided the bigger one was too big and the only

piece for him was the one Shane was eating. Shane said, "Forget it," and Andrew started crying, said he wouldn't eat any, then, and the pizza was stupid.

Shane offered me a piece, but I wouldn't touch the damn pizza. I said, "Brad's got two more hours. You said we could wait."

Lloyd's hand traveled to his breast pocket where Sharon's picture lay. He patted it the way people who have given up smoking will when they forget they've given up smoking. "We can't handle police questions, Maurey. Brad hasn't come back all day. Two more hours is too big a risk."

To be honest, I had a higher priority than Brad. Alcohol does that. When you need it, other loyalties fly right out the window. "Can we stop at the first liquor store and trade some Coors for a bottle? A half-pint will hold me over."

Lloyd didn't make me beg. I have to give him that much. Never once the whole trip did he make me beg. "Sure," he said. "We'll get you a bottle."

36

WHAT MAKES PEOPLE FALL IN LOVE WITH SPECIFIC OTHER people? Sam Callahan says it's a combination of timing and brain waves. Our brain waves snap into place with other random brain waves like pieces of a jigsaw puzzle. And we fit with an amazing variety of people the same as one jigsaw piece fits with different-shaped pieces depending on which side they lock into. Only the jigsaw metaphor crashes at this point because human brain waves change every so often, so people who click like magic the moment they meet can fall in love, get married, and seven years later be total strangers.

Sam says the way to deal with romance is to find someone you fit with on the passion level, then try like hell to become friends before the irrational, fluttery-heart stuff wears off.

Park and I snapped together. When I was with him my stomach trembled, I hyperventilated, and my crotch put out enough lubrication to grease a pickup truck—STP Vagina Treatment. No logical reason existed for basing the worth of my life on this pale, curly-headed, soft-fingered sophomore. He was from the East Coast, didn't know squat about horses, and, same as Sam Callahan and Lloyd Carbonneau, Park wore his vulnerability like a shirt. If you ask me, guilelessness for its own sake is a form of guile.

Probably, if I'd been a virgin when Park and I met, we would be positioning ourselves for a divorce about now— fighting over who gets the Dutch oven and the Remington prints and how much I'm gouging him for child support. We'd have split up over his mother, I bet. Or my alcoholism. In-laws and alcoholism are God's gift to lawyers.

You notice I admitted to alcoholism there.

Breakthrough! Breakthrough!

First they say it's a disease, not a character flaw, then they say admitting you have it is half the battle. Admitting you have cancer isn't half the battle. Or mumps. If this is nothing but a disease, what does the sick person's stance toward it matter? Huh?

Alcoholics don't all expire on the sidewalk in a pool of vomit. Hardly any of them do. Some alcoholics lead rich, full lives surrounded by love and family. Witness Errol Flynn, W. C. Fields, and Calamity Jane. Okay, forget Calamity Jane.

They can't take your children simply because you drink through Paul Harvey and masturbate. I could dry out—hide up in the mountains and live off fish and rabbits and huckle-berries for the summer while my body detoxed. By reducing all conflict to survival I could sweat out the poison as I grow spiritually and find a private peace.

If whoever's in charge let me return to Go, collect my two hundred dollars, and start again, I could control it this time. The bad stuff snuck up on me before; now I'd know the signs of slippage. Given another chance, I would make definite rules for myself—a one-pint limit with no drinking before Auburn went to bed at night. Who could ask for more than that?

There on Highway 64, rolling through the darkness of Tennessee, sipping discreetly on my half-pint of George Dickel, I made a pact with God: Give me back Auburn and I'll never touch alcohol while he's awake. I will stay in control. What a deal. I get what I want—my baby and a relationship with Yukon Jack—and God gets what he wants—a good mom.

The moon illuminated a countryside littered by countless varieties of trees and houses that glowed silver behind long front porches and open windows with no curtains. I could see the rooms the people lived in, the couches and flickering television sets. As Moby Dick wallowed east the dash lights threw a shadow from Lloyd's upper lip across his nose. When he blinked the spider lines around his eyes glittered.

I felt good about admitting to alcoholism and making the covenant with God, and I almost told Lloyd, but the nice feeling was too precarious. Lloyd might scoff. He might say "I used to make deals with God," as if everything I tried to cope with the situation was old hat.

Reformed people are such a pain. "I did it, so you can." How the hell do they know that? I can stand up on a galloping horse; Lloyd can't. I can make a baby; Lloyd can't. Personal capabilities are highly individualistic. Lloyd was weak and couldn't control himself, so he assumed I couldn't control myself, either. With him, drinking had to be all or nothing. But I wasn't Lloyd; I was capable of compromise.

———

Dad used to say I was stubborn as a hare-lipped mule— one of those nifty yet basically meaningless phrases he learned from his father, who learned it from his father, and so on back into the Middle Ages. Ever notice how the stupid stuff is passed on but the valuable lessons must be relearned by each generation?

Anyhow, every Pierce family reunion Dad told this story about how he gave me a Red Ryder BB rifle for my fifth

Christmas. Wyoming's one of those places where it's considered normal for Santa Claus to bring guns to little girls. I was riding horses solo at four. I guess Dad figured I might as well be shooting animals at five.

An hour after I unwrapped gifts I was *pow-pow*ing at Petey, and Dad told me always take for granted the weapon is loaded.

I said, "It's not loaded."

Dad said, "That doesn't matter. Always pretend it is, and never point it at a person."

I said, "I'll point it at Petey if I want to."

Same conversation you read in the newspaper next to a photo of a redneck with his head blown apart. In my case, Dad took the gun away and I ran to my room and wailed all morning, screaming angry denunciations of all my presents, my parents, and Christmas itself. Bad as Andrew.

Finally Dad decided I'd learned my lesson and gave back my rifle. I said, "Any numbskull knows this gun's not loaded," and fired a round through Mom's beehive hairdo into an angel ornament atop the Christmas tree.

That's the last I saw of my Red Ryder rifle. Looking back, it seems fate that any girl who rides at four and shoots (once, anyway) at five will get pregnant at thirteen. Thirteen is the age when Mom and I stopped laughing when Dad came to the part of the story where he said, "That's the day Maurey nailed her mother and an angel with a single bullet."

———

I woke up in a campground beside a dull silver river somewhere in Tennessee. The campground was deserted except for a pickup camper next to us and a station wagon surrounded by five Boy Scout tents. Birds chirped like mad, and down by the river a raccoon waddled along a trail, stopping now and then to sniff the air.

Lloyd was asleep with his head back and his hands on the steering wheel. Shane's rumble was louder than ever; his sleeping lungs had taken on the grunt of a bugling elk. If I told people around here Shane sounded like a bugling elk, they would say "Huh?" I missed Wyoming. I missed my own bed and my fuzzy blue bathrobe and the window seat where I could look out at the mountains. If anything, Tennessee had more trees than Arkansas. Made me claustrophobic.

The camper door opened and a large, hairy man came out, stretched, and made chew motions with his mouth. He had on slacks but no shirt or shoes. He faced the horse trailer, unzipped himself, and started peeing—didn't bother checking to see if anyone else was awake and watching.

"You'd think he would cover himself," Lloyd said.

"You awake?"

"I don't care where he is, a man should shield himself when he urinates."

"Dad said a man should be able to leak off his porch in the morning without shame."

"There's a difference between without shame and showing off."

The hairy man went an awful long time—sounded like a horse going on gravel. With his free hand he rubbed the hair on his chest, then scratched his beard. Only after shaking his thing twice and zipping it back up did he look around and see me. There was no sign of embarrassment, even though he must have known I'd watched. He stared at me a long time, almost as long as he'd peed, then he went back to the camper. He opened the door, but before climbing inside he stooped to throw a rock at the raccoon. Missed by two feet.

"Rude fella," Lloyd said.

The truck was an off yellow with Tennessee plates and half-bald tires. "Seemed okay to me."

"Well, look at that," Lloyd said.

Hugo Sr.'s Oldsmobile pulled off the highway and stopped fifty yards or so downstream. Brad got out the passenger side. I *whooped* and jumped out the door. I don't know why I was so glad to see the kid, it's not like we went way back or anything. It's just that I felt responsible, what with helping him escape Freedom and cutting his hair and all. Losing him was a minor form of losing Auburn and Shannon.

Brad waved so long to Hugo Sr. and walked toward us carrying a brown paper sack. You could tell he was happy to be home. Moby Dick's side blew open and Andrew flew out. He ran down to Brad, yelling, "The grown-ups ditched you. I told them I'd break windows if they did, but after pizza they ditched you anyway. They never listen to me."

Everyone's reaction was way overblown, considering we hardly knew each other. Shane grinned and bobbed, Lloyd waved a thank-you to Hugo Sr., Marcella straightened a place in the junk pile for Brad to sit.

He'd sold his hair. Walked way out in the suburbs to a wig joint and sold the sunshine-colored mane. The sack was full of presents—spark plug wires for Lloyd, Oreos for Shane, a stack of Marvel comics for Andrew, and a box of pink bubble bath for Marcella.

Marcella was amazed. "No one ever gave me toiletries before. Every year I ask, but Hugo Sr. gets me scissors or Tupperware or something he thinks I need. How'd you find him?"

"He was sitting in the parking lot. Said he knew y'all had left without me, so he waited." Brad turned to Marcella. "He feels real bad about Annette Gilliam."

Marcella's hands did a nervous twisting thing. "You're good with men, Maurey. What should I do?"

I'm good with men? "Let him feel bad. We all feel bad— why should Hugo be different?"

Brad dug into the bottom of the bag and came up with a fifth of Yukon Jack. "Is this your brand?"

I could have kissed the boy. Instead, I kissed the bottle.

———

Dear Dad,

People are trying to make me want things I swore off and swear off things I want, i.e. family and whiskey. I expressed enthusiasm this morning and afterwards floundered in guilt that I can feel joy without Auburn. What kind of mother am I? What kind of father were you? How should I behave?

Get your ass back here,
Your daughter

———

As morning wore on, I found myself free-falling into depression. For one thing, I'd missed Paul Harvey. And for the other thing, I was irritated with Moby Dick's little gang of lost souls. Didn't they know we were almost to the destination? What then? I'd go on to Greensboro to find Sam Callahan and Shannon, Lloyd was off to Florida searching for the holy grail or whatever, Lord knows what would happen to Brad. I'd lost everyone I ever cared for, and now, after this bunch tricked me into liking them, it was fixing to happen again. As always, nobody gave a flying hoot. They all acted as if we were driving to the moon and back. I was tempted to find a bus stop and bail out.

"Most people are unaware that Hank Williams had leukemia when he passed away," Shane said. "A doctor in Mobile prescribed heroin to kill the pain, and Hank overdosed, thus making him the first superstar, white superstar, anyway, to die of drugs."

"What about Jean Harlow?" I asked.

"Jean Harlow was a tramp."

Brad offered to buy lunch with what was left from the hair sale. Lloyd pulled Moby Dick into a Sonic drive-in on the main strip in Pulaski. Because of the trailer, we had to park in the end slot, and even then our butt stuck out on the highway shoulder. A wide-load truck could have creamed the Coors.

Everyone but me had cheeseburgers and Tater Tots, which are nothing but cardboard shredded up, then pressed into lumps. Because I was depressed I ordered a chocolate malt to chase the Jack with. Chocolate malts in those drive-ins aren't ice cream at all but some runny poop-colored chemical that oozes from a machine. I named the bottle Injun Joe after a character in *Huckleberry Finn* because Mark Twain named himself after a unit of depth in the Mississippi River.

I passed Brad his Tater Tot boat and the little packets of ketchup. "Lloyd said they don't sell Yukon Jack down here. It's illegal, like Coors."

"Right," Brad said. He was checking out the carhop who was checking out him. Short hair hadn't killed off his allure.

"How'd you find this bottle, then?"

Wasn't easy to check out the carhop from the back end of an ambulance. Brad had to pretzel himself and lean between the front seats, pretending to need a napkin. "My education wasn't a complete bust back in Comanche. If it's illegal, I can score."

I don't criticize younger women as a rule, but the carhop could have used a flea collar. Brad smiled at her and leaned back. "Can I have the cat?"

I said, "She's a dog."

"No." He held up the half-whiskered kitten. "This cat. I never had a pet."

Andrew yelled, *"Mine,"* spilled his Orange Crush, and burst into tears. Hugo Jr. joined in. In the confusion the hairy man parked his pickup camper opposite us, facing me.

"Here." I handed Andrew my malt. I wasn't hungry anyway. Marcella soothed Andrew in her lap while he sucked down my chocolate-flavored chemical stuff.

"It would be real Christian of you to share your kitty with Brad. I'm sure he'd let you play with him any time you want," Marcella said.

"My kitty!"

"You have not bothered to name the animal," Shane pointed out. "He's not legally yours if you haven't named him." Andrew eyed Shane with suspicion. Shane lifted his hands, palms up, as if the matter were out of his control. "That's the law, buddy. It's not your cat."

"My name's not Buddy."

"Either let Brad keep the cat or give me back my malt," I said. The malt won.

Brad held the cat in his lap and fed it a Tater Tot. The cat dropped the tot, then made scratches on Brad's leg, trying to bury it. "I'll name him Merle," Brad said.

I was touched. "That's my name."

"I know."

I started to ask how he knew but skipped it since I'd probably told him during a blackout. Blackouts put drinkers at such a disadvantage. One time I called Delilah Talbot to say I wouldn't be over that night to watch *The Carol Burnett Show* because I was stuck in Jackson with a broken car, then the next day I told her I'd missed the show because I had the flu and the phone was out of order. Even Delilah saw the discrepancy.

"What is that shady character staring at?" Shane asked.

I looked out the front windshield across the carhop island into the eyes of the hairy man. He had fierce eyebrows.

"He pissed on the trailer this morning," Lloyd said. "Maurey likes him."

"I do not."

"You said he seems okay."

"Seems okay doesn't mean I like him."

Shane clucked with his tongue. "Does if you have observed his genitalia."

———

The man in the pickup wore a short-sleeved Hawaiian shirt open at the neck so you could see hair bubbling up from his chest. He chewed gum and his fingers tapped a rhythm on the steering wheel, which I took to mean he was listening to the radio with his engine off. The black hair on his head wasn't exactly curly, but it sure wasn't straight. It grew all over the place the way it grows on real smart men like Einstein, Schweitzer, or Kurt Vonnegut. My dad had the same hair.

"Wouldn't you hate being stuck on a chain gang with that fellow?" Shane said.

I took a slug of Injun Joe. "What's the matter with him? You don't make such a hot first impression yourself."

"If that primate dated my daughter, I wouldn't allow him in the door or her out. I better not catch you encouraging his affections."

Injun Joe made me overreact. "Who are you to tell me what to do?"

"I'm the one of us with fit judgment."

"To hell with your fit judgment. If I want that man, or any other man, I'll take him. Who made you my guardian?"

"Someone has to do it, young lady. Lord knows you can't take care of yourself."

"Fuck you, Shane." Right away I felt bad about saying "fuck" in front of Andrew, but, Jesus, I never let my own father tell me who not to sleep with. I'd be damned if I'd listen to an old, fat cripple. I hadn't even considered encouraging the hairy man's affections until Shane told me not to. Before that he was just another cute guy like you see across a parking lot somewhere and waste five seconds on in fantasy. But one more crack from Shane and I'd have switched vehicles.

Shane knew it, too. As I glared at him he set down his Coke, dug around for that stupid knife of his, and busily went into trimming his toenails. Brad stared at me as if I might bolt. Everyone else pretended to ignore me the way you pretend to ignore a horse who may or may not be fixing to kick the tar out of you.

I looked from Shane to Lloyd to the man in the truck. He acknowledged my look without a smile. Keeping my eyes burning on his, I brought Injun Joe to my mouth and drank.

37

ONE SPRING MORNING WHEN I WAS THIRTEEN AND FIVE MONTHS pregnant, Sam Callahan and I rode our bikes from town up to the TM ranch. Estelle had just foaled and Dad let me name the colt, so I named her Dad, kind of like Brad naming the kitten Merle.

Sam and I played around Miner Creek a couple hours, then I told him it was time to break our secret to Dad and he should ride home alone, that I would be along later. As I walked across the west pasture my stomach got all tight and nervous. Telling your father you're pregnant must be the high-stress moment of a girl's teenage years.

I found Buddy—Dad—in the kitchen cleaning up after his lunch. One plate, one coffee cup, and one fork sat in the drainer. Dad was wiping his hands on a towel, looking out the window toward the horses when I told him I was pregnant. At first, I didn't think he heard, so I repeated it.

"Dad, I'm going to have a baby."

He turned and walked to the table, where he sat in one of the straight-backed chairs. With that beard, you never could tell what he was thinking.

"What do you want from me?" he asked.

I moved forward a half step. "I was hoping you'd hold me and tell me it's going to be okay."

He exhaled so sharply the hairs on his upper lip jumped. "Is it that kid from this morning?"

"Yes."

For the first time I could remember, Dad's posture made him appear tired. "Guess I'll have to whip him."

"It's not Sam's fault. I made him do it." Dad looked at the linoleum on the table while I gave him a two-minute summary of the last year and how I came to this point. I left out the near abortion.

After I stopped talking we slipped into a long silence. Dad looked at the table; I looked at his hands on his legs. The right thumbnail was dark purple. Some blood or placenta or something stuck to his left wrist. The whole time he sat and I stood, neither of his hands moved a muscle.

Dad's throat finally rumbled and he spoke. "Does your mother know?"

"I think so."

He looked back out the window. "I never thought I'd raise a child to grow up a slut."

I lost my breath. "Daddy."

He turned and looked directly at me. He said, "You are a whore, Maurey. I'm ashamed to call you daughter."

———

The far side of Chattanooga Lloyd announced we needed gas, although I don't know how he knew since the gas gauge and mileage doogie were both broken. I guess after Lloyd lost his wife, then his bottle, he'd bonded with his car. You have to bond with something.

The rest of us waited in near darkness in the parking lot of Junior's Truck Stop and Cafe while he went inside to negotiate. I'm not a good waiter, especially when I've been drinking. I get antsy and need to take action—any action. I'd rather take the wrong action than piddle my time away waiting for something to happen.

Andrew was whiny and Shane was back on his harmonica. He'd played the Elvis medley all day to the point where I was dangerously close to fed up. I offered to hold Hugo Jr., but Marcella said, "No, thanks." She knew I'd been drinking. People treat me different when I've been drinking, even when I act the same.

Lloyd finally came back to say he'd traded three cases of Coors for a tank of gas and six chicken-fried steaks with soup or salad and potatoes.

"I don't feel an affinity for chicken-fried steak," Shane said.

Andrew threw a D-volt battery against the ambulance wall. "I hate chicken-fry steak."

"I'll eat yours," Brad said.

Andrew broke down in tears. "He's stealing my supper." Typical outing with the Moby Dick gang.

The first door we tried was too narrow for Shane's chair, so we had to go way the hell and back around by the diesel pumps to get him inside. Whoever builds buildings is prejudiced against people with fixed dimensions.

As we turned Shane around to yank him up the double steps, he nodded in the direction of the TRUCKER'S ONLY overnight lot. "Speaking of the devil."

"What devil?" Brad asked.

"Maurey's."

I knew before I looked, it was the off-yellow pickup camper. I didn't say anything. This dude showing up all the time was a little eerie, and partway through my afternoon drinking bout I'd decided not to nail him just to spite Shane. He was probably okay and wondering why we were following him, but I'd been nailed by enough weirdos not to take chances. No more sleeping with non-friends.

"Freedom's Dallas connection drives a truck like that," Brad said.

Shane said, "Wouldn't surprise me if he keeps a corpse in the camper." I fought the urge to push Shane off the steps.

At the booth Brad and Andrew spat over who got to sit on the inside by the jukebox wheel. I traded sides with Andrew, and Marcella moved to the aisle so both of them could be on the wall, but that hacked off Andrew because he hated sitting next to his mother. Life with kids is complicated. I decided to hole up in the John until the group sorted out seating arrangements.

"Order me coffee," I said as I slid out the booth.

"Can your system take it?" Shane asked.

In the bathroom I did the mirror routine again. Gruesome, but not terminal. I didn't look all that drunk. The bruise on my arm was turning brackish purple outlined by lime green. Otherwise, my eyes were semi-clear and my hair combed, sort of. Considering all I'd been through, Shane had no right to give me guff. The turd. Wasn't a thing wrong with me a three-day nap wouldn't fix.

I tried to add up the days. Mother's Day, then Monday when they stole my Auburn. I was unconscious till Friday and left GroVont Monday night. Since then, there'd been two showers, one in Amarillo and one in Memphis. That made today Wednesday, but I didn't think so. Somewhere I'd miscounted.

"What day is this?" I asked back at the booth. Lloyd had finished gassing up and was plopped down in my place. I had to scoot in with Marcella, Hugo Jr., and Andrew.

"See that fellow behind the cash register?" Lloyd asked. I turned to look at an angular midlevel-management type in a blue suit and white tie with a pitch-black dress shirt. His neck had a bad rash spreading up from the collar. Lloyd continued, "That's the shift manager I traded the Coors with. How long has he been on the phone?"

Brad said, "Saturday."

I thought he was kidding. Coming back from the can, I'd upped my guess to Thursday, possibly even Friday, but Saturday? "Are you sure?" I asked.

Brad nodded. "No school today."

Shane adjusted his body in the chair. "Maurey, are you cognizant to the fact that you are sloshed out of your gourd?"

"That's a damned lie."

"I don't like the way he's watching us and talking on the phone at the same time," Lloyd said.

Shane rotated his chair so he could see the situation. When the manager realized we were staring at him, his face went the color of his rash and he looked quickly at the floor.

"The gentleman is definitely discussing us with someone," Shane said.

Marcella made Andrew stop screwing around with the salt and pepper shakers. "Sure, it's Saturday," she said. "Jewish people go to church on Saturday. Everybody else goes on Sunday."

"We should move along now," Lloyd said.

"Personally, I believe in better-safe-than-sorry," Shane said, which wasn't true. "We shall reach Granma's by midnight. I'm certain she will insist on feeding us."

Shane spun his chair and headed for the diesel doors. Lloyd stood up. "Don't run, but let us leave as quickly as possible."

Andrew set up a howl. "I'm hungry."

"We have to go," Marcella said. "There's graham crackers in the ambulance. You can have those."

"I want chicken fry!"

I said, "Shut up."

The manager abandoned the phone and hustled over. "Is there anything I can help you people with, a larger booth, perhaps?" Some guys are totally out of place in a suit. They look like they're wearing a costume, Halloween or something.

"We have to be leaving," Lloyd said.

"But you haven't finished your meals. You haven't started your meals." He sucked up to Andrew. "How would it be if I served complimentary cherry pie for everyone."

Andrew was happy—"Yea!"—but the rest of us moved out fast. Any man offering free pie has an ulterior motive. Brad and I followed Shane the long way while Marcella carried one kid and dragged the other one after Lloyd. The manager couldn't decide who to try to stop.

"What's our problem?" Brad asked as we pushed Shane past the lit pumps.

"I imagine he telephoned the police. He looked like the scuzzy type," Shane said.

"I am not sloshed out of my gourd."

38

THE PATROL CAR CAUGHT US ON A DARK ROAD A COUPLE miles west and south of Junior's. Lloyd had thought we stood a better chance doubling back toward Chattanooga where there were more side streets, but it didn't do any good. On a straightaway at the bottom of a vine-covered hill Lloyd glanced in his side mirror and said, "Rats." Red-and-blue flashing lights reflected off his face.

"What is it?" Marcella asked.

Lloyd stopped the ambulance and sat there a moment, rubbing his hand on his overalls leg. "Everyone stay put. Whatever happens, let me handle it." He gave me a meaningful look. I shrugged. "No sweat."

After Lloyd slammed the door, I hit Injun Joe a big slug, then waited maybe ten seconds before slipping out. Behind me I heard Shane call something unintelligible that ended in "*fool.*"

Even though the moon was nearly full, the low cloud cover made for a milky-dark borrow ditch. I walked quietly along Moby Dick and the trailer and came up behind the policemen. The one shaped like a 7Up bottle had his flashlight beam in Lloyd's face while the short, slim guy examined my trailer. They were doing that smug patter cops do when they know you're nailed.

"Hey, Bernard, you ever seen anything like this? They got a horse on the license plate."

The big one was considerably older. "Probably because that's a horse trailer, A.B."

"I never met anyone from Wyoming. I heard cowboys out there fuck sheep."

"You fuck sheep?" Bernard asked.

Lloyd said, "No."

"He's lying," A.B. said. "All cowboys fuck sheep. I bet his mama was a sheep." A.B. walked off toward Moby Dick. I heard him up by the hitch. "I bet he's got himself a trailer chock full of illegal aliens."

"Or whores," Bernard said. He kept his flashlight in Lloyd's eyes. "We don't hanker to whores in Hamilton County. This ain't Nashville."

Lloyd didn't try to shield his eyes from the blinding light. His voice was resigned. "We're not carrying illegal aliens or whores."

"Must be contraband, then," Bernard said. His light traveled down Lloyd's body. "Drugs. Them's just the kind of shoes drug smugglers wear."

A.B. opened Moby Dick. "We could radio for the dogs. Sniff out their marijuana."

"We're not hauling marijuana," Lloyd said.

Bernard flipped up the bolt in the trailer's double doors. "Let's see what illegal substances you are hauling."

I said, "Beer."

Bernard dropped the flashlight, twirled, yelled "*Shit*," and pointed his gun at me. "Who the hell are you?"

"It's my trailer. Put down that pistol."

A.B. called from inside the ambulance. "Bernard, we got us three kids, a mama, and a cripple back here."

Bernard answered. "We got us a crazy bitch back here."

"Watch your tongue, mister."

Lloyd sent me a look, but I wasn't in the mood. When cops act abusive, men should cooperate, women shouldn't. That's how America works. I pointed to their car. "You're Chattanooga city police. You have no jurisdiction on this road." Bernard raised his gun higher. "This is all the jurisdiction I need. You snuck up on a law officer. I could legally shoot you. Do you want that?"

"Not particularly."

"So, shut up."

A.B. hurried over. He had this little, skinny mustache no thicker than the fuzz on Sugar Cannelioski's lip. "Where'd she come from?"

I said, "Wyoming."

Bernard said, "I said shut up."

Lloyd joined in. "Shut up, Maurey."

I plowed right on through. "We're moving to North Carolina where they don't sell Coors, and I love Coors beer." Biggest lie I ever told in my life.

"So do I," A.B. said.

"Well, I filled the trailer with Coors so I could always own a taste of the mountains. It's all for personal consumption. We'll never sell a drop. You officers are welcome to a bottle if you wish."

Bernard had the posture of a pregnant woman—splayed feet, shoulders holding up too much weight, left hand resting on his gut. The right hand still pointed a pistol at me.

"We'll take more than a bottle if we wish. I think you're a smart broad." He stared directly at my breasts. "I hate smart broads. Open that trailer, A.B."

A.B. swung open the doors and two bales of straw fell out on the road.

"Looks like you're hiding something," Bernard said.

"We've got horses to feed," I said, figuring the idiot didn't know straw from hay, either.

A.B. ran his light over the batteries and tires to the stacked beer. "There she is, as promised," he said. It was worse than I expected—fifty cases, tops. Because Freedom ripped us off for three hundred dollars we'd traded away two thousand dollars' worth of Coors. I almost could have pulled off the personal consumption defense if they'd been intent on arresting us.

Which they weren't. Arresting us meant turning in the Coors as evidence, and these were good ol' southern boys. They viewed beer with a finders-keepers mentality.

Bernard holstered his gun and picked up his flashlight. "You." He motioned to Lloyd. "Inside."

"Think it'll all fit?" A.B. asked.

"If it don't, we'll make two trips."

———

They formed a bucket brigade. Lloyd brought a case to the rear of the trailer and passed it down to A.B., who carried it to Bernard, who stacked it in the backseat of the Chattanooga patrol car. I stood off to the side and felt helpless. That was my Coors those jerks were stealing. I'd gone to a lot of trouble to get that beer and keep it, and now two cracker Tennessee cops were taking it away from me. If I only had Charley, I could have tried a bulletless bluff, but I'd gotten drunk and lost him, too. All my life I'd felt helpless because all my life I'd been helpless.

Bernard was an efficient stacker. He squeezed cases in four across and three high on the seat plus another six on the floor. When the interior filled up he pulled out his keys and opened the trunk. That's when he saw me hovering in the darkness.

"Quit hiding like a nigger," he said. "You make me nervous. Go on up and stay with the others, and no funny business. I won't tolerate sneaking around."

"Yes, massah."

"Git."

I thought about running for help. A few house lights glimmered at the far end of the straightaway. One thing I'd noticed about the South is you're practically always within a mile or two of a house. Nothing like Wyoming. But what would I say to the people in the houses—"Two policemen are stealing my illegal beer. Call the cops"?

I climbed in the driver's side and sat behind the wheel.

"What's going on out there?" Marcella asked.

"They're taking the Coors."

Shane made a sound like a little dog when you step on its tail. "That's my beer. They can't steal my beer."

"Go tell them that."

"I might condone an arrest. Criminality was an accepted risk, but for lawmen to steal from us..." For once, Shane ran out of big words.

Andrew was on his feet. "We should always obey the policeman. He is our friend."

"That's a lie they teach you in the first grade," I said. "The police hate you and will hurt you whenever they can."

Popped that little sucker's bubble. He turned to Marcella for the truth, but she could hardly deny it. "Where's Hugo?" she asked.

"I suppose we lost him. He didn't expect us to double back," I said.

I studied my crew. Andrew was scared, Brad defiant. My guess is he'd been involved in rip-offs before. Marcella's hands kept traveling from Andrew to Hugo Jr. and back, either reassuring them or herself.

Shane's face was a torment of twitches. "The villains can't take all the beer. It won't fit."

"They're planning several trips. I imagine one will hold us here while the other one goes off somewhere to unload."

Shane said, "Abomination"; after that we were quiet. I found Injun Joe, but only to hold him, not to drink. Normally, I was a pint woman because real alcoholics drank fifths and I wasn't a real alcoholic. Being a fifth, Joe had thrown me off the pace of my buzz.

I thought of a fact. "They can't arrest us or they'll lose the beer."

"First thing tomorrow I shall report this behavior to their superiors," Shane said.

Andrew was more direct. "If I had my pistol I'd shoot the policeman."

"That's the way," Brad said. "Freedom wasn't wrong about everything. He told me a million times, 'Never trust a pig.'"

Marcella protested use of the word *pig* even if they were thieves. Shane told about nailing a policewoman in her squad car in Ogden, Utah. Andrew pretended to shoot cops— "BANG, BANG-BANG."

The babble roiled around my already confused brain, but like a drowning victim on a stick, I held on to my fact. "If I drive off, there's nothing they can do to stop me without losing their beer."

Nobody spoke. From behind us came the sound of Lloyd walking up and down in the trailer. Way off to the right the lights of Chattanooga soaked into the clouds. I thought I heard thunder.

"So drive off," Brad said.

Shane was nervous. "Maurey's too drunk to drive."

I pulled out the choke, pumped the gas pedal twice, and flipped the ignition switch. Moby Dick coughed to life. I yelled, "*Banzai, motherfuckers!*" then I jammed the Dick into first and we got the hell out of Dodge.

39

GOD KNOWS I TRIED TO PEEL OUT IN A WAIL OF SQUEALING rubber, but Moby Dick didn't have it in him. Probably for the best, his tires had no squealing rubber to spare.

We did move right along, though. Lloyd's tinkering and Brad's new spark plug wires had the engine humming, not to mention by now most of the trailer weight was long gone. Hard to say without a speedometer, but I'd estimate we hit sixty before old Bernard even stuck his key in the keyhole.

"Hope we didn't lose Lloyd out the back end," I said, gearing down for the first turn.

"Watch out, for Christ's sake," Shane yelled as I swerved to miss a possum. I should have splattered it. Nobody risks death to save a possum.

Brad climbed between the seats into the passenger spot. "Think we can outrun the pigs?"

"Hell, no. But we can get far enough ahead for them to figure one carload of beer is enough."

"Are they following?"

I checked the side mirror. Sure enough—red, blue, red, blue. "Shit."

"Coors isn't worth dying for," Shane shouted.

"I have children back here," Marcella called, unnecessarily since they were both howling.

"This is like being in a movie," Brad said.

It would have been except chase scenes in movies were choreographed and driven by sober guys in helmets. As we blew over a hill I remembered something Shane might find interesting.

"Did you know Herbie the Love Bug Volkswagen had a Porsche engine?"

Shane yelled, "I don't give a fuck." I hit a mother of a chuck-hole that bounced him off his perch onto the floor. Marcella scrambled to upright him, but from the sound of things Shane and the entire junk pile were rolling out of control back there. Marcella passed Hugo Jr. up to Brad so the baby wouldn't get killed by a flying jack.

"I never held a baby before," Brad said.

"Hold his head so it doesn't flop."

"This diaper's all wet."

Bernard and A.B. caught us on a hill full of tight curves. I moved Moby Dick dead center of the blacktop, figuring anyone coming down would have the brains to get out of my way. Hunter-and-prey stalemate—they couldn't stop us and we couldn't escape.

"What are you going to do?" Brad asked.

"I don't know. Let me think."

Their advantage was they knew the roads and we didn't. For all I knew, we could be hurtling down a dead end into a brick wall. Our advantage was they didn't want other law enforcement attention any more than we did. That's why they hadn't turned on the siren. Also, if this thing lasted all night, we had a full tank of gas. Neither one was much of an advantage.

"Look at the map and see where the hell we are," I said to Brad.

Instead, he peered out at the mirror on his side. "Someone else is chasing us."

I looked and didn't see anything, then we hit a flat spot and I saw it—behind the police car another set of headlights, closing fast.

"You think it's Hugo Sr.?" I asked.

Brad rolled down his window for a better look. "I don't know. Maybe."

In the middle of the flat spot we flew up and over a railroad crossing that sent Shane spinning back to the floor. The trailer jumped clear off the ground, came down, bounced, went up, and came down again.

"I bet this is real exciting for Lloyd," Brad said.

"Hand me that bottle."

I heard a noise and looked in the mirror just as the police car swerved to the wrong side of the road, hit the ditch, and rolled.

"Holy shit," Brad said.

It rolled all the way around onto its roof, then onto its wheels, then onto its roof again. I hit the brakes hard.

———

Life simply stopped for about five seconds. It was kind of eerie, as if everyone froze in the moment, afraid to go on to the next moment, which might be even more bizarre than this one. I looked in back where Shane, Marcella, and Andrew were sprawled on the floor under an avalanche of magazines, used clothing, and automobile parts. They were all breathing, and I didn't see any blood. The three were alive and would stay that way, although I doubt if that fact had dawned on them yet.

"You shouldn't stop so fast," Brad said. He'd behaved like a hero—gathered Hugo Jr. in his arms and twisted at the last instant so his shoulder, instead of the baby, banged the glove box. The jar seemed to have knocked the tears out of Hugo. He looked content.

"They flipped," I said.

"Us going through the windshield won't make them unflip."

I jumped out and ran to the back of the trailer. Lloyd stood on the road, leaning forward so he wouldn't bleed on his overalls. He had a nasty cut across his upper lip.

"He didn't have to do that," Lloyd said.

"What he?"

The Jesus eyes flashed like heat lightning. "You didn't have to do that, either."

"I was trying to save the beer."

"You broke most of what was left."

I squinted through the pale darkness toward the police car and saw the pickup camper. The driver stepped out and walked to the far shoulder to view the damage. He carried a flashlight in his left hand and a pistol in his right.

"What'd he do?" I asked.

"Shot their tires, I imagine."

Brad came up carrying a torn T-shirt, which he handed to Lloyd. "Marcella has her baby."

"Thank you," Lloyd said. He pressed the T-shirt against his cut.

"That truck was back at the cafe," Brad said.

Our savior returned to his cab and drove up to where we stood next to the trailer. He rolled down his window and smiled at me. I smiled back. His eyes were amused, and he had this tiny gap in his front teeth that made him appear impish.

"Hi," he said.

"Hi."

He turned his attention to Lloyd. "Are you okay?"

The shirt muffled Lloyd's voice. "It wasn't worth killing anybody."

"You folks were in trouble and I had to help." He waved the pistol vaguely back in the direction of the upside-down patrol car. "Neither one is hurt—just shook up some. They won't be pursuing anyone else today."

Bernard was stooped over with one hand on the car and the other hand on his lower back. A.B. pulled himself out a broken window. When he stood up I heard a groan. Both had that stunned posture men get right after they've been popped in the face with a baseball bat.

The man in the truck leaned a hairy arm on the windowsill. "Their car is full of broken glass and smells like a brewery. Why were they after you?"

Lloyd said, "Long story."

I figured somebody should thank the guy. Even though I wasn't nuts about his methods, he had just saved our asses. "Thanks for helping us," I said. "I don't know what we'd have done if you hadn't come along."

He stared right at me. For the first time all trip I was conscious of the no-bra deal. "Glad to have been of service. I specialize in saving damsels in distress."

Lloyd spit blood.

There didn't seem like anything to do but watch Bernard and A.B. stumble around their car. They were looking for something—an upper bridge or a contact lens or something, I don't know what. The air had that smell like right after it starts raining, the same smell you get when a neighbor changes his oil. The road glistened, so it must have been raining lately and stopped. I wondered what was supposed to happen next. Bernard had to come up with a story explaining a tits-up patrol car full of broken beer bottles. Would he leave us out, or would the countryside soon be crawling with armed-to-the-teeth cops with orders to shoot to kill anyone in a big white ambulance pulling a horse trailer?

The hairy man must have read my mind. "You folks better follow over to my place. It might be a good thought to lay low for a day or so."

Lloyd was studying our rescuer. "We don't have much choice," he said.

The man nodded, as if the plan were settled. He kept his eyes on me while he talked. "I live thirty miles up the Hiwassee River. It's remote, they'll never find you."

As Lloyd, Brad, and I walked up front to Moby Dick, Brad said, "I don't trust that guy. He smiles like Freedom."

I couldn't decide if I trusted him or not. He was intriguing—dangerous and southern—the way I always pictured Stonewall Jackson.

"So far he's behaved like a gentleman," I said. "He saved us when we were in trouble. He didn't have to save us." I opened the driver's door. "What do you think, Lloyd—evil snake or knight in shining armor?"

"I think..." Lloyd dropped the blood-soaked T-shirt into my hand. His eyes were angry. "I'll drive from here on."

40

His name was Armand Castle. He was a sculptor. To prove it he led Marcella and me into the barn-turned-studio, where iron skeletons lay around in various levels of completion. What Armand did was he found scraps of metal and junk in old dumps and welded them into these conglomerations he gave names like *Mobocracy* and *Pain*. The camper was full of bed frames and brake shoes and unidentifiable angle iron he'd picked up driving across the state.

"I will wager you could use a drink," Armand said.

"How'd you guess?"

"That was one heck of a job of driving. One heck of a job. How about you, Miss Marcella, ready for a toddy?"

Marcella touched her bun. "Maybe just one." Shocked the hell out of me.

Armand stuck his head in the trailer, where Brad held two flashlights while Lloyd sorted through the chaos. "You fellas hungry? You want a drink?"

Lloyd said, "No." Not "No, thank you" or "Thanks just the same." His voice held no hint of politeness. Rudeness wasn't like him. In fact, rudeness was less like Lloyd than any other person I knew except maybe Dot Pollard back at the Killdeer Cafe. I decided he was jealous. Armand was good-looking and creative and he'd rescued us, and Lloyd couldn't handle not being top dog on the block.

From Shane, on the other hand, I expected rudeness.

"Are you kin to the family who founded the White Castle restaurant chain?" He was bent over loosening his ankle clamp so he could drain onto the front yard.

"I believe the White Castle restaurants are named after the shape of their first building, not the family who owns them. I'm kin to the Virginia Castles," Armand said.

"You look as if you own White Castle. They sell the worst hash browns in the food industry, although the term *bad hash browns* is redundant."

"I avoid hash browns altogether."

"Did you make your money on square hamburger patties?"

Armand was being amazingly patient, considering he's the kind of man would shoot the tires off a cop car. "I made my money by outliving my father."

"That explains a lot about you."

"Pay no attention to my friends," I said. "They're ex-alcoholics, and ex-alcoholics are always holier-than-thou jackasses."

Shane turned his head to give me a hard look. I expected a mean shot back, but it was more like he decided I wasn't worth fighting with. That's the feeling I got, anyway. Instead, he said, "Your escapade seems to have affected the seals on my reservoir."

"Did that rolling around make you spring a leak?" Marcella asked.

He retightened his clamp. "I would appreciate the use of strong tape, electrical tape might be best."

Armand started up the steps. "I imagine we can find you some electrical tape, old-timer."

"Call me old-timer again and I shall leap from this chair and flail you."

Armand stopped and his eyes jerked back around to Shane. He seemed about to say one thing, then switched to something else. "It was only a term of respect."

Shane's hands went white on the sides of his wheelchair. "I don't need your respect."

"You're just mad 'cause you peed on yourself"—I smiled at Shane—"again."

———

Armand's house was a three-story brick box at the bottom of a long hill. In the dark, you couldn't see the Hiwassee River, but I knew it had to be close by because I could smell it. Smelled like Dothan Talbot's crotch.

The inside of his house was the cleanest inside of a house I've ever seen, which is saying a mouthful considering my mother dusted her light bulbs daily. Mom at least left two *Reader's Digests* on the lazy Susan so people would think our family kept up on current trends. Armand's house didn't have a magazine, not a plant, not a family photograph. The front room was mostly black couches and glass-topped tables with a few pole lamps. A foot-high statue of an armless woman with her robe around her hips stood on a lapis lazuli column. The coolest thing about the room was the marble floor. Houses in Fred Astaire movies had marble floors, but I'd never seen one in person.

"I believe the tape is stored in the laundry," Armand said.

The statue had polished tits. I said, "Your maid must have known when you'd be back."

He stood with his hairy arms crossed next to a door leading off into the rest of the house. "I have no maid. Domestics gossip, and more than anything, I cannot stand gossip."

Marcella's face took on a lost puppy eagerness. "You're rich, aren't you, Mr. Castle?"

He smiled that urbane look. "I'm comfortable."

While Armand was off digging up tape I circled the room, inspecting his tastes in art. I couldn't figure this guy out, which frustrated me because I can almost always figure guys out. He talked too polite for a man with a full, untrimmed beard. The art on the walls was primarily Impressionist landscapes with some Picasso-like fragmented animals thrown in—no people pictures. Maybe he was gay. Sometimes gay guys live alone in clean houses.

Marcella wallowed in embarrassment. "I can't believe I asked him if he was rich. What got over me? This is a room out of *House and Garden*."

"I can't stand up anymore, Marcella. You think an alarm would go off if I sat on one of these couches?"

"No, that's not likely. Why would an alarm go off?"

"I was joking, Marcella."

She wrinkled her nose. "I'm sorry, I missed it."

———

Armand returned wearing a different Hawaiian shirt and rubber flip-flops. You could see hair on the tops of his big toes. He carried a silver tray with a role of electrical tape, a decanter of dun-colored liquid, three cut-glass glasses, and a covered candy dish. "Your friends do not approve of my company," he said.

"They're jealous because you're a gentleman and they're not," I said.

Marcella stepped toward him. "We don't have gentlemen in Texas."

"Come now, I'm certain a few gentlemen dwell in Texas, perhaps around Beaumont."

"I don't know Beaumont, but there's not a one in the Panhandle." Her hands were wringing each other like wash rags. "I'm truly sorry I asked if you're rich. You must think I'm gauche. It's just this house is so *clean*, no one but a rich person would have a house this clean."

He filled the bottom of a glass and handed it to her. "I thought your question showed both rare candor and grace. Here, drink this, it'll help you relax."

"Only one, though. I'm nursing." Marcella took a sip. "Jesus in heaven, what is it?"

Armand poured three fingers in each of the other two glasses. "Something my neighbor cooks up. The recipe has been in his family for generations. I shall explain the process after I give Mr. Rinesfoos his tape."

"You better let me do that. I need to check on the boys— they're asleep. Besides, Shane doesn't like men seeing his tally-whacker." Marcella carried her glass and tape out the door.

"Charming woman," Armand said, sitting next to me on the couch.

"Her husband's followed us a thousand miles so far. I think we lost him this time."

The hand that held a glass out to me had a big diamond ring on the fourth finger. "Moonshine, my dear?"

"I've heard of this stuff all my life but never tasted any. Isn't it amazing the stuff you hear about all your life but never come in contact with? Take hookers and Communists. I met my first hooker yesterday, I think it was yesterday, but I've heard stories about evil Communists since the day I was born and I've never yet met one." The moonshine tasted sweet, like Yukon Jack, only it had a touch of cough syrup-kickback.

"I'm sorry my friends are being turds," I said.

He drank from his glass. "You are a beautiful woman. I cannot blame them for not wanting to share."

The beard was animalistic, but the fingers were delicate. I didn't know what to think, and my stomach was showing signs of whirlies. "If I was sober I wouldn't trust you, Armie. I don't think I trust you anyway."

With a small flourish, he opened the candy dish. "Try one of these, they'll help you appreciate my finer traits."

"Those are green pills."

"How right you are." He tossed two in his mouth.

"I've got enough problems, I don't need pills. What are they?"

"Something else my neighbor whips up in his bathtub."

"You've got quite a neighbor."

"I have him on retainer. They're weak relaxants, the Appalachian home-remedy version of a tranquilizer."

"I could use a relaxant."

"You've had a hard day, little lady. You deserve to relax."

The moonshine was smoother on the second sip. "I get real angry when Shane calls me 'little lady.'"

He touched my hair with his hand. "I mean it only as a term of respect."

I popped a pill in my mouth and slugged it down with moonshine. Washing tranquilizers down with whiskey is hard core. Made me feel like Judy Garland.

———

Time lost sequentially. Which is to say I got fucked up and made a horse's ass out of myself. Most of the night is lost in blackout, thank God, but I remember Marcella throwing up after one drink. I had a loud fight with Shane in which we called each other names you can't take back; Lloyd's face floated somewhere away from his body, judging me with the sad, Jesus eyes; I must have set a personal record for banging shins on furniture.

I broke some glass, and something I did or said made Brad cry.

Then I was alone, lost in Armand's hair. I was clutching at him, trying to tear the hair out or get back through it or something. I wanted Auburn. I thought if I found my way through the hair into skin, I could breathe, I could be with my baby. The last thing I remember is holding Armand's chest and screaming, "*Daddy!*"

41

I SHIFTED MY WEIGHT FORWARD ONTO FROSTBITE'S SHOULDERS *as he waded through deep snow up Red Rock Peak. It was a warm day in early April, and the snow was softening into a pudding texture that made rough going for a horse—no going for a person on foot, snowshoes, or probably even skis. Frostbite progressed up the hill in thrusts, gathering his back legs and springing into the snow. I wore a penstemon in my hair, which was long again, the length it had been when Shannon was born. A pair of bluebirds hop-scotched from fence post to fence post ahead of us. The posts didn't look connected because snow covered the top line of barbwire. I was watching a mouse skim across the snow when I heard a quiet* Thock *and the snow started to move. Frostbite screamed and went over. I clutched the reins with both hands as the avalanche swept us down the mountain. Frostbite hit a tree and screamed again, then he was lost. I cupped my hands over my nose to give myself an inch of breathing space as the snow rolled over me deeper and deeper, then everything was still, dark, and heavy. To find which direction was up, I spit in my hand, although, buried alive, up doesn't matter from down and snow doesn't matter from earth.*

———

I gasped awake, struggling for air. There was pain in my head, a very specific pain in a very specific spot, as if a bolt had been screwed into my forehead, right over the bridge of my nose. I squeezed my eyes shut and listened to the rain and fought both for and against remembering. Nothing came at first, then Memphis, then a police car chasing an ambulance. Armand shifted an arm across my breasts, and several more pieces fell into place.

Jesus—another social blunder. Where was Lloyd? I'd woken up bare-assed and dry-mouthed before, but not in a long, long time. Had we fucked? Did it matter? Armand lay on his stomach, facing away, with one arm over my body. The hair on his back was a furry shawl across his shoulders with two thinning lines running down either side of his spine. He seemed clinched and asleep at the same time.

In the bathroom, I held my hand under the tap and drank, then I splashed water on my face. When I peed I lowered my head between my knees and stared at the floor tile. Spotless. Nothing snotty dribbled down my thighs, but that didn't prove anything. He could have nailed me and not come. Or, for all I knew, he nailed me and I got up afterward and danced on the tables. God, I hate blackouts. What had I done to Brad? I can't stand questions everyone but me knows the answers to.

Hangovers are best handled by three aspirin, a gallon of water, and twelve extra hours' sleep, but this didn't feel like your everyday puking-shivering hangover. This hangover was unique in my experience. I fought to remember—Injun Joe, moonshine, the little green pill. I'd mixed whiskey with pills. The woman who'd lost her baby had sunk to an all-new low.

———

Still avoiding the mirror, I fumbled open the medicine cabinet in search of aspirin. The bottles were lined up in alphabetized categories with each category marked on a piece of plastic embossing tape—AMPHETAMINES, AMYL-NITRATE,

ANTIDEPRESSANTS, ANTIPSYCHOTICS, BARBITURATES. My green pills from the night before were down at the bottom under QUAALUDES. I pride myself on self-abuse sophistication, but I'd never heard of half Armand's pharmaceuticals.

"Don't touch my property." He was behind me, angry.

"I was looking for aspirin."

"If you need aspirin, ask for it. Don't snoop."

"This is an amazing collection, Armand. My mother would marry you to get at this drugstore."

Armand stood with his hands on his hips, glaring at me. He'd passed out wearing a rubber—a third explanation for the lack of dribble. I hate being glared at by a man in a rubber.

"I'm sorry, Armand. May I please have three aspirin?"

Careful not to touch his body, I moved aside while he yanked open a drawer next to the sink. The drawer was full of stuff regular people stock in bathrooms—toothpaste, deodorant, aspirin. Down south they're big on ground-up aspirin. Armand gave me three packets of Goody's Headache Powder.

As Dad used to say, his breath could have knocked a coyote off a flyblown calf. "Your friends are outside behaving strangely."

"What's that mean?"

"I think they're leaving."

Back in the bedroom, I looked out the third-floor window at Moby Dick and Dad's trailer. Lloyd and Brad stood in the rain with their hands in their pockets. Through the open loading doors I could see Shane in his chair, playing his harmonica.

"What makes you think they're leaving?" I asked.

Armand appeared at the bathroom door with a glass of water in one hand and three different-colored capsules in the other. Condoms look silly on limp dicks. "They turned the rig around."

"That doesn't mean they're leaving."

"Last night the skinny one said y'all would clear out as soon as you could travel."

— —

Only two days ago I'd been proud of myself for never having stooped so low as to wear dirty underwear, and now I was faced with a choice between dirty and none. I put the question in Mom's terms: If I got hit by a truck and rushed to the hospital on the verge of death, which would be least mortifying? Dirty. There goes another standard.

Downstairs as I crossed to the front door I noticed a large burn hole in one of the black couches and broken glass on the marble floor under a topless table. Must have been a hell of a party. Too bad I couldn't remember it.

Lloyd stood in the slow rain looking up the hill away from the river. I followed his line of sight up to Hugo Sr.'s Oldsmobile. Hugo got out and waved, so I waved back. He was proving to be a tough little sucker, a lot tougher than he'd come off in Amarillo.

Marcella's and Andrew's faces peeked from the ambulance, behind Shane. I smiled at the gang. "What's going on, guys?"

Brad turned away. Andrew and Lloyd were the only ones who would look at me. "It's time to go," Lloyd said. "Get in the ambulance."

Behind me, Armand said, "She's staying here."

Shane snapped. "Don't be a fool, Maurey. Get in the ambulance."

"Whoa," I said. If everyone was in the mood for ugliness, hung over or not, I'd take them on. "I will do whatever I want."

Lloyd's eyes weren't Jesus now—they were black ice. "No, you won't. You'll come with us."

"You're not my father."

Shane spit a laugh. "Neither is he."

"What's that supposed to mean?"

"Come off it," Shane said. "You've wanted to fuck your father all your life, and now you have."

"To hell with you, Shane." I'd expected ugly, but this was

terminal. Marcella looked frightened. Brad glanced at me, then down at the mud by his feet.

Shane kept coming. "What else could you see in this pretentious drip? He's your father."

"Be careful, old-timer," Armand said. In his gray slacks and no shirt or shoes, he did look a tiny bit like Dad, at least in hairiness and size, but that wasn't why I'd slept with him.

No one likes being accused of having the hots for a parent. I advanced on Shane until I was about six inches off his face. "What a sick, perverted, slime-ball thing to say." I almost had my one chin against his three. "I wouldn't leave here now if you paid me."

"Paid you for what, father-fucker?"

Marcella grabbed the wheelchair and pulled him away from the edge. "Shane doesn't mean it," she said. "We're just all tired and tense."

I stared into his purple eyes and saw no trace of humor. "He did too mean it, he's a pig."

Andrew burst into tears and kicked the hell out of Shane's ankle. "Ouch," Shane yelped. He tried to backhand Andrew, but Marcella caught his wrist. If he'd hit Andrew, I think I'd have plastered the son of a bitch, wheelchair or no wheelchair.

Lloyd touched my arm and I jumped like I'd been cattle-prodded. "Will you get in the ambulance?" he asked.

The ice was gone from Lloyd's eyes, and he was back to vulnerable—which is a stronger weapon. The cracks on his face were like a relief map demarking grief. Lloyd had been my friend, he deserved a better explanation than "Fuck you," but I didn't know how to explain to him something I couldn't explain to myself.

"What's the point?" I said. "Granma is two-hundred-something miles away. What then? You dump me and rush off to Florida in search of your precious Sharon, who almost surely isn't even in Florida. I'm sick of getting dumped. What's the difference if we break up the gang here or tomorrow?"

Brad walked up behind me. "Please come with us, Miss Pierce."

I turned to him. Even without hair, he had the face of an angel. He reminded me of the Little Prince from the Saint-Exupéry book. I touched his jawline. "I can't."

Rain ran down his forehead into his eyes. "You're the first person I ever trusted. Don't leave me."

Jesus, this was too much. "I can't."

Lloyd walked past me to the back of Moby Dick, where he bent down and disconnected the wiring and safety chains from the trailer.

"What are you doing?" I asked.

"It's your trailer."

"If you guys need it, take it. How will you haul the beer?"

He flipped the doobie that released the trailer from the ball. "There's only fifteen cases and a six-pack left. We'll leave five cases and two bottles with you. The rest will fit in back."

"Lloyd, there's no reason to be a dick about it. Take the beer and the trailer. What am I going to do with a horse trailer and no way to pull it?"

He turned a crank that made the trailer tongue rise off the hitch. "What were you planning to do with the trailer once we reached North Carolina?"

"I hadn't thought about that. I've been afraid to think past Shane's grandmother's house."

Lloyd straightened up. "Well, now you don't have to."

———

I walked back over to Armand and stood watching Lloyd and Brad unload the trailer. After stacking my cases and two bottles by the barn, they opened Moby Dick's rear doors and crammed in the spare tires, Marcella's suitcase, and the beer.

They left my stuff and Sam Callahan's tent on the dry porch. Neither one looked my direction. They just sloshed back and forth, being efficient and non-emotional.

I could hear Andrew crying inside Moby Dick. For a six-year-old he sure did cry a lot. Seemed like that's all he'd done since the moment I saw him. Marcella was next to Shane, holding Hugo Jr. and staring across the yard at me. She was wearing a green print dress my grandmother would have bought at J.C. Penney's. Her hair was in a perfect bun.

Armand put his hand on my arm. "Come inside, Maurey. You're getting wet."

I shrugged off his hand. I felt manipulated, but I didn't know who'd manipulated me. I didn't want to stay in this rain forest with a hairy pill popper. I wanted to hold Hugo Jr. I wanted to sit in the front seat beside Lloyd. The two-bottles thing seemed especially petty—a crappy note to end on. From somewhere in Moby Dick I heard Merle *mew*ing. How had I managed to fence myself into this stupid situation?

I was all set to swallow my pride and say "Forget it, guys, I was only joking," when Shane spoke.

"Maurey, you've been nothing but a bitch and a drunk since we allowed you to join us. I am glad to abandon you with this psychotic thug."

Slam—last door shut. Last bridge burned. I stood in the rain and watched Moby Dick climb the hill and roll out of sight. Hugo Sr. drove across the road, then backed, then turned and followed. I stared at the spot where they'd disappeared, wishing my headache would go away. It felt like Dad's funeral.

Armand draped his arm around my shoulders. "How on Earth did you ever get mixed up with that bunch of losers?"

42

I STAYED IN THE SHOWER UNTIL THE WATER TURNED COLD, which must have been over an hour. I imagined a huge, two-hundred-gallon water heater hidden somewhere in the house, heating water as fast as house inhabitants could use it. The shower stall itself was the opposite end of the scale from the Calhoun Arms. Two spigots gave the option of rinsing your front and back at the same time or separately without having to turn around. The walls and floor were covered by heavy, dark tile with no gunk in the grout. I sat on the floor, leaning back against the wall, holding Armand's soap-on-a-rope with both hands and letting the twin streams of water rain down on my body.

My God, I was tired. And hollow. I didn't care if I ever saw alcohol again. At that moment I didn't care if I ever saw anything again. Once I left Armand's shower, life would resume itself. People would come at me and people would go away. I would drink and pee, eat and shit. Getting by would take every drop of energy I would ever have, then someday I would stop getting by and be dead.

Big deal.

Armand came in the bathroom and opened and closed the medicine cabinet. "You alive in there?" he asked.

"Compared to what?"

"I'll be working in the barn. Find whatever you can to eat." Guess he didn't mind my touching his property in the refrigerator. "I'll probably take a nap."

The bathroom door closed and he was gone.

———

I slept most of the day, dreaming variations on the smother motif—snakes wound around my neck; my tongue swelled up and closed my throat; Dothan Talbot tied a plastic dry-cleaning bag over my head; I drowned a dozen deaths. Some dreams take all the rest out of sleep.

Every few hours I awoke to find Armand in the bathroom mix-and-matching his pills. I'm not sure if he was inbibing primarily in ups or downs, but whatever they were made him sweat.

Once he saw me awake and asked, "You want medication? I can make you feel any way you want to feel."

"No, thanks, I feel like sleeping."

"How about a drink? After last night you must need a drink."

"No, thanks."

Late in the afternoon I stood at the window and watched him work. He had the double barn doors thrown open and he stood before a misshapen mass of metal in the full welding mask and no shirt. With his hair, muscles, and sweat, and his torch spitting a white-blue flame, Armand took on an unsavory Greek god look—Vulcan, maybe, or Hades.

———

The kitchen downstairs had ivory-colored walls and pastel green appliances. I found an unopened jar of peanut butter and a spoon and poked around while I ate. The upright freezer contained about fifty steaks and a gallon of Scotch.

I'd seen two or three microwave ovens before and heard pros and cons about them, mostly cons, but I'd never been in a spot where I could try one out. I put the spoon globbed with peanut butter in and turned the dial. The microwave made a popping sound and tiny lightning bolts flashed inside; I didn't eat the peanut butter.

Outside the rain had let up temporarily, so I walked past the barn down to the cliff overlooking the river. The rocks were wet, but I sat on one anyway. I always think best when I can hear running water. Dad taught me that. I told Sam Callahan and he fixed Lydia's toilet so it ran all night. He said Shannon slept better that way and she would grow up to be a calmer person. I don't see how anyone could grow up calm being raised by Sam and Lydia.

The river shot through the gorge gray-green with sprays of whitewater. I was surprised to find Whitewater in the East. Stephen Foster Sewanee River-type songs gave me the impression eastern rivers were lazy. High up on the other side a wooden flume ran parallel to the river. I'd seen a flume over near Dubois, but it ran straight down the side of the mountain. Old-timey timberjacks sent logs to the river that way. I couldn't figure out why anyone would build a flume parallel to a river. Growing up in Wyoming is great, but it leaves certain holes in your education.

———

Our senior year at GroVont High Sam Callahan's grandfather, Caspar, started having little strokes. I guess they're like alcohol blackouts. He was driving down the highway and suddenly woke up high-centered on the median fifteen miles away. As a bribe, he offered to pay for Sam's college if Sam would move to North Carolina and live in what Lydia called the manor house. Anybody with eyes and brains could tell

Sam would never move anywhere without Shannon. They were inseparable. He took her on dates and everything, which tended to put off local girls. Teenagers don't like the guy showing up with a toddler.

I knew Sam would want to take her, but I didn't think about it. My mind was on more important things—senior play, the prom, graduation. I was enrolled in UW next fall, mostly to escape Dothan Talbot, and I just figured Shannon would be taken care of the same as she had been all her life.

Sam brought her over the Saturday afternoon before the prom. He knew I'd be too busy with my hair and formal and all to put up much of a fight. Sam's sneaky that way. Everyone thinks he's all intellectual and spacey, but a lot of that oblivious doo-dah stuff is an act.

I was sitting in front of my vanity mirror, performing damage control on a zit. Shannon squealed and ran across the room, hugged me, and crawled in my lap. "How's my little girl today?" I asked.

"She has a new tooth," Sam said. "Show Mama your new tooth."

Proudly, Shannon opened her mouth wide for me to inspect the little rows of teeth. I couldn't tell which one was new, but I *oohed* anyway. "Will the tooth fairy bring you a dime now?"

"That's when she loses teeth, not grows them," Sam said. Shannon looked disappointed in me. What kind of mother doesn't know tooth fairy protocol?

"Do me," she said. She pointed to her eyes. Our favorite—in fact, our only—mother-daughter game was putting on makeup.

"I like your hair better down," Sam said.

"I just spent two hours putting it up. What do you think of my dress?" This pink satin number with a dipping neckline, low back, and spaghetti straps hung on a hanger on the closet door. I was doing the vanity thing in my bra and panties. Ever since seventh grade Sam and I have walked in on each other in underwear or the bathtub or wherever the one being walked in on happens to be. Mom didn't like it at first. To me, it's nice being able to talk to a guy without sexual tension.

Sam didn't compliment my taste in dresses. Instead, he sat on my bed. "I'm starting writing school in Chapel Hill next fall," he said.

With my right-hand little finger, I rubbed shadow on Shannon's lids. "You're going to hate North Carolina," I said. "The humidity will kill you."

"Shannon is going with me."

I stopped to look at him. Sam had that false casualness he assumes when he's tense. "But she's my daughter."

"When was the last time you saw her?"

I tried to remember. I'd been awfully busy lately, but I seemed to recall sometime the end of last week.

Shannon stirred on my lap. "Mama?"

"Okay, eyeliner next, honey." I looked in the mirror at her face below my own. We look amazingly alike, except she has brown eyes and I have blue. "Sam, that's not fair. You can't make a decision like this on your own."

"They won't let you keep a child in the freshman dorms."

"I thought she'd stay with Lydia." Which wasn't exactly true, I hadn't thought anything till that moment. "That way we can both see her when we come home for holidays and summers."

Sam's nose wrinkled. "My mother can't raise a child."

He had a point there—just look at Sam. I drew a dark line across her lower lids, then applied mascara to her lashes. They were dark and beautiful even without mascara. Shannon was an extraordinarily beautiful child, and I'm not saying that because I gave birth to her. Solid cheekbones, long neck, thick hair—she was much cuter than that prissy little girl in the Breck ads. I'd always pictured Shannon and me growing up together. I'd teach her horsemanship and how to control boys. She'd brush my hair while I explained the facts of life. Sam couldn't explain the facts of life to a little girl. The only facts of life he'd ever known got me pregnant.

"Listen, Sam, can we talk about this later? Dothan's coming any minute."

"I thought you deserved to know."

"We'll talk later. Are you going to the prom stag?"

Sam stood up. "I promised Shannon I'd read her William Blake's 'Visions of the Daughters of Albion.' She gets a kick out of de-flowerment scenes." Shannon leaned her head back, looked up in my face with her beautiful eyes, and laughed.

Of course, we never talked later. That August I waved good-bye from the terminal building as my best friend and my daughter boarded a plane and flew away, and child number one slipped through my fingers.

––––

When you drink it's easy to lose track of the point of what you've been doing. The point of this damn journey was not some fat sicko's grandmother's farm. I didn't come all this way to bond with a band of roving vagrants, and I sure didn't come all this way to wind up mistress to a pharmaceutical welder. I came to see Sam Callahan and Shannon. By seeking out two of the three most important people in my world, I'd hoped to gain strength for the battle to get back the most important person—Auburn. Instead of gaining strength I'd wallowed in alcoholic self-pity and lost track of my point.

Okay, now—find the track and get back on it. Sam and Shannon were in Greensboro, North Carolina, so I had no business sitting on a wet rock in Tennessee.

––––

Back upstairs, I dumped the contents of my suitcase and day pack on the bed and took stock. Wasn't that much, really, as the two pairs of boots I hadn't worn yet filled most of the suitcase space. I gathered panties, socks, shirts, and the spare Wrangler's into a pile and went in search of this laundry room where Armand found Shane's tape. The washer and dryer were the same pastel green as the refrigerator and stove. Everything must have arrived at once, which is the rich-person way of decorating.

After starting the washer, I took another shower—a real one this time, where cleanliness counted more than psychological collapse. I washed and conditioned my hair, shaved my legs, and sudsed up my crotch to root out any residual weirdness from last night. Just because Armand woke up in a rubber doesn't mean he penetrated with one.

The clothes dried in a half hour or so, then I brought them back up to repack. For some reason, when I dressed I put on a bra and my town cowboy boots. I think the reason had to do with Armand. I was fixing to walk out there into the barn and say "Gee, Armand, it was swell, but do you mind running me into town now?" and I wasn't totally comfortable about his reaction. You never know, he might have interpreted last night's whatever-it-was as romance.

Armand being a southern gentleman, I figured if I dressed properly, he would behave properly. More than once I've heard men say any woman not wearing a bra "wants it."

———

Because I was a little nervous, and a little queasy, I circled through the kitchen and poured myself a juice glass of Scotch. One snort wouldn't knock me off track.

The rain had picked up again into a steady downpour. I stood outside in the gathering darkness watching Armand work. Rivulets of sweat ran down his back, staining the butt of his gray slacks. He moved in quick jerks and metallic clangings. Empty Coors bottles littered the concrete floor beneath his work area, which I took as a bad sign. No matter what disgusting depths I'd sunk to the last couple of weeks, I'd never stooped so low as to drink Coors.

Armand turned and faced me straight on. He held the flaming torch in his right hand and a piece of angle iron in his left. The structure he was cutting on reminded me of those molecule models we made in high school, only this one had been run over by a bus. With his hooded mask pulled down and his body slick with sweat, Armand produced a threatening, alien effect. Everyone says don't look at the welder's flame or you'll go blind, and like anything else people tell you not to look at or you'll go blind, the overpowering urge was to look.

"You mind shutting that thing off?" I asked.

He didn't move a few seconds, then he bent over a tank and turned a valve, and the flame sputtered out. I hadn't realized until it was silent how loud the hiss had been.

"I was hoping to talk to you a minute," I said. "If you have time."

More seconds ticked by. The rain drizzled on the roof and wet ground behind me. This wasn't going well. I couldn't see his face. All I saw was my own face, blurry in his mask, and talking to a mirror with someone behind it is intimidating.

"I need to be getting on to my daughter's place," I said, "in Greensboro. That's North Carolina. And I was wondering if you'd loan me some money for a bus ticket and a motel room tonight. I can leave the beer and horse trailer to cover the loan."

Armand didn't move. I was afraid the pills had blown his hearing.

"Or maybe you'd rather buy the trailer. However we do it I'd like to thank you for your help with the police and all, but I really need to be going now."

The sucker had turned statue. Made me nervous.

"Or if a motel room is too much, you might just drop me off at the bus station."

This was getting ridiculous.

"I don't even have to borrow the money. If you can give me a lift into town, I'll call my daughter's father and have him wire enough for a ticket."

Now he was pissing me off. The only way to fight intimidation is with intimidation. I walked right up to him and knocked on his hood like it was a door.

"Anybody in there?"

Slowly, Armand's hand rose and he lifted the mask off his face. "You're not going anywhere."

"Come on, Armand. Get real. You can't kidnap me, my friends know where I am."

"No woman cock teases Armand Castle."

I should have known. If you're not friendly, it's cunt; friendly but not friendly enough, cock tease; friendly as can be, slut. Those are the categories—take your pick.

"What cock tease, Armand? You got your action last night, now take me to town."

His chin stuck out like Andrew's when you don't feed him. "No woman cock teases Armand Castle."

I leaned one hand on my hip. "You already said that. Did something happen last night I don't know about?"

"You were a cock tease. You were all over me, then when it came time you said you'd lost your pills and made me go put on a condom. When I came back to bed you were passed out."

The scenario sounded funny, so I laughed. "You mean we didn't fuck last night?"

He blinked about ten times in a row—like a machine gun. "Yeah, we fucked."

I stared at his black eyes. Yesterday he'd been suave, urbane, a little dangerous; now he was just stupid. It took a minute for what he said to sink in. The son of a bitch nailed me while I was unconscious.

I slapped him hard. He looked surprised, blinked three or four times real fast, and slugged me in the stomach. When I gasped and bent over he hit me in the back of the head with his mask. I fell at his feet and bit the shit out of his big toe.

The man went insane. He kicked and I saw bright red pain in my eyes. He stomped again, driving my chin into the concrete. I tried to crawl away, but he pulled me upright by my hair and drove his knee into my spine. Blindly I found a Coors bottle and swung it into his body; I couldn't see well enough to know what part I hit.

The weird thing was the noise. There wasn't any. Neither one of us made a sound other than heavy breathing and the fist-on-flesh *thonks* when he hit me. A person hiding in the corner would have thought we were making love.

Which to Armand, in some sick, rotted part of his mind, we were. The blows came with a sexual rhythm. After working on my face, he moved on to the breasts, then lower. He tore my shirt off, then the bra. I kneed him in the crotch, and he hit me with a backhand that sent me sprawling across the floor. My hand landed on the hot end of the welding torch and I jerked away, smelling of burnt skin.

Then he was on me again. As he tore at the buttons on my jeans, I gave up and stopped fighting. When Armand realized this he stood over my inert body and dropped his pants. He knelt, pulled off my right boot, and threw it across the barn. He did the same with my left boot, then he lifted my legs to pull off my jeans.

That's when I nailed him in the balls with the welding torch. Armand screamed and fell to the floor. I took off.

43

THINGS WERE SCREWED UP INSIDE MY BODY. BREATHING hurt real bad, and something warmer than rain flowed in my eyes. I slipped and slid on my face through mud, then crawled a few feet and came back up, running for the lights of the house.

At the porch, I stopped a moment to will away panic. Think. Should I go in the house? He would be after me soon, and he knew where the guns were kept. Unless I found one fast, the house was senseless.

I turned and ran up the driveway toward the road. If I made it to the highway, I could hole up off the side, wait for someone to pass by. Coming in, I'd been too drunk to notice how far away the nearest neighbors lived, but it couldn't be more than a mile or so. Easterners aren't spread out like back home.

I risked a look at the barn and saw Armand silhouetted in the double doors. He was bent over with his hands on his knees, trying to see through the rain. He shouted something and came toward me. I headed up the hill.

I was scared and hurt, but there was more—a sense of unreality. I could not believe Maurey Pierce would ever be in this much pain and this frightened. How had I come to the point where this was real? The thought struck that I could actually die. His reaction to a slap had been rape, then I burned his crotch. Death was not abstract here.

I hit a rut and fell again. My socks gave less traction than bare feet, but I had no time to yank them off. Behind me, Armand's footsteps splashed across the yard and started up the drive.

As I scrambled uphill, a voice came from the ditch. "I could use a hand, if you don't mind."

"Shane?"

"Maurey. You look like death with tits."

"God, Shane, I love you."

His wheelchair was stuck in the mud. Shane was shaking badly, his hair and shirt, everything soaked through. Running to him, I slipped again and slid down the short embankment into one of his wheels.

"Don't you dare move a muscle," Shane said.

I looked up at the barrel of a pistol. Shane was pointing it behind me where Armand stood, breathing like a wounded bear.

———

Shane leaned over to offer me his spare hand. As I lifted myself upright, he said, "What seems to be the problem here?"

"Lovers' quarrel," Armand said. "Maurey overreacted."

Shane looked at my face. "As a rule, lovers' quarrels don't involve this much blood."

I finally got some control of my breath. "He beat the crap out of me."

"Beating women is unethical," Shane said.

"No shit, Sherlock."

Armand took a step toward us, but Shane stopped him with a lift of the pistol. "Maurey is exaggerating," Armand said. "She forced me into kinky sex and things got a little out of hand."

I said, "Rape is more than a little out of hand, you prick."

"Now, now." Shane patted the inside of my elbow. "Why don't we get in out of the weather and sort it all out?"

This was too civilized for me. I wasn't brought up to handle violence with "Now, now."

Armand came forward two more steps. "At least let me free you from the mud."

"Freeze," Shane ordered. "One more step and I blow your nuts off."

I said, "That's more like it."

"Thank you, Maurey. Now help me out of this mire."

"That's my pistol, isn't it?"

———

Took some pushing and tugging—and pain in my burnt hand—but I finally got Shane back on the driveway and down the rest of the hill. I couldn't see my own face, thank God, but Shane looked in bad shape. He was coughing his guts out. Each cough spasm ended in what sounded like gagging, and I was scared to piss he might pass out.

"You want me to hold Charley?" I asked.

"I am perfectly competent with a gun."

"I can't believe you stole him. Then you lied, you swore to God himself you didn't take Charley."

"Lying to alcoholics is mandatory, especially where firearms are concerned," Shane said.

Armand lurched ahead of us like a spoiled child. He even had hair growing out his butt, the jerk. My greatest fear was that he might call a bluff and realize Charley wasn't loaded. We'd be in big trouble then.

"I'll never trust another sober man," I said.

Shane spit something up. "Aren't you glad now that I lied?"

I rubbed my hand over the top of his wet head. "You think

because you're saving my life I'm going to forgive those ugly things you said?"

"Yes, I think so."

———

Back in the dry, lit barn, Arrnand stood over by the art nouveau junk pile, eyeballing me. He had the ugliest penis I'd ever seen—looked like those Chinese handcuffs we played with as kids. He breathed at hyperventilation speed. Between the blood-pounding excitement and running, his pills must have been flat sizzling. A heart attack might be appropriate.

Shane kept Charley pointed at Armand, but he looked at me. "Holy Hannah, child, what did he hit you with?"

"You don't look so healthy yourself. Did you see a phone inside? Maybe I should call someone."

Armand gave a bark laugh. "Who could you call? The police are after you both."

Shane started to speak but went into a coughing fit that lasted thirty seconds and left drool hanging off the corner of his mouth. Finally he asked, "Did he rape you?"

"He was going to." I picked my torn shirt off the floor and wiped Shane's mouth. He smiled weakly at me.

"I wasn't going to rape her. Why should I rape something I'd already had?" Armand's voice was full of disgust.

Shane pointed the shaky gun. "You. Shut up." He took the shirt from my hand and gently dabbed my chin. It came away soaked in blood and dirt.

"Hold your pistol," Shane said. "It's time this villain paid for his sins."

I took Charley. "Let's charge the villain a lot. Beating me up should be expensive."

"If he'd raped you, I would have cut out his reproductive system."

Armand paled noticeably. I had the urge to point Charley at his crotch and pull the trigger, just to watch the jerk faint. "He fucked me while I was unconscious last night. Is that rape?"

"What am I, a lawyer?" With effort, Shane wheeled toward Armand. "If he moves, shoot him."

"Gladly."

Shane stopped out of the line of fire. He motioned to one of the two tanks connected to the welding torch. "Place your foot up here."

Armand fastened his eyes on mine. "You can't hurt me. I'll call the police. She slept with me last night, and she stayed when you left. No court in Tennessee would convict me of rape."

"You're not going to court," Shane said. I saw him dig in his pocket. "Now put your foot here."

Armand's mouth formed a red sneer inside his black beard. "Look at her. She enjoyed what I did. She wants more. You always wanted a real man, didn't you, bitch."

He screamed and dropped like a stuck pig. Shane flashed that wicked little knife of his, said, "Banzai, motherfucker," and leaned over Armand's writhing body. Five seconds later Armand screamed again, worse than when I stuck a hot welding torch to his testicles.

Shane turned the wheelchair a half circle and slowly made his way back across the floor. He held out his hand to show me two big toes, each with hairy growth behind the yellow nail.

Shane kind of sighed. "I always wanted just cause to do that. Being a cripple makes you mean sometimes."

I said, "Jesus Christ, will he die?"

Shane looked at Armand, who lay on his back, weeping and holding the ends of his feet with both hands. "Not if he seeks treatment. Are you aware if you slice the big toe off a person you effectively cripple him?"

"Armand had it coming."

Shane looked down at the toes in his hand. "I know. Still, if I weren't dying, I probably would have taken only one."

"You're not dying," I said.

Shane bent close over his hand. "Good Lord, Maurey, this toe has bite marks."

44

"YOU DEFINITELY SHOULD SEEK PROFESSIONAL TREATMENT," Shane said to Armand. "The human body has only so much blood to give, then it runs dry."

For the advice, Armand's face returned hatred.

"Think he can drive a truck without toes?" I asked.

Shane hacked out a couple coughs and a spit. "Sure, he can drive. I knew a cowboy named Tim Butler, tried to commit suicide by sticking the barrel of a .410 over-under shotgun in his mouth and pulling the triggers with his toe. Shotgun backfired and snapped that toe like the pully bone off a turkey. Tim drove a stock truck sixty-two miles to a clinic in Cedar City, Utah."

I pulled up a milk crate and sat down. It was highly entertaining watching Armand crawl around trailing blood. He seemed to have lost his orientation.

"So where's the cowboy now?" I asked.

"Tim decided God blew off his toe instead of his head for a reason. He joined up with Church of Christ missionaries in Patagonia. The natives made him a set of viper-headed crutches that he's quite proud of."

Shane rolled over by Armand. "Listen closely, son. Go in the house and wrap clean cloths around your feet to clot the flow. Then take a couple of painkillers—do you have any painkillers?"

Armand didn't answer.

I said, "He's got more than enough painkillers."

"That's fine. Take your painkillers and drive into a hospital and tell the nice nurses you ran over yourself with a lawn mower. You don't want authorities involved in this any more than we do."

From his hands and knees, Armand stared up at Shane, who continued the lecture. "It's not the end of the world, son. Without your feet to hold you up, you shall grow a stronger base. Your life will be much fuller, spiritually speaking. Believe me, I have traveled the road and I know the destination."

If Armand could have killed, Shane would have been dead in a heartbeat. Instead, he began the long crawl from the barn to the house. As the worm slithered past me, I fought the urge to kick him.

I said, "That'll teach you to mess with women from Wyoming."

I don't think he heard me. Watching him grope his way across the mud, I thought of something. "You sure we should let him go? He has guns in there, at least the one he used on the cop tires."

Twin lines of blood followed Armand across the yard. Shane's eyes took on a reminiscent glow; I suppose he was thinking about his own lack of leg function.

"Your friend is in no shape for a shootout," Shane said. "Besides, we have Charley if he tries anything."

"Yeah, but Charley's not loaded."

I aimed Charley at Armand's hairy ass as he pulled himself up the steps. He reminded me of road-kill badger.

"What makes you think Charley has no bullets?" Shane asked.

"Hell, any numbskull knows this gun's not loaded." I squeezed the trigger and—Boom!—Armand's porch light exploded over his head. The noise was terrific.

Shane said, "Simply because you can't buy bullets doesn't mean everyone can't buy bullets." He took Charley away from me.

———

A light came on up on the third floor. "Imagine him climbing all those stairs," Shane said. "The boy must be more resilient than I thought."

"His stash is on the third floor," I said.

"That explains it. Do you think he realizes the loss of his toes was a consequence of what he did to you? So few people connect actions with consequences. Take yourself, for instance."

"Aren't you too wet to pontificate?"

"Whenever a man saves a woman's life the rules say he must tell her how to live it."

"Does the woman have to listen?"

"Have you considered that losing your child and being beat to a pulp are both direct consequences of alcohol consumption? We're not talking bad luck here; everything that's happened happened because you are a sot."

I stood up. "You'll be sick if we don't dry you off. I'll look around, see if he hasn't got a rag pile or something."

"Denial is more than a river in Egypt."

"Yeah, right. You better move out of the doorway. Armand might be resilient enough to pull a trigger."

Shane's snicker rapidly deteriorated into coughing followed by violent shivers. As I moved through Armand's junky art, it occurred to me the situation might still be dire. I'd have a hell of a time explaining to Lloyd how Shane saved my butt, then keeled over dead. Where was Lloyd, anyway?

"Where is Lloyd, anyway?" I called.

"They're camped a mile or so back toward Chattanooga. Lloyd said we had to wait in case you came to your senses. I informed him you don't have any senses."

Armand had an amazing inventory of iron trash—everything from barbwire to girders. Several antique tractors had been disassembled back by the horse stalls. "So why are you here instead of Lloyd? No offense, but you're not built right to play cavalry."

Shane bent over to take off his shoes and socks. "I told Lloyd he should check on you, but he said you had to make the choice and take action. You had to save yourself."

"Then why let you come alone? Did he say 'Maurey's in trouble, go out in the rain and get sick'?"

"It wasn't raining when I left, and Lloyd doesn't know where I am. In case you haven't noticed, he's had maybe ten hours' sleep spread over the last five days."

"I haven't noticed much of anything lately."

"Everyone is lost in slumber, thus they won't know I'm gone until tomorrow. Lloyd hid the campsite most effectively. You'd never find it in the rain at night."

I looked back at Shane. "Is that your way of saying we're stuck here till morning?"

He raised his head. "My tube is filled with mud."

———

In a far corner of the barn I found a tack room full of riding saddles, horse blankets, and a few bridles. None of the saddles had been oiled recently, and spiders had spun webs in the stirrups. Seemed kind of strange to have all this gear and let it go to pot. One of the saddles was a kid's English rig. I couldn't imagine a scenario that fit a man living alone in a big mother of a house with all this horse equipment he seems to have walked away from. Sam Callahan would have come up with a story, but he basically lives in his fantasies. I've always been more of a reality woman.

Time to behave like a reality woman. Shane, the bum, was

right. My ribs burned when I breathed, my breasts were covered with dried blood, my back felt as if someone had hammered on my lower spine, and, worst of all, I still didn't have Auburn. And every single misfortune was my own damn fault.

Shit.

The weird thing is at that moment I didn't need a drink. You'd think a person who dealt with the daily humdrum by staying soused would race to the bottle after major violence. Maybe major violence was too much trauma even for Yukon Jack. Lying on my back on the concrete, looking up as that hairy monster dropped his pants and prepared to rape me—something inside had died. Or gone away. The powerlessness changed something.

I lifted a horse blanket and looked down on the hugest set of jugs I'd ever seen. This floozy on a magazine cover crawled toward the camera with her tongue hanging out like a thirsty dog and—no lie—her tits dragging the floor. It was disgusting. She had hair the color of Armand's toenails. The whores of Memphis were rank amateurs compared to this hard-ass woman. Shane would love it.

———

"This ought to make you feel more human," I said, carrying a load of horse blankets with the girlie magazine on top.

When Shane saw the floozy his eyes sparked with the old flame.

"Nothing in all nature compares to the woman's breast," he said. "The combination of beauty and nutrition is unrivaled."

"Only a pervert would call those things beautiful. They're nothing but hanging pumpkins."

Shane examined me, then the magazine cover, then me again. "Do I detect a note of jealousy, little missy?"

"You better dry fast, you're getting delirious."

The horse blankets were fairly high quality to have been

abandoned to mice—mostly plaid Baker blankets and coolers with a couple of Australian rugs. I spread the Australians on the floor.

Shane asked, "Have you ever considered implants?"

"I gave birth to two children with this pair and they work fine. Now, take off those wet clothes, Lloyd'll kill me if you die on us."

He stared at my blood-encrusted breasts. Up to then I'd been too busy for self-consciousness about the hanging tits thing, but now I crossed my arms. "Off with the clothes."

Shane started unbuttoning his shirt. "You just want to see my phallus."

I covered his shoulders with a blanket and rubbed his hair. "I've seen your phallus, you should consider an implant."

Shane started to laugh and went into a gag. His whole body was shivering. He tried to work out of his pants but couldn't manage it. I straightened his legs to help with the process, and together we got him naked. Touching his legs was like handling firewood.

"Is there any chance of you answering a question honestly?" I asked.

"I am always honest."

I'd turned out the overhead lights and moved Shane back from the open doors, out of the wind and rifle range, but I could still see the front door and the light up in Armand's room. "When you stopped drinking, did your social life suffer?"

I had Shane's middle wrapped like a mummy, but he still shook. "You mean did I get laid less?"

"I'm thinking seriously about quitting alcohol, but I'm afraid interesting men won't like me anymore."

"To be strictly frank, women have always found me irresistible. However, after I stopped drinking, the quality of woman who did so rose several meaningful notches."

"I wonder if I could find higher-quality men."

"My child, you could search the world over and never find lower-quality men than the ones you've chosen recently."

The bedroom light went off. Armand was probably up there at the window, with his rifle, waiting for us to leave the barn. Let him wait—we had nowhere to go, and he was losing blood too fast to stay.

"Armand was nice at first. How was I to know he was a paranoid, sadistic psychopath?" I asked.

"If you'd been sober, you would have known."

As I knelt on the concrete to dry Shane's feet, the adrenaline high suddenly crashed and everything that had happened the last few weeks came down on me at once. Dothan, Auburn, Lloyd, Shane, Yukon Jack—the weight was unbearable.

I started to whimper. "Shane, life isn't turning out right."

He touched the top of my head. "It never does."

"I try to keep going and act happy, but nothing I do works. I'm helpless."

"You are only helpless if you refuse to ask for help."

"Jesus"—I rested my head on his knees—"another bumper snicker to live by."

I cried while Shane ran his fingers through my hair. Shane's touch brought back a feeling of Dad when I was real little. Had Dad ever brushed hair out of my face while I cried in his lap, or is that one of those memories you want so much you make it real?

"Why did you come back?" I asked.

"You are worth saving."

"Oh." I felt the horse blanket on my face. It reminded me of Frostbite and the ranch.

"I don't think I'll listen to Paul Harvey anymore," I said.

Shane did his chuckle sound where all three chins seem to contract at once. "The postcards to Papa have to go, too," he said.

"They do?"

"Let him die, Maurey."

———

We were both quiet a long time, until Shane exhaled one of his freight-train snores. He slid down on his back, and I was afraid he would fall out of the chair, so I eased him onto the Australian rug pallet. His face seemed waxy and melting, like a red candle in an oven.

I thought about what he'd said about asking for help. Life must be pretty desperate for me to be listening to Shane Rinesfoos's advice, but, let's face it, my life had been pretty desperate lately. At the moment, I had more faith in other people's judgment than my own. Which is a frightening moment to find yourself in. The time had come to stop dicking around and admit the way I'd done things so far didn't work.

I seized on the idea of changing every element of my life. I would start over at the last point where I'd liked myself, which was before I lost my virginity and before I took my first drink. Then I would do every single detail differently; I'd get up on the other side of the bed, brush my teeth sideways instead of up and down, only sleep with nice guys who liked me—that would be a switch—stay sober, and stay on the ranch.

Armand's truck sputtered and kicked on. In my new-life rapture I'd forgotten to watch the front door. It was just dumb luck he didn't crawl in the barn doors and shoot us both dead. When he shifted into first, the truck jerked forward and died. The engine rumbled again, and, delicately, Armand turned it around and headed up the hill.

Shane came awake with a wheeze. "Tell him to clutch with his heel, not his toes."

"He'll learn," I said.

"Holy Hannah, I'm freezing." He was in bad shape, shivering and coughing. His face felt clammy cold and hot at the same time.

I talked as I wrapped blankets around his arms. "Shane, I've decided to start all over at the beginning."

"I wish I could do that."

"I'll stop drinking by pretending I never started. I'll stay home on the ranch and won't go to college. I'll wear too much makeup instead of none, I'll die my hair blond. If I'm blond, I won't have to drink to attract men."

Shane made a weak smile. "Do you know why gentlemen prefer blondes?" he asked.

"All I know is they do."

"Because they're tired of squeezing blackheads."

We both laughed way out of proportion to the worth of the joke. I lay on my back, next to him on the pallet, and laughed, looking up at the corrugated metal ceiling. Shane turned his radish color and went into a coughing fit that ended in a choking sound and loads of bloody drool.

"Don't tell any more jokes," I said. I tried to play it blasé, but coughing up blood was scary. Shane looked real sick, and I was helpless to make him better. *Helpless* seemed to be today's theme word. Maybe I'd been helpless all my life but too stupid to know it.

"In Alaska, while I was serving on the Antarctic Rescue Squad, we used to find victims of hypothermia, and the only way to warm them was to wrap them in blankets with a naked person. The body heat transferred to the victim and often saved them," Shane said.

I didn't for a minute believe that Antarctic Rescue Squad jive—for one thing, it's Arctic in Alaska, not Antarctic—but the naked-body-in-the-blankets trick works. You read about it in a Wyoming newspaper once or twice a winter.

"Only a suggestion," Shane said.

I stood up. "The panties stay on. And one lewd move from you and I throw you out in the rain."

"When have I been lewd on this trip?"

"About as often as I've been drunk."

"I have one other problem. In the ditch, while I was risking my precious health to save your pretty skin, my catheter sprung a leak. There's tape in my pants, the pocket with the harmonica."

Shane looked like a plaid caterpillar with a fat, human head. He wouldn't meet my eyes. "This entire escapade is a trick," I said. "You've been scheming to get my hands on your penis since the moment we met."

Shane's chest made a rattle sound. "Would I go so far as to die for a hand job from you?"

I dropped my jeans. "Yes."

45

THE NEXT AFTERNOON I DROVE MOBY DICK BETWEEN A double set of railroad tracks and endless green fields of something southern—tobacco or cotton, maybe. The day was a beautiful blue, and room temperature, a warm room, anyway, and the trees hovering over the farmhouses were covered with pink and white flowers. Brad sat next to me in the front seat, although we hadn't made up yet. He answered my statements or questions with moody monosyllables—*yep, nope, uh.*

Lloyd was in back helping Marcella take care of Shane. There wasn't much taking care they could do besides wiping his forehead with a wet rag and turning him sideways when he coughed blood. Andrew made a *Popular Mechanics* into a fan and stood at Shane's feet stirring the air around until he got bored. Then he read *Spider-Man* out loud.

Shane had been delirious for several hours. At least I think he was delirious. He seemed to be reliving amorous escapades from his youth. "Try some butter, Jeanie." "That's not my finger." "Let me on top, I never get to be on top."

Knowing Shane, he may have been faking delirium as an excuse to show off.

"I think that's it." Brad pointed up ahead at a two-story yellow house with white trim. The house fit what Granma had told us when we called from Brevard—full-length porch, twin magnolias out front, field out back. That description matched every farmhouse we'd passed for miles, but this was the only one next to a burned barn.

"Uncle Shane keeps talking dirty," Andrew whined. "Make him stop."

"Uncle Shane doesn't know what he's saying. He's having a dream," Marcella said. She'd been trying to coax Shane into drinking water. Loved ones are always trying to strong-arm food, drink, or medicine into sick people. When I'm sick all I want is stuff out.

"We'll get you a Coca-Cola at Granma's," Lloyd said to Shane. "Coca-Cola made you feel better that time in Mexico City."

Brad turned to look back at the others. "I hope his granma has Coca-Cola, I'm thirsty."

Shane raised up on his elbows. "Miss Hepburn wants me on a horse!"

I hit a big pothole in the road that bounced first Moby Dick, then the trailer. Yes, it's true. We'd rescued my trailer from the evil rat Armand. Got back what was left of my beer, too.

Lloyd snapped, "Take it easy, you're shaking him."

Normally when I'm criticized like that I snap right back, but today I eased up on the accelerator. "I hope Granma has an extra bed. I could sleep for a week," I said.

I pulled Moby Dick and the trailer into Granma's red dirt driveway. She had a pink stone birdbath next to one of the magnolias and flagstone steps from the driveway to the front door.

"Don't stomp the brakes," Lloyd said.

"Yeah, right."

A tall woman in a baseball cap, long-sleeved plaid shirt, and green pants came around the house, pulling off her cotton gloves. Her complexion matched the off-red dirt on the driveway, and she had eyes could drill holes in sheet metal.

"You get lost?" she demanded.

When you've been trying to get somewhere a long time, and suddenly you're there, it's like a tension collapse. The pressure you didn't know was so heavy is released, but it leaves a vague emptiness. High school graduation gave me the same depression as switching off Moby Dick in that yard.

"We took it slow for Shane," I said. "Will you tell Granma we're here?"

She drew up ever taller. "I am Granma."

That was a surprise. I figured Shane in his mid-fifties, which put Granma at late eighties, at least. Gravity is supposed to wear a body down after eighty years or so, but this woman had the posture of a dancer.

"Is Lloyd Carbonneau in this vehicle?" she demanded.

"Yes, ma'am." I'd never called anyone "*ma'am*" in my life.

"Andrew always said I could trust Lloyd Carbonneau."

"Andrew said that?"

Lloyd opened the side doors and asked, "Where should I put him?"

"The downstairs bedroom is made up. You and Marcella help me bring Andrew inside."

"Hello, Granma," Marcella said.

I figured it out. Shane was Andrew. He'd lied through his teeth about Shane being his real name. That explained why Hugo Jr. was the second kid.

"You." Granma addressed Andrew, the child. "Go in and wash your face. This isn't Texas, we do not behave like Indians in the South."

All right. A take-charge person. That's exactly what I'd hoped to find at the end of the road—someone with the strength left to know what to do.

"You two, start picking," Granma ordered.

Brad looked at me. "Does she mean us?"

"Picking what?" I asked.

"Strawberries!" Granma glowered with her hawk eyes. "I'm coming off the line, someone has to go on."

I stepped out of Moby Dick into the sunlight, thinking maybe the old lady had cataracts in her eyes and hadn't noticed my bruises. "I'm not in very good shape to be picking crops," I said.

Granma was clearly disgusted. "You're at least sixty years younger than I am. If I can pick, you can pick."

"But—"

"Don't but me, little missy."

From the ambulance, Shane's voice rose in an erotic fever. "Mount it, little missy. My rod's hot as a firecracker."

———

A very black man named Patrick gave us each a wooden frame that held six quart baskets. He looked at my face and sort of recoiled. "What happened to you?"

"I fell down."

Patrick studied me a moment, then nodded, either satisfied with the explanation or figuring it was none of his business. "We pay twenty-five cents a quart. Fill them to overflowing. If I find any rocks or soft strawberries, you don't get paid for that quart."

"How do we pick them?" Brad asked.

Patrick spit. "The row on the end is yours. You'll have to hurry to catch up."

Just like that—*Zip*—I became a farmer. What would my father do if he knew I was picking fruit off bushes? He'd laugh so hard he would fall off his horse, that's what he would do. Hank Elkrunner would adopt that sly Blackfoot smirk and innocently say, "Farming suits you, Maurey. Puts color in your cheeks." Then he would fall off his horse. Lydia

Callahan would throw some ironic twist on the deal, like "We all end up being what we fear most," and Sam Callahan would ask, "What's the difference between ranching and farming?" The cluck.

Me, I was almost too tired to be embarrassed. Brad and I stood over our first strawberry plant, staring down at it the way you stare at fairly exotic and smelly food your mom is making you eat. Four little black kids—who I was later to learn were all sons and daughters of Patrick—were forty or fifty feet ahead of us, picking their way across the field. Since Brad and I shared a row, theoretically anyway, we should be able to catch them somewhere along the horizon.

"You think they're good to eat?" Brad asked.

"Try one."

He bent over and tasted a strawberry. "They're just like the strawberries in the stores."

"What'd you expect?" I still hadn't moved on my first berry.

"I don't know, I thought they treated them with chemicals or something."

I looked over at the yellow house. In the backyard, sheets and pillowcases hung limply from a clothesline that was looped around these pulley deals so a person standing on the screened-in porch could reel in the wash. I don't know how Wyoming women dried clothes in the olden days before electricity. Some years we'll go four months without cracking thirty-two degrees.

"So, what'd I say the other night to piss you off so bad?" I asked.

"We better pick. I don't want that lady mad at me."

Getting the strawberries off the plants was easy—you pinch the stem and pull—but the bending over, straightening up, moving the quart baskets, and bending over again was agony-on-parade for my back and ribs. Let's not forget I'd been stomped recently.

Brad was picking two or three plants ahead, with his back to me, when he said, "You told me my drawings stunk and I was no better than my father."

I stopped work. "I was drunk, Brad. I'm sorry, sometimes when I'm drunk I say mean things that aren't true. You are a very talented artist and you're nothing at all like your father. Maybe I was talking about me and my father. Whatever I said was a lie."

He turned profile, still not looking at me. "That's not what you said the other night. You said when you drink you tell the truth, and when you're sober you're afraid to be honest."

Had I said that? I looked at the strawberry in my hand. "It's the other way around, Brad."

"I don't get it. Freedom was a bastard all the time, but you're nice to me when you haven't been drinking and a real stoolhead when you have. Which is the real you?"

"They're both the real me." I made it to my feet. "Sometimes when I love people I treat them badly so they'll have an excuse to go away."

At the word *love*, a strange look crossed his angel face. He glanced at me, then back at the red dirt. "Why?"

I shrugged. "I guess I'd rather drive them off than get left. Hell, I don't know. I don't analyze why I do the crap I do."

Brad didn't say anything for a while. Grown-up approach-and-flee behavior must be confusing to a kid. I know it's confusing to me. Finally Brad asked, "Does that mean you love me?"

I took a deep breath. "Sure, I love you."

Brad turned to look at me. Lord knows what he thought. He probably hadn't run into much love before and hadn't realized how people who feel it hurt each other. He shook his head side to side. "Beats me," he said.

"Beats me, too."

He gave me an uncertain smile. "Whichever is the real you, I'm not buying her any more Yukon Jack."

———

"How'd you enjoy picking strawberries?" Lloyd asked that evening at supper.

I glared with all the venom I could muster, but it wasn't enough for him to notice. He kept buttering his corn and salting his okra. Delilah Talbot was right about the South and vegetables. Outside of Thanksgiving and Christmas, I never sat at a western table with more than one non-potato vegetable. Down south they eat more vegetables than beef. The part of meals I don't approve of in North Carolina is the pre-sugared iced tea. I think people deserve a choice, but southerners say sugar won't dissolve right unless you dump it in when the tea's hot. Dothan Talbot and I used to go round and round on the subject and, other than one more excuse to hate each other, nothing was ever decided.

"You make much money this afternoon?" Lloyd asked.

"I made seven dollars, and Maurey came in with three fifty," Brad said. "She had three quarts disqualified for soft strawberries."

Nobody had noticed I was giving them the silent treatment, so I blew it off. I said, "That's for five hours' work. Three dollars fifty cents for five hours is cheaper than slavery."

"Amos made thirty-six dollars," Brad said. Amos was eleven years old and a show-off. The only good thing about him was he sang Stevie Wonder songs while he worked.

Marcella brought in a bowl of field peas, which you have to be from the South to tell from black-eyed peas. Andrew had been fed earlier and sent outside to play. Hugo Jr. was asleep in the same crib Shane used to sleep in. Isn't that amazing?

"Where were you hiding all day?" I asked Lloyd. "We could have used another hand in the field of hell."

Lloyd's eyes were worn out. It must be rough when the person who saved you goes down. Even though Shane seemed dependent on Lloyd, my guess is that need stuff flowed both ways. "Granma sent me out to inventory the barn."

"The cur what's-his-name burnt it down."

"Ashley Montagu," Marcella said.

"Wasn't that the guy in *Gone With the Wind*?"

Marcella poured milk from a glass milk pitcher. "Wilkes. The guy in *Gone With the Wind* was Ashley Wilkes."

"She wants the barn rebuilt," Lloyd said. "I went through to see if there's anything worth keeping and what it would take to clear the foundation."

"Did you ever do any carpentry?" I asked.

He shrugged his bare shoulders. "She just needs to know what's out there. I won't be here to drive the nails."

"Where is Granma, anyway?" I asked. "She's passing up a chance to criticize us."

Even though I hadn't asked, Marcella cut me another chunk of ham. "She's with Shane and the doctor. Dr. Keller drove out after his regular office closed for the day." Marcella smiled. "When you're ninety, doctors still make house calls."

Brad couldn't believe it. "That lady is ninety?"

I said, "Shane hates doctors. He'd never allow one to touch him." We'd tried to drag him off to a doctor in Chattanooga that morning and he'd thrown a Shane fit—threatened to make all our lives miserable if we didn't take him straight home.

"He didn't have much choice this time," Lloyd said. "Granma's in charge."

Brad got up with his dishes. "Now that I've met Granma, I'm not so certain Ashley Montagu was a cur."

Lloyd said, "You're starting to talk like Maurey."

I took that as a compliment.

After supper I carried my coffee out on the front porch to watch the light change. Hank Elkrunner once told me you can't go crazy if you take the time each day to sit quietly and watch the sun come up and go down. I'd almost as soon go crazy as wake up for sunrise, but I've found half the deal helps a lot.

Andrew waved at me from across the yard. He'd made it his personal mission to knock down the birdbath, which meant running as hard as he could and hurling himself into the base. He wasn't having any effect on the birdbath, but he had managed to scare away the birds.

I felt drained. It had been almost twenty-four hours since I drank anything alcoholic, and that was only a juice glass of Scotch, but I didn't feel the usual knot in my stomach and nail in my spine. My spine hurt, sure, but that was from being kicked. Maybe one pain blew away the other pain. The physical symptoms when you want a drink and can't have one are way different from the physical symptoms when you don't want a drink. In the end, the addiction wins either way, but that first forty-eight hours or so, mental attitude has a major influence on physical discomfort. So to speak. As it were.

The screen door banged and Marcella came out to stand next to me and watch Andrew climb the birdbath. She was wearing a sweater, which is what people from warm climates do when the temperature dips below seventy. Somehow, Andrew had gotten his feet up in the basin and was hanging upside down by his heels, hollering for help. Neither one of us took it seriously enough to leave the porch.

"The doctor is still with Shane," Marcella said.

"How's it look?"

She used her hands to pull her hair behind her ears. "You know doctors, they won't tell you anything until they're ready. Shane's awake, anyway, he's not delirious anymore."

Some kind of cricket or locust or something we don't have back home started buzz sawing in the trees. That's the kind of noise, if you're raised on it, you find comforting, but if you're not, it gives you the willies. Marcella hugged her elbows with her hands and stared up the road toward the tracks. I turned to check out what she was watching and saw the Oldsmobile.

"Let him come in," I said.

Marcella rocked back a few inches. "Are you sure?"

"It's time to forgive. Hugo's had enough."

"But you said throw him out on his ass."

It was my turn to be taken back. "Marcella, I'm amazed. A week ago you'd have choked if you tried to say *ass*."

She blushed from the neck. "You said never forgive a man who fools around."

"I changed my mind."

"One of the reasons I've been so strong with him is because I'm trying to be more like you."

"Oh, Lord, Marcella, don't do that."

Andrew fell off the birdbath on his head. He rolled over and got up shaky, then he kicked the stone, which hurt his foot so he had to sit down again.

"You think it can ever be the same between me and Hugo?" Marcella asked.

Watching Andrew and being sober made me ache for Auburn more than ever. "It can't be the same, but you can make it okay."

Marcella walked across the yard and lifted Andrew onto the birdbath. He stood with a foot on each side of the rim, his arms held high, and shouted, "*King of the mountain.*"

Marcella looked back at me and said, "About Armand. It wasn't all your fault. He fooled me at first, too, and I wasn't even drunk."

"Thanks."

She smiled, then turned and walked up the driveway toward
the Oldsmobile.

46

LLOYD SAT ON A COUCH IN THE LIVING ROOM, WATCHING
television and eating frozen grapefruit juice from the can with
a spoon. It was odd, seeing him on regular furniture, watching
regular television. I'd never connected Lloyd to normal things
people do.

"It's called *Bridget Loves Bernie*," he said, gesturing at the TV
with his spoon. "One's Jewish and one's Catholic, and their
parents can't adjust."

I sat in an antique rocker that would have been great for
nursing babies. It creaked gently as I leaned back. "Which one
is Jewish?"

"Bernie, I think. That's more a Jewish name."

"Only Jewish kid I knew growing up was named Pete. Once
a year he passed out crackers to everyone in class."

Bridget wore her hair the way I did before I went crazy and
attacked myself with the scissors.

"Will Shane die?" I asked.

The spoon stopped moving. "I think so."

Bernie's mother yammered at Bridget a mile a minute in real
condescending tones. If I'd been Bridget, I would have said,
"Go fuck yourself, bitch."

"Should I stop drinking?"

Lloyd glanced at me, then back at the TV. I've noticed most people do best in serious conversations if you don't look at them and they don't have to look at you. "That's your decision. If you do stop, I'll be here to help."

"The way Shane helped you in Mexico City?"

His eyes clouded, I suppose thinking of those days in Mexico City. "Yes."

I leaned forward, toward Lloyd, looking right at him. "But you're going off to Florida."

On the television, a cartoon penguin urged us to smoke Kool menthol cigarettes. He wore a green stocking cap and glissaded down a chunk of ice. "I'll stay with you till you don't need me anymore," Lloyd said.

"Shane stayed with you three years."

"You won't need me three years."

"How do you know?"

Still without looking at me, he said, "If you do, we'll look for Sharon together."

That would be an odd way to live, driving around the countryside, partners with a man searching for his wife. A permanent Moby Dick trip. I studied Lloyd's face with its web of lines and crucified eyes. He slid a spoonful of frozen juice between his lips, swished it around, and swallowed. Had I missed something, or had we just sworn to a major commitment?

———

Dr. Keller came through the living room after he left Shane. The doctor wore a suit vest but no coat. His glasses were the kind without ear pieces that hang from your pocket by a ribbon. They clipped on his nose and made his forehead wrinkle when he focused on something. People in Agatha Christie books wore weird glasses like these, but no one I'd ever seen or heard of in real life did. Maybe the doctor read too much Agatha Christie and became one of her characters. I've known cowboys to do that with Louis L'Amour.

"Granma gave orders I was to look at you before leaving the house," Dr. Keller said.

"She did?"

"Hold your face to the light."

The doctor inspected my chin and burned hand, then felt the knot on the back of my head. He had me lean forward while he poked at my lower back, asking, "Does this hurt? Does this hurt? How about here?"

I answered, "Yes, yes, yes," but he didn't seem impressed.

He had me unbutton my top two shirt buttons and breathe deeply while he listened for gurgles in my lungs.

"How is Shane?" Lloyd asked.

The doctor slid the cold stethoscope across my chest. "Mr. Rinesfoos might live through the night. I wouldn't bet on tomorrow."

"He's dying?" I asked.

As he listened to my chest, the doctor cocked his head to one side, like a bird. "Oh, yes, he's dying all right."

"Shouldn't we take him to a hospital?"

"I have done everything possible to make him comfortable. There is no real point to admitting him, and, evidently, he wants to die at home." Dr. Keller gave a soft chuckle. "The man has quite a forceful personality, you know. Not unlike his grandmother."

He finished and put away his doctor tools. "No broken bones or internal bleeding. That cut on your face should have been stitched, but it's too late now. Better to leave it open, let it breathe. I'm afraid you'll have a rather nasty scar."

"You think it would help my back if I don't pick strawberries tomorrow?"

The chuckle came again. "Oh, no, work is the best thing—keep you from stiffening up." He snapped his black bag shut. "You're the woman Mr. Rinesfoos rescued, aren't you?"

"I'm the woman."

"I wouldn't feel too badly if I were you. He would have died in another year or two anyway."

———

Too tired to sleep. Desperate to sleep. Granma or someone equally sadistic would bang on the door at dawn to drag my ass into the strawberry fields. Panic sets in—knowing you're exhausted beyond human endurance yet you must be back on your feet in so many hours makes every moment of rest too precious to waste lying there wishing you could sleep.

I stared up from my bunk bed at the bottom of the top bunk bed. This was Shane's very own room from God knows how long ago when he was a boy. Those were Shane's hangers in the closet and Shane's chest of drawers with the framed black-and-white photographs of Shane, upright, in a graduation gown and funny hat. Those stains on the box springs two feet above my nose were no doubt made forty-five or fifty years ago when a thinner Shane, who was Andrew then, lay right where I was now and whacked himself off in the dark. It staggers the imagination to picture people of an older generation masturbating.

Sounds of *Gunsmoke* drifted up through the floor. Lloyd and Brad were down there in the living room, held captive by Matt Dillon and Miss Kitty. Did Matthew and Miss Kitty hump? That was the crucial question of an entire decade of American history. First there was the atomic bomb, then the Cold War, and finally Matt Dillon's sex life. And why bunk beds? Had there been another Shane, a brother who died or didn't die or what? If Granma really was his granma—which was debatable since everyone from the doctor to the black guy in the field called her Granma—then that implied a middle generation, a Mom and Dad. No wonder I couldn't sleep. I was going crazy.

I rolled over facedown with my arms tucked at my sides, then back over with both hands clasped on my belly, like a laid-out corpse. Nothing worked. I didn't need a newspaper to tell me Granma was one of those hated fanatics who claim it's a sin to sleep past sunrise. Which I wouldn't mind if they kept it to themselves, but in my sleepless heart I knew Granma accepted no internal clock but her own. Sunrise—get up. Sunset—sleep. Do it my way or else. That's how grouchy people get to be so old while pleasant people who don't bother anyone die young.

"It's no bother." Those were Dad's last words to me. He'd called to see if I wanted some gourds they'd picked up at a farmers market in Idaho. Auburn was two months old and I said I couldn't drive out to the ranch until Thursday, and Dad said he'd bring them in after he rounded up a couple of cows the next day. I said, "Don't make a special trip to town," and Dad said, "It's no bother." I should have told him I loved him or would miss him or something, but, Jeeze, you can't walk around every day thinking, What if my loved ones die before I see them again? You'd go nuts.

If Shane died in the next hour, his last words to me would be "My rod's hot as a firecracker." He probably planned it that way.

The last time I saw Sam's grandfather, before he died, I'd flown to Greensboro for Christmas my sophomore year at UW. It was right after the Park heartbreak thing, and I thought Sam and Shannon would help me find sanity. Sam's grandfather Caspar had already suffered a couple of mini-strokes, and he wasn't in great shape. Christmas morning he leaned on his cane next to the tree and recited Henry Wadsworth Longfellow's "Hiawatha." I read the directions while Sam and Shannon tried to assemble a L'il Miss Doll House. No one paid any attention to Caspar. Two weeks later, he was dead.

When lightning killed Molly, my whole world was devastated. If I ever go to a shrink, I think I'll tell her that was the moment the happy part of my life ended. I still mourn that horse, and the deal is even more complicated because I mourn her in a way I don't mourn Dad. So I feel guilty that my grief for Dad isn't as pure as my grief for my horse. When Molly died, I felt horrible; when Dad died all I felt was hollow. And to prove I really loved Dad the way you're supposed to, I adopted self-destruction as a personal style—made myself ugly by cutting my hair and stupid by staying drunk.

Let's cut to the crux of all this sleep-avoidance mishmash: My mistakes ended someone else's life. Shane would die because I screwed up. I didn't want to ever forget that.

A knock so gentle it had to be Marcella came at the door. "Maurey, are you asleep?"

"Yes."

She cracked open the door. "Shane is asking to see you."

I rolled over on my side to consider what that meant. Accusations? A deathbed forgiveness scene? Shane had squeezed drama from every situation in his life, no reason to think he would stop at this point.

Marcella slipped through the light into the room. "He said to wake you on account of he'd probably die before morning."

"I'd have come without extortion."

"Shane wanted to be certain."

47

WHEN I CUT THROUGH THE LIVING ROOM LLOYD AND BRAD looked up from the couch but didn't say anything. Merle lay curled in a fur ball, asleep in Brad's lap. From the rocker, Hugo Sr. smiled through his rectangular glasses. He nodded at the TV and said, "I liked Festus better."

On *Gunsmoke* a cowboy named Newley or Muley or something like that helped an overdressed lady into a stagecoach. I said, "Everyone likes Festus better."

Hugo Sr.'s box head bobbed up and down. "Ain't it the truth."

———

Granma sat under a semicircle of light at a rolltop desk doing whatever paperwork people who run farms do. She one-finger-punched her calculator with the force of punching out eyeballs, then scowled through bifocal wire rims at whatever results the calculator had the audacity to cough up. So far as I could tell, the bifocals were Granma's only admission that time touched her body or mind.

"I was just thinking about Mary Beth," Shane said. "She was such a lovely, energetic girl. I wonder if there's not something we could do to help her."

"Who?" Shane's side of the room was so dark it took a few seconds to locate him under the massive quilt that must have been passed down from the Civil War. "Mary Beth. Critter. She's much too vivacious to attach herself to that manipulative snake with the ridiculous name." Shane's forehead and upper lip glistened with sweat. Drops collected on all three chins and ran into the creases in his neck. His eyes glittered like purple lights on a Christmas tree, but they seemed to be withdrawing into the flesh beneath his eyebrows. I slid into a chair still warm from Marcella and picked a damp washrag from a bowl on the nightstand. I guess it's an automatic response to wipe sweat off sick people's brows.

"Critter was wonderfully happy and curious when I met her. One look and I knew she was the one to make me feel young again. I wish I could have kept her. You probably are unaware that she loves strawberries. Of all my women, I recall Critter most vividly."

"I guess you always remember the last one most vividly."

"Critter was not the last woman I slept with, you know."

I wasn't sure if that meant he didn't sleep with her or he'd slept with someone since. I held his hand. "Tell me about the last one."

He gave my fingers a weak squeeze. "She was a confused girl with a raging fire inside that had been so insulated by her fear of love, no warmth came to the surface."

Didn't take any idiot to tell he was talking about me. "That was first aid, Shane. Don't go around saying we've slept together."

"When I am in heaven and called up to testify before God concerning the many beautiful breasts I've taken comfort between, yours shall lead the list. You should see Maurey's tits, Granma. Show Granma your tits."

Granma glared at me with blatant hostility. You'd have a monumental battle if you threw her hawk eyes up against

393

Lloyd's Jesus look. Could he absorb anger faster than she fired it out? Would her drive to judge saturate his capacity to accept? Las Vegas could lay out the odds.

"I love women." Shane made a sound like a sigh interrupted by a dry heave. It didn't seem to bother him or alarm Granma, so I pretended not to notice.

"God, I love women," Shane repeated. "Did you ever watch a woman apply makeup? Or stockings—I nearly cry when I see a woman sliding stockings over her legs."

"I generally don't wear makeup or stockings."

"It's not so much the sexual act, although that is wonderful. I still get chills up my back when I recall a blow job given me by Dessie DuBose in 1953. My God, what a mouth on that woman." He kind of drifted off for a while, reliving a pleasant moment from 1953. I mopped his forehead again and squeezed the washrag into the bowl. Shane's lips parted as he tried to breathe, and I could see his yellow-pink tongue on his bottom teeth. What would I relive as I lay dying? Bathing my babies, maybe, or one spring day when I took off my clothes and sat in Miner Creek feeling the water on my legs and sunshine on my shoulders.

"It's not so much the sexual act." Shane took up where he left off. "What I'll miss is putting my face against a woman's neck and falling asleep. The smell is delicious. I hope heaven smells like a female's collarbone."

"Maybe you better get some sleep now," I said.

His eyes shifted and landed on me. "Why? I'll be gone soon enough. Why can't I spend my last hours of consciousness conscious? Did you know I once jammed with Son House? Son said 'Take it, white boy,' and God, did I take it. I was in heaven that day."

"Sounds nice," I said, even though I'd never heard of Son House.

"I'm going to miss my harmonica almost as much as women."
Later he added, "And Oreo cookies."

Back in the eighth grade I read every death-of-a-major-character book in Teton County Library—*Little Women*, *Charlotte's Web*, *Daisy Miller*, *Bambi*, I devoured Dickens—searching for a clue as to what happens next. Eternal blankness was impossible to understand, but all the other theories struck me as silly. What happens next is the most important question there is, but no one knows the answer, and the only way to have any semblance of a life is to ignore the question.

Through college and into the drunk years, I got caught up in my personal life and managed to ignore the question easily, but sitting in a dark room next to a dying man made the deal hard to beg.

All the individuals I trusted deflected the unspeakable stuff with jokes. Lydia Callahan once told me that when I commit secret, disgusting acts—like ditching gum under a chair or peeing in a swimming pool—an alarm goes off in heaven and the angels gather to laugh at my social blunder. In Lydia's world, religion and proper douching go hand in hand.

Dad said when people die they go to San Francisco, which makes as much sense as pearly gates and streets of gold. At least San Francisco is real.

"And Jimmy Stewart movies," Shane said. "The westerns, not the ones where he plays Charles Lindbergh or the guy who went to Washington."

"What's that?"

He held up his hand to show me four fingers. "Women, my harmonica, Oreos, and Jimmy Stewart westerns."

"How about horses?"

"No, I won't miss horses."

"My most favorite thing is the sound geese make when they fly over the house in fall."

"I like campfires," Shane said.

We were silent awhile, thinking of things we would miss if we died. My list was theoretical.

Shane cleared his throat. He dug under the quilt for a handkerchief, which he spit into, then he folded the handkerchief over whatever he spit and slipped it back under the quilt. The doctor had done something to stop the coughing, but not coughing scared me more than coughing because I could picture his lungs filling with blood.

"Let us review Maurey's last few weeks," Shane said.

"Oh, no, surely there's a better way to spend your time."

He did the four fingers thing again. "You drove a car with your baby on the roof, you attempted suicide, you got yourself beat to smithereens, not to mention almost raped and murdered, and you killed me."

"Shane."

"Frankness is expected from a dying man. It's the only time in life when honesty goes unpunished."

"Wouldn't you rather conserve your strength than talk about this?"

His chins jiggled, causing rivulets of sweat to run onto the quilt. "Do you know why all these disasters happened?" he asked.

I looked at my feet. "Alcohol."

"Correct. Now, since you caused my demise, I have the right to demand a promise."

I kept my eyes on the hardwood floor and didn't say anything. Whatever atonement he had in mind would be brutal. Shane wasn't the type to ask for small favors.

"Do you agree you owe me a promise?"

"I agree already."

"I want you to promise you won't take another drink until I am dead."

I exhaled. I'd been expecting a dry-for-life pledge. This was short-term enough to deal with. "I was planning to quit forever, Shane."

His smile made him look ghoulish. The man was melting before my eyes. "Quite admirable, and I hope you follow through," he said, "but what I demand is a solemn oath—cross your heart and hope to die—that you won't touch a drop of alcohol while I am alive. If you honor the vow, I shall forgive you for killing me and, even better, give you permission to forgive yourself."

I looked over at Granma, who was furiously writing in a ledger. She didn't care if I promised. Shane watched me from sparkly eyes that seemed to be sinking into his flesh. Normally, I don't care for commitments, but the guy was dying, and it was my fault.

"Okay."

"Okay what?" he asked.

"I solemnly swear not to touch a drop of alcohol while Shane Rinesfoos lives."

He nodded. "Cross your heart and hope to die."

"Don't you think we're a little old—"

"Cross your heart and hope to die."

"Okay. I cross my heart and hope to die." Interesting phrase for someone who recently attempted suicide.

Shane took my hand again. "Send Lloyd in. Opportunities such as this are rare."

Feeling dismissed, I stood up. His hand tightened on mine. "Good-bye, Maurey, take care of them."

"Take care of who?"

"Lloyd and Brad. Marcella and Andrew. They'd be in big trouble without you."

How was I supposed to take that? "I'll look in on you later."

He squeezed my hand one more time. "Life is lovely, Maurey. Don't forget."

48

SHANE DIDN'T DIE THAT NIGHT, OR THE NEXT DAY WHILE I was crawling around the strawberry fields, feeling sick. When we stopped for lunch—which Granma called dinner—Marcella said he was in and out of delirium, mostly in. One of the times he was out, he'd had the strength to ask about me.

"I told Shane you were picking," Marcella said.

"Was he entertained?"

"He said you must be having kittens. I don't know what he meant by that."

My stomach refused to accept fried okra or corn bread. It's like I looked at the glistening grease and a fist grabbed my belly. Instead, I drank a half gallon of pre-sweetened iced tea.

That afternoon Lloyd finished whatever it was he'd been doing in the burned-down barn and came out to help Brad, Hugo Sr., and me with our migrant worker act. Lloyd looked right at home in those white overalls with no shirt, all he lacked was a tattoo—BORN TO FARM. He worked the row next to mine, which made me somewhat nervous because I knew he was on the lookout for crash symptoms. So was I. I kept expecting the earth to boil over with spiders and cockroaches, but all I saw were a couple of worms that I suspect were real.

"You ever get DTs?" I asked Lloyd.

From the crouch position, he rubbed his overalls leg. "I never hallucinated that much, but for a couple weeks there whenever I tried to sleep I felt rats running over my body. They would bite me in the face and I'd come to screaming."

"How did Shane handle it?"

"Made me sleep in a bathtub full of cold water while he watched to keep me from drowning. It was his own technique. I've asked people in AA, and no one ever heard of his therapy."

"Whatever works," I said.

"Once I felt a snake crawl up my anus."

"You think that'll happen to me?"

"I'd been drunk twenty-three years, you've only lost eight months."

I went to turn in a rack of strawberries, and Patrick told me I wasn't picking fast enough. He compared me to molasses. His family owned a place down the road where they grew green peppers and tomatoes, but every May he and the kids came over to help Granma harvest. Patrick's respect for a person was determined by their ability to do farm work, so he didn't have much use for me.

"You'd never last a day in peppers," he said.

"Yeah, but I can dehorn steers. And I'm a whiz at castration."

I'd made nine dollars twenty-five cents on the morning shift—price of a midlevel bottle of Canadian whiskey. I wish. At least the temperature was nice. It would have been an okay day if I hadn't been farming sober.

"Has it occurred to you that Shane drug us across the country simply because Granma needed help getting the crops in?" I said to Lloyd.

He straightened and put both hands on his back. "He had more on his mind than picking strawberries."

"I mean besides nookie."

Lloyd took off his cap. "You're not the only one sworn to carry out Shane's last requests."

This was interesting. Shane was using his own death to blackmail his friends. "What's he got in mind for you, a statue in the town square?"

Lloyd wiped his hairline with his arm and put his cat cap back on. "I can't leave Granma until the barn is rebuilt."

"He's making you give up Sharon?"

"Shane and I stopped a few months now and then to earn money. He's not making me give up the search, just call an intermission. I figure if we don't take any days off, we'll have it built by fall."

"We?"

———

That night I sat in the rocker watching *Columbo* while Brad and Hugo Sr. played chess and Lloyd and Andrew played Candy Land. They tried to get me involved, but I wasn't in the mood. Alcohol withdrawal and Candy Land don't mix. Columbo had something wrong with one eye, which made him look at everything sideways. For some reason, that chipmunk head twist irritated me. And he carried this pitiful beagle-looking thing around in his arms, like the dog couldn't walk by itself or something. That irritated me, too.

I wondered what Lloyd would say if I asked for the keys to Moby Dick.

"You're a cheater," Andrew yelled. He was wearing his red pajamas with the black oil derricks. Granma had made Marcella cut his hair.

"I am not," Lloyd said.

"Are too, are too."

"Am not, am not."

"Shut up!" I said considerably louder than I'd meant to. Both games halted while the males stared at me, but I didn't care. I felt reckless. "Nobody in the whole world gives a hoot about your stupid game, so don't argue about it. You're taking up too much air."

After a moment of silence, Brad said, "Mellow out, Miss Pierce."

I could have used that blatant insult as the excuse to storm out and go get drunk, and a month ago I would have, but this time I stayed put. Let's all give me some credit here. I bit my lip, forced back the leaky eyes, and rocked the chair for all its worth. Marcella made unnecessary noise bringing in a huge bowl of popcorn—exactly the same as my mom would have done in the situation. Most moms think snacks relieve tension.

"Shane woke up a while ago." Marcella stood behind Hugo Sr. with one hand holding the popcorn and the other touching his neck above the collar of his Ban-Lon shirt. Something about their domestic casualness made me resentful. I hate it when people are casual while I'm tense.

"He asked if you've had a drink yet," Marcella said.

"Tell him I'm sober as he is."

Marcella brought the popcorn over. I refused to touch the stuff. "It's so wonderful what you're doing for him," she said. "Shane knows that every hour he can keep going is one more hour you stay sober. All his life, he loved to help people, especially alcoholics, and now you've allowed him one last chance to save somebody."

I rocked violently. "Your brother is a damn saint."

Marcella seemed surprised. "Why, no, you are, Maurey. You've given Shane a reason to live."

———

After a while, Lloyd and Marcella traded places with Lloyd going in to sit by Shane and Granma, and Marcella dealing with Andrew. Hugo Sr. had been winning most of the chess games before Marcella came in the living room to stay, but after that Brad blitzed him. Hugo was too busy making goo-goo eyes at Marcella for either of them to concentrate on their boards. Andrew gave up on Candy Land and crawled into my lap on the rocker and fell asleep. When Marcella brought Hugo Jr. in to nurse, I thought Sr. was going to drool on his pawns.

Personally, made me sick. I tried to picture the two of them in bed, but in my wildest imagination I couldn't strip Hugo of his black socks and glasses. A week ago I couldn't have imagined Marcella making a peep during the act, but the last week had shaken my basic assumptions about human behavior. Maybe meek women have orgasms, too.

Brad got disgusted with his worthless opponent and went out to Moby Dick, where he and Lloyd slept last night. Before he left, he kissed me on the cheek, just like I was a regular mom.

"You're doing fine, Miss Pierce," he said.

"Yeah, right."

Between Brad's kiss and the smell of Andrew's hair, the tear duct thing was a constant threat. Dad never had much patience with tears—said they weren't cowboy. Or maybe he didn't say it but I assumed he felt that way because he was a cowboy and I never saw him cry. I was getting more and more confused over what people expected of me and what I'd made up along the way. Columbo's loyalty to the stupid dog had me puddle-eyed, too; then there was a commercial about a mother and daughter that no one could tell apart because their hands were equally soft. By eleven o'clock, I was a mess.

Some domestic signal I didn't catch passed between Hugo and Marcella that sent them packing off to bed with their flock.

Marcella said, "Sleep tight."

Hugo Sr. said, "Don't let the bedbugs bite."

"What's that mean?"

He looked at me without understanding. "Don't let the bedbugs bite?"

"You think I'll hallucinate, don't you."

"It's a saying," Marcella said. "Goes with 'Sleep tight.'"

"I don't appreciate these snide little remarks about my condition," I made my voice high-pitched and tacky. *"Don't let the bedbugs bite."*

Marcella loaded up the baby and Hugo loaded up Andrew, and they disappeared up the stairs with Hugo repeating, "What'd I say? What'd I say?"

The news had a story about a family of six who perished together in a trailer fire, tobacco futures were either up or down, and the governor of Wisconsin wanted Nixon to resign. Lloyd came in midway through the weather report and caught me crying like a child.

He rubbed his leg while staring down at the pieces on the chess board. "I don't think Granma has slept since we showed up yesterday," he said. "She's a remarkable woman."

"Lloyd, I don't feel so good."

He looked at me and said softly, "You're not supposed to, Maurey. If it was easy, there'd be no alcoholics."

"But it's not supposed to be like this."

He came over and knelt in front of me and took my hands. "Just think about how much better your life will be afterwards."

"Will it?"

"Yes."

I looked at his face. "I hate myself for thinking it, but sometimes I wish he would die so I could drink in peace."

"I know. So does he and he understands. It's normal."

"Normal? Wishing someone you love would hurry up and die is normal?"

He looked down at our hands. The tears felt kind of nice, in a sick way, and telling him what an ogre I was helped, even though I didn't believe for a minute it was normal to choose whiskey over someone's life.

"I'm scared to death I'll fail," I said.

"But you're equally scared you'll succeed."

I nodded. "I can't conceive of my life without Jack. I can't go on like this forever."

"Just go on for today. We'll make it through tomorrow tomorrow."

I got angry. "Don't spout AA slogans at me. I'm no wino off the street."

As soon as I said it I knew the words were bullshit. I was a wino off the street—or something just as bad. Looking at the lines on Lloyd's face, I had that same powerlessness feeling I'd had when Armand prepared to rape me.

"So, how do people quit?" I asked.

Lloyd's eyes were totally Jesus. It was as if he'd felt all the pain anyone anywhere ever felt and knew there was more to come. "Most alcoholics do something so awful, they scare themselves off the binge," he said. "You hit bottom hard and say to yourself 'My God, what have I become?' and you stop for a while."

"I've been there. I am there."

"But I've never known fear alone to cause a long-term cure. In a few weeks the denial sets in and you take another drink. To really quit, you must replace the fear with something that lasts. You've got to change your entire self."

I wiped the tears from my eyes so I could see him. "I'm so whacked out tonight I don't know what the hell you're talking about."

"I know."

We sat there not talking clear through the sports. Basketball.

First of June and I was in a place where the sports guy talked about basketball. Everything was upside down.

Lloyd fished a bandanna from his overalls pocket. I blew my nose with a sound like a honker. "You said you'd stay with me."

"I will."

"There's bunk beds in Shane's room. Will you sleep on top of me in case I need you?"

"We'll talk all night if you want."

I tried to smile and screwed it up. "I probably won't talk. I just want you close by."

49

Dear Dad,

Because I was selfish I didn't let you go. I held on for nine months, same as it takes to make a baby. I love you, I won't forget you, but life and death are separate and I must choose for both of us.

I choose life for me, death for you.

Good-bye,
Maurey

———

Wednesday—Shane still lived. Strawberries aren't like potatoes or wheat where you harvest a field and go home. With strawberries, the same field has to be picked every other day for nearly two weeks as the berries ripen. To my horror, I found myself bent over the same plants I'd bent over two days ago. That night I used Marcella's foundation powder to cover my scar. Made me look like a corpse.

Thursday—Shane slipped into a coma, but he still lived. At noon, I heard Paul Harvey's voice coming from a transistor radio in Patrick's breast pocket. Maybe it was the radio speaker the size of my thumbnail, or maybe it was my new expectations, but Paul no longer resembled God or Dad either one. I dropped off my six quarts and walked away.

That night Lloyd and I sat with Shane three hours while I prayed he would and wouldn't die. The cough was back, and his skin had gone mushroom-colored. I talked like a maniac—told Shane everything I could remember about my life up until the day I lost my virginity. Granma and Brad got in a fight over Merle in the house. The kid stood up to her, but both boy and cat ended up in Moby Dick for the evening.

Friday—My appetite showed up. Even though I ate a number of strawberries, I still cracked twenty-five dollars for the day. Lloyd never left my side. I made him sit on the closed toilet lid and talk to me while I took a shower. He told me about his wedding. He and Sharon got married at the Chapel of the Little Lamb on the Strip in Las Vegas. The "Wedding March" record had a bad scratch, and he drank two magnums of champagne. I asked Lloyd if I bought him a pair of jeans and a shirt, would he wear them? He said, "No."

That night I got suckered into a game of Chutes and Ladders with Andrew. Granma let Brad and Merle back in the house. Lloyd said tomorrow was the day Shane would die.

"How do you know?"

"He told me."

"Shane told you he would die Saturday?"

"The night he made you make the promise, he asked me how long you could be forced into sobriety and I said a week."

"But I was planning to quit forever anyway."

"Would you have made it this long without the promise?"

I didn't need to think about that one. "Hell, no."

"See."

Although my brain sizzled like a walking case of emotional hives, the only physical symptoms left over from the cold turkey experience were messed-up sleep patterns and a sense of smell about ten times better than anyone needs. Maybe my nose was only normal and it'd been numbed so long I couldn't remember what normal smelled like, but I don't think so. Sober people don't usually smell each other coming from sixty yards. Sticking my head in Moby Dick was like morning sickness all over again.

The messed-up sleep pattern had me dozing off at midnight, then snapping awake around three-thirty. I'd lie on my back, hyperalert, mind racing like a revved-up truck with a blown clutch, until six when I fell into the sleep of the dead. Lloyd yanked me out of bed a half hour later.

Friday night, early Saturday morning, I was dreaming about Frostbite and another horse I didn't much like named Buster Keaton. Buster bit horses, dogs, and people, mostly people. In the dream they were swimming across a river toward me. Frostbite stayed downstream with his head pointed up, facing Buster, and when he reached dry land he pulled himself out by his front legs, and the truth hit me: it hadn't been a week.

I came awake in a heartbeat. Outside, the rain did a soft background number, while Lloyd's gentle snore made the air above me familiar. The blowout with the fifth of Yukon and pills had been last Saturday, but I drank a juice glass of Scotch late Sunday afternoon. Shane must have forgotten, and Lloyd never knew. Shane didn't have to die yet. I owed him another day.

Careful not to wake Lloyd, I slipped into my jeans and shirt and padded downstairs barefoot. The house had a museum smell in the dark, as if it were being preserved for future generations of tourists. The air was like inhaling that blue stuff Mom put in our toilet tank. I hesitated before pushing open the door to Shane's sickroom. My mission smacked of irrationality. Why was it important to tell a man in a coma he'd miscounted the days? What's a day to the dead, anyway?

Granma was asleep at her desk. She hadn't slumped forward or anything you'd expect, just sat there sleeping with perfect posture. The circle of light from the lamp made her appear etched, which enhanced the closed museum feel. I wiped Shane's forehead and the twin tracks of blood coming from his nostrils. He'd lost flesh and color in his face; his hair looked dirty. When I touched his forehead with the damp washrag, his shallow breathing stuttered, then went on.

"It hasn't been a week," I said. "You told Lloyd you'd keep me sober for a week." It's so weird watching a person die. It's magic—I mean, the definition of magic is to make things appear and disappear, right? And birth and death are the only times things appear and disappear from nothing into nothing. Doesn't seem possible.

"I'm sorry," I said.

"Andrew had an interesting life," Granma said. "No matter where he's going next, he said being here was worth the trouble." Her eyes were open—other than that, she hadn't moved.

"Where does he believe he's going next?" I asked.

"Andrew agrees with my views on that question. We're both taking a wait-and-see attitude."

I sat watching his face, trying to memorize it so I could draw a picture of him in my mind after he was gone. I'm not good at picturing people after they're gone. I see Dad, and I don't know if I'm seeing Dad as he was at the end or earlier when I was little or the face is something I remember from a photograph.

"Where is Shane's mother?" I asked.

"Gone. She was the daughter of a hired man. Pretty girl, had curly hair, but she couldn't take criticism. She gave birth to Andrew and fled. He and Marcella have different mothers. My son had a way with women."

"Where is he now?"

"Dead."

The door opened and Lloyd slid in. He took a stool from Granma's desk and sat next to me, only lower, on the same level as Shane's face. No one said anything. A half hour later Brad came in, carrying his charcoal and sketch pad. He stood behind me with his hand on my shoulder, looking down at Shane. After a while, Brad went over by Granma and sat on the floor with his back against the wall and his knees up, supporting the pad.

Just after dawn, Marcella came in. I gave her my chair and moved over to the wall, beside Brad. From the floor I could no longer see Shane's face, but I could see Marcella's and Lloyd's in the gray-pink light. Lloyd blinked with slow deliberateness; Marcella leaned a little forward with one hand touching the quilt. Losing Shane would change the way I looked at people and things around me, and I'd only known him a couple of weeks. For Marcella and Lloyd, this must have been one of those intense moments that only happen four or five times a life.

Brad was drawing a picture of Shane tipped back in his chair while I lowered him over a curb. I recognized Memphis in the buildings behind us. Shane held the harmonica to his lips with one hand while the other hand controlled the wheelchair wheel. His eyes rolled upward, toward me. My mouth was open. Brad's fingers moved with amazing speed, shading and filling, capturing a moment I couldn't remember.

The light changed to a morning greenish yellow. I heard Hugo Sr. and Andrew slamming drawers in the kitchen. Out in the yard a pair of birds we don't have at home argued over something territorial. Or maybe they were doing a mating thing— who can tell the difference between arguing and foreplay?

The room was really quiet for a long time, then Marcella said, "He's gone."

I discovered I'd been holding my breath. Granma stood up, walked over to the bed, and touched Shane's eyes. I went over to look at him. I can't say he looked at peace or like his spirit had flown or any of that other stuff you hear. Right then, he just looked like Shane, only not breathing.

Lloyd patted his shoulder and said, "So long, pal." I didn't know what to do.

———

Lloyd and I wandered out on the porch to look at the new day. The rain had stopped, but the trees still dripped and the sky looked washed. The birds I'd heard earlier were perched on the bath, jerking up and down and walking with a tic. They resembled what we call ouzels back home, but they weren't ouzels, probably some Appalachian form of sparrow.

Lloyd stretched with both his hands in his back pockets. He squinted into the sun. "I suppose you're off for the nearest liquor store?"

"I suppose."

"If you're willing to wait long enough for me to find my shoes, I'll give you a lift into town. I'm heading in for an AA meeting."

"AA, huh?"

He nodded and rubbed his hand on his leg. Lloyd's Adam's apple was more pronounced than ever, looked like he had a rock in his throat. "Seven-thirty morning meeting for the working folks. Starts their day with a boost."

A milk truck went by on the highway. The more colorful male bird took off west, followed quickly by the female. I felt as if I were telling a life good-bye.

I mumbled to Lloyd, "Mind if I tag along to the meeting?"

"What's that?"

"You heard me."

Lloyd's eyes got smoky, as if he were looking at things I couldn't see. When he swallowed, that Adam's apple took on a life of its own. "I'd be honored. So would Shane."

"Just one thing. You mind if we borrow a cup from Granma? My stomach goes queasy at the thought of drinking coffee out of Styrofoam."

Lloyd turned toward me. "I'm certain we can arrange something you'll find acceptable."

I bit my lower lip and thought of Auburn. "Let's do it."

Lloyd smiled and said, "Banzai."

I smiled and said, "Motherfucker."

50

THREE MONTHS LATER, LABOR DAY MORNING, THE GANG lined up for the good-bye scene from the *Wizard of Oz*. Or I tried to line them up. The entire city and all major characters paid strict attention when Judy Garland clicked her heels. I couldn't even get my primary three to cooperate. Marcella chased Andrew through the brand-new barn, Brad sat on the steps playing "Tumbling Tumbleweeds" on Shane's harmonica, and Lloyd was on his back under Moby Dick, doing whatever he did on his back under Moby Dick.

I loaded my day pack, suitcase, and Sam Callahan's tent into the ruby slippers—in this case, Hugo Sr.'s Oldsmobile—which would take me on the first step home. The day was hot, by my standards, anyway, but for a change the humidity had dropped into the livable range. Maybe that's autumn in the South— summer with less humidity.

Granma had a man out from a tavern in Gastonia to give her an estimate on the fourteen cases and then some of Coors. Lloyd and I had been too sentimental to sell it or even talk about selling it. Plus, now that I was what us AA types call a recovering alcoholic—we're not allowed to use the word *ex*—I didn't feel like making money on booze. Even if Coors is cow piss in a can, no one can deny it passes for booze. I wondered if back in Wyoming Dothan had filed the necessary papers to make himself my recovering husband.

Granma, on the other hand, wasn't a woman who allowed sentiment to interfere with working capital. Now that she had a barn, she aspired to chickens and a milk cow. I was bailing out in the nick of time. Hamburger cows are labor intensive enough, but at least in the summer you can turn them loose on the national forest and let them eat. Milk cows require attention every single crack-of-dawn year-round. And don't even get me started on the living nightmare that comes with chicken ownership.

Granma haggled. "My grandson said you would receive five dollars a bottle, therefore I want three fifty."

"Your grandson was wrong, ma'am." The beer man wore a GAMECOCKS cap and had that pot belly guys in the South seem to equate with manhood. "I can't get more than three, so I'll give you two." As I recall, Shane planned to sell the stuff for ten bucks a six-pack. We bought it for four eighty-five a case.

Brad jumped in from the steps. "He's lying like a dog. Any less than three and you're getting screwed."

Granma cast her hawk eyes on Brad. "I know he's lying like a dog. You don't have to tell me he's lying like a dog. And I won't have you using disgusting language on my property."

"What's disgusting about screwed?"

Brad and the old lady had adopted a kind of domestic churliness toward each other, like a married couple who've been ragging for fifty years and no longer hear the words. Lloyd and I had never quite reached that depth of homey familiarity. We still listened to each other.

Since the Tin Man wouldn't come to me, I went to the Tin Man.

"I hear you're starting school tomorrow," I said to Brad.

He blew a flat note. "Granma says if I skip a single day, she'll throw me off the farm."

"Wouldn't want that."

"She also says I have to cut my hair again."

I sat next to him and touched his golden hair, right above the ear. "I like it a little bit long."

Brad shrugged. "Grown-ups rate moral fiber by hair length."

"That's just Freedom and Granma. Not all grown-ups are crazy."

"Show me one who's not."

"Me."

Brad laughed. The notion was too bizarre even to argue. He reached down a step for a large manila envelope. "I made you a going-away present."

It was the picture of me helping Shane up a curb in Memphis, only this one had been done in pastels. "Brad, it's color."

"Shane wanted me to try it. He said everything isn't shades of black."

"I think he was speaking symbolically." Shane had lost weight from the original, but my mouth was still open. Every picture Brad drew of me, my mouth was open. I don't know why.

"You never could tell with Shane." Brad blew a single note, then lowered the harmonica. "Everything he said came out sounding like he meant something else. That's why I like Granma. There's only one way to take her."

Granma and the pot-bellied man were arguing over the horse trailer. I'd given it to her in hopes she'd buy a horse to make the farm a tad classier, but all she wanted was a better tractor. After a summer in and around her fields, I had to admit a tractor might be handier here than a horse.

Brad and I stood up and hugged. He'd grown two inches over the summer and put on twenty pounds of muscle. Farm work may be a pain, but it's a lot healthier than sitting on the couch watching hippies fall down.

I felt the muscles in his back. "Come to Wyoming when you grow up. I'll give you a job."

He shook his head. "I'm going to Paris to be an artist."

"Where'd you get that idea?"

Stupid question. Together Brad and I said, "Shane."

———

Marcella handed me Hugo Jr., then hugged me with him between us so her arms were around me but mine were busy with the baby. She looked right at my face, which I was still a little self-conscious about because of the scar.

"What'll Andrew do without you? What'll I do without you?"

"Andrew'll be in love with his second-grade teacher within a week. And you've got Hugo Sr."

She nodded toward the house. "He's got the trots again. Working with kids always gives him the trots, I don't understand why he does it." Hugo Sr. had a job selling children's shoes at a Kinney's shoe store in Gastonia. He was supposed to give me a ride to the bus station if he could ever get off the pot.

Hugo Jr. reached up and pulled my hair. His head was getting boxy, just like his father's, and his ears seemed to be growing faster than the rest of him.

"Remember what I told you," I said to Marcella.

She set her mouth in a line and recited, "Accept no shit from my man."

"That's the spirit. If he ever takes you for granted, remind him what it's like to drive cross country alone. Did you look at that book I bought you?"

Her neck reddened. Even though she could say *shit*, Marcella still had modesty limits. "I can't believe people do those things to each other. What if they got stuck and had to call an ambulance?"

"Getting stuck is physically impossible. I think. All I'm saying is, if you introduce a new position or game every three months, he'll stay intrigued and won't go nail any sleazeball with cotton flowers in her hair."

"Hey!" Andrew leaned way out of the barn loft and aimed Charley at me. *"Bang, bang-bang. Bang!"*

I pointed a finger at him and hollered, *"Bang* back at you."

"Your finger's not loaded."

"I still can't believe Shane gave him that gun," Marcella said.

"Me either, it's my gun." Before he went comatose Shane had removed the firing pin and trigger and presented Charley to Andrew as some kind of heirloom. I spent the summer arguing with Andrew that Charley wasn't Shane's to give, and Andrew spent the summer ignoring my arguments. Not that I missed Charley—surrogate pricks were no longer cool—but I'd rather give the kid the gun.

"If you go away, I'll track you down and shoot you," Andrew shouted.

"Be careful you don't fall out that loft until I'm gone." This was one hell of a loft, too. Built by hand, one board and one nail at a time, by Lloyd Carbonneau and Maurey Pierce. My dream was to drag all my friends and family down here and say, "Look what I did, doubters." They would fairly swoon at my competence.

Andrew went back to *Bang, bang,* then he threw a chunk of lumber at Merle—missed by two yards.

"Bye, Andrew," I yelled.

"Bye, Murray."

"Maurey."

I walked over and kicked the soles of Lloyd's bare feet until he slid out from under Moby Dick. He probably wasn't even fiddling with ambulance underbelly parts down there but hiding from me because he knew I'd try to guilt trip him into coming to Greensboro.

"Sharon's just as likely to be in North Carolina or even back in Wyoming as Florida," I said. "You have no reason in the hell-bitch world to think she's in Florida."

He stood up, wiping grease onto his overalls leg. "I have a feeling in my gut," he said.

"What if I need you? After you leave here I won't even have a phone number. I bet you're the kind who says 'Sure, I'll write letters' and never writes."

His eyes avoided mine. "I'll write, I promise. I'll send postcards, and after I find Sharon we'll have you over for Christmas some year."

"After you find Sharon? You men are all alike, get a woman dependent on you, then run off to Florida or some godforsaken land with oranges."

One trick I learned from Sam Callahan—whenever you say what you really mean, make it sound like a joke so people won't believe you. The corollary to that one is whenever you lie, be sincere.

"You slept above me every night for three months, and the whole time you were thinking of another woman," I said.

The eyes went perplexed. "Well, yes."

Since I was leaving, I could be semi-audacious. "Didn't you ever have one lascivious thought about me?"

"No."

Lloyd sounded so sincere, I took for granted he was lying. I gave him an extended hug that was as emotional as anything I've ever done with a person I didn't give birth to.

"What do you say to someone who saved your life?" I asked.

Lloyd smelled like barn wood. "Shane always told me to pass it on."

I looked into his eyes and saw pain, tolerance, humor, the ability to love—pain more than any of the others. I suddenly wanted Lloyd to find Sharon and her to be the same person she was all those years ago. I also wanted world peace, a cure for cancer, a GMC four-by-four, and true love—any of which seemed more likely than Sharon taking him back even if he pulled off the impossible and found her. But, hell, you have to start somewhere.

"How would it be," I said, "if I write a testimonial note to Sharon. I'll tell her she's amazingly lucky to have you and amazingly stupid if she doesn't take you back in a heartbeat."

Lloyd took off his cap and scratched behind one ear. "Can't hurt. I've got some paper and a pencil in Moby Dick."

51

AT THE BUS STATION IN GREENSBORO I NEGOTIATED A CAB
and headed across town to one of the snootier neighborhoods, where Sam Callahan's grandfather had built the
manor house. The cabdriver had an unfiltered cigarette
tucked behind his right ear and a tattoo on his shoulder—
SEMPER FI. He didn't care that I was going to one of the
snootier neighborhoods; to him I was another faceless fare in
an afternoon of faceless fares.

Greensboro itself was so typical you'd think a Hollywood
committee dreamed it up for a movie set in Real Town,
USA. Wide streets, big hardwood trees, grocery stores
where you can buy milk and be back in your car in forty-five
seconds. It was one of those towns where the high school
kids think everyone in the world lives the way they do.

"Do you know of an AA meeting later tonight or in the
morning?" I asked the driver.

He glanced in the rearview mirror, suddenly aware that
I was an individual. People like it when you admit to being
Alcoholics Anonymous. It's confessing a flaw. They compare
your looks and personal hygiene with their own, searching for
that detail that makes them morally superior.

The cabdriver more or less grunted, "The Presbyterian

church rec hall has a ten o'clock meeting. First one in the morning is VFW."

Here's one of the lessons Lloyd taught me: When in need of a meeting in a strange town, ask a taxi driver. That's because a high percentage of alcoholics have legal problems where driving is concerned.

Lloyd said, "Taxi drivers know where the next meeting is, only to find out you'll have to sit through anecdotes of the driving-drunks-home variety."

Sure enough, the driver went into a story about a three a.m. fare who had to be carried into the house where a pissed-off wife almost shot them both. Fairly tame stuff after you've heard it from the drunk's point of view.

"I haul a lot of alcoholics," the cabdriver said. "They have me drop them off at a meeting, then pick them up an hour later and take them to a bar. I want to say, 'What's the use?' but it's none of my beeswax."

"Maybe they don't know where else to go."

"My old lady wanted me to join AA, but I don't like all that religious stuff. If she can't accept me the way I am, to hell with her."

"You sound like a scratched record," I said.

He didn't know what I meant, so he decided I was a nutcase and dropped the conversation. I was categorized again—nutcase—back to nonindividual.

Not that I cared. I was more interested in being nervous about Shannon. Seeing your child who doesn't live with you is a lot more nerve-racking than people who haven't tried it think. There's a guilt ratio involved. Will my daughter hurl accusations of abandonment? And a fear of discomfort. What happens if we're strangers? I'm supposed to have a deep bond with this person I hardly know. What if we have nothing to say to each other?

Here's another lesson Lloyd taught me: Just because you stop being a drunk doesn't mean the world will turn hunky-dory overnight. Sober people have problems, too.

The driver took the cigarette from behind his ear and tapped it on the dash. "She thinks I can't control it," he said. "I can control it, I just don't want to."

"Yeah, right."

———

I stood on the manor house steps between two fake Greek columns, concentrating on my breathing. Lloyd says if you focus on deep inhale-slow exhale, your brain won't explode. It's very important that recovering alcoholics avoid brain explosions. I wanted to waltz into Sam Callahan's front room tanned, strong, and self-assured, which is how I felt, sort of, but feeling like your shit's together and acting that way aren't always the same.

The neighborhood seemed colored from an eight-color box of crayons—green yard, blue sky, paper girl riding a red bicycle, wearing a yellow sweatshirt. Piano music came from inside the house—*Für Elise*. Music for daughters. Across the street, lawn sprinklers circled slowly clockwise, whirred back counterclockwise, then circled clockwise again, and far off a siren chased down someone else's emergency.

I imagined I'd just dyed my hair blond and was poised on the edge of a room full of friends and family who weren't expecting a change. The most pain-free way of making the transition would be to slip in unnoticed and get on with life, but they won't let you do it that way. They have to make a big deal over the new you—touch you and say that you're much improved, even though you know a certain percentage are lying through their teeth. Everyone who was once one way I could count on would be different now. And I wouldn't know if they really were different or it was me.

The girl's arm cocked back and she threw the newspaper in

a graceful arc across the lawn onto the front walkway, where it slid gently against my day pack. In a single, fluid motion, the girl waved to me, then dipped her hand into the bag for the next-door neighbor's paper. Two doors down a kid yelled, "No way!" as his dad slammed the trunk of the car. Time for me to either move forward or backward—some direction. Wouldn't do to hyperventilate out here and be found passed out on the doorstep.

As I bent to pick up the newspaper, Sam Callahan's old cat, Alice, came bounding around the side of the house, giving mean excuse to put off the entrance deal. I knelt and said, "Kitty, kitty," and scratched under her neck. Sam and I got Alice from Pud Talbot almost ten years ago. She and I had always been friends in spite of her one and only trick, which was peeing in open suitcases.

"Well, Alice," I said. "Time to dive in."

She flipped onto her back and *mew*ed.

When I rang the doorbell *Für Elise* stopped and I could hear the clatter of a piano bench being shoved back and someone young running across the room. Biting my lower lip, I touched my hair, inhaled deeply as possible, and made my face smile. The door was flung open and there stood my Shannon, taller than I remembered, wearing a sky blue jumper and white leotards. She didn't recognize me for a half second, then her eyes lit like sunlight on the Rockies and she said:

"Mama."

About the Author

Rebecca Stern

REVIEWERS HAVE VARIOUSLY compared Tim Sandlin to Jack Kerouac, Tom Robbins, Larry McMurtry, Joseph Heller, John Irving, Kurt Vonnegut, Carl Hiaasen, and a few other writers you've probably heard of. He has published eight novels and a book of columns. He wrote eleven screenplays for hire; two of which have been made into movies. He turned forty with no phone, TV, or flush toilet, and spent more time talking to the characters in his head than the people around him. He now has seven phone lines, four TVs he doesn't watch, three flush toilets, and a two-headed shower. He lives happily (indoors) with his family (wife, Carol; son, Kyle; daughter, Leila) in Jackson, Wyoming.

Coming in 2011, Tim Sandlin returns to GroVont with Lydia, available at booksellers everywhere.

1

My mother, Lydia Callahan, walked out of the Dublin, California, federal women's penitentiary at noon on Mother's Day, 1993, a free woman, with nothing but the clothes on her back and a Land's End fanny pack full of credit cards. She took a taxi to the Holiday Inn in Walnut Creek where she checked in as Lydia Elkrunner and gave her address as hell. Then she washed her hair in complimentary Pert and fell asleep. Lydia was fifty-eight years old; in her dreams she was twenty.

The next night, she telephoned my daughter Shannon in Greensboro, North Carolina.

Lydia said, "I'm out of stir."

Shannon said, "Stir?"

"Prison. They let me go."

"That's wonderful, Lydia. I can't wait to see you."

"I want you to pick me up at the airport Thursday afternoon. I don't know what flight I'll be on, so you'll have to meet them all."

"Which airport is this where you want me to meet every flight?"

"Jackson Hole. I want you to be the one waiting when I come home. No one else."

"Lydia, Dad lives right there, almost next door to that airport, and I live two thousand miles away."

"Are you going to do this for me or not?"

Shannon said, "I was being practical." Then there was silence. In the past, before going underground, Lydia would have flown into a tirade at the suggestion that practicality might take precedence over her will. But prison had taught her the power of silence. Noisy intimidation works on men; women respond to a quieter approach.

After twenty seconds, Shannon said, "I'll be there."

Lydia said, "I would also like you to organize a community get-together. No use sneaking back into town."

"You want a welcome home party?"

"Put up a notice at the GroVont post office. Tell them chicken wings and shitty beer for all. That'll bring the yokels out."

"Anything else, Grandma?"

"What?"

"Lydia."

"Dress nice. This is my triumphant return. I don't need to come off the airplane and see a slob."

———

Lydia's phone call came while Shannon was in the process of breaking up with her tenth boyfriend in ten years. This one's name was Tanner. They had made love with a device Tanner bought for seventy-five cents from a machine in the truckers-only washroom at the Dixie Land Service Center near Highpoint. Tanner was proud of his device, and, in his mind, he had just given Shannon the sensual experience of the epoch.

Tanner kissed her left breast and said, "My God, that was great."

Shannon rolled over on her back to face the ceiling. "I don't feel the way you're supposed to feel when you're in love."

Tanner said, "Yeah, but the orgasm makes up the difference."

"There's more to love than orgasms."

Tanner was confused. His belief system was based on the concept that sexual prowess and popularity go hand-in-hand. "What the hell does that have to do with us?"

"I do not love you, Tanner. You're interchangeable with others."

"But I'm here now."

Shannon rolled back to look at Tanner, who had a little scar on his chin she was fond of. She realized the scar was why she had chosen him in the first place. It lent Tanner a sense of vulnerable danger, but vulnerable danger is not enough in the long haul. "Tonight was fun," she said. "I want you to move out tomorrow."

He said, "No."

At that point, the phone rang.

———

Tanner pouted throughout Shannon's conversation with Lydia. After they said their good-byes and hung up, he said he was sorry he wasted his youth on a woman with the emotional capacity of a mud flap. He asked her if their time together meant nothing to her, and she said, "That's right." He asked her if she was made of stone. Shannon realized Tanner would not leave her until tears flowed and glass shattered. She would have to make him believe the break-up was his idea, and at the moment she simply didn't have the energy. Instead, she telephoned her father, Sam. This is where I enter the story.

———

I answered midway through the first ring.

Shannon said, "Grandma's out of the slammer."

There followed a moment of silence as I adjusted to the idea of a free mother. It's not as easy as you would think. "I knew it was happening this month; I wasn't sure when."

"They let her go yesterday. Seems strange to do it on a Sunday."

"We express mailed her a loaf of pumpkin bread for Mother's Day. Do you know if she got it?"

"Lydia didn't say." Tanner flounced off to the bathroom and slammed the door. Shannon knew he was angry, but it was hard to take him seriously with a condom dangling between his legs. "She did say I'm supposed to pick her up at the Jackson Hole Airport Thursday afternoon."

Sam said, "I can be there."

"She said I have to be the one. Nobody else." Shannon could hear Tanner's electric toothbrush. First thing, after sex, Tanner always brushed his teeth. "Grandma's nuts. Prison hasn't changed her."

"I didn't think it would."

"She wants me to organize a party at the GroVont house."

"Am I invited?"

"I guess so. She didn't say invite everyone but Sam." Tanner came from the bathroom, minus the condom. He picked his jockey shorts off the floor, snatched the seventy-five cent device from the night stand, and left the room.

I said, "Will you need a ride from the airport yourself?"

"Leave Lydia's BMW in the parking lot with the keys behind the gas cap cover. I'll pick it and her up at the same time."

"The BMW hasn't run in ten years."

"Better have someone look at it. Grandma's coming home."